He

MW00446155

Her Name in the Sky

Copyright 2014 by Kelly Quindlen
All rights reserved.
Printed by CreateSpace, an Amazon.com company

ISBN 978-1495335297

Cover art and design by Eric Ehrnschwender

For Mom, Dad, Freida, Gorb, and Cakes,

with all my love

Table of Contents

Chapter One: Birthday

Baker is wearing her least favorite pair of knee socks. Hannah can tell even from here—even from halfway up the bleachers, where she stands between Wally and Luke and looks down to where Baker stands in the center of the gym floor—because Baker keeps reaching down when she thinks no one is looking and tugging her knee socks up her calves. Hannah knows that Baker must have woken up this morning and realized that none of her good pairs of knee socks were clean—perhaps they were still in her laundry basket, untouched since before Christmas break—and that she must have dug into her sock drawer, her nimble fingers brushing against the cherry wood, and pulled out the old cotton pair, the ones she swore back in 9th grade that she would never wear again because they were always falling down.

"They'd better hurry up," Wally says, glancing at his wristwatch. "It's 2:17 already."

"It's Friday, Wall," Hannah says. "No one's gonna care if we have to stay an extra minute." She scans the gym and spots their ill tempered vice principal brooding beneath one of the basketball hoops. "Except maybe Manceau. He looks like he's gonna faint if he doesn't get his end-of-the-day sticky bun soon."

"I feel him, for once," Luke says. "I'm starving and I want a burrito."

Hannah's about to respond when a deafening buzzing sound swells outward into the gym. Students all around the bleachers jerk their hands up to their ears. Then there's the distant sound of a microphone falling over, and Hannah, clutching her ears, sees Mr.

1

Gauthier, the half-blind old technical director, raising his palms in apology. Several feet away from him, Mrs. Shackleford, the principal, rolls her eyes up into her head.

"Think they finally got it?" Hannah says.

"Mr. Gauthier looks confused," Wally says.

"He looks the same as ever," Luke says. "Like he's high and doesn't know what he's doing here. Gotta love old Goach."

"—say something to test it?" a clear voice says through the speakers, and they all swing their eyes to Baker, who stands at the half court line holding a cordless microphone in her hand. "Oh," she says, half-laughing at herself, her earnest expression visible even from the bleachers. "I guess it's working now—"

"'Bout time!" one of the football players in the lower bleachers yells. From where Hannah stands, it sounds like Clay.

Baker laughs along with the rest of the gym. She runs a hand through her hair, her smile relaxed and unguarded like it is when she tells Hannah stories late at night. "Hi, y'all," she says.

"Hi," the hundreds of students laugh.

"Thanks, Mr. Gauthier," Baker says, with no trace of irony in her voice. "Okay—so should we have this pep rally?"

The student body breaks into whooping and applause. It starts in Hannah's section, with the senior class, and moves all around the gym as the juniors, sophomores, and freshmen echo their older peers. "Yeah!" Luke shouts amidst all the cheering. "Bring on the burritos!"

Several of the seniors on the bleachers below them turn around with quizzical smiles on their faces, but Luke just grins and pumps his hands in the air, making everyone around them laugh.

"Before we start," Baker says, and at her words, the gym falls quiet again, "Father Simon is going to lead us in prayer."

The energy in the gym turns restless and agitated. Boys crack their necks; girls pull their shirtsleeves over their wrists. Father Simon steps toward the microphone, his neck straining against his white clerical collar.

"Kill me now," Hannah says under her breath. The seniors all around her shoot her conspiratorial smirks.

"Let us bow our heads and pray," Father Simon says. The mass of freshmen to Hannah's left obeys his order, their skinny, acne-heavy faces tilted toward the bleachers. Across the gym, most of the sophomores and juniors follow suit. It is only here, in the senior section, that Hannah senses resistance. The anxious resistance of young adults, of people caught between the crayon drawings of Sunday school and the cognitive dissonance of grown-up theology.

"Heavenly Father, we thank you for this day..."

Hannah doesn't listen to him. She lets her mind wander as she picks at the chipped green nail polish on her thumb. Next to her, Wally scratches at his forearm, his calloused knuckles hinting at too many nights spent wrestling with his little brothers.

Hannah's mind slips back to the pep rally they had in August, when everyone had fresh haircuts and neatly pressed skirts and slacks, and when she, Baker, Wally, Clay, and Luke had organized a surprise skit for the student body in which their teachers had dressed up as the more memorable students in the senior class. She can still see Mr. Akers' impression of Clay's cocky strut, can still hear Mrs. Paulk's attempt at Baker's laugh, can still remember the thrill she felt when

Ms. Carpenter—her favorite teacher—adopted Hannah's own mannerisms and spoke with her phrases.

"...We thank you for our athletes, these young men who will represent our school tonight and who will seek to glorify You with their performance," Father Simon says. "We know You have endowed them with a special gift—"

"Hagh," Luke says, shaking his head. "Jeeze. Sorry, everyone. Got a little cough here."

The seniors all around them snicker and brush their hands over their mouths. Hannah tries in vain to stop her shoulders from shaking with laughter.

"...In Your name we pray. Amen."

"Amen," Hannah mutters, tossing the word into the great rush of "Amen" that sweeps across the gym. She raises her hand to her forehead to make the same Sign of the Cross that everyone else is making, the words and actions ingrained in her brain, her movements mirroring those of every other person in the gym.

"Thanks, Father Simon," Baker says, taking the microphone back. She pivots toward the senior class and her mouth twitches with a smile, like she can read their discomfort all too plainly. "Alright," she says. "So. Does anyone want me to bring out our St. Mary's football team?"

The energy in the gym changes instantly: the crowd erupts, the band launches into the school fight song, and the center of the gym is flooded with color as the football players, decked out in their blood red St. Mary's jerseys, spill onto the gym floor and throw up their hands at the crowd around them.

"Don't you just love when we hero-worship our own classmates?" Luke says.

"You know, I actually do," Hannah says. "I'll probably ask Clay for his autograph after this."

"He'll think you're serious," Wally laughs.

Baker holds the microphone low in her right hand and cranes her neck to talk to some of the football players. The rest of the student body, watching from the bleachers, continues to shout and stomp and cheer, until Mrs. Shackleford pats her hands over the air to indicate that she wants quiet. The gym falls into a relaxed silence, and Baker redirects her attention to the student body, biting her lip as she transitions from a smile to a serious face.

"Tonight's expo game will be a crucial event in the race for the Diocesan Cup," she says. "We're already leading the pack with community service hours and our Adoration log, but winning this football game will really put us over the top. And I think the leaders of this diocese know exactly what they're doing in pitting us against Mount Sinai, because there is no better rivalry in Baton Rouge. So tonight, let's set ourselves up for a Diocesan Cup victory and ensure that the St. Mary's legacy continues to grow stronger.

"Those of us who are seniors—" she pauses to wait for the inevitable hollering from the senior class—"first set foot on this campus three and a half years ago, back when the football team had an overall losing record, most of us still had braces, and Clay Landry was about four-foot-seven."

There's a great outburst of laughter, particularly from the senior class section of the gym. Clay, who stands at the front of the football team, laughs good-naturedly while several guys hit his arm.

"All of that has changed now," Baker says. "We had an overall winning record this past fall, all of our seniors are braces-free and beautiful, and Clay now stands at—what are you, four-foot-eight?"

Everyone laughs again, as does Clay, his smile huge and bright. "Pretty close," he calls to Baker.

Baker's smile stretches up to her eyes. She tips the microphone away from herself and lets out a series of short, repeated laughs, the kind that always overtake her when she's trying not to find something funny. She casts a look behind her before speaking into the microphone again. "Sorry," she laughs. "Mrs. Shackleford wanted me to use that joke—Sorry! Sorry! Anyway. We beat Mount Sinai back in the fall, and tonight we're going to beat them again, right here in our own stadium, with the whole diocese watching. We're going to show them what it means to be a St. Mary's player, student, fan, and believer, and what it means to be the very best school in this diocese. So, before I turn the mic over to Clay, I just want to say: Geaux Tigers!"

And again, the crowd of students roars, stomps, and throws their hands in the air. Some of the girls near Hannah are practically shrieking. The teachers sitting along the first row of bleachers on the other side of the gym shake their heads and laugh, and Mr. Gauthier actually pulls his hearing aids out of his ear. Ms. Carpenter claps her hands and leans over to say something to Mrs. Shackleford, and they both laugh.

The noise dies down as Baker beckons Clay over to the microphone. He hugs her and whispers something into her ear, earning a smile from her, and then he takes the microphone and pivots his body so he can address the entire gym.

"Our student body president, everyone," he says in his deep, rumbling voice. "Hey, y'all know it's her birthday today, right?"

Suddenly the whole gym swells with an impossible level of cheering and shouting. Baker smiles big and tugs on her earring, tilting her head to the floor. Clay lowers the microphone and turns back to look at the football team, holding his fingers in the air—3-2-1—and then the team begins to sing *Happy Birthday*. Within a half-second, the whole school is singing with them.

Hannah sings quietly under her breath, keeping her eyes on Baker the whole time, watching her tuck her hair back behind her ear. Toward the end of the song, Baker raises her eyes to the bleachers. She meets Hannah's eyes, and Hannah waggles her eyebrows and grins as big as she can, and Baker shakes her head and fights a smile just as the song ends.

It's a standard pep rally after that. Clay pumps up the crowd until the cheering around the gym is so amplified and everyone's emotions are so heightened that Hannah feels almost delirious with excitement. Luke starts to crow where he stands, his eyes wide and his cheeks flushed, and then he sets his hands on Hannah's shoulders and shakes her back and forth until Wally leans forward and jabs him in the stomach to make him stop.

"Dude!" Luke rasps.

"You deserved that," Hannah laughs, shoving Luke's shoulder.

"Joanie would have hit you harder," Wally says, hiking his eyebrows high above the rims of his glasses.

Luke pulls up his t-shirt in a fit of mania so that the red *Tiger Spirit!* imprint catches around his armpits and his white undershirt is on full display to everyone across the gym. He makes to take the shirt all the way off, but Hannah elbows him and points down at Mr. Manceau, whose small, beady eyes are glaring daggers at Luke from beneath the basketball hoop.

"Alright, alright," Luke says, pulling his shirt down and holding his palms up in surrender.

The cheerleaders take to the floor to lead everyone in organized cheers while the band plays the fight song again. Clay holds the microphone in his left hand and grins out at the display like it's entirely for him. The band reaches the end of the fight song, allows for a minute-long intermission, and then plays the fight song all over again.

The pep rally ends when the costumed school mascot—a yellow tiger sporting a red St. Mary's shirt, and whom the administration officially refers to as "Mr. Tiger" but whom the entire student body calls "Hot Little Mary"—bursts onto the center of the gym floor and dances to the fourth repeat of the fight song. The gym goes crazy with cheers and shouts to the costumed tiger, and the noise level peaks so high that Hannah's ears ache.

Then the music abruptly stops, and the cheerleaders and football players and students look around for the source of the disruption. Mrs. Shackleford stands on the court sidelines, slicing her hands back and forth over the air in an *Enough* kind of gesture, and then she walks to the center of the gym and takes the microphone from Clay.

"What are y'all on today?" she says. "Save some of this energy for the game tonight! Let's all bid farewell to Mr. Tiger, and then we'll start dismissal with the freshmen."

"Bye, Hot Little Mary!" "We love you, Hot Little Mary!" "Get it, Hot Little Mary!" the students around the gym shout, and Mrs. Shackleford frowns at the bleachers, her mouth pulled tight in disapproval.

"Were you planning on giving the whole school a strip tease?" Joanie asks Luke when she joins them in the hallway. Around them, other students drum on each other's booksacks and push each other down the hall, and the whole vicinity has that air about it like something is going to happen.

"It was only for *you*," Luke says. "But considering you were on the other side of the gym, what was I supposed to do?"

"You should have let him take it all the way off, Han," Joanie says. "You deprived us all of another great Luke-Manceau showdown."

"There'll be more," Hannah says.

"A whole semester's worth of them," Wally says.

"Can we talk about how the band played the same song like twelve times?" Joanie says. "Do they not know anything else? I felt like I was riding in the car with Hannah, being forced to hear the same song on repeat for twenty minutes."

"Oh, I'm sorry," Hannah says, "would you like me to choose something else from my library of three-thousand songs *that you accidentally deleted when you were wasted?*"

Joanie rolls her eyes. Luke takes her hand and says, "Aw, do you not know how to respond when we publicly shame you?"

"I am above conflict," Joanie says.

Wally snorts, and Hannah shoots him a sideways smirk. Luke looks down at Joanie with exaggerated pity, almost like she's not in her right mind.

"I hate all of you," Joanie says. "Come on, Luke, let's go before I change my mind about wanting to hang out with you. Han, will you take my bag home?"

"Take it yourself, lazy."

"Come on, it's like two books. Can't you at least put it in the car?"

"Fine."

"Tell Mom I'll be home to change before the game."

"I'm going to tell her you're fornicating in the park and she'd better buy you a new chastity belt."

"Shut up. You are disgusting. Bye, y'all," Joanie says, and then she grabs Luke's hand and pulls him toward the senior parking lot.

Hannah swings Joanie's bag over her arm and looks to Wally, who leans against the white cinder block wall. He smiles knowingly at her. "Does she really only have two books in there?" he asks.

"Of course not," Hannah says, rolling her eyes. "Feels like she's been lugging a dumbbell around."

"Want me to carry it?"

"I got it."

"Don't tell me you two were waiting around for me," someone calls. They turn to see Clay striding toward them, his football jersey stretched taut over his chest. "What'd y'all think of the pep rally?"

"It was awesome," Hannah says. "You were as *dashing* as ever."

"Don't make me blush, Han," Clay says, clapping a hand to her shoulder. "Where's everyone else?"

"Joanie and Luke just left," Wally says. "Can you hang for a bit, or do you have a team meeting?"

"Nah, I can hang. Where's Baker?"

"Haven't seen her yet," Hannah answers.

"Let's go out to the parking lot," Clay says, brushing past them. "It was crazy in there. I need some air."

Hannah and Wally lean against the back of Clay's truck while Clay talks up his excitement for the game. He bounces up and down on his toes and pounds his fists against each other, his statements getting increasingly repetitive. Hannah blinks against the late afternoon sun. The parking lot has mostly cleared out and only a few stragglers linger around the remaining cars. The air tastes crisp and clean, like it always does in January, and Hannah breathes it into her lungs while she rubs her hands over her bare knees to warm them.

"But how lucky am I that I get to play one last game for St. Mary's?" Clay says. "This whole Diocesan Cup thing is awesome."

"I find the whole thing weird," Hannah says. "Making schools vie against each other for something that doesn't even mean anything?"

"Doesn't mean anything?" Clay says, his expression incredulous. "Are you kidding? Dude, like Baker said, it's a chance to show we're the best. Fifty years of competition with Mount Sinai and we can finally prove we're better. We'll have bragging rights for the next 50 years! Besides, think about that prize money. If we could pour that into the football program—"

"Everyone talks about Mount Sinai like they're the enemy," Hannah interrupts, "but we're part of the same diocese. The same *Catholic* diocese. Don't you find that a little hypocritical?"

"Mount Sinai people suck," Clay says. "Half the kids Wally and I went to middle school with ended up going there, and they were all douchebags."

"That's true," Wally says, lifting his shoulders.

"Anyway, I just have this feeling about tonight," Clay says. "I can't explain it, but I know we're going to win. You know?"

"Yeah," Hannah and Wally say together, Hannah giving up on arguing with Clay.

Clay runs a hand through his dark hair and mutters "Big night" for the third time, and then a building door opens several yards behind him.

Baker walks slowly out to the parking lot, her eyes glazed over in thought, her hands pulling on her booksack straps.

12

"Hey," Clay calls to her. "What took you so long?"

Baker jerks her head up, seemingly startled by the question. "Hey," she says. "Clean up. You know how OCD Mrs. Shackleford is. And then Ms. Carpenter wanted to debrief with everyone on student council afterwards. Y'all weren't waiting on me, were you?"

She's looking at Hannah; Hannah meets her eyes and shrugs easily. "We were just hanging out. How do you feel?"

"Pretty good," she smiles.

"No points this time, though," Hannah grins. "Such a wasted opportunity."

"I know, I'm kind of ashamed of myself."

"What are you talking about?" Clay says.

"Hannah wrote me a list of Dares for the assembly," Baker says, unfolding the notebook paper Hannah had slipped her that morning. "Look at this."

Clay takes the note from her, and Hannah and Wally walk up beside him to read the message:

Bake,

Here are my suggestions for your speech today. I think you'll find this list comprehensive and inspiring. Ten points to you for each one of these gems you manage to work in—

- *Deliver the entire speech with your eyes closed. Never explain why*

- *Ask for volunteer Tributes to come forward*

- *Shake the microphone cord at Mrs. Shackleford and tell her you challenge her to a jump rope competition. Loser has to do body shots off of Manceau*
- *Interrupt yourself halfway through, make your eyes go wide, and shout, "OH MY GOD! I JUST SAW JESUS UP THERE IN THE STANDS!"*
- *Tell the student body we are going to "clobber the fuck out of those Mount Sinai douche-bitches"*
- *Call Fr. Simon "Mother Simon," then pretend you just got confused*
- *When Clay speaks, stand at the back of the gym and shout, "He doesn't even go here!"*
- *When Hot Little Mary runs in, tackle him/her/it to the ground, then yell for back-up*
- *End the speech by invoking prayers for the football players' herpes outbreak; proclaim your faith that their discomfort will not prevent them from winning*

Good luck, you'll be awesome.

PS please don't lose this note, as it might result in my being suspended and/or expelled.

PPS now that you're 18, you might actually be held accountable for this stuff...so keep that in mind. Happy birthday!

"You are crazy," Wally laughs, looking at Hannah. "What if someone had found that?"

"That's why I didn't sign it," Hannah says.

"Han, it would take about two seconds for anyone in this school to figure it out," Clay says. "Who else would give Baker a note like that?"

"Nobody," Baker says, taking the note back. "Only Hannah."

The temperature drops to the low 40's that night. Hannah watches Wally squeeze his shoulders tight together as they walk into the football stadium. She burrows her hands into her jacket pockets and clutches the warm screen of her cell phone, feeling it vibrate with a new text message, knowing that it's Baker wondering where she is.

"You want something from concessions?" Wally asks her.

"I'm good."

"You sure? I'm getting a Coke. You want one too?"

"Alright," she says, reaching into her purse for her wallet.

"Don't," Wally says, lightly knocking her arm. "My treat."

They hike up the stands with their drinks in their hands, the paper cup burning Hannah's fingers with cold. The sea of people around them—students, parents, siblings—moves like one mass in response to the game. Hannah climbs upward and upward until she sees Baker, her dark hair reflecting the light of the stadium lampposts, sitting in the middle of a row, surrounded by people on all sides. "Here," Hannah says, tugging on Wally's sleeve and leading him into the row of people.

"Hey," Baker breathes when she sees them. "Hey, Colby?— Katie?—Would y'all mind moving down a little bit?"

"How are we doing?" Hannah asks her.

"Clay just threw a perfect pass to Jackson and Jackson scored a touchdown."

"Excellent."

"Regular or Diet?" Baker asks, tapping Hannah's cup.

"Regular," Hannah says, offering it to her. They spend the next few plays trading the drink back and forth, and Hannah's stomach hums with the familiarity of it all.

Clay throws a 20-yard pass to Danny Watkins, who runs the ball another ten yards into the end zone for the second touchdown of the game. The stands erupt with noise, the St. Mary's band leading everyone in the fight song, and Clay gallops backwards with his hand in the air, his finger pointing at the goal posts as if to say *Told you we'd make it happen.*

Wally leans down close to Hannah, his eyes bright and his mouth open in a big smile. "Remember the first time Clay talked to us about football?" he says.

Hannah laughs as she claps her hands hard together, her skin burning against the cold. "When he told us he'd be quarterback by junior year? And we'd be the most popular kids in school?"

"And you said 'That's nice' and went back to your Geography homework."

"Guess he showed us."

"What are you two laughing about?" Baker asks, passing the Coke back to Hannah.

"Clay," Hannah says, the one-word answer sufficient enough to make Baker smile knowingly.

The crowd falls hushed as they wait for the kicker to score the extra point. Hannah watches the boys on the field, white light

16

illuminating their bodies and making the whole game look more special than it is. Miles, the kicker, surges forward and kicks the football, and it spins a perfect arc through the goal posts, setting off the crowd into a fresh flood of cheering.

"Hola, amigos," Joanie says, shuffling into their row, oblivious to the screaming people all around her. "Sorry we missed the big play."

"We paid a visit to concessions," Luke says, holding a carton of nachos in his hands, "and I'm happy to tell you that we've already eaten two hot dogs and a pack of Sour Patch Kids."

"And now you're gonna share those nachos with the rest of us?" Hannah asks.

"Hell no," says Joanie.

"Sorry," says Luke, "but they're *not-chos.*"

"I'm stealing one because that joke was offensively bad," Hannah says.

"Back off, demon sister," Joanie says, swinging the nachos toward herself. "They're only for us."

"Joanie, I will scoop up some of that fake cheese and put it in your hair."

"You are disgusting. You will not do that."

"Just give me one."

"Fine." Joanie bites a nacho in two and hands Hannah the smaller half. "Don't say I never did anything for you."

Before Hannah can eat her small half of the nacho, Baker swipes it from her hand and eats it herself. "Are you kidding me?" Hannah half-shouts, and the dad in the row below them turns around in confusion, thinking Hannah is responding to the game.

Baker shrugs and looks at Hannah with a straight face. "Sorry. I was hungry. Big speech earlier today."

Joanie, Luke, and Wally crack up laughing. Hannah rolls her eyes and shoves Baker lightly until she breaks her straight face and grins. "At least give me my drink back," Hannah says.

"Okay." Baker takes a long gulp, her eyebrows raised as she waits for Hannah to smile. "Here you go."

St. Mary's wins the game, mostly due to Clay's efforts, and the St. Mary's fans make so much raucous noise that it drives the Mount Sinai fans out of the stadium like demons out of a possessed person. Hannah stands in the middle of her friends and cheers the team off the field until her throat starts to ache, watching Clay raise his helmet into the air while he cranes his neck up at the stands, looking to the parents, to the teachers, to the student body, to the senior class, and, Hannah knows, to them.

"Hey, how are y'all celebrating?" Colby asks as he hugs them. "Are you having a party? Or know of any going on?"

"We have to head out, actually," Hannah says, gesturing at Baker, Wally, Joanie, and Luke. "We have some stuff to take care of."

"Is Clay going with you?"

"Yeah, he's meeting us," Wally says.

"Aw, c'mon, you're gonna take the MVP away from us?" John Strawburn says.

"We thought y'all would organize something," Katie says.

18

"That's what everyone's been saying."

"Sorry," Hannah says, leading the way out of the stands. "I'm sure tomorrow night or next weekend we'll be doing something!"

"What's going on?" Baker asks as the five of them clamber down the bleachers.

Hannah turns around and places her hands on Baker's shoulders. "I have a secret errand to take care of."

"A secret errand?"

"Yes. It may or may not involve your natal day celebration."

Baker's eyes fill with light. "What are we doing?"

"Just something small. Just the six of us. I didn't think you'd want anything crazy, especially after that pep rally and the game—"

"I don't—"

"Good, then drive to my house and I'll see you in a bit."

"Where are you going?"

Hannah raises her eyebrows but doesn't answer, and Baker assumes her challenge smile—the one that means Hannah has surprised her and she wants to see what's next. Hannah locks eyes with Joanie and Luke, and Joanie grabs the arm of Baker's jacket and tugs her away. Baker looks back just once, so Hannah shrugs—*You'll see*—and then turns to follow Wally in the opposite direction.

Their friends are standing around the front yard when Hannah and Wally drive up to Hannah's house. Luke and Clay look up from throwing a tennis ball back and forth and Luke waves his arms overeagerly at them as they turn into the driveway. Baker stands with a hand on her hip, her purse slung across her body, talking to

Joanie on the front walk.

"Food time!" Joanie sings when Hannah and Wally step out of the car.

"Luke, are you seriously standing on our dad's flowers?" Hannah says as she crosses the driveway, balancing the cake box awkwardly under her arm. "Don't you know better by now?"

"Hannah, it's *January*," Joanie says. "I doubt Dad cares. What took you so long?"

"What? We were quick."

"I did three thousand push-ups in the time you were gone," Clay says. He tosses the tennis ball to Wally and runs out into the street. "Throw it long!"

"Clay, get back here!" Hannah shouts. "It's birthday time!"

"Hold on, just let me get a few more throws in! I'm trying to stretch out my arm!"

Wally cups the tennis ball in his palm and looks to Hannah for permission. Hannah looks to Baker, who smiles. "I don't mind," she says.

"Come on, Wall!" Clay shouts from across the street.

Wally throws the tennis ball out into the night, and they all strain their eyes to see Clay catch it triumphantly. He lets out a whoop and holds the ball above his head; Hannah sees a sphere of neon green against a black backdrop.

"Alright, man, come on," Wally yells.

"I'm coming, I'm coming," Clay says as he hustles back to the yard. He tosses the tennis ball to Hannah. "Are you gonna hug me, or what?"

20

She grins and allows him to sweep her up in a hug. "Awesome game," she says into his hair.

"Best we've ever seen you play," Wally says, clapping Clay's hand.

"Thanks," Clay says, his smile stretched wide.

"Okay, and now..." Hannah says, turning to Baker, "cake time! Ready, Birthday Girl?"

"Ready," Baker grins.

Hannah leads Baker and their friends back toward the carport and in through the side door. She can hear Clay and Wally lagging behind them, their voices joining in laughter with Luke's and Joanie's.

"I'm going to cut them small pieces for making us wait," Hannah whispers.

"Tiny slivers," Baker says, playing along.

"Maybe we can throw Clay's to him."

"He would probably go for that."

"Probably. And then you and I can have all the leftovers for breakfast tomorrow."

Baker's eyes brighten just before the boys run in and wrap her in a hug. "Deal!" she says, grinning at Hannah over Clay's shoulder.

Hannah's mom walks in from the family room to say hi to them all, and Baker and the boys hug her while Hannah and Joanie gather everyone's jackets. "So how's the birthday girl?" Hannah's mom asks, her voice thin but warm, and Baker leans her forearms on the kitchen high counter and tells Hannah's mom all about her day at school and her dinner with her family. Luke, Wally, and Clay step around her to walk into the family room, where Hannah can just see her dad's bristly gray hair poking out from his armchair, and Hannah watches out of the corner of her eye as the boys shake hands with her dad.

"Heard you gave 'em quite a show tonight," Hannah's dad says.

"Yes, sir," Clay says, his deep voice vibrating with pride.

"That's great," Hannah's dad says, and then he says nothing else. Hannah strains her ears past Baker and her mom's conversation to listen to the pocket of silence in the family room. She pictures her dad shifting his eyes from boy to boy, wondering what to say, his mouth half-open around another pleasantry. Joanie gives her a look.

"We'd better get back in there for cake," Wally says, his voice more robust than normal. "Good to see you, Mr. Eaden."

"See you later, Mr. Eaden," Luke and Clay say.

The boys come back into the kitchen and there's a spike in volume from the TV in the family room. Hannah looks automatically at Wally. His mouth curves in a simple smile to let her know everything is okay.

There are remnants of Christmas littered all throughout the kitchen: a plate of stale gingerbread cookies that Joanie never finished decorating; a collage of holiday greeting cards tacked up with magnets on the fridge; a dying poinsettia in the middle of the table, its blood red petals withering right in front of them, though none of them notice. Hannah gathers silverware from the drawer in the counter and her mom's mint green dessert plates from the cabinet above the coffee maker, and all the while she feels a beating thrill in her stomach, that same thrill she feels every year at the start of Carnival season, when the King Cakes first appear on store shelves and the neighbors on the corner hang their purple, green, and yellow flag off the side of their house, and her classmates at school talk about which Mardi Gras balls their older siblings are going to or where their family plans to go skiing during the long weekend. "It's the best damn time to be a Louisianan," Clay always says, and Hannah, glancing at her friends, agrees.

"How can I help?" Baker asks, appearing at Hannah's side.

"You can go enjoy your unofficial birthday party."

"I *am* enjoying it," Baker says, "but let me help you."

"I'm pretending to be a domestic goddess right now," Hannah says. "Just let me have my moment."

"What kind of cake did you get?"

Hannah slides the cake box toward her. When Baker glances down at it, Hannah says, "Open it."

"You got a King Cake?" Baker exclaims, looking down at the icing-coated cake ring.

"Are you surprised?" Luke calls from the table. "We're obviously going to use your Epiphany birthday to kill two birds with one stone. What kinds of friends would we be otherwise?"

"I can't wait to eat it," Clay says, reaching his hand out.

Hannah slaps his hand away. "I will punch you if you try to eat this before we sing."

"Sorry, Mom," he says, licking his finger and sticking it in her ear.

"Stop! Stop! Oh my god, just go make sure everyone has their drinks!"

"Did we get candles?" Luke asks. "Or are we gonna sing without them, hard-ass style?"

"We got some," Wally says, fishing them out of the grocery bag. He places them carefully into the King Cake, spacing them equidistant from each other and taking pains not to mess up the icing more than he has to, and Hannah imagines him doing this for his mom or his little brothers with the same deliberate care.

"You really didn't have to do this for me," Baker says, resting her eyes on the cake, then glancing up at Hannah.

"Of course we did, goober," Hannah says, taking Baker's glass from the table and refilling it with sweet tea for her. "This is actually probably the lamest birthday party we've ever had for you."

"Well, nothing tops the one at California Pizza Kitchen," Luke says.

"When you and Clay got her that *Hannah Montana* card and walked around the restaurant asking everyone to sign it?" Joanie asks.

"And then we went over to Urban Outfitters and Wally and I got her that book about hamsters dressed as Renaissance painters?" Hannah says.

"I still have that book," Baker says. "And that card. My mom keeps trying to steal it off my dresser and throw it away, but I always catch her."

"How could she ever want to throw away something like that?" Joanie says.

They light the candles and gather around the cake, each of them leaning in on their elbows and yelling at each other not to breathe too hard over the 18 tiny flames. "Ready?" Hannah says in a hushed, excited voice, and then five of them start to sing, with Clay and Luke affecting bullfrog voices and Wally pretending to conduct them, and Joanie laughing at Luke across the top of the cake, and Hannah watching Baker the whole time, watching how her eyes get even softer and her face looks disbelievingly happy, and how she tucks her hair self-consciously behind her ear when they all sing her name.

"Make a wish!" Hannah reminds her, and Baker glances at her for a lightning-quick second, happiness evident in her eyes, before she blows out the candles on her cake.

"How has nobody found the baby yet?" Joanie says, stabbing her fork back into her cake. "Someone *always* finds the baby during the first cut."

"This Baby Jesus is holding out on us," Hannah answers around a cream cheese-filled bite. "Playing hard to get."

"I'm cutting seconds," Clay says with his mouth full. "I want that baby."

"*I* want that baby," Hannah says.

"Careful, Clay," Joanie says. "Hannah gets really competitive about finding the Baby Jesus. She once pushed our cousin Warren into the refrigerator just to beat him to seconds. He had a bruise on his chest for a month."

"That's an exaggeration," Hannah says.

"Not so much. And I bet everyone here can believe it."

"I can absolutely believe that," Baker says, catching Hannah's eye.

Wally ends up cutting seconds for everyone—"We need a fair judge," he says, elbowing Clay out of the way—and they all eat eagerly, watching each other's plates to see who unearths the plastic pink Christ child hidden within the cake.

"Bam!" Hannah says, digging the Baby Jesus out from beneath layers of bread and cream cheese. She holds the inch-long plastic figurine up for the others to see. "I got him!"

"Goddamn it," Clay says.

"Well, how does he look?" Luke asks. "Do we have ourselves a bouncing baby boy?"

"Does he look like the Messiah?" Wally adds. "Think he's got the potential to save us all from our sins?"

"Doubtful," Hannah says. "But you know, this is probably the best Baby Jesus I've ever found in a King Cake."

"Better than that one we found last year?" Baker asks.

"Are you referring to the one you 'accidentally' threw away?"

"Don't bring that up," Baker laughs, lowering her eyes back to her cake. "I still feel bad about that."

"You know who else feels bad about that? Jesus. Because you *denied* him."

"Hey now," Clay says. "Let's get this mocking under control."

They finish their cake slices—Clay finishes Hannah's and Baker's second pieces for them—and sit around the table for another hour, long after Hannah and Joanie's parents have gone up to bed, just talking and making fun of each other, and asking Luke to do

26

impressions of their teachers, and asking Baker to tell the story about the time she walked into Mrs. Shackleford's office to find her talking aloud to the curtains, and indulging Clay with his questions about how the St. Mary's crowd reacted to the game tonight ("A couple of old women started speaking in tongues every time you got the ball," Luke says; "It's true," Joanie says, "I sold them a nacho with your face imprinted on it"). Wally pushes discarded sprinkles around his plate while he listens to the conversation, and Joanie leans her head against Luke's shoulder and starts to doze off, and Hannah stands the plastic Baby Jesus on the table and dances him over to Baker's plate until Baker, her eyes swinging sideways to meet Hannah's, tugs him out of Hannah's hand.

"We should probably go," Luke says, his voice uncharacteristically hushed as he watches Joanie doze against his side.

"Yeah," Wally says, rising gently from the table. "Here, everyone give me your plates."

The boys leave just after midnight. Hannah stands at the sink and rinses the plates and forks, watching Baker hug the boys goodnight. Clay's hand lingers at the small of Baker's back and Hannah concentrates on scraping a stubborn piece of icing off one of the plates.

Then the boys have gone, and Joanie has lumbered upstairs in a half-sleep, and now the only thing in the room seems to be the water pouring forth from the sink. Baker turns where she stands and casts Hannah a gentle, sleepy smile before she wordlessly walks to the sink, takes the other sponge, and starts to wipe down the table.

"You don't have to," Hannah says, more out of polite habit than anything else, but Baker just sends her a look—*Don't be ridiculous*—and continues to clean.

They walk up the wooden stairs in silence, their feet tracing the familiar path to Hannah's room, and Hannah feels content just to be together, just to have another Friday night sleepover in which Baker will borrow one of Hannah's t-shirts to sleep in, and Hannah will turn the ceiling fan on high because Baker likes it that way, and they'll fall asleep with some sitcom episode playing through Hulu on Hannah's laptop.

"Do you want your birthday present?" Hannah asks when Baker pulls the sheets back on the bed.

Baker stills. "I thought this impromptu party was my present?"

Hannah smiles. She walks to her desk and retrieves the carefully wrapped gift from her second desk drawer, and in some part of her mind she thinks about how she's opened this drawer to check on this present every day for the last two weeks.

Baker removes the daffodil-yellow wrapping paper very gingerly, her slender piano player's fingers working under the tape with an easy grace. When she finds the book, her face alights with an expression Hannah cannot name.

"Han," she says as she trails her fingers across the cover.

"I know you lost your copy," Hannah says, stepping nearer to her. "And I thought you might want a hardcover edition."

"I love it," Baker breathes. She opens the book and flips to a random page, sliding her fingertips down the hard paper, the black ink words—*Scout. Atticus. Boo.*—breathing off the page with the mysterious power of gospel. And in the dim light of the room, with the fan guiding currents of air across the leaves of the book and the phantom taste of King Cake on her tongue, Hannah is wrapped in magic.

"Think it'll make it onto the sacred shelf?" Hannah asks.

"Front and center," Baker says, drawing her fingertips across the cover. She shifts her footing to face Hannah. "Thank you."

They crawl into bed and prop up Hannah's laptop between them. They choose an episode of *Parks and Recreation* and play it with the volume on low. Baker rolls onto her side and nestles her head into Hannah's shoulder, and Hannah falls asleep to the rhythm of Baker's breathing and the smell of her hair.

Chapter Two: Ordinary Time

The following week at school, during Hannah and Wally's unassigned period, Wally asks her if she wants to go somewhere off campus. "Off campus?" she asks. "What, like, just to experience the thrill of maybe getting caught?"

"To get some food," Wally says, his sinewy arms moving over his Calculus textbook as he packs it into his booksack. "I'm bored and hungry."

"You sound like Luke."

"I feel like Luke."

Hannah taps her pen against her Calculus binder. "We could bring food back for our friends."

"We could."

Hannah pictures her friends' faces lighting up when she and Wally surprise them with food. She sees Baker's eyes growing large with her smile.

"You're driving," Hannah says.

They sneak out the back entrance and drive down South Acadian in Wally's old Toyota Camry. Wally plays one of his standard mixed CDs—the one with a lot of tracks by Eli Young Band— and lowers the windows so the fresh, wintry air rushes into the car.

"Where do you want to go?" Wally asks, looking over at Hannah.

"You wanna do Coffee Call?"

"For beignets?" he asks, with a spring in his voice.

Hannah smiles and changes the CD track. "For beignets," she says.

Wally opts for the drive-through so their school uniforms will be less conspicuous. He orders six beignets and a cup of coffee and they pull up to the window to wait. The smell of rich processed sugar wafts out from the kitchen, making Hannah lightheaded. An older woman opens the window and smirks knowingly at Wally's red tie and Hannah's plaid skirt.

"Thank you, ma'am," Wally says, accepting the white paper bag from her.

The woman looks at them from under raised eyebrows. "You'd better get back to school."

"We're home-schooled," Hannah says. "Our mom just makes us dress up so it feels more authentic."

The woman raises her eyebrows even higher, and Wally moves the car into gear, bursting with laughter as soon they've pulled away.

They take the long route back to campus, driving down Perkins until they can turn right into the Garden District. The mid-morning sun colors the trees and houses in wintry light, illuminating the purple and yellow LSU flags that hang from the porches. Wally lowers his window all the way to swim his hand through the air, and Hannah looks at him, carefree behind the wheel, his russet brown hair lifting with the oncoming rush of air.

"I don't think I've ever seen you look so happy," Hannah says.

Wally stares ahead through the windshield. After a moment, he says, "Yes you have."

Hannah clutches the warm paper bag in her lap and turns to look out the window.

To: Baker Hadley & 4 more...
Jan 12, 2012 9:54 AM

> Wally and I request your presence in the senior lounge. We have beignets from coffee call. Hurry bitches!

Joanie: How did you go to coffee call??

> The way most people go...in a car

Wally Sumner: We snuck out like secret agents. Come eat!

Clay Landry: This is awesome, coming in a min, waiting for Akers to shut up so I can ask to leave, save me at least 4 beignets

Baker Hadley: Beignets?! But I'm in computer systems. I'm learning how to use the space bar

> As stimulating as that must be...we have SUGAR

Baker Hadley: Space...bar...space...bar...

Joanie: Coming now. Luke where are you

Wally Sumner: He probably fell asleep in class again

Luke Broussard: O ye of little tiny baby faith. I'm walking down the hall now! You know if you bring me food then I'm there. Joanie hurry up or I'm going to steal yours and I won't regret it

Joanie: And I will break up with you. Beignet > boyfriend

Luke Broussard: How long did it take you to find that symbol on the keypad

Joanie: ...a while

Luke whoops with laughter when he bursts into the lounge. Clay and Joanie follow close behind him, Clay clapping his hands together and Joanie whispering "Bitches and hos" with giddy reverence. Baker comes last, her long hair swinging behind her as she closes the door and turns to face the table. She meets Hannah's eyes and her smile grows even larger than Hannah pictured.

"You really weren't kidding," Baker says.

"I really wasn't," Hannah says.

The six of them circle around the table and feast together. Clay and Luke end up with powdered sugar on their mouths and chins and Wally loses his coffee cup to the mercy of the group, all of whom drink from it without asking. Wally catches Hannah's eye and rolls his eyes up into his head, pretending to be annoyed, but Hannah can tell he's not bothered in the slightest.

"Y'all hear about Cooper?" Clay asks. "He sent his deposit in to Alabama."

"He's going to *Alabama*?" Luke says. "Are you kidding me?"

"He said LSU losing the championship pushed him over the edge. Said he'd rather root for the Tide for the next four years. Asshole."

"I always thought that kid was an idiot," Joanie says.

"Okay, to be fair, both his parents went there," Wally says.

"Yeah, but he grew up *here*," Clay says. "Anyway, the hell with him. I'm glad I don't have to spend another four years dealing with his shit. He always challenged just about every decision I made as captain."

"God forbid," Hannah says, smirking.

Clay crumples up his napkin and tosses it at her. "You know what I mean."

"I'm just kidding. You know I don't like Cooper anyway. Not since that time I saw him lock Marty in a storage closet the first time Marty got drunk."

"Or when he kicked that dog at our community service site," Baker says, her voice bitter.

"Tell me this, Han," Clay says. "Have you decided on LSU yet?"

"I told you, I'm waiting to hear back from the other schools I applied to."

"It won't matter," Clay says, sprawling back in his chair. "When it comes down to it, you'll want to go to LSU with Baker and me."

"Can we not have this conversation right now?"

"Don't pressure her," Baker says.

"I'm not pressuring," Clay grins. "Just predicting."

Hannah opens her mouth to retort, but just then, the lounge door opens. The six of them, taken by surprise with their fingers still covered in powdered sugar, swing their heads around to the front of the room. Michele Duquesne stands in the doorway, one hand on the metal door handle and the other hanging limply at her side. "Oh," she says, her eyes narrowing as she spots the beignets on the table. "Am I interrupting?"

Clay, his mouth hanging open in uncertainty, rakes his eyes over the group before he shifts in his chair to face Michele. "Not at all," he says. "We were just having a delayed celebration. You know, for the big win last week."

"Are you all on unassigned?" Michele asks.

"Yep," Clay says, pulling his lips together.

She frowns at him. "You don't have to lie to me, Clay."

"Are *you* on unassigned?" Hannah asks.

Michele stares at Hannah as if trying to decide whether Hannah is worth her words. "I *am*, actually," she says after a moment. "But I think it's better to spend my unassigned period helping in the front office, rather than leaving campus illegally." She flits her eyes away from the group and continues, in a lofty voice, "Father Simon asked me to come pick up the rosary bags. We have prayer group after school today. Maybe you all should come."

"Mm, maybe not," Hannah says.

Michele glares at her before flashing her eyes in Baker's direction. "I thought you said you had unassigned during fourth block."

Baker tightens her mouth and looks into the corner of the room.

"Isn't that what you said?" Michele presses. "So you could take care of student council stuff at the end of the day?"

Baker raises her eyes. "Yes. That was the plan."

Michele hikes her eyebrows as she crosses the room to fetch the rosary bag. "Probably should set a better example for the student body," she says under her breath.

Baker tenses. Clay pokes his tongue into his cheek and says, "Come on, Michele. We're just taking a five-minute break."

"I have to get back to the front office," Michele says, clearing her throat. "But y'all have yourselves a lovely time. And Clay—you're welcome to come back to prayer group whenever you're ready."

Clay pulls his lips together again and nods. Luke, who sits with his back to the door, mimes throwing up on the table.

"See you later," Michele says. "Oh—but Joanie? I'm not trying to be mean, but the lounge is exclusively for seniors. If we start letting selective juniors in, then all the other underclassmen will think they're entitled to use the lounge, too, and it kind of defeats the purpose, don't you think?"

Joanie's face flushes red as crawfish. "Yep," she says, her voice prickly.

"Thanks," Michele smiles. Then she shuts the door behind her and leaves.

Joanie slumps down in her chair. "That dumb bitch."

"Don't listen to her," Luke says.

"Everyone knows you're basically a senior anyway," Wally says.

"She's not trying to be a bitch," Clay says. "She's just kind of a rule girl."

Hannah trades looks with the other four. Clay crosses his arms and asks, "What?"

Hannah shakes her head. "Thank God you dumped her."

"Seriously," Baker says.

"Aw, come on," Clay laughs. "She's not that bad."

"She's pretty bad," Luke says.

"Wally," Clay says, gesturing to him, "You always liked her, didn't you?"

Wally balances on the back of his chair and tilts his head in thought. "I could never figure her out."

"She's gonna tell Ms. Carpenter that I was skipping," Baker says, raking her hair back as she adjusts her headband. "She'll probably tell her before I even get to the student council office."

"She needs to get over her jealousy," Hannah says. "I mean, how long ago was that election? Like four months, at this point?"

"Yeah," Joanie says, "but between that and Clay dumping her ass, I doubt she's gonna be our best friend anytime soon."

"Come on, we should go," Wally says.

"Yeah," Luke says, sweeping crumbs into his hands, "everyone's going to think I've been taking a huge shit or something."

"Thanks for the nice surprise, y'all," Clay says, looking between Hannah and Wally as he stands up. "You know I love family meals."

"Especially illegal family meals," Hannah says.

Baker leans down and hugs Hannah from behind while the others talk and gather their trash. "Thanks," she says quietly into Hannah's ear.

Hannah ignores the somersault in her stomach. "You're welcome," she says, keeping her voice even, and then Baker and the others are gone, and Hannah reminds herself to return Wally's smile.

The days go on. The sun rises earlier and sets later, and the afternoons grow warmer degree by degree, and the whole earth starts to trill with anticipation of spring. The live oaks that line the streets of the Garden District lean forward to whisper to each other, and the Spanish moss that hangs from their branches droops like heavy shawls they are ready to discard.

But Hannah clings to the static of winter as long as she can. She and her friends meet in the school parking lot each morning, the group of them thumbing their booksack straps while they wait for Luke to show up just before the bell rings with his Oxford shirt unbuttoned and his tie not yet fastened; they gather in the senior courtyard at lunch time and dare Clay to eat French fries with yogurt or apple slices dipped in ketchup; they untuck their uniforms and lean against their cars at the end of the day, exchanging jokes and stories before Clay has to leave for basketball practice and Wally and Luke have to leave for track and field; they text each other late at night while they study their Theology notes and solve their math problems.

They spend every weekend together, wrapped securely in the knowledge that it is still early in the semester, that they do not have to worry about college and new lives until spring is in full bloom, that for now they are simply six high school kids allowed to plan their lives around Friday night hangouts and Saturday night parties. Hannah knows the terrain of her kingdom: she knows what it is like to steal away to Waffle House to meet her friends late at night, to lie on the floor at Clay's house and throw ice cubes at him when he tries to make them all talk about sex, to spend her Friday afternoons riding in Baker's car with the country station playing and the vanilla scent of the car freshener seeping into her clothes.

On Saturday mornings Hannah and Baker take Baker's handsome Saluki, Charlie, to the dog park on Dalrymple Drive. They sit on the circular bench that wraps around the tree in the center of the park and watch Charlie gambol around the park with the other dogs.

"He's really happy today," Hannah says.

"He is," Baker agrees, her eyes gentle. She pulls at the threads on her scarf as a thoughtful expression comes over her face. "Sometimes I wish we could shut down all the roads in Baton Rouge," she says, "so there would be no cars, no traffic, and everyone could just walk around beneath the trees, and the dogs could run and play wherever they like."

"Charlie would probably run all the way down to New Orleans," Hannah says.

"As long as he came back."

"He would. You know he would."

They go to Zeeland Street Café for breakfast afterwards. Baker leads the way to their favorite booth, the one in the back left corner beneath the painting of an old Cajun man. She sits like she always does, with one leg pulled up on the seat so she can lean against her knee.

"Your mom would yell at you for sitting like that," Hannah says, tapping her foot against Baker's.

"My mom's not here," Baker says, her brown eyes dancing.

They eat bacon and eggs, hash browns with Tony's seasoning, and biscuits with jelly. Baker spreads the jelly onto her biscuit in that quirky way she always does—with grape jelly on one half and strawberry on the other. Hannah catches her eye and shakes her head, and Baker grins and asks, "What?", even though she knows what, so Hannah just shakes her head again.

"I'm getting you a coffee refill," Baker says, lifting Hannah's empty paper cup.

"I'm stealing your hash browns while you're gone," Hannah says.

They talk about the boys and Joanie and their classmates, and neither one of them mentions how the semester is ticking by, though Hannah knows they must both be thinking about it. Hannah taps the salt and pepper shakers together and watches Baker sweep her long brown hair over her shoulder while she talks, and all the while Hannah feels that happy, sweet feeling in her stomach—the one she always feels when she's with Baker, the one that's been growing stronger and stronger inside her lately.

On Saturday nights they play music in Hannah's bedroom while they dress and do their makeup for whatever party they're going to that night. Joanie breezes in and out of the room, asking them which flats she should wear and whether they can see her thong through her dress, and all the while Hannah cannot stop looking at Baker, cannot stop yearning to take her hand or touch her waist, cannot stop wanting to make her laugh or hear what she's going to say next. When they stand next to each other at the dresser mirror—when Baker is so close that Hannah can marvel at the length of her eyelashes, can breathe in the scent of her hair, can glance at her eyes and wonder what exact shade of brown they are—when they stand next to each other, all of the goodness inside Hannah swims to the surface of her skin and shines outward into the air, until she feels like a conductor for light and electricity.

"You look happy," Baker says.

"I am happy," Hannah says. "It's Saturday night and we can do anything we want."

Baker smiles and taps her eyeliner against Hannah's arm. "Let's get dressed for the party."

They stand before Hannah's closet and try to make sense of the kaleidoscope of clothes. Summer dresses hang next to winter sweaters, green pieces next to black, brilliant scarves next to worn away sweatshirts.

"This would be a lot easier if you color coded and separated everything by season," Baker says.

"But then I'd be a dork like you," Hannah says.

Baker looks sideways at her, then pulls a scarlet dress down from the closet and drapes it over Hannah's head, and Hannah isn't aware of anything except Baker's laugh, a laugh with a life force all its own.

They go to parties, and the six of them fall into the same routine every time: Luke and Joanie team up against another couple in a game of beer pong, Wally sips his beer slowly and catches Hannah's eye every once in a while, Clay walks over and talks to every person in the room, every person in the room walks over and talks to Baker. And Hannah, standing in the kitchen with Wally, looks over to Baker and feels drawn to her by a force so powerful, so lovely, that she can almost see it shimmering in the air between them. She wants to go to Baker immediately, to walk on water across the space that separates them, to wrap her in a hug and hold her forever. Instead, she stays planted where she is, clutching a cheap beer and talking to Wally and some friends from their A.P. Calculus class.

"You look pretty tonight," Wally says when the others aren't listening.

"Thanks," Hannah says, affecting as much nonchalance as possible. "So do you."

Then he laughs in that shy way he has, and Hannah turns away from him and talks to whoever is on her other side.

Baker always finds her after a while, whenever she manages to break free from other conversations, and Hannah's heart skips when Baker touches her wrist to get her attention. "It's loud in here," Baker always says. "Do you want to go outside?"

So they step onto the back porch when no one is looking, and they shiver in the early February air, and Baker looks over and asks, "Are you having fun, Hannah-bear?" with an expression that means she wants to know the real answer.

"Yeah," Hannah says, because she's always happy just to be around Baker. "Are you?"

Baker smiles her half-smile, and then, looking down at her drink, she says, "I'm bored."

"You do realize you don't have to whisper that like it's a guilty secret, right? It's not a sin to be bored."

"I just feel like I should be more excited to be here. Aren't parties supposed to be, like, a teenager's dream?"

"What would you rather be doing right now?"

Baker turns to look at her. They blink at each other for a moment, the crisp air cutting the space between them, and then Baker's lips turn upwards.

"Eating macaroni and cheese at your house," she says.

"Yeah?"

"Yeah."

"Let's do it," Hannah says, throwing the rest of her beer into the grass.

They work out the logistics, deciding which one of them should drive—"I'm way more sober than you," Baker says, "you know I only had one drink"—until Clay pokes his head out onto the porch and says, with an edge to his voice, "What are y'all doing?"

"We're star-gazing," Hannah says with a straight face. "Baker's really into *Ursa major* right now."

Clay stares at her like he doesn't know whether he's being made fun of or not, and Baker bites her lip to contain her smile, and finally Clay shakes his head and leaves them on the porch.

"Come on," Baker says, tugging on Hannah's arm. "Let's go home."

They say goodbye to the boys and to Joanie—"Don't come home too late," Hannah tells her, "I don't want another joint lecture from Mom"—and then they make their way through the house, their classmates parting for them like the two halves of the Red Sea, everyone begging them to stay, to have one more drink, to listen to one more song.

Baker drives them down moonlit, oak-towered streets. They drive in peaceful silence, carrying the emotions from the party in their stomachs and their lungs. Hannah looks through the windshield and begs the sky that her life will always be like this—large and loud and brimming with youth, but always followed by the quiet drive home and the promise of ending the night with her favorite person in the world.

The house is dark and silent when they walk inside, but Hannah's mom has left the kitchen light on for them. Hannah pulls the cooking pot out from under the stove while Baker pulls out bowls and silverware, and then Baker hops up on the counter, tapping her bare heels against the yellow kitchen cabinets, while Hannah stands at the stove and turns the heat up so the water will boil.

"How do you think they choose the shapes?" Baker asks.

"What?"

Baker holds up the macaroni and cheese box. Scooby Doo smiles in all his dopey cartoon glory, and Baker points at him and repeats her question.

"Maybe there's a secret society," Hannah says with mock seriousness, "of people whose sole job is to choose the shapes for kids' macaroni."

"You think so?"

"Oh, yeah. They spend their nights agonizing about whether Dora the Explorer or Superman would make a better macaroni noodle. And if they make the right choice, they get an award trophy that says, 'Congrats, You Really Used Your Noodle!'"

"But who gives the award trophy?" Baker asks with equal mock seriousness. "Who gets to decide whether they chose the right noodle or not?"

"Children, obviously. Don't you read?"

Baker laughs and tosses the macaroni box at her. "Tend to our food, brat."

"Get me the milk and the butter, brat."

Hannah pours the macaroni into the pot and stands still while the steam rises to her face. She watches the water dance around in an always-changing formation of bubbles while the macaroni lays helpless on the bottom of the pot, sunk forever by the laws of density.

"Milk," Baker says, hoisting the gallon jug onto the countertop, "and butter."

Hannah says nothing in response, just stands above the stove and watches the water boil. And then Baker comes to stand behind her and hugs her around her middle, and suddenly the steam from the pot spreads all over Hannah's body, settling into the hammock of her torso and finding its way to her ears and fingertips. She feels Baker's touch everywhere, and when Baker drops her head onto Hannah's shoulder and watches the boiling water with her, Hannah's heart climbs in her chest and peeks out over the water too.

"Can we still do this when we're in college?" Baker asks, her voice bare.

Hannah nods very carefully, not wanting to betray her insistent heart or the steam inside of her. Then Baker turns her head—Hannah can sense it with every nerve inside of her—and kisses Hannah's cheek. Hannah stills all over, begging the steam not to spill out, begging her heart to stay balanced where it is, until Baker moves away from her, as casual as a breeze on the bayou, and opens the refrigerator.

Hannah picks up the ladle for something to do and swirls the macaroni around the pot. Her body feels flushed all over, but she answers as nonchalantly as she can when Baker asks her if she wants some Coke.

"Sure," she says. "But is there any caffeine-free? I don't want my heart to start racing."

They fall into bed with their stomachs full of macaroni and cheese and their teeth coated with sugar from their Coca-Colas. Baker wears one of Hannah's old t-shirts—the softest, best-loved one—and a pair of her Victoria's Secret PINK shorts. She lies on her stomach and starts to breathe on a sleep cycle almost right away—before Hannah even has a chance to ask her which TV show she wants to watch—so Hannah lies down next to her and re-memorizes the familiar sound of her breathing. The fan blades circle overhead, moving the air in the room so that it washes over them in gentle waves, occasionally carrying Baker's scent to Hannah like a bee carries pollen to a flower.

Sometimes, with her heart beating strong in her chest, Hannah realizes that Baker does not belong to the rest of them. "You're too good," Hannah tells her, meaning every word sincerely, offering this truth with a degree of wonder she's never felt for any other human. "I'm not," Baker insists, her long, dark eyebrows drawing together in surprise. But Hannah knows it from fall semesters spent cheering Baker on at her volleyball matches, when Baker would score serve after serve after serve while the crowd and her teammates screamed their applause, and then Baker would approach the opposite team's captain, the girl who had been crying at the end of the match, and whisper in her ear at the corner of the court when no one was looking. Hannah knows it at a party in mid-February, when she walks upstairs to find Baker sitting on her knees in the hallway with her arm wrapped around a sophomore girl. "It's okay," Baker soothes while she rubs the girl's back. "Your name's Ally, right? You're going to be okay." "I feel sick," the girl says, her voice coming out like the compressed cry of a feverish child, "I want to go home." "We'll take you home," Baker says, her voice light and gentle and filling up Hannah's heart. "We're going to get you some water first. My friend Hannah's here, and she's the best person you could ever know. She'll help me take care of you."

"You're too good," Hannah says after they take the girl home.

"I'm not," Baker promises. "You would have done the same."

"I don't know that I would have," Hannah says honestly.

"But I do," Baker says with her deep, dark eyes.

Hannah knows that Baker does not see in herself the same miracle of goodness Hannah sees in her. She knows that Baker struggles to measure up to her brother, that she desperately craves her mother's approval, that she worries constantly about whether or not she's a fair team captain or an effective student council president. "You're amazing," Hannah wants to tell her. "You're the best thing that's ever been." But Hannah knows that Baker, when she's not smiling at parties and laughing with their friends in the parking lot, carries these secret worries in her heart, worries that Hannah wishes she knew the full extent of, worries that Hannah sees in Baker's eyes when Baker thinks no one is looking.

"You're so much better than you even know," Hannah says one afternoon when they're sitting in Baker's car, talking through Baker's latest argument with her mom. "You're just—you're so—I wish you could believe me—"

"What's funny," Baker says, blinking down at their sun-spoiled sweet teas in the console, "is that, when I tell you these same things about yourself, I wish you could believe me, too."

Chapter Three: Mardi Gras

"I'm having a Mardi Gras party," Clay tells them in mid-February. "Tuesday night. My parents will be in New Orleans."

"You sure you want to volunteer for that?" Hannah asks him. "Those parties are notoriously crazy—"

"No they're not. Think about how many people go out of town for Mardi Gras. You know, skiing and shit. And then you've got the people that go down to New Orleans. But we're all staying here, and a lot of prime people are staying here, so why not make something out of it? Ethan threw a Mardi Gras party when he was a senior and he said it was the best party St. Mary's had ever seen. Besides, my house is all the way at the end of that cul-de-sac, so it's not like we'll piss off too many neighbors."

They trudge through the last few days before Mardi Gras break, swamped with quizzes and tests and essays but buoyant at the thought of the five-day weekend. The hallways swell with noise on Thursday and Friday as students trade information about which krewes are going to have the best floats this year and whether or not it will rain at Spanish Town and whose parents are going to let them drink at the parades. In Hannah and Wally's A.P. Government class on Friday, Mr. Creary actually throws his Expo marker up into the air when a third student is called to the office to check out early for a family ski trip. "Not sure why I'm even trying," Mr. Creary says, his droopy eyes roaming to his desk in the back of the classroom, where everyone knows he keeps his Reese's Pieces stash. "Y'all do whatever you want. But keep the noise level down, and if Mrs. Shackleford or

Mr. Manceau comes around, you'd better look like you're working on those essay outlines."

Father Simon leaves them with a special sign-off message during afternoon announcements on Friday. "Please remember," he says, his voice hovering on each syllable, "that while this is a joyous time to celebrate our Louisianan and Catholic heritage, the purpose of Mardi Gras is to prepare for the Lenten season, when we must remember our Lord and His greatest suffering. Remember to conduct yourselves like children of Christ."

"Wasn't it Jesus that turned water into whiskey?" Luke asks at the lockers afterwards. "So, I mean, we *will* be acting like children of Christ."

"It was wine," Baker laughs, her arms folded as she leans against Hannah's locker. "But yeah, I see your point."

"Just make sure you don't hook up with Joanie in my pantry again," Clay tells Luke.

"Ew," Hannah says.

"Maybe you should worry about your own hookups," Luke says. "Who's it gonna be at this year's Mardi Gras? Gonna go for Sammy Hebert again?"

"Shut up, man," Clay laughs, shoving him playfully, but his face tinges with color and he turns away from them. "Not interested in Sammy."

"Who are you interested in?" Hannah asks.

Clay blinks his eyes shut and shakes his head rapidly. "Nothing. No one. Come on, let's get some food."

They meet Joanie and Wally in the parking lot, and from there they drive to Zippy's for chips and queso. They sit on the outside patio, where it's warm enough for them to take off their jackets, and they roll up their shirtsleeves and fight over the chips and talk about the party on Tuesday, and all the while Hannah tries not to notice how Clay leans forward to talk to Baker with a different look in his eyes than she's ever seen before.

Hannah and Joanie spend the first few days of break hanging out with Wally and Luke while Baker and Clay are in New Orleans with their families. They go to the Spanish Town parade on Saturday and stand in the rain catching beads and doubloons from the passing floats, everyone around them wearing hot pink t-shirts and tutus and latex, the policemen watching from horseback and little kids watching from atop their dads' shoulders. On Sunday they go to Wally's house to build forts with his little brothers while Ms. Sumner runs errands, and on Monday the four of them help Hannah and Joanie's dad plant new flowers in the backyard.

"It was really nice of you to come over," Hannah tells Wally afterwards. "I know my dad's not the easiest guy to talk to."

"He's neat," Wally says, wiping his brow with the back of his hand. "I like him. We talked a lot about engineering. What he does at work and everything. It's the most he's ever talked to me."

"Yeah, well, he's pretty quiet," Hannah says, rubbing at the dirt on her forearms.

"That's not a bad thing," Wally says. "It just means when he says something to you, you really listen, you know?"

He stares directly at Hannah until she stops scratching her arm and looks up at him. His eyes are intense behind the lenses of his glasses, and Hannah gets the strange feeling, like she sometimes gets around Wally, that he sees her differently than she sees herself.

"I'm really glad I came over," he says, one corner of his mouth lifting upward in a smile.

"Yeah," she says, trying on the skin of the girl he must see when he looks at her. "Me, too."

Hannah and Joanie lie around watching TV on Tuesday, neither one of them having showered, both of them rocking messy buns, both of them waiting for word from Clay. He finally texts their friend group around six o'clock, asking them to come over to help him set up. "I get shower first," Joanie says, jumping up from the couch and sprinting upstairs, and Hannah runs after her, yelling at her to hurry up and to not spend ten minutes conditioning her hair.

They tell their parents they're going to Clay's house to watch a movie. "It's a really long one," Joanie says. "Like, longer than *Titanic*, even, so we won't be home until late."

"What's the movie?" their dad asks, sincerely curious.

Joanie's mouth hangs open for a long second. "I don't know— some weird one Clay wanted to watch."

"Text us when you get there," their mom says. "And *no drinking.*"

Hannah texts Baker just before she and Joanie walk out the door. *We're heading over, are you there yet?*

At Albertson's getting Sprite for the drinks, Baker writes back. *Be there soon. And I'm bringing you a surprise* ☺.

What's the surprise? Hannah asks.

Baker replies a minute later. *Nope,* she writes, *don't even try.*

Wally and Luke's cars are already in the driveway when Hannah and Joanie arrive. They find the three boys in the family room, moving furniture against the walls and listening to booming music—Madonna's "Like a Prayer," which radiates outward from Clay's speakers system. Hannah pauses in the hallway when she realizes that all three boys are singing and haven't noticed her yet. Joanie bumps into her from behind and opens her mouth to yell at her, but Hannah pinches her arm and points at the boys.

"Best part," Clay says, pushing back from the sofa he and Wally are moving. "Listen—this part, right here."

Clay starts to jump in place, singing the lyrics, at the same moment that Wally leans forward and drums his hands on the air. Luke ambles over to them, adapting his voice to a high pitch to match the singing of the background choir. The three of them stand in a loose triangular formation, each one of them playing some kind of air instrument while they sing. Hannah holds her hand over her mouth to keep from laughing.

Luke jumps onto the sofa and holds his arms out to the open space of the room while he belts the song. Clay and Wally each grab one of his arms and wrench him down so that Luke gives an inadvertent yelp that sends all three of them into a fit of laughter.

"Oh my god," Joanie laughs behind Hannah, and the boys look up from the sofa, all three of them startled.

"So manly," Joanie says when she realizes she has their attention.

Luke recovers first. "Very manly," he says, walking over to kiss Joanie hello.

"Do y'all always listen to Madonna like this?" Hannah says.

"No," Clay says, holding his hands at his waist. He grins sheepishly. "Only sometimes."

"You surprised us," Wally says, sliding the bridge of his glasses back up his nose. "If we'd known you were coming over this soon, we would have played some Tina Turner, too."

He walks over and hugs Hannah, and she can smell the cologne on his clothes. *It's good*, she tells herself, breathing in his scent. *It's good. It's good.*

Baker breezes into the house a few minutes later, grocery bags cutting into her arms and long brown hair falling over her floral-patterned dress, and Hannah concentrates hard on the lingering smell of Wally's cologne. But then Baker pulls her aside and sneaks her a pack of Peanut M&M'S—Hannah's favorite—out of one of the grocery bags, and Hannah forgets Wally altogether.

They finish clearing the space in the family room and start with their party preparations. Luke and Wally fill two ice coolers with beer while Hannah and Baker set up card tables and Joanie opens bags of Solo cups.

"Elixir de Landry," Clay says haughtily, peering over the punch bowl.

"Oh my god, you made that again?" Joanie says.

"I did."

"I thought we told you to stop calling it that," Hannah says.

"Why would I do that?" Clay says, looking back at her over his shoulder.

"Not sure why we're having this discussion," Luke says, stepping away from the coolers to fill a cup with Clay's punch. "I love this shit."

"It's going to get us all obliterated," Wally says, "but I love it, too."

The three boys stand over the punch bowl and sip from their drinks while Hannah, Baker, and Joanie shoot looks at each other. "That is some fucking good shit," Clay says, tapping his cup against Wally's and Luke's.

Minutes later, just before the party starts, Hannah notices Clay has taped a sign below the punch bowl.

Elixir de Landry, the sign reads. *Bringing you unprecedented pleasure since 2011.*

Hannah pours herself a cup of the orange beverage and takes a long sip of it, resenting how good it tastes.

"Damn him," she says.

"I know," says Joanie.

Clay invites Baker to light the outdoor torches with him, so Hannah nudges Wally and says, "Come on, let's go with them." Clay's face shows a half-second of irritation before he smiles and says, "Yeah, come on, let's all go."

The six of them traipse across the sprawling backyard and walk along the perimeter of the property, where a rickety old fence separates the Landry's yard from the steep decline into the woods below. They stop at each torch and watch Clay create fire out of his hands, and for a few minutes none of them speaks.

Joanie is the one to break the silence. "Not to be an ass," she says, her face scrunched up in the orange-gold glow of the torches, "but what's the point of this? Aren't we going to be inside? It's cold out tonight."

"Because it looks awesome," Clay says. "Plus the party might get really crowded and people may want to come outside. We don't know who all's gonna show up."

"It's a neat effect," Wally says, sliding his palm across the air, his hand following the curving line of torches as if he could make each one light up with magic. "I always love when your dad lights these in the summer."

"It's really pretty," Baker says, her expression pensive. "It's almost mystical."

They continue along toward the center of the torches, each of them following Clay's steps like a group of preschoolers playing Follow the Leader, until they stop at a particularly pathetic-looking section of the fence. "That's where Ethan and I crashed Dad's lawn mower through the fence," Clay says, pointing at the thin planks of wood. Hannah peers closer and sees that these planks have a fresher color than the rest of the wooden fence. "We wanted to see what would happen if something fell down that hill."

"It's a steep drop," Wally says, craning his neck forward.

"Yeah. Ethan used to say he was gonna kick me over it. Probably would've killed me."

"What happened to the mower?" Baker asks.

"It crashed and burned," Clay shrugs. "The body of it was all contorted and there was smoke coming out of it and everything."

Luke laughs. "You and Ethan did some dumb shit when you were kids."

"We weren't even kids," Clay says. "We were, like, 12 and 17."

"Your mom must've wanted to kill you," Joanie says.

"Yeah, sounds about right," Clay says. "She freaked out over the whole thing. She never even wanted to buy this house just 'cause of that stupid hill."

Hannah crouches down to examine the fence. In the dancing glow of the torch fire, the wood seems pained and helpless, a break in the chain that never full mended.

"Careful," Clay says. "It's not very sturdy. Dad made Ethan and I repair it and we took to it like a couple of girls."

"Hey," Hannah says, kicking dirt at his legs. "Watch it."

"I'm just messing with you," Clay says. "But seriously, we had no idea what we were doing. A butterfly could land on that thing and it would probably fall over."

"You two are idiots," Joanie says.

"Yep," Clay says, arching his eyebrows, but there's a peculiar strain of pride in his voice. "Anyway, let's get back inside. I want to test the Elixir one more time before everyone gets here. Got to make sure it's Landry standard."

The house has swelled with people by ten o'clock. The music is ear-achingly loud, and the air is humid with breath and sweat, and Hannah feels that she might be drunk just by standing in the middle of the party.

"Let's get drinks," she says, touching Baker's arm, and Baker nods and follows her toward the punch table. They wind their way through a dozen people, all of whom want to hug them and ask how their break has been so far, and scoot past Michele Duquesne, who eyes them warily as they go by.

"It's crazy in here," Baker says when they're standing by themselves.

"I know. I didn't expect it to be at this level already. Do you want some of Clay's punch?"

"Sure. Not too much."

"I won't," Hannah promises, and she makes sure to measure out a small amount.

Everything starts to look softer and warmer—all yellow and gold and orange hues—and the music starts to get even louder, standing as it is on the shoulders of teens. Hannah's arm muscles slacken and her vision dims, but the magic of the night, the rawness of it, starts to grow in contrast.

"You okay?" Baker asks, setting her dark eyes on her.

"Yeah," Hannah answers, "just a little tipsy."

Baker touches her wrist. "I'll watch out for you."

Clay finds them after a while. His face is ruddy and bright, the way it always looks when he's in his element like this, walking around and courting people, finding classmates who validate him and smile at all of his jokes. "Let's get drunk, y'all!" he says, and when Baker gives him a hesitant smile, he places an arm on her waist and says, "What are you holding back for? It's our last high school Mardi Gras."

"I'm not holding back," she says. "I'm just pacing myself."

"Let me make you a drink. I promise it won't be too strong."

"Says Mr. Elixir-de-Landry," Hannah says.

Clay shoots her a look. "We're talking about Baker here," he says. "I'm not going to get her wasted or something."

"I didn't say you were."

"Alright," Baker says, offering her cup. "Mix me something. But nothing too strong!"

"You got it," Clay grins as he turns away.

"Clay—" Hannah says.

"Yeah?"

Hannah hesitates. "Watch out for Michele. She's had her eyes on you all night."

Clay's expression darkens. "I know. She's already sneaked up on me twice."

"Be careful," Baker laughs. "She'll get you."

Clay's happy look returns. "Yeah," he says, resting his eyes on her, "I guess I do have to be careful, huh?"

Luke and Wally find them, their smiles eager like little boys', their temples glistening with sweat. Wally sports an orange stain on his white shirt—"Luke knocked my cup over," he says, self-consciously following Hannah's eyes—and Luke wears Joanie's scarf around his waist, tied low and carelessly like a pirate's sash.

"This orange shit is getting to me," Luke says as he hangs his arms over Hannah's and Baker's shoulders. "The hell did Clay put in that mix?"

"Insecticides," Hannah says.

"And maybe some bleach," Baker says with a glance to Hannah.

"And just a dash of Kool-Aid to make it taste good."

"He's a master," Luke says reverently.

Hannah drinks another cup of Elixir de Landry, and now her muscles feel even slacker and her chest feels heavier. "You alright?" Wally says, placing an arm on the small of her back, and she swats at him and says "I'm fine, Wall," until he drops his hand.

The room continues to darken and the shouts of Hannah's classmates get louder and looser. Hannah sips from her drink without thinking about it, until it's empty once again and she has to mix a fourth drink. "I'll do it," Clay says, holding out his hand for her cup. "Baker, you want another one too?"

The music changes to a song they all love. They throw themselves into the crowd, hugging and shouting and singing, Luke hopping from one foot to the other in a bizarre dance, Wally nodding his head over and over in a kind of trance, and Clay returns with fresh drinks and a roar of delight, and Joanie jumps on Luke's back from behind, and they all sing the lyrics together, clapping for each other's melodramatic gestures, drinking from their cups when they're not sure how to match their dancing to the beat, but most of all falling into the music, into the crowd, into each other.

Hannah feels exuberant—freer in a way than she has ever been before. She clutches her drink and bobs where she stands, watching the people dance all around her, and for just this moment, for just this second of her life, she feels whole, she feels at ease, she feels like she could exist in this cocoon of time forever and ever. She looks at Baker, standing there with her long brown hair falling over her shoulders and her dark chicory eyes blessing everyone around her, and tenderness pours forth from Hannah's chest like light from a broken vessel.

"Outside?" Baker says, catching Hannah's eye.

They step out onto the back porch and close the door on the party behind them. Hannah knows the air is cold, but she doesn't feel it. Her body is warm and her muscles feel like jelly. She steps forward, closer to the yard, and watches the mesmerizing torches in the distance.

"Baker," she says.

"Yeah?"

"I might be drunk."

Baker laughs. "I can tell."

"What? No you can't."

"You keep combing your hair over your face. You only do that when you're drunk."

Hannah smiles. She extends her hand toward Baker. "Come sit with me."

Baker takes her hand, and Hannah pulls her toward the porch steps. But when Hannah spins back around to sit down, she loses her balance and knows a split-second's terror as she falls forward off the steps.

But then Baker is there, quick and steady in her movements. She wrenches Hannah back, gripping her left wrist and the right side of her waist. "Whoa, drunky," she says, guiding Hannah to sit down on the steps. "Let's not ruin the night with a bad fall."

"Sorry," Hannah laughs.

"You okay?"

"I'm good. Thanks."

They sit still for long minutes, simply breathing. Baker pulls absentmindedly on the hem of her dress until Hannah grabs her hand and stills her fingers.

"Thanks," Baker says. "Hey, Han?"

"Yeah?"

"Do you think Clay likes me?"

Hannah stops breathing. "I don't know." She hesitates. "Why?"

"I think he does," Baker says, her eyes narrowed at the dead grass in the yard. "But I don't think I like him. Do you think that's bad?"

"Why would that be bad?"

Baker doesn't reply. They sit in silence in the cold air, and Hannah feels Baker's energy all around her.

"Sometimes I can't wait to graduate," Baker says after a long minute.

Hannah lets the words wash over her. "I never want to graduate," she says.

Time passes over them. They walk back inside and the party absorbs them again, and Hannah marks the minutes by the songs that play through the speakers. She loves every song that comes on, even the ones she usually skips when she hears them on the radio, and as she looks around the room, she feels elated to see Joanie and Luke belting out lyrics until their faces turn red; to see Clay raising his cup into the air in the middle of the crowd; to see Wally, who rarely sings, throwing his arms around his track teammates and letting them pull him into the song; and to see Baker, who stands next to her, laughing hard as she mixes up lyrics, her skin flushed and her eyes bright.

Hannah's not sure how it happens. One moment her friends are all walking toward them, and then the six of them are singing in a circle, their arms laced around each other's waists and their drinks spilling onto each other's clothes, and the next moment Clay's trying to kiss at Baker's cheek. Hannah watches, in a drunken daze, as Clay's lips graze Baker's face once, twice, and as Baker jerks back and gives him a look that's entirely sober, and entirely unlike any look Hannah has ever seen her give before. And then Baker's gone, and Clay's looking in confusion at Wally and Luke, and Hannah finds herself suspended in time, until all of a sudden she blinks herself back into awareness and moves into the crowd, following Baker's path out of the room.

It's like she's in a trance. She sees Baker pushing ahead of her—the dark hair, the sharp movements—and she vaguely registers the people all around them trying to stop Baker, and then Hannah, to ask what's going on. Hannah keeps moving, moving, moving, her legs and her heart carrying her, until she's face to face with a tall door and the whip of Baker's hair disappearing behind it.

"Hold on!" Hannah says, throwing her hands against the door to keep it from shutting. "Bake—you okay?"

Baker allows her into the bathroom with her. Hannah shuts the door behind them and locks it without thinking about it. "What's wrong?"

"Nothing."

"Something."

"I'm fine."

"You're not fine."

"I'm fine."

Baker sits down on the edge of the bathtub. Hannah walks toward her until she's standing above her, able to look down at Baker's eyelashes and the serious expression on her face. "Hey," she says softly, tucking Baker's hair back behind her ear. "What's going on?"

Baker breathes in. Her eyelashes still; her lips stay parted around her breath.

"Is it Clay?" Hannah asks.

Baker closes her eyes. Hannah keeps tucking her hair back behind her ear.

"Bake, it's alright. Tell me what's wrong. Tell me how we can fix it."

"Nothing's wrong," Baker says, keeping her eyes closed. "I just—do you ever just feel not right about something, but you don't know why?"

Hannah sits down next to her on the edge of the tub. "Sure," she says. "I think it just happens at our age. You know?"

"Maybe."

"Was it—was it him trying to kiss you?"

Baker's eyes open. Her eyes are dead; her expression is vacant. She doesn't answer the question.

They sit in silence for a long minute. Outside of the bathroom, on the other side of the door, Hannah knows that the party is carrying on, that the music is pulsing, that people are laughing and singing and drinking and waiting to welcome her back. But she has no desire to leave this bathroom. So she looks down at her dark-washed jeans, at her black ballet flats, at the bathmat below them, and she waits.

"Maybe I'm just drunk," Baker ventures after a few minutes.

"Maybe," Hannah says.

"It's a weird feeling. I like it, but I—I feel scared. Does that make sense?"

Hannah looks at her. The expression in her eyes is vulnerable and uncertain, and Hannah wants nothing more than to gather her in her arms and tell her that everything is alright. She takes her hand instead.

"It makes absolute sense," Hannah says. "I feel the same way."

Baker's mouth shifts slowly into a smile. She presses her thumb against Hannah's fingers. "Really?"

"Really."

Baker raises her free hand, the one not holding Hannah's, to Hannah's face. She brushes her fingers down Hannah's cheek, and Hannah's heart beats faster. "I'm really glad you're my best friend," Baker says.

"Me too," Hannah says. She leans forward and wraps Baker in a tight hug, losing herself to the smell of Baker's perfume and the beat of Baker's heart against her chest. "You're the absolute best," Hannah says, and then she kisses Baker's cheek.

Baker pulls back from her until they're looking at each other full on. And it's startling, because all Hannah can see are deep, dark eyes, the eyes she has trusted for years, but tonight there is something blazingly different in them, something ancient and yearning, something that calls to a feeling deep inside of Hannah. Baker leans in and kisses Hannah's cheek very slowly and gently—like she means it—and when she draws back Hannah sees that same something in her eyes again, and it prompts her to lean forward and kiss Baker's other cheek. Baker's skin is soft under her lips, and when Hannah pulls back she feels Baker touch her face again, her fingers gentle but commanding on Hannah's jaw, and then they're moving towards each other again, both of them wanting to kiss each other's cheeks, except this time they're facing each other directly.

They kiss each other's lips, and Hannah feels the spring of creation in her body and blood.

It's a bursting, awakening feeling. It's so potent that it almost hurts, the way it feels to eat a morsel of food after a long period of starvation. Every nerve beneath Hannah's skin—every deep, hidden crevice in her body—every tiny atom that makes her who she is—they all jazz to life, as if they had been long ago buried and were simply waiting to be called upon to arise. Hannah opens her eyes and finds Baker looking at her with a kind of breathless, frightened desire, like a child who just got caught with her hand in a cookie jar, so Hannah leans forward again before either one of them can think about it. She kisses Baker's lips, and once again all her nerves spring to life, and her heartbeat quickens in her chest, and the drunken part of her sings *Oh, yes* even while the sober part of her warns *Oh, no.* Baker's mouth moves against hers, and now they're full on kissing, their lips sliding against each other's while Hannah's heart rises up to fill the room around them. And it's magic, it's sacred ritual, it's God.

And now Baker's making small noises, and her hands are running up and down Hannah's arms, and her breathing is as erratic as her kisses. Her lips are wet and Hannah wants to kiss them, kiss them, kiss them, and in some distant, forgotten part of her mind, she finally understands what the big deal is, why people *want* to kiss, why this action communicates so much more than words ever could.

"Han," Baker says against her mouth, and never before has Hannah heard her name pronounced with such fear and such reverence. She answers with another kiss, with a turn of her head, and Baker receives her kiss with a desperate eagerness Hannah never knew she possessed.

And then their tongues are involved, moving into each other's mouths with exploratory fervor, and deep inside of Hannah there's a voice that says, *This is your best friend, this is your best friend,* over and over, and it seems to intensify the physical feelings even more. They kiss and kiss and kiss, and Hannah hears soft whimpers and breaths escaping from Baker's body, or maybe from her own, and she can't think of anything except how much she loves this.

"Hannah," Baker says, her voice more fearful than reverent. She draws away and wipes her fingers across her mouth, and Hannah sees that her hand is shaking.

"Baker—"

"Let's go back out to the party," Baker says, standing up and walking toward the door, her voice high and panicked like it is when she thinks she said the wrong thing to someone.

"Are you okay?"

"I'm just drunk—I think you're pretty drunk, too—I think we're both really wasted—"

"We're okay—" Hannah says.

Baker looks into the mirror and rubs her fingers over her lips again. Her hand is still shaking. "I need some water," she says. "I think I'm pretty drunk."

Then she leaves the bathroom, and Hannah's left sitting on the tub with her heart in her throat.

Joanie drives them home. "I'm *fine,*" she assures Hannah. "I only drank two beers and Luke made me drink, like, six cups of water before we left. What's up with you, Baker? Are you okay?"

"I'm fine," Baker says, her voice high and breathless from the backseat. "Just drank too much."

Joanie snorts. "That's a first."

Hannah's mom calls down to them when they walk into the house. Hannah tries hard to sound sober and is grateful to Joanie for doing most of the talking. "Yes, Mama, we're all heading to bed," Joanie says, sounding exasperated as she kicks off her shoes. Under her breath, she says, "You're driving next time, Hannah."

Baker doesn't speak to Hannah as they get ready for bed. They change in silence—both of them turn away into opposite corners of the room—and brush their teeth without looking at each other's reflections. When Baker gets into bed and turns on her side away from Hannah, Hannah steps toward the door and says, "I'll get us some water."

"Thanks," Baker says.

When Hannah returns with two plastic tumblers full of ice water, Baker is fast asleep, or at least pretending to be.

Chapter Four: Dirty

When Hannah wakes in the morning, she finds Baker packing up her overnight bag, the tumbler of water next to her.

"Hey," Hannah says.

Baker doesn't look up. "Hey."

"You feeling okay?"

"I think I'm hungover."

"Yeah. Me too. Just drink that water. Want me to put on some coffee for you?"

Baker hesitates; she snaps in an earring and looks down at the floor.

Hannah sits fully up in bed. "Look," she says, tying her hair into a bun, "I know we're both being weird about last night—"

"Don't," Baker says, her face scrunched up.

"Don't?"

"Just—don't try to bridge last night and this morning. You always do that. You always try to bring things out in the open. Just let it be, okay? It was a party, it was a late night, we were both really drunk, so let's just leave it alone. I don't want to talk about it."

"But we—"

"Hannah."

Baker's voice is sharp when she speaks. Hannah feels something sink in her stomach.

"Okay," she says.

Then they exist in silence, and Hannah feels like they are two little kids sitting in a mud puddle, unsure of how this submersion feels, unsure of whether they'll ever be clean again.

"I need to take Charlie out," Baker says, standing up and swinging her bag over her shoulder. "I'll see you later."

"Have fun," Hannah says, her voice sounding fake to her own ears.

Baker leaves the room, and Hannah retreats under the covers.

Later that morning, Hannah's mom drags Hannah and Joanie to Ash Wednesday Mass at St. Mary's. "We don't want to *go*," Joanie whines from the backseat of the car.

"Too bad," their mom says.

"We don't want dirt on our foreheads," Hannah says.

"Stop calling it 'dirt.' Be respectful. With all the blessings in your lives, you should *want* to go thank God for everything you have."

Hannah sits through Mass with knots in her stomach. Father Simon delivers a homily about the start of the Easter season, about what it means for them as Catholics, about how they should remember Christ's deliberate sacrifice every day for these next six weeks. Hannah averts her eyes from the life-size Crucifix that hangs above the altar.

She falls in line to receive ashes, feels Father Simon thumb the ashes into a cross-shaped pattern on her forehead, hears the words—*Remember you are dust, and to dust you shall return*—murmured all around her.

She returns to her pew and tries not to touch her forehead. To her left, Joanie and her mom seem unfazed by the ashes: Joanie picks at her nails and her mom closes her eyes in prayer. But Hannah cannot resist raising a hand to her forehead and pressing her fingers against the mark there. When she draws her hand away, her fingers are tainted with dirty charcoal. She does not look up at the Crucifix.

She still feels unsettled when they get home from Mass. Her mom pours herself a glass of sweet tea and goes into the study to check her e-mail. Hannah and Joanie shuffle around the kitchen, making themselves chicken salad sandwiches, Joanie chatting about how funny Luke was at the party last night.

Hannah pours herself a glass of water. Just as she's about to take a sip, she remembers, with a jolt, how it felt to kiss Baker.

No, she tells herself, blocking the feelings. *You don't want that. No.*

She plops down on the couch with Joanie, trying hard to feel carefree, trying not to look back at the memory she just discarded in the kitchen. Joanie turns on the TV, scrolls through the guide, and chooses an *E! True Hollywood Story* episode.

"So what are you gonna give up for Lent?" Joanie asks at commercial.

Hannah takes a bite of her sandwich to buy herself some time. She drinks another sip of water.

"Nothing," she says.

She falls into an uneasy sleep that night, her face buried in her arm and her body sweating under the heavy comforter. She sees Baker's eyes again, dark and deep and startling, and then she is awash in the tactile memory of kissing her last night. Her body starts to ache all over—her chest aches, and her stomach aches, and, most concerning, the area between her legs aches. She tries to shut it down, to think of something else, but she wants to give into it, she wants to feel that mystical experience again.

She wakes, hours later, in terror. She sits straight up in bed with her heart sprinting in her chest. Her face and neck are damp with cold sweat. She sweeps the back of her hand across her forehead and remembers, with the force of a stone slinging down into her belly, that she had been dreaming about God.

School resumes on Thursday. Hannah's esophagus burns with nausea as she drives into the parking lot and spots Baker's car.

But Baker steps out to greet her with her usual smile. "So get this," she says, launching into conversation before Hannah can even fully look at her, "Charlie has figured out how to open doors with his paws."

Hannah hesitates for only a pocket of a moment, recognizing the offering for what it is. *This is normal. We can be normal.*

"That's crazy," Hannah says, her voice sounding only slightly affected. "What'd your mom say?"

Baker's eyes relax. "She's freaked out. Worried he'll get into her china cabinet or something."

"That's ridiculous," Hannah says, her voice sounding normal as they walk into the building. "If she understood Charlie's personality at all, she'd know he has no interest in frilly ceramic china."

Baker laughs. "Exactly."

The hallways are subdued, with most people talking lazily to their friends or whining about how they want to go back to bed. The bell rings to get to first block, but while the freshmen scurry to heed it, most of the seniors just roll their eyes and drag their feet to their classrooms. Even the teachers seem reluctant to be back: Mr. Montgomery makes no effort to hide his yawning, and Madame Rowley, Hannah's French teacher, leans against her doorframe and chugs a 24-ounce coffee as students walk by. There's an unspoken agreement that today and tomorrow don't count as real school days because they comprise a two-day workweek coming on the heels of a five-day party.

After second block ends and the bell rings for lunch, Hannah and Wally walk slowly down the hallway, feeling lethargic after their unassigned period. They're about to reach the main lobby when they come upon Baker and Luke leaning against the white tiled wall outside the front office, their shoulders slumped and their expressions downcast.

"What's going on?" Hannah asks.

"Clay's in Manceau's office," Luke says.

"Michele went to Father Simon about the party," Baker says.

"Oh, Jesus," Hannah says.

"Are you serious?" Wally says.

"Yep," Luke says. "Why does she even go to these parties if she's just gonna rat us all out afterwards?"

"She's probably pissed because Clay didn't pay attention to her," Hannah says.

"Apparently she told Father Simon she was upset by how much drinking our class does," Baker says.

"Yeah, as if she didn't used to be right there with us," Luke says.

The four of them stand with their backs against the cold tile and listen to the din of chatter coming from the underclassmen in the cafeteria. The front office secretaries on the other side of the office windows glance up at them every other minute, their eyebrows arched and their lips pursed.

Finally Clay comes out of Manceau's office, a grimace on his face. They watch through the front office windows as his tall form weaves around the secretaries' desks—he smiles politely at the secretaries, then frowns again as soon as he's past—and exits into the main lobby.

"What happened?" Wally says.

Clay fidgets with the knot in his tie. "They can't prove that I had the party, but they're using 'an anonymous student's word' to go on—"

"Michele," Hannah says.

"Yeah," Clay grumbles. "So then Manceau gave me a bunch of bullshit about how St. Mary's expects better of me because I'm football captain and all that. Oh, but then get this, he interrupted his lecture halfway through because his wife called and wanted to know whether he'd prefer 'teacup pink' or 'butter yellow' paint for their bedroom, so then he spent like six minutes debating the options with her, and then finally he gets off the phone and tells me that he wants to suspend me but can't because he has no proof. So then Father Simon comes in and is all, 'I'm praying for you during this time of reflection' and some other bullshit."

"So what's going to happen?" Hannah asks. "Anything?"

"No," Clay says, with a trace of a smirk. "Other than them calling my parents. But you know my dad would sue the fat rolls off Manceau if he tried to suspend me with no proof—"

"Yeah, but your dad will skin you alive," Wally says.

"Nah. He'll be pissed, and my mom will probably cry a little bit, but they've already been through this kind of thing with Ethan. They'd only care if something really bad happened. But it's not like I had a party and someone died."

"Let's go outside," Baker says, peering over their shoulders at the front office. "Mrs. Adler's sending us death glares."

They shuffle out to the senior courtyard and take their place at their favorite table, where Joanie sits waiting for them, tapping her foot against the table leg. "Where the hell were y'all?" she says. "I look like an idiot sitting here by myself."

"Yeah, because that's the only time you look like an idiot," Hannah says.

"Clay got in trouble with Manceau," Luke says, rubbing Joanie's back as he sits down.

"What happened?"

Clay launches into the story again, and Joanie's features elongate in astonishment at all the right parts, and when Clay has finished, the six of them turn in their seats to search out Michele amongst the courtyard dwellers.

"She's not coming to any more parties," Clay says, his face souring as he looks in Michele's direction. "Tell everyone you can. Make sure the whole class knows not to invite her to things."

"Amen," Joanie says, and Luke nods vigorously at her side. Wally regards Michele with a thoughtful look on his face—the one Hannah has seen him wear when he tries to solve a challenging new calculus problem—and Baker, when Hannah shifts her head to look at her, wears the same expression Hannah has seen her wear many times before: the one that means her heart is battling with her head, that her instinct to empathize is wrestling with her compulsion to keep social order.

Mrs. Shackleford announces an impromptu assembly the next morning. Hordes of students sweep into the gym and plop themselves down on the bleachers, and Mrs. Shackleford and Father Simon stand in the middle of the gym floor, their eyes watching every movement.

Mrs. Shackleford speaks for three minutes about the standards of behavior she expects from St. Mary's students. She never mentions Clay's Mardi Gras party, but the sophomores, juniors, and seniors avert their eyes, all of them understanding the message. Only the freshmen look blankly around at each other, and Hannah, sitting on the end of a row in the senior section, hears a freshman several feet away whisper, "Is this about Marshall passing around that dirty cat comic yesterday?"

Then Father Simon steps forward to address the gym. He stands still with his left hand gripping his right elbow and his fingers raised to his lips, as if figuring out how to counsel a death-row prisoner. He remains silent for a full 30 seconds, until the freshmen start to rustle in their bleachers, and then he raises his head, finally looking around at them all, his expression solemn.

"Here we go," Hannah mutters under her breath.

Father Simon berates them for a quarter of an hour. "I'm disgusted," he tells them. "I am at a loss for what to say. And to think that this behavior took place right on the cusp of Lent, and when we're in the midst of a competition for the Diocesan Cup...."

Mrs. Shackleford stands off to his side, her expression hard to read. Across the gym, Ms. Carpenter sits with her arms crossed and her brow furrowed.

Five minutes into the lecture, Hannah looks over at Clay. His cheeks have colored with only the lightest tinge of pink. When he catches Hannah looking at him, he takes his hand away from his mouth and chews on a smile like he's about to burst out laughing.

The student body is unusually quiet after the assembly. They return to their classrooms without talking much, the boys walking with their hands in their pockets and the girls tugging insistently on the sleeves of their sweaters. But many of the seniors smirk knowingly at Clay and nod conspiratorially at Hannah, Baker, Wally, Luke, and Joanie, and there is an inherent understanding that the whole thing is a big joke rather than anything to worry about.

78

They cross paths with Michele when they reach the senior hallway. She has the grace to look ashamed when she sees them. "Clay," she says, her voice barely audible, "I—"

"Don't even," Clay says, cutting her off. He pushes past her, and Hannah and her friends follow, and Michele stands limply at the lockers, her head bowed against the looks of revulsion the other seniors throw her.

The bell rings for second block, and Hannah and Baker step into their English classroom to find their classmates leaning on the backs of their chairs and complaining to each other. Hannah joins in with the griping and gossiping while Baker sits with her chin on her hand, her brow furrowed as she absorbs her friends' outrage.

Ms. Carpenter shuts the door to signal the start of the class period, and the murmuring in the room trails off. Ms. Carpenter leans against the door with a funny smile on her face. "I guess we didn't enjoy the assembly, huh?" she says.

Hannah's classmates launch into loud complaints. Ms. Carpenter's eyebrows arch comically as she listens to them all.

"Okay," she says. "So you all didn't appreciate Father Simon's tone. To be honest with you, neither did I. But what about the substance of what he said? Don't you think he had a point?"

"Come on, Ms. C, high school parties are just a given thing," Michael Ramby says. "He can't get mad at us for doing something that teenagers have done forever."

"What's the big deal, anyway?" Jessica asks. "What's so bad about parties? Adults always act like they're the worst thing in the world."

"Adults are afraid of teenage partying," Ms. Carpenter says.

"Why? Like, what do they think is gonna happen, we're all gonna be in the bathroom doing lines of coke?"

"Some of your parents probably worry about that, sure."

"Ms. Carpenter, you know we're not doing that kind of crap," Harrison says.

Ms. Carpenter shifts onto her high wooden stool at the front of the classroom. Her long skirt falls over her legs. "Adults are afraid of parties," she says, leaning forward to look at them all, "because they remember, very acutely, what parties are like. The madness that pervades. How powerful it makes you feel, how special, but also how untethered it can make you feel. The things that can happen when you let it go too far."

Hannah breathes in the silence.

"What do you mean?" Jackson asks.

"Someone tell me how you feel when you're at a party," Ms. Carpenter says.

"Really good," Michael grins. "I feel really good."

Ms. Carpenter gestures at him to indicate that she expected that response. "The way I see it, parties can be very liberating, and that's their appeal. Alcohol can be liberating, music can be liberating, the absence of parents can be liberating. The normal rules don't apply, right? It's just you and your friends acting on impulse. And sometimes, when a party makes you feel especially liberated, you'll start acting from your deepest nature. The part of you that's still an invincible little kid—that does whatever you want to do, that takes the world as if it's all yours. It's a return to your most basic nature, before you knew rules. So you find yourself acting with either earliest innocence or earliest evil. And sometimes it's hard to tell them apart from each other. And *that* is what scares adults."

The classroom of students sits in rapt silence. Everyone around Hannah has his or her face turned toward Ms. Carpenter with a hungry, childlike expression, and Hannah remembers story time in elementary school, when her teacher would lead them to the rectangular blue carpet in the back of the room so she could read to them about talking animals and magical children and nightmarish monsters.

So you find yourself acting with either earliest innocence or earliest evil. Hannah's gut twists beneath her skin, and her heart rate increases like she's preparing to sprint out of the classroom and through the hallways. To her left, Baker's face is sickly pale, the way she looked just before she fainted at her volleyball match in ninth grade.

"I don't believe that," Hannah says into the silence. Her classmates turn to look at her as if jarred from a daydream, and Ms. Carpenter's eyes skip to her in surprise.

"I don't think Father Simon has thought about any of that stuff," Hannah continues. "I doubt he's ever even been to a party. And if he has, then he's probably just yelling at us out of bitterness because he couldn't get a hook-up to save his life."

The classroom breaks into shocked laughter. Some of the boys pound their desks with their fists, and the girls' mouths go wide with delighted disbelief.

"No ladies for Father Simon?" Jackson says, his expression gleeful.

"No dudes, more like," Hannah says. "You know how half these priests are."

The laughter in the room surges to a high pitch, and the boys pound harder on their desks, and the girls cover their mouths for just a fraction of a second before leaning towards each other to whisper *Oh my god.*

Ms. Carpenter sits absolutely still on her wooden stool. Her eyes burn into Hannah's until Hannah looks away and joins in with the laughter she created.

The laughter dies when Ms. Carpenter stands up from her stool. Her sharp eyebrows draw together in anger. "This discussion is over," she says, her voice tense. "Hannah, I will speak to you after class." She purses her lips and clears her throat. "For now, we're going to spend the rest of the hour on *Their Eyes.* Take out your books, and someone tell me: What is Hurston trying to do with the scenes of Janie beneath the pear tree?"

There's a flurry of activity as everyone digs their books out of their booksacks. Ellie Thomas raises her hand to answer the question, and Marty Carothers speaks after that, and within minutes, the classroom has returned to its normal, relaxed state. But Hannah sits with her shoulders hunched and her throat full of bile, and to her left,

Baker spreads her fingers over her book as if she can draw strength from its leaves.

Ms. Carpenter meets Hannah's eyes when the bell rings for lunch. "My desk," she says, pointing to the back of the room.

Baker casts Hannah a quick look before she leaves with the rest of the class, but Hannah cannot discern what her look means.

"I'm sorry," Hannah says before Ms. Carpenter can sit down.

"I'm not interested in hearing an apology," Ms. Carpenter says. She settles herself in her desk chair and burns Hannah with her eyes. "I'd rather hear what prompted you to say those things."

They sit in silence while Hannah tries to articulate in her head. "I just...don't like Father Simon."

"Liking and respecting are two different things."

"Well, I don't respect him, either. Him or his religion or his faith. Any of it. It's all just a huge fabrication that's been used to oppress people for ages."

"Cynicism doesn't look good on you, Hannah."

"I'm not being cynical, I'm being truthful."

Ms. Carpenter gives her a knowing look. "Whatever you are being, it's not truthful."

Hannah inhales from her stomach.

"I don't know what's bothering you," Ms. Carpenter says, "and I don't need you to tell me. But I do need you to understand that words mean something, and the words you used just now were very damaging."

Hannah's heart hammers in her chest. "I wasn't being *damaging*, I was just speculating. Besides, so what if I'm right about him? How is that damaging? Because he's not supposed to be that way?"

Ms. Carpenter's eyes rest steadily on Hannah's. Her sharp, dark eyebrows crease inward again. "Damaging because you insinuated it would be a bad thing."

"No, I didn't."

"You weren't going for the laugh? You weren't trying to wound? Your words were meant to hurt. Not just Father Simon, but anyone who could have been listening. What if one of the boys sitting around you yearns to be with a 'dude,' and you just made it clear to him that that option is repulsive?"

"But—but that's not what I—"

"Just answer this question: What was the purpose behind what you said? Was it to wound? Was it to hurt? Did your words come from a place of hatred?"

To Hannah's horror, her eyes start to sting with tears. Her face and neck heat with blood.

"I wasn't—" she croaks. "I wasn't trying to—"

"I know," Ms. Carpenter says. "And I know you weren't acting like yourself. I've known you for four years and I've never heard you say anything like that. But Hannah—we have to take ownership for our words. Words are powerful. They can be devastating. If your words carry hate—if they shame others, if they make them doubt that they are loved—Hannah, you don't want to own words like that."

84

Ms. Carpenter pauses to watch her for a moment. She offers Hannah the box of tissues on the corner of her desk. Hannah does not take one. She looks away from Ms. Carpenter and swallows down the bad things in her throat. "Can I go?"

Ms. Carpenter nods quickly and repeatedly, as if remembering herself. "Go ahead," she says. "I'll see you later."

Hannah hurries out of the room and into the empty hallway. She pushes into the bathroom and checks the floor beneath the stalls to make sure there are no pairs of saddle-shoed feet in the room. Then she shuts herself into the handicap stall, leans her head against the cold tile, and breathes.

"I heard you got in trouble in Ms. Carpenter's class today," Joanie says after school. She stands across from Hannah in their mother's yellow kitchen, snapping pretzels in her mouth. "What'd you do?"

"Nothing."

"I heard you said some shit about Father Simon."

"Everyone's been saying shit about Father Simon."

"So did Ms. Carpenter give you detention?"

"No."

Joanie snaps hard on a pretzel. "What'd she do?"

Hannah turns her back on Joanie to heat a bowl of leftover rice in the microwave. "She just talked to me."

"Talked to you? What, like, lectured you?"

"Yeah. Kind of."

"Ms. Carpenter's so cool," Joanie says. "I can't wait to have her next year."

"She's alright."

"She's awesome. You've been saying that for years."

Hannah shrugs.

"Jeeze, what'd she do, shout in your face?" Joanie says. "I thought you loved her."

Hannah pushes the microwave to stop it from beeping. "She just spewed a lot of bullshit."

"Bullshit," Joanie repeats. "What kind of bullshit?"

"Jesus, stop being so nosy. She just irritated me, okay?"

Joanie bites a large pretzel in half and stares Hannah down. "You're probably just pissed because she was right about whatever she said."

"Shut up, Joanie."

Hannah takes the rice up to her bedroom and shuts the door with her foot. She sits on the end of her bed and stares across the room at her bookshelf. *A Separate Peace. To Kill a Mockingbird. The Catcher in the Rye.* All the books she read as a freshman in Ms. Carpenter's English 1 Honors class—back when Ms. Carpenter still taught freshmen, before she switched wholly to seniors—stand side-by-side on the top shelf. They are small and unassuming, their spines crinkled in a way that makes Hannah nostalgic for the 14 year-old girl who had not yet opened them. The other books that Ms. Carpenter gave Hannah to read outside of class—*The Perks of Being a Wallflower, The Book Thief, The House on Mango Street*—books that Hannah then passed on to Baker—stand next to them. Hannah sets her rice bowl down on the bed and walks over to the bookshelf, running her fingers across the tops of the books, touching the dust that has settled over them to prove to Hannah just how long ago she read them, just how long ago she was that bright-eyed freshman girl. She trails her finger down the spine of *A Separate Peace* and remembers, with the soft coloring of memory, the first moment Baker existed in her world.

Hannah can still see the configuration of the classroom—the plastic-topped desks separated into two rectangular formations, each one facing the center of the room. She can still see Ms. Carpenter, the first teacher who showed them that high school would not be scary, sitting on her wooden stool in the middle of the tiled floor. And she can still see the back of the head of the girl sitting in the desk in front of her—the girl wearing a yellow headband over her long dark hair— who, on the third day of class, when they were supposed to be taking notes on Ms. Carpenter's discussion of *A Separate Peace*, turned around and looked at Hannah with big, anxious eyes.

"Can I borrow a piece of paper?" she had asked, her voice nervous but earnest. "I gave my last piece of loose-leaf to someone in first block. I can just use, like, a torn-off piece of your paper—" she had pointed at Hannah's sheet—"if you want."

"Sure," Hannah had said, sliding her paper forward, "but are you sure you don't want *a separate piece?*"

Baker had faltered for the briefest second, not getting the joke, but then she had smiled like she'd just found the best surprise in the world. Hannah had given her a fresh sheet of paper, and after class they had walked to the cafeteria together and waited for each other in the lunch line, and by the end of the day Hannah couldn't remember what life had been like before her.

Hannah closes her eyes against the memory and leans into the bookshelf, breathing in the musty scent of the books. Her mind drifts to a different memory of Baker—the one from the bathroom at the party on Tuesday night—and her heart and body hum to life before she can shut the memory down.

"No," she whispers through gritted teeth. She weaves her hands into her hair and tugs hard. "Stop it."

She leaves the rice on her bed and pulls her skirt, blouse, and knee socks off her body. She turns the shower on with the faucet switched all the way to the left—heat—and waits for the humidity to seep across the bathroom, hiding the mirror and drawing sweat from her body. Then she steps into the near-scalding water and sucks air over her teeth in response to the pain.

There is an ache in her chest. It stretches from the left side of her torso across to her right. It hurts but she doesn't know why. It feels like the tears inside of her are trying to breathe but can't.

She presses her forehead to the tile wall. The burning water pelts her body and she knows her skin will be pink and raw when she looks at herself in the mirror. She studies the water droplets that cling to the shower wall and she wishes she could cry out thousands of tears to stick there with them.

She lathers soap over her hands and scrubs at her heart, at her stomach, at her inner thighs, eradicating earliest evil from her body.

Things go back to normal with Baker. They talk at their lockers and laugh at inside jokes at lunchtime. They work together in Ms. Carpenter's class and hang around each other's cars in the parking lot. They spend the last day of February working on papers at Garden District Coffee, and when Hannah looks up and sees Baker mouthing words at her laptop, a large mug of dark roast clutched in her hand, she has a hard time remembering the girl from the bathroom: all she sees is her best friend.

The only new thing—the thing that's not normal—is the unspoken new rule: they can never talk about it.

Chapter Five: Girl and Boy

During the first full week of March, when Hannah drops by the student council office after school, she finds Baker holding a single red rose in her hand.

"What's that?" Hannah asks, the scene not making sense to her.

"Clay asked me to prom," Baker says, leaning back against the whiteboard and twirling the stem around her fingers.

"Prom?"

"Yeah," Baker smiles.

"And he gave you a flower?"

"A rose. Look, smell it."

Hannah holds the rose up to her face, but she can't smell anything. "Awesome," she says, the word scraping up from some hollow place inside her stomach.

The door opens and Michele hurries into the office, heading straight for the vice president's desk without looking at either of them.

Hannah hands the rose back to Baker. "I'll see you later."

"I'll call you about the AP Lit homework," Baker says, her eyes touching Hannah's only briefly before she looks at the rose again.

Hannah has her hand on the door when Michele's grating voice stops her. "What is that?"

Michele is looking at the rose. Her jaw hangs loose from her face.

Baker eyes her without blinking. "It's a rose..." she says slowly, as if speaking to a child.

"Who gave it to you?"

"Clay. Why?"

Michele pushes her tongue against her front teeth. After a long second, she says, "Did he ask you to prom?"

"Yes," Baker says, "and I don't see why you care. He broke up with you almost six months ago. And then you ratted him out to Father Simon. Remember?"

Michele's face flushes pink. She breathes heavily through her nose as her eyes fill with tears.

"He asked me to go with him," Baker continues, her eyes still unblinking, "and I want to. So I'm going."

Michele wrenches her booksack off the desk and storms out of the room, pushing Hannah with her shoulder in her haste to get out the door.

Baker blinks very fast, her eyelashes fluttering like bird's wings. She sets her lips hard against each other and tosses the rose onto her desk.

"That wasn't like you," Hannah says quietly.

Baker drops down into her chair and slumps her shoulders over her desk. "A lot of things haven't been like me lately," she says.

On Thursday morning, when Hannah pulls into her parking spot, she notices Clay standing with Baker at her car. Baker holds a skinny, rectangular white box in her arms.

"What's he doing here?" Joanie frowns. "He never gets here earlier than us."

"'Morning," Clay says when they step out of the car.

"Hi," Hannah says. "You're early today."

Clay shrugs and looks over at Baker. "Felt like it."

"Clay brought us donuts," Baker says, opening the white box's lid. Inside, there are half a dozen donuts, glazed and covered in chocolate icing.

"Baker's favorite," Clay says.

"Wow," Hannah says, nodding at the donuts. "That was nice of you. What's the occasion?"

"No occasion, just wanted to."

"Wow," Hannah says again.

"Do you want one, Han?" Baker offers. "Joanie?"

"I'm good," Hannah says while Joanie shakes her head.

They hang around the car and wait for Wally and Luke to arrive. When the first bell rings and they all start to walk inside, Joanie jogs up to Hannah and knocks her elbow. "The hell was that about?" Joanie snickers. "Are donuts supposed to be romantic or something?"

"Ha," Hannah laughs, her stomach hollowing out, "Yeah. I don't know."

Though Baker offers her a donut three more times that day, Hannah can't bring herself to eat one.

The six of them spend Friday night hanging out at Clay's house, finalizing their plans for their spring break trip to Destin. They drink Coke and eat Doritos while Joanie flips through the TV channels to find a good movie.

"I'm still trying to convince them not to come," Clay says.

"They're going to," Wally says.

"Yeah, that's not gonna work," Luke says. "Besides, if your parents don't end up going, I doubt any of ours will let us go."

"Our parents definitely won't," Joanie says.

"My mom's already uneasy enough," Baker says. "I think the only reason she feels okay with it is because she thought your mom was like the most religious person ever in their bible study group."

"Not too far off," Clay smiles.

"I don't see why you don't want them there," Hannah says. "We like your parents."

"It's not that, it's just that I think we'll have more *fun* if they're not there."

"Clay, we don't always have to be drinking," Hannah says. "I think we're all perfectly okay with a chill week at the beach."

"I didn't say we always had to be drinking, I just wanna be able to have a beer here and there."

"Your parents' house is our best bet."

"Yeah, I get that, I just still think they might come around to the idea of us being there without them."

"Your mom won't go for that," Wally says. "You know she won't."

Clay huffs in frustration. He looks down the couch, to where Baker's sitting. "What do you think, Bake?" he asks.

"I think it'll be nice to have them there," Baker says. "Your parents are great people. I think we all just appreciate that they're willing to have us down there."

Clay is quiet for a minute. "Alright," he says finally, "you're right."

When they go to leave that night, Clay hugs Baker for much longer than he normally does. Hannah waits awkwardly by the front door and stares at the fleur-de-lis symbols in the Landry's wallpaper. When Baker finally breaks free of the hug and joins Hannah and Joanie in the car, Joanie turns around from the front seat and waggles her eyebrows.

"That was a beautiful hug," Joanie says. "Did he give you more donuts, too?"

"Shush," Baker says, and Hannah watches, in the rearview mirror, as Baker leans her head against the window and frowns.

On Sunday, Wally asks Hannah to meet him for coffee so they can work on their AP Government essays. They sit at the spindly black tables outside Garden District Coffee and argue about the structure of Wally's essay, until Wally finally leans forward in his chair and watches Hannah reorganize his paragraphs.

"*That* works better," Hannah says.

Wally tilts his head sideways to look at his paper. Sunlight reflects off the lenses of his glasses. Behind the lenses, Hannah can see his eyes, calm but serious as they read what she has written.

"I think you're right," he says.

"I know I am," she says.

"Hannah," he says, and suddenly he looks breathless. "Will you go to the prom with me?"

Hannah's stomach hops. Wally looks earnestly at her, the question still showing in his eyes.

"Yeah," she says, and then she has the comforting sense that she is in a story, that she is correctly playing her part, that she has brought her personal touch to the role of *Girl*. She looks at Wally, at how he fits the role of *Boy* in his own way, with his fern green eyes and his square jaw and his hint of cologne, and she feels good.

"Yeah," she says again, smiling. "I'd love to go with you."

Wally smiles. He continues to look at her with that earnest way he has, like he might just tell her that she made the sun rise that morning, until Hannah breaks eye contact.

"Here," she says, "let me look at your conclusion one more time."

They stay there for another hour, comparing essays and suggesting ideas, Hannah correcting Wally's grammatical errors and Wally pointing out flaws in Hannah's arguments. Just as Hannah starts to pack up her things, her phone chimes with a text message alert.

Hey, Baker writes, *want to get fro yo?*

Can't, Hannah replies, *still at gd coffee with wall. He just asked me to prom.*

She goes back to packing up her notes and drafts. Wally stands at the corner of the table, thumbing his booksack straps while he waits for her.

That's great, Baker writes.

Yeah, Hannah writes as she and Wally walk to the back lot where they parked their cars. *Now we can all go in the same group.*

"Bye, Han," Wally says when they reach their cars. "Thanks for your help."

"No problem."

He shifts his weight from one leg to the other, still thumbing his booksack straps, before walking forward to pull her into a hug.

"Bye," he says.

"Bye," Hannah says.

She reads Baker's reply after she turns her car on. *Yeah,* Baker writes, *it's perfect.*

The following week at school, the whole student body buzzes with excitement for Baton Rouge's annual St. Patrick's Day parade. Hannah and Joanie make plans for their friends to come over after the parade, since they are the only ones who live in the Garden District, close to the parade route. "Maybe we can sneak in some drinking afterwards," Joanie says, her eyes bright. "Mom and Dad have that party to go to."

"Maybe," Hannah says. "If Dad actually ends up going."

On Saturday, the 17th, a large portion of the Garden District and a long stretch of Perkins Road are shut down for the parade. Hannah, Joanie, and their friends walk to the intersection of Terrace and Perkins, where hundreds of people mill about, all of them dressed in lime green or hunter green or Kelly green, all of them waiting for the parade floats to roll by.

Hannah stands between Wally and Baker at the front of the crowd, waving up at the floats as their riders throw down slabs of green beads and random trinkets. Luke catches a purple stuffed penguin, Joanie catches an Irishman's hat, and Wally snags more beads than the rest of them put together. Clay manages to catch two

Jello shots, thrown down to him in white paper cups quivering with green gelatin.

They gather together after the parade has passed through and compare their treasures. Joanie takes pictures of them all, weighed down by beads and sweating in the early spring heat, everything around them green and lively.

They start the trek back to Hannah and Joanie's house on Olive Street, darting their feet onto clear patches of asphalt, occasionally slipping on rogue strings of beads. Above them, tangled on tree branches and street lamps, hang the far-flung beads that never made it into the hands of parade-goers. They sparkle in the sunlight, each one of them seeming pathetic and desperate on its own, but the whole scene magical when taken together.

"My neck hurts," Joanie says when they get home. "I need a drink."

"Are your parents home?" Clay asks.

"No," Hannah says, "why?"

Clay takes on that look he gets when he knows he's about to get his way. "I have some stuff in the car."

"What kind of stuff?"

"Alcohol, Han, what do you think?"

"I don't know if we should—"

"Come on, Hannah," Joanie says in a lofty voice. "You know they're at the Mason's. They won't be home for hours. We can drink on the porch and clean it all up before they get back."

"Sounds good to me," Luke says.

"Hold on, I'll go get it," Clay says, hurrying out to his car.

He comes back in with a handle of Absolut and a two-liter bottle of Sprite. Joanie sets about filling glasses with ice while Luke grabs snacks from the pantry.

"You alright?" Baker asks Hannah under her breath.

"We can still shut them down," Wally offers.

"It's fine," Hannah says, not looking at either of them. "We just have to be careful."

They sit around the table on the back porch and drink their vodka Sprites, all of them still wearing green, Luke wearing Joanie's Irishman hat. Joanie produces a deck of cards for them to play Kings, with Clay reminding them of the rules and Luke attempting to change them. "Why does it have to be '3 is *me*'?" he says. "We should make it, like, '3 is *naked spree*,' and everyone has to run around naked."

"How much vodka have you had?" Joanie says, rubbing his hair. "No way in hell are we doing that."

"Dude, just shut up for a second," Clay says. "Okay, one more time: 2 is you, 3 is me, 4 is floor, 5 is guys, 6 is chicks—"

"We *know*," Hannah says. "Can we just get started? I have no idea what time my parents will be back."

"Hannah, they are at a *party*," Joanie says, regarding her with distaste. "And they'll probably stay there for a while because, unlike you, they actually know how to have fun."

"Shut up, Joanie."

"Alright, hey, let's just get started," Wally says.

They play several rounds of Kings, with the vodka diminishing faster than Hannah anticipated. She starts to feel the alcohol and knows that her friends are feeling it too. Wally laughs much more readily than he normally does, Clay's voice gets louder and louder, and Baker's eyes get smaller and smaller.

"Dude, Clay, you're up," Wally says, hitting his shoulder. "Get a good one."

"Okay...8," Clay says as he reads his flipped card. "8, Pick a Date. Alright, who thinks they can keep up with my drinking?"

"Don't pick me," Luke slurs. "Joanie's making me drink too much."

"Sorry, man, but you're not what I envisioned for a date anyway. Okay, how about...Baker?"

Baker looks across the table at him. "You want me to match your drinking?" she asks, her voice carrying her smile. "I don't know if I can."

"I think you can," Clay grins.

They hold their drinks up to each other and cheers over the table. Hannah shakes the ice in her glass and takes another swig of her vodka.

By the late afternoon, with the sun beating down on them and two-thirds of the vodka gone, Hannah knows they are all drunk. Luke and Joanie lie slumped against their chairs and Clay rubs at his eyes every other minute. "I think everyone needs a nap," Baker says, her eyes small and glazed over.

"You want to send everyone off to a bed and I'll get this stuff cleaned up?" Hannah says. "Just try to keep them, like, hidden."

"Sure thing," Baker says, rising from her chair. "I'll be back in a minute to help you."

"I can do it," Wally says, sitting up straighter. "Go ahead, Bake, I'll help Hannah."

Baker hesitates, looking back and forth between Wally and Hannah, but then she turns and taps the other three to lead them inside. Hannah turns to Wally, who's looking at her.

"Y'okay?" he says.

"I'm good. Are you?"

"Yeah. Thanks for letting us hang out."

They clean up the table without talking. Hannah rinses the glasses and watches Wally through the kitchen window: he wipes down the porch table with a deliberate attentiveness, his arm muscles straining as he scrubs away a spill.

"Thanks," Hannah tells him when he comes back inside. "Can you get rid of that vodka bottle? I'm going to check on everyone and make sure they're okay."

She finds Joanie asleep in her bed, with Luke sprawled out on the floor, a blanket covering him. She imagines Baker tucking the blanket around him, touching his shoulder just before she pulls away, like Hannah has felt her do many times before.

The guest room door is slightly ajar. Hannah tiptoes toward it, not wanting to wake Clay, who is probably asleep in there, or Baker, who is probably asleep in Hannah's room next door. She's about to nudge the door open when she catches sight of something in the room.

Clay and Baker are both in there, but they're not sleeping. They're making out.

Clay stands against the bed, the backs of his legs scraping against it, and Baker stands with her body pressed into him, her hands rubbing over his shoulders while they kiss. Hannah ducks away from the door before they can notice her, her heart beating hard in her chest, but even as she hurries quietly back down the hallway and down the stairs, the image of them kissing burns itself on her mind: all she can see is Clay's mouth on Baker's, and Baker's mouth on Clay's, and the way their bodies had moved against each other.

"Hey," Wally says when she returns to the kitchen. Then, upon seeing her, he says it again. "Hey," he says, his voice softer and more concerned. "What's up? You look upset."

"Oh—nothing. I thought I saw a stain on the hallway carpet. I thought somebody had spilled."

"But it's all good?"

"Yeah," Hannah says, her heart aching. "It's all good."

Baker never mentions the kiss to Hannah. They go all through the following school week without her saying anything about it, even though Clay flirts openly with her and tries to grab her hand when they all hang out in the parking lot. Hannah thinks back on the previous conversations they'd had about boys—after Baker kissed Joey Dietzen, and that boy Lance in New Orleans, and Luke's cousin who came to visit; after Hannah kissed Ryder Pzynski, and Jonathan Owens, and Wally at the end of last summer—and Hannah wishes desperately that they could talk to each other now. She wants to talk about it, wants to hear it from Baker herself, even though at the same time she wants to push it from her mind, wants to remove it from her memory forever.

"Want to go to Sonic?" Baker says after school on Friday, and Hannah assumes that Baker wants to tell her now.

"Only if you let me pay this time," Hannah says, and then they're in the car and on their way.

They park at the Sonic on Perkins and roll their windows down to the smell of grease and fried food. Baker orders a Butterfinger Blast and Hannah orders a chocolate shake, and they trade the desserts back and forth while the traffic rushes past behind them.

"I'm surprised you got Butterfinger," Hannah says. "I thought you liked Oreo better."

"Yeah, but you like Butterfinger better," Baker says.

They talk about school and the test they had in Ms. Carpenter's class yesterday and what they're going to do on spring break. Hannah waits for Baker to tell her about Clay, but Baker never does.

"Want to hang out later tonight?" Baker asks when she drops Hannah off.

"Can't," Hannah lies. "I promised my mom we'd do a mother-daughter night."

Baker's expression falls just the tiniest bit. She licks her lips before she speaks. "That's great," she says. "Your mom will love that."

"Yeah."

"Okay, well, text me tomorrow."

"I will."

"'Bye, Han," Baker says, and then she puts on her sunglasses and backs out of the driveway.

Want to hang out? Hannah writes.

Wally replies seconds later. *Yeah, I'd love to. What do you want to do?*

They end up on Wally's back porch, his little brothers asleep in their room inside, his mom still out with her speech therapist friends. It's a cool night and Hannah shivers from the breeze.

"Here," Wally says, scooting closer to her. He wraps his arm around her shoulders, and she feels warmer.

"Thanks," she says.

They are quiet for a minute. Hannah can smell Wally's deodorant, musky and boyish, carrying her back to last summer when they made out on the dock.

"I'm glad you wanted to hang out," Wally says. "I love hanging out with all our friends, but it's nice to hang out with just you."

"Yeah," Hannah says. "Same."

He wraps his arm tighter around her, and she looks up at him, and then they start kissing. And it's exactly as she remembered: a series of motions, a mouth pushing against a mouth, a tongue sliding against a tongue, and that desperate voice, somewhere in the depths of her heart, wailing in panic.

Why aren't you liking this? Why aren't you liking this?

They make out for long minutes, and Hannah holds onto the hope that she will feel something, that something will trigger in her lower body, that she will respond like any other girl. She remembers how Baker looked when she was pressed up against Clay, so Hannah places her hands on Wally's shoulders and leans into his kiss, telling herself *She liked doing this, and so do I.*

They don't stop until they hear Wally's mom's car in the driveway. They jolt away from each other, and Wally says "Wow," and Hannah wipes at her mouth with the back of her hand.

"Where've you been?" Joanie asks when she gets home.

"Nowhere."

Joanie tilts her head, narrows her eyes. "Were you with Wally?"

Hannah busies herself with opening the refrigerator. She scans the items inside—orange juice, chocolate pudding, leftover jambalaya—before she answers in a deliberately distracted voice.

"Yeah, we were just babysitting his little brothers."

Joanie says nothing. Hannah grabs the orange juice for something to do. She pours the juice into a glass, still pretending like she's just breezed in with nothing on her mind. When Joanie still remains silent, Hannah turns around to look at her. Joanie has her eyebrows raised high and her lips pulled into her mouth.

"What?" Hannah asks.

"You know *what*, dummy. Wally. And you. Did something happen? Was there a *love* connection?"

Hannah can feel her face heat. "Shut up, Joanie," she says, meaner than she meant to sound. She shoves the orange juice back into the fridge and stalks out of the kitchen. By the time she reaches the top of the stairs, her throat is thick with unexpected tears.

The last days of March hang full with anticipation. At school, the whole student body seems to be holding its breath, waiting for Easter break. The seniors are especially on edge, waiting for their decision letters from colleges all across the country.

On the last Tuesday of March, Hannah pulls two envelopes out of her family's mailbox. The first, from Duke, contains a letter telling her she was not accepted.

The second envelope contains a letter from Emory. Hannah reads it carefully, her face pulled tight in concentration.

"What's it say?" Joanie asks.

Hannah looks up from the letter to see Joanie leaning breathlessly over the kitchen counter.

"I got in," Hannah says, the words vibrating in her throat as she laughs with relief.

She calls her mom and dad even though they're both at work. "Oh, Hannah!" her mom says, her voice louder than it ever is when she's at the office. There's the sound of something hitting wood, and Hannah pictures her mom smacking her palm against her desk. Her dad, when she calls him, reacts with quiet joy. "That's beautiful, honey," he says, his voice warm with pride just like it was when she would bring home her report cards in elementary school.

She texts her friends after that.

BALLERRRR, Luke replies. *Way to go han!!*

So awesome, Clay writes. *But this better not mean you're ditching us!*

I'm not surprised at all ☺, Wally writes. *Congratulations!*

Baker responds separately from the group thread. *You are amazing,* she writes, so that only Hannah can see. *I am so unbelievably proud of you.*

Hannah re-reads Baker's text message seven more times that night. She falls asleep with her phone clutched in her hand and Baker's face in her mind.

She wakes the next morning with a pit in her stomach.

She knows she should feel excited about her acceptance to Emory and the promise of spring break. She should feel infinite and hopeful, like the growing earth around her. Like the sunlight, which stretches longer each day, asking for one more minute, one more oak tree to shimmer on. Like the late March mornings, which arrive carrying a gentle heat, rocking it back and forth over the pavement in the parking lot, letting it crawl forth over the grass and the tree roots, nurturing it while it is still nascent and tender, before it turns into the swollen summer.

But while the whole earth prepares for spring, Hannah feels a great anxiety in her heart, for something dangerous has grown in her, something she never planted or even wanted to plant.

It's there. She knows it's there. If she's truthful with herself, she's probably known all along. But now, as the days grow longer and the Garden District grows greener, she can actually see it. It has sprung up at last, and it refuses to be unseen.

She tells herself it's passing. It's temporary. It's intensified only because she's a senior and all of her emotions are heightened. It's innocent. It's typical for a girl her age. It's no more or no less of a feeling than everyone else has had at 17.

But deep down, deep below the topsoil of her heart, she knows it's not.

Still, she pushes it down inside of her, buries it as far as it can go, suffocates it in the space between her stomach and her heart. She tells herself that she is stronger, that she can fight it, that she has control. That no one has to know.

I can ignore it, she thinks. *I can refuse to look at it. I can stomp on it every time it springs up within me.*

So she lies to herself that everything is normal. That she is normal. She carries herself through the end of the school week by refusing to acknowledge it. By refusing to align her heart with the growing sunlight and the nurturing heat and the flowering plants and the tall, proud trees.

"You alright?" Baker asks, when Hannah says goodbye to her after school on Friday.

Hannah stomps, buries, suffocates, wishes for death. "Yeah," she says. "I'm good."

Chapter Six: Spring Break

On the first day of spring break, Hannah steps outside to a mild blue sky. She stands still on the front porch, holding her sunglasses in one hand and her travel bag in the other, until Joanie lumbers out behind her and says, "Move your dumb ass, can't you see I've got an economy-sized duffle bag here?"

Baker shows up right on time, swinging her car into the driveway with country music pouring out of the open windows. Hannah drums her fingers on the hood of the car and offers her a smile. "Are you pumped?"

"So pumped," Baker says, stepping out of the car with her long legs and long hair.
She wears her favorite white shorts from Banana Republic and the old Raybans she inherited from her brother, and Hannah tries not to look at her for too long.

Hannah's mom steps out onto the porch behind them. "Do you have everything, girls?"

"I think Joanie has everything and then some," Hannah says, watching Joanie struggle to zip up her bag.

"And I think Hannah has *such* a great sense of humor," Joanie pants.

"Did you print out directions?" their mom asks. "You know where you're going?"

"We'll use our phones, Mom."

"Okay. Well, be safe. Call me when you get there. Use your manners and make sure you help Mrs. Landry with everything. And *no* drinking."

"We *know*, Mom," Hannah and Joanie say in unison.

"Drive carefully, Baker."

"I will, Mrs. Eaden."

"And if these two start fighting, just give me a call."

"I will," Baker laughs.

They all hug Hannah's mom goodbye, and she gives them *the look* and tells them to behave, and then they're in the car and on their way to meet the boys, and Hannah feels the promise of spring break growing in her belly.

"Adventure," she says, turning to grin at Baker.

Baker keeps her eyes focused on the road, but her mouth curves into a smile. "Adventure."

"I think we're *Destin*ed for greatness this break," Hannah says.

"I think you're right," Baker says.

"I hate both of you," Joanie says, and they all laugh.

They pick up Luke from his mom's house—she kisses him goodbye and waves at them from the porch, still wearing her bathrobe—and then drive to the Landry's to meet Clay, Wally, and Clay's parents. They park in the driveway behind Clay's dad's Audi.

"Hold on," Baker says, grabbing Hannah's arm to stop her from getting out of the car. "He wanted us to text him first."

"Why?"

"He wants to stash his alcohol in here before his parents come out."

"Genius," Joanie says.

Clay takes forever to come outside. Hannah, Baker, Joanie, and Luke sit in the car, their windows rolled down and their legs pulled up on their seats, swapping guesses about what's taking him so long.

"He's pooping," Joanie says.

"Stop projecting, Joanie," Hannah says.

"He probably lost his wallet again," Baker says. "But we're being rude just sitting here. We need to go in and say hi to his parents."

"I'm texting him again," Hannah says.

Clay walks out of the house a minute later, small duffle bag thrown over his shoulder and winning smile on his face.

"That's it?" Joanie says. "Look at the size of that bag. There's no way he fit all the alcohol in there. What's he bringing, those dinky little sample sizes of Firefly?"

Baker hangs her arm out the window as Clay strides up to the car. "Feel like going to Destin?" she asks.

"Absolutely," Clay says, his voice loud and rumbling. "Sorry I took so long. My mom made sausages."

"Where's the stash?" Joanie says, leaning forward from the backseat to address him.

"I have to go around to the backyard to get it. Hold on."

He disappears around the back of the house, then returns a few minutes later with a navy blue booksack in hand, Wally at his side this time. Clay waggles his eyebrows and gestures at the bag. Wally walks with his hands in his pockets, squinting behind his glasses. Hannah, Baker, Joanie, and Luke get out of the car and meet them on the driveway.

"This better?" Clay asks, opening up the booksack for them to see. Inside, Hannah can see two handles of whiskey and a fifth of vodka.

"Much better," Joanie says.

"We'll have to be careful," Baker says, "with your parents around and everything."

"We'll keep it hidden in our room," Clay says, gesturing to Wally and Luke. "Don't worry."

They stow the booksack in Baker's car, right in the middle of Luke and Joanie's seats ("It's like our baby," Joanie says; "Our beautiful, boozy baby," Luke says), and then head into the house to help Clay's parents bring their things out to the car. Mrs. Landry greets them warmly, pulling each of them into a hug, and says, "Look at this beautiful day—can it get any better?"

After the Landry's car is packed, their phones are set with the Destin address, and Clay has doubled back inside to use the bathroom, their caravan of cars reverses out of the Landry's driveway and heads toward the interstate. Hannah settles into the passenger seat, tucking her legs up underneath her, watching Clay and Wally's heads bob against the seats of Dr. Landry's car in front of them.

They cruise down I-12 East, laughing and joking and arguing over the music. Joanie convinces Baker to lower the windows so they can "appreciate the rush of the oncoming air and how it makes our hair blow in the wind like models." And then for a while they all sit quietly, subdued by the music and the stretch of the bright sun. Hannah picks up Baker's iPhone, connected to the stereo through the auxiliary jack, and scrolls through the playlists until she finds the one she wants—the one she discovered by accident a few months ago, and which made Baker blush and steal the phone back.

Songs han loves.

She plays Coldplay's "Strawberry Swing" and leans back against the leather seat, letting the sound and lyrics wash over her. No one says anything—they all sink into the song with willing submission— but Baker turns the stereo volume up, and Hannah glances over at her, at the way she looks behind the steering wheel, sunlight on her neck and shoulders, dark hair spilling over her cotton tank top.

"Perfect song," Baker says, her voice soft in the way it is when her mind is far away.

Hannah doesn't respond for a long beat. The lingering notes of the song echo in her head, until she blinks hard against the sunlight and shifts in her seat.

"Truth," she says, and scrolls through the playlist to find another song.

Their rental house is four stories tall, narrow, stucco, with windows that look out over the wrap-around balcony. Baker parks on the driveway behind Dr. Landry, and the four of them step out of the car and stretch in the sunlight, mimicking Clay, Wally, and the Landry's as they stare up at the house. Hannah can smell and taste the saltwater air all around them.

"Alright," Clay says, with quiet satisfaction. "This is definitely where I wanna be right now."

"It's a beautiful house," Baker says.

"Well come on," Dr. Landry says, climbing the stairs to the second-story entryway. "Let's have a look around."

The eight of them tour the house together, Hannah and her friends trailing the Landry's through the kitchen, the hallway, the basement bedroom, and the pool area. Clay tugs off his t-shirt and Sperry's and jumps into the pool right then and there, splashing them all with water.

"Clay—!" his mother starts.

"Come on!" Clay calls to Luke and Wally. "We don't need to see the upstairs anyway, we're not sleeping up there."

Wally looks to Mrs. Landry. She rubs a hand down her face and rolls her eyes. "Go ahead, Wally, Luke," she says. "You're on vacation, anyway."

They leave the boys in the pool and tour the upstairs. "This must be the master," Dr. Landry says, circling around a bedroom on the third floor. "Nellie, I'll get our things and bring them up here."

"Okay," Mrs. Landry says, popping her lips, "and let's see the other bedrooms—"

She leads them into a room across the hall from the master bedroom. It has a queen-sized bed and a Jacuzzi in the bathroom.

"Oh my god," Joanie says, eyeing the Jacuzzi. "I have to sleep in here."

Mrs. Landry laughs as she crosses the room to open the curtains. "So does that mean Baker and Hannah want to take the fourth-floor bedroom? Or do you want to share with your sister, Hannah?"

Joanie spins away from the group and heads into the bathroom, her eyes on the hot tub, unconcerned with Hannah's answer. Hannah looks to Baker before she can help it, realizing too late that she is asking a question with her eyes. Baker meets Hannah's eyes for only the sharpest second before she looks away.

In the time it takes her to inhale, Hannah knows an infinite moment of turmoil as her mind wrestles with her heart.

"I'll go upstairs," she says.

"Great," Mrs. Landry says. "Let's go on up and see it."

Hannah and Baker follow Mrs. Landry up the stairs to the very top floor, where they find a small landing with a white door leading off of it. Mrs. Landry nudges the door open with a light touch of her fingers to the wood, murmuring "Let's see" under her breath.

This room is smaller than any of the others in the house. The walls are sea green, with a paper border of seashells cresting along the top. There are two rectangular windows with pearl-colored, airy curtains that transform the bright sunlight streaming through them into something gentler, less powerful, so that it coats the room in a tempered glow. Hannah notes a dresser, a white wicker rocking chair, and, to the right of the door, a queen-sized bed with a seashell pink comforter. To her left, she sees a small bathroom.

"Oh, this is so cute," Mrs. Landry says, stepping toward the windows and parting the curtains. "I think you two got the best room in the house!"

"It's perfect," Baker says, her eyes shining as she surveys the room.

"It is," Hannah agrees.

"Well, I'll get out of your hair so you can unpack and get changed," Mrs. Landry says, crossing the room with a pleased smile on her face. "I'm going to make some sandwiches for y'all to take to the beach. Turkey okay?"

Hannah flops back on the bed after Mrs. Landry leaves. She stretches her arms above her head and listens as Baker unzips her tote bag and pulls items from within.

"You unpacking already?" Hannah asks, her eyes on the ceiling.

"If I don't do it now, you know I'll stress on the beach."

"True. Hey, did you bring toothpaste? I forgot mine."

Baker laughs softly. "Yeah. I brought every toiletry I could think of because I knew you'd forget something."

Hannah sits up on the bed, a smile already on her face. "What? I never forget anything."

"Freshman retreat, your deodorant. Sophomore summer—at the lake—your razor. And remember skiing with my family last year? You forgot your toothbrush and Nate had to go buy you one?"

"Fine," Hannah laughs. "You're right. As usual."

"I know," Baker says, a smirk on her face as she holds up her toothpaste. "Okay, let's get changed and head downstairs. We should help Clay's mom with those sandwiches."

They pull their swimsuits out of their bags, and now the energy in the room changes from giddy to awkward. They haven't thought about this part—about how to change in front of each other after what happened on Mardi Gras. Hannah digs further into her bag, pretending to search for something else, buying time to figure out what to do. But then Baker stands up and heads into the bathroom, swinging the door after her so that it doesn't fully shut, but doesn't remain open, either. And Hannah understands, as she hears the rustle of Baker's clothes falling to the floor, that she is supposed to change out here, in the bedroom, in her own space.

"Are you finished?" Baker calls through the bathroom door.

Hannah finishes tying the top of her turquoise two-piece. "Yeah, I'm good."

She merely glances at Baker when she comes out of the bathroom: a glance just long enough to see that she is wearing her favorite red bikini. "All set?" Hannah asks, just for the sake of making conversation, just to keep herself focused on something other than Baker's toned olive skin.

"Yeah. Are you bringing anything?"

"Couple of books."

Baker's eyes land on Hannah's skin for a lightning-quick second. "Yeah. Good idea."

The beach sand is hot under Hannah's feet as she and her friends saunter down toward the water, their towels slung over their shoulders, Baker and Joanie carrying beach bags, Clay carrying a food cooler.

"Feel that sun," Clay says, arching his neck skyward. "So awesome."

"Good thing we brought SPF 50," Joanie says, "or Hannah and I would fry like bitches."

"Joanie, what does that even mean, 'fry like bitches'?" Hannah says.

"You know what I mean. Don't ask me to explain my genius mind to you."

They drop their towels and bags on a patch of hot, smooth sand about twenty feet from the water, and without further ado, Clay, Wally, and Luke sprint down to the ocean, shouting and waving their arms as they go. Hannah, Baker, and Joanie spread out their towels and survey the beach to see who else might be here, but they don't recognize anyone from St. Mary's.

"Okay," Joanie says, pulling twin bottles of sunscreen from her bag and tossing one to Hannah, "let the sunscreen process begin."

"Should I time this?" Baker says.

"You should probably put some on," Hannah tells her. "Remember last summer? How burnt your shoulders got?"

"I know, Mom," Baker says, smiling as she crouches by her bag. "But I'm not using your bottle. I brought SPF 30. I want to get *some* color." She pulls a bright orange bottle from her bag, then lifts her tank top over her head. Hannah stares pointedly at the floral pattern on her beach towel.

"The boys are gonna burn," Baker says, squinting toward the ocean as she rubs white lotion all over her upper arms.

"Wally will make them come back in a minute," Hannah says. "You know he will."

"Here," Baker says, watching Hannah struggle to apply her sunscreen. "Let me get your back."

She spins Hannah away from her, and after a long second, Hannah feels the startling cold of sunscreen lotion on her skin. Then Baker's hands are there, warm and soothing, rubbing over her shoulders and upper back, then trailing down to her lower back and her hips.

"Are you using the 50?" Hannah asks, struggling to keep her voice even.

"Of course," Baker says, her voice bordering on tender. "I don't want you to burn at all."

And then Hannah feels Baker's fingers on the back of her neck, playing with the stubborn wisps of hair that have escaped from her ponytail. "All set," Baker says, her voice still harboring some of that tenderness.

"Thanks," Hannah says, turning around to offer her a half-smile.

"Can someone do my back?" Joanie says.

Baker's eyes tick away from Hannah, and for a shining hot second she seems to be looking at nothing, but then she blinks and focuses her eyes on Joanie. "Sure," she says, her voice back to its normal cadence. "Did you get your shoulders yet?"

On that first night at the beach, hours after Clay's parents have gone to bed, Hannah and her friends sit by the pool and drink whiskey-Cokes. Hannah can feel the sun's latent heat trapped beneath her skin, can taste the salt on the air when she takes a breath, can hear the ocean's rhythm playing deep in her ears.

She sits in a love seat with seashell-patterned cushions, and Baker sits next to her, her legs pulled up toward her chest and her arms wrapped around her calves. Clay sits on the ground with his whiskey glass secured between his feet, and every other minute he lifts the glass, shakes it, takes a swig from it, and spits the ice cubes back. Joanie and Luke sit tangled up in the same chair, her knees bumping into his stomach and her elbow resting on his shoulder, and Hannah watches as Joanie plays with one of Luke's curls. Wally sits opposite them, in the other chair, occasionally catching Hannah's eye and smiling in his steady way.

They talk for hours, one of them always heading inside to pee, another always heading inside to fill the ice bucket, another always carrying the thread of conversation so that nothing ever truly stops. They take turns shushing each other so as not to wake Clay's parents, and Baker and Wally take turns announcing the time and insisting that they should all go to bed, but they continue to sit in the cooling air while Clay tells the story of the time he broke a classroom window in second grade, and Luke tells the story of the time he got a crayon stuck up his nose in kindergarten, and Baker tells them about the boy she punched at Vacation Bible School. They laugh hard at each other's stories, leaning forward in their seats to point at each other and say "You *would* do that," and all the while the ocean plays for them in the background, quiet music in the their teenaged cathedral.

"I'm getting tired," Baker says, bumping her shoulder against Hannah's. "You ready for bed?"

"Want me to make you one last drink?" Hannah asks, her heart beating happily, her fears quelled by the alcohol and the ocean's magic.

A tipsy smile plays across Baker's face. She shakes the ice cubes in her glass, then shakes her head with that same lax smile. "Just sleep for me," she says.

They say good night to the others. Clay whines that they ought to stay down here for a while longer, 'cause don't they know they've got a whole handle of whiskey and a whole ocean of water to keep them company?, but Baker yawns and shakes her head no.

"Tomorrow night," she promises. "When we don't have to get up for Mass the next day."

"Fuck," Clay says, at the same time that Luke says "Shit."

"What time is it?" Joanie asks.

"Almost four," Baker says. "And Clay's mom said we had to leave by 9:15."

"I don't know why they can't give us a Sunday off," Clay says, wiping a hand down his face. "I'm sure the Good Lord would understand that we're on vacation."

"And drunk," Luke says.

"It's Palm Sunday tomorrow," Baker says, her voice flat, her eyes glazing over.

"Alright, whatever," Clay says, picking himself up off the ground. "I guess we should all head to bed and continue this tomorrow night."

"Let's get some water first," Wally says. "We're gonna be hungover in the morning."

"This is why I don't like Catholicism," Luke says as they clean up their glasses. "It seems to get in the way of everything."

Upstairs, in the quiet of their bedroom, Hannah and Baker get ready for bed with a comfortable calm between them. They stand in front of the bathroom mirror and brush their teeth together, crossing their eyes at each other's reflections. Baker washes her face while Hannah changes, then Hannah washes her face while Baker changes. They peel back the covers of the bed and shimmy their bodies beneath the sheets, and the linens are cool on Hannah's bare feet and legs.

"I feel tipsier than normal," Baker whispers.

"We had a lot of whiskey," Hannah whispers back.

Baker closes her eyes, then shifts closer to Hannah so that they're lined up, front to front, like two hands meeting in prayer.

Hannah smoothes Baker's eyebrow with her thumb, then runs a hand down the back of her head. Baker shifts even closer, until her face is on the edge of Hannah's pillow.

"You okay?" Hannah asks, her heart beating fast, fast, too fast.

Baker opens her bleary eyes. "Yeah," she says, her voice drunk and only half-there.

They stay like that, facing each other, until Hannah touches Baker's cheek and tells her to go to sleep.

"Only if you do," Baker whispers.

Hannah closes her eyes and dreams.

They are all hungover the next morning. Mrs. Landry watches them warily while they cross the church parking lot, her eyes somewhat suspicious, until Clay tells her the partial truth: that they were awake until four in the morning, hanging out by the pool.

"Well, you made a choice, now you have to make due with it," Dr. Landry says in his gruff voice. "The important thing is that you all got up for Mass this morning."

The church is much smaller than St. Mary's. The eight of them walk in a line up the center aisle, stepping carefully over the stone floor, ceiling fans whirring high above their heads, the air in the room humid and stale. Mrs. Landry leads them into a pew and Hannah sits down between Clay and Baker. Clay closes his eyes and breathes deep through his nose, and Hannah wonders whether he might be sick.

Hannah listens to the first two readings and the Gospel—the one about Jesus riding a donkey into Jerusalem, days before his Crucifixion, while the townspeople lay palm fronds at his feet—but she zones out during the homily. She stares instead at the family seated in the pew in front of them. Their two small children, a girl and a boy, alternate between crawling all over their parents' laps and coloring the

122

pages of the church missal. The little girl—maybe three or four years old—zigzags her crayons back and forth over the book, replacing age-old church hymns with rainbow creations. Hannah watches as the girl's father, upon noticing what she's doing, leans down and snatches the crayons from her with a reproving glare.

At once, the little girl's face changes from artless happiness to concentrated anger. She smacks her hands down onto the wooden pew and, scrunching up her face until her cheeks puff out in a near-cartoonish manner, huffs so forcefully that snot shoots out of her nose. The commotion catches the attention of everyone around her, so that the people two pews in front of Hannah turn around in confusion, and the people sitting in the right-side section of pews look over to see what's going on. The girl's mother starts rifling through her bag, probably searching for tissues, but the father picks the girl up and carries her out of the pew, an embarrassed scowl on his face, while the girl kicks her legs and beats her tiny, chubby fists against his shoulders.

The church goes back to normal as everyone pretends like they hadn't just been watching the little girl's tantrum. The mother in front of Hannah straightens her back and pulls her son close to her side, wrapping her arm tightly around him. The priest, up on the altar, continues his homily like nothing happened.

But on Hannah's right side, Baker starts silently laughing. Hannah can feel Baker's arm shaking, can see, out of the corner of her eye, that Baker lifts a hand to her face to smother her smile. Hannah tilts her head very slightly and shoots her a look—*What are you doing, you goober?*—but Baker, upon catching Hannah's eye, just shakes harder with silent laughter. And now Hannah can't seem to reel in her own smile, can't slow the giddiness that starts to overtake her, can't hold in the laughter that climbs to the top of her throat. "*Stop*," she whispers through her teeth, still catching Baker's eye, watching as Baker, with tears in her eyes, tries to fight down the hilarity that has overtaken her.

Clay leans forward on Hannah's left. He looks across Hannah to Baker, a cheeky smile on his face, and winks. Baker stops laughing for the space of a moment, just long enough to shrug her shoulders and send him a look that says *I don't know what's gotten into me.* She looks across Hannah as if she doesn't see her.

They each pick up a palm frond on their way out of the church. They walk back through the parking lot, following the Landry's to the cars, and Hannah experiences a strange exhaustion— the kind that comes after a giddy high.

Luke starts to swordfight Joanie with his palm frond when the Landry's aren't looking. Joanie reciprocates, a flirtatious smile playing on her face. Wally walks next to Hannah, tying his palm frond into a compact shape, his eyebrows knit together in concentration. And in front of Hannah, Clay walks in step with Baker, teasing her about her church giggles.

"We should get you tired more often," he says, poking her arm with his palm frond.

Baker squints at him in the sunlight. She assumes the playful expression Hannah has seen on many a weekend night—after Baker has stolen a bite of Hannah's ice cream, or when they've taken pictures of cats and photoshopped the boys' heads on top—and says, with a graceful shrug of her shoulders, "Just wait 'til I start laughing at *you*."

Clay grins like she's just told him he's the strongest man on earth. "Guess I'd better watch myself," he says.

They cook a late breakfast when they return from Mass—Hannah helps Baker make scrambled eggs while Wally prepares the toast—and then change so they can go down to the beach. The boys find boogie boards in the garage and carry them awkwardly over the sand: Clay over his head, Wally under his arm, and Luke dragging his behind him over the sand until Joanie sits down on it and demands a ride. They settle in the same area they occupied yesterday, and today Baker insists the boys apply sunscreen before they go down to the ocean. "This is because of my ears, isn't it?" Luke says, pointing at the burnt red tips of his cartilage. "Nah," Clay says, grinning where he stands while Baker rubs sunscreen over his shoulders, "it's just so the girls have an excuse to touch us."

Baker shoves him. "You can get the rest," she says. "Good luck reaching your back."

"Aw, come on, you're not gonna let me burn, are you?"

"You would deserve it."

"I would."

Joanie and Baker stretch out on their backs after the boys go down to the water. Hannah spreads her towel down next to them, trying hard not to look at Baker's long torso glistening with the oil from her sunscreen. She eases down onto her stomach and flips to her bookmark in *A Lesson Before Dying*, but she only manages to read one sentence before Joanie distracts her.

"Do you think I should keep dating Luke after y'all graduate?"

Joanie's expression, even with her eyes closed, is uncharacteristically anxious. Hannah keeps her thumbs over the pages of her book, unsure of whether she wants to engage in this conversation. Baker, lying between the two of them, speaks first.

"Where is this coming from?" she asks gently.

"Just something I've been thinking about."

Baker sits up on her towel. She pushes her sunglasses off her face and gives Joanie an open, sympathetic look. "Are you okay?"

"I'm fine," Joanie says, but Hannah hears the tremor in her voice and notices the old telltale sign: Joanie starts rubbing her left elbow, the way she used to when they were young and she was afraid to step onto the school bus.

"What's wrong, J?" Baker asks.

"I just—I mean—I have to start thinking about going through my day-to-day without him. He wants to stay together but I don't know if I can—not when he's going to be in a different state, making all these new friends, and meeting new girls—"

"Joanie," Baker soothes, setting a hand on her wrist. "Don't think about that yet."

"It's only April," Hannah says loudly. "Why are you worrying about this now?"

"It's spring break, Hannah," Joanie says.

"Exactly. We have so much time left—"

126

"No, we don't. It's basically the end of the year, whether you want it to be or not."

"It is not the end of the year. And even if you did break up with him, you wouldn't have to do that until, like, August."

"He's going to running camp for most of the summer," Joanie says. "I might have to do it before then."

"Still," Hannah says, opening her book again. "You're wasting your time worrying about this. Luke's awesome, and you like him, so why are we even having this conversation? Why don't you just enjoy being with him?"

"I am enjoying being with him, but I'm not going to act like things aren't about to change—I don't want to be stupid that way, like you—"

"Shut your mouth, Joanie," Hannah says, snapping her book shut.

"Learn some empathy, Hannah," Joanie growls, standing up and glaring down at her. "And start accepting that you're going to graduate soon."

She stalks away, her cell phone in her hand, and Hannah tosses her book into the sand in frustration. She wipes her hair back from her face and glares at Joanie's retreating figure.

"You okay?" Baker asks.

"I'm fine."

Baker is quiet for a moment. Then: "I'm scared, too. About graduating."

"I'm not scared."

"I'm worried I'm going to miss our friends too much. And St. Mary's."

"Why would you miss St. Mary's?" Hannah says, grating the words against the lump in her throat. "It's repressive, and close-minded, and nobody can go a minute without talking about *God*—"

"Hannah," Baker says. She smoothes her hand over Hannah's hair, starting at her hairline, moving across the crown of her head, and trailing off at the apex of her braid. She does it again, going more slowly this time, and Hannah feels the lump in her throat grow thicker.

"It's okay," Baker says.

Hannah swallows. She lowers her eyes to the pattern on her towel—yellow suns on a midnight blue background—and collects herself for a moment before she speaks.

"I don't want anything to change."

"I know," Baker says. "Me neither."

"I don't know where to go to college. Emory, or LSU, or even one of the other schools I got into...."

Baker drops her eyes. She rubs sand between her forefinger and thumb, her eyebrows creased in a frown.

"What should I do?" Hannah asks.

Baker sprinkles sand onto her towel. "Do you have a gut feeling about this?" she asks. "Where do you think you'd be happiest?"

"As of this moment..." Hannah says slowly, "my gut tells me Emory."

Baker moves her jaw around, still sprinkling sand onto her towel.

"But," Hannah continues, "I have a hard time believing I'd be happy without my best friend."

Baker looks up. Her eyes are sad. "You know if it was up to me," she says, "I'd probably be selfish and choose LSU for you. Just so we wouldn't have to be apart."

"I know."

"But when I think about it unselfishly, I want you to go to Emory."

"Why?"

"Because I had a feeling your gut was telling you Emory. The way your voice sounds when you talk about it—I can just tell you want to be there."

Hannah says nothing. Baker brushes the sand off her towel. The seagulls fly above them, filling the silence with their high-pitched squawks.

"Can we go back to pretending we have a lot of time left?" Baker asks.

Hannah clears her throat. "Yeah. Did you bring a book?"

"Yeah."

"Do you want to have a reading party?"

Baker smiles like Hannah has said the most wonderful thing in the world.

They drink by the pool again that night. Clay starts them in a game of Truth-or-Dare, which then evolves into a game of dares, which then evolves into them anonymously calling their teachers and administrators to say ridiculous things.

"Hi, yes, hello," Luke says, affecting a high, squeaky voice as he speaks into Clay's cell phone. "I'd like a large pizza. A very large pizza. The largest pizza you have. Pronto."

Mr. Manceau's agitated voice crackles through the speakerphone. "This isn't a pizza company. You have the wrong number."

"What? Oh, my good sir, I am so sorry, I seem to make this mistake frequently—if you only knew the extent of my ignorance! But hey, while I have you, could you recommend a good pizza place?"

"Goodbye," Mr. Manceau says.

"NO! Wait! I need my pizza!"

They hear the dial tone through the speaker, but before they can regroup, Luke dials the number again.

"Okay, fine, if you can't give me a large pizza, I'll just take a medium—"

"Stop calling me!" Mr. Manceau yells. "This is a personal cell phone number!"

"Then why is it listed online as the number for 'Chubby Charlie's Pizza Palace'?"

"What? Where did you see that?"

"Sorry, I've gotta go—"

"No—hold on—is this a prank call? Is my number really listed online?"

"Catch you later, Chubby Charlie."

Clay doubles over with laughter as Luke hits the red "End" button on his phone. Joanie leans her head against her hand and watches Luke with a fond look in her eyes.

"Alright, I've gotta go to bed," Luke says. "I'm exhausted from Mass this morning."

"Yeah, me too," Joanie says, standing up next to him.

"Right, so the rest of us will just stay out here and pretend like you two aren't hooking up inside," Clay says.

"Thanks," Luke says, taking hold of Joanie's hand. "We appreciate it."

Clay pours another round of whiskey after Joanie and Luke go inside. He holds up his glass for a toast, and Hannah, Baker, and Wally oblige him, each of them holding up their glasses in turn. "Cheers," Wally says, nodding at Clay, and the rest of them echo the sentiment.

"Let's keep this game going," Clay says as he settles back on his chair. "I love Truth-or-Dare."

"You just like to talk about sex," Hannah says.

"Yes I do," Clay says, smacking his lips together after taking a drink. "Even though it's not very fun with you all, since *none of you* can talk about it with me."

"Hey," Wally says, and in the dim porch lights, Hannah can see his blush. "You need to stop bringing that up."

"I'm just messing with you, man."

"Alright, Clay, I've got a Truth-or-Dare for you," Hannah says.

"Dare."

"I *dare* you to tell us what song was playing when you lost your virginity."

"I—" Clay falters. He shakes his whiskey glass and grins down at the patio, almost in amusement at himself. "I told you that in confidence, Han."

"And now you can tell all three of us in confidence."

"Alright, fine. So...when it happened, Michele told me to put some music on, so I just hit play on my iPhone, and the last song that had been playing was 'Colorblind' by The Counting Crows. I didn't really care what we listened to, so I just started going for it, you know, but then the song ended and replayed, and I realized I'd somehow put it on repeat."

"Are you serious?" Baker smiles.

"I'm serious."

"Why the hell had you been listening to 'Colorblind'?" Wally asks.

"Dude, I don't know, I just was."

"So you never took a break to change the song?" Baker asks.

"I was busy," Clay says emphatically, leaning forward in his chair. "And besides, it ended up being kind of nice. Kind of, you know, emo-romantic."

Wally chuckles into his hand. "Oh, man, I can't believe you never told me that story."

"Well now you can thank Hannah for bringing it up."

"Hey, you were making fun of the three of us," Hannah says. "All I did was put it back on you."

"I'm not ashamed," Clay says, taking a long pull from his whiskey glass. "I made love beautifully that night."

"Do you have the song on your iPhone right now?" Wally asks.

"Probably."

"Play it," Hannah goads.

"No chance."

"Play it," Baker says, nudging him with her foot.

Clay fixes her with a look; her teasing smile grows bigger until Clay smiles in turn. "Fine," he says, making a show of fishing his phone out of his pocket. "But y'all are not allowed to laugh."

"Why would we laugh?" Hannah says innocently.

"Can you do a reenactment in time with the song?" Baker says.

"I don't know why I'm listening to you," Clay says as he sets his phone on the table and hits play.

Within the first three sad, somber notes, Baker starts to giggle. She holds her hand over her mouth, much like she did in church that morning, and shakes with barely-restrained laughter. Her laughter is contagious, so that Hannah starts to giggle too, and then Wally starts to outright laugh, actually slumping back in his chair and holding his stomach.

"I'm sorry," Baker gasps, seeing Clay's fake-wounded face, "it's just, like, the depressing sound of this song, and the lyrics—"

"How did you not pause it?" Hannah laughs. "What did Michele say?"

"She didn't *say* anything," Clay says, grabbing his phone off the table and stopping the music. "She was too busy moaning."

"Oh, god," Hannah says distastefully, at the same time that Baker says, "Okay, wow."

"Dude," Wally says, shaking his head.

"What?" Clay says. "It's true. Someday soon you'll all get laid, and then we'll be able to have a real conversation about this. But anyway, it's my turn to ask Truth-or-Dare."

"Can we veto that?" Hannah says. "I have a feeling you're going to keep mocking us."

"I'll be nice," Clay says. He shakes his whiskey glass back and forth, and they all wait.

"Baker," he says.

"I knew I shouldn't have laughed," she says, pinching the bridge of her nose.

"Don't worry, I'll go easy on you," Clay grins. "Truth or Dare?"

"Truth."

"What's the best make out you've ever had? More specifically, *who* was the best make out you've ever had?"

Baker freezes, her mouth falling open in surprise. Hannah's whole body tenses up and her heart speeds in her chest. She clutches her whiskey glass in both hands, telling herself to take a drink, to act nonchalant, but she feels unable to do anything other than wait for Baker's answer.

"I should probably add that you *are* allowed to name someone here," Clay says haughtily, raising his eyebrows.

Color floods Baker's cheeks, and Hannah realizes that Baker feels trapped by the implication, as she never told Hannah about making out with Clay.

"Come on, really?" Clay says, his shoulders slumping.

"I—" Baker says.

"Damn," Clay says, sprawling back against his chair. "Who was better than me?"

Now Baker looks absolutely shamed: her cheeks are tinged dark, and her whole expression seems to retract in on itself. She opens her mouth to answer Clay, looking as mortified as the adulterous woman who was to be stoned in the bible, but there's something else in her reluctance, too: an elusive kind of hesitation, like she's fighting inwardly against something.

"It was you," Baker says finally, with an air of shoving the words out if only to keep breathing. She makes fleeting eye contact with Clay before looking down at the patio stones, her mental attention clearly focused on something else. She taps her tongue against her front teeth, bracing to say something she doesn't want to, and then mumbles, "I hadn't told Hannah yet."

"Oh," Clay says, his eyes shifting uncomfortably from Baker to Hannah. Hannah doesn't look at him. "Sorry. I told Wally, and I just assumed you told Hannah—"

"Sorry," Baker whispers, turning her head toward Hannah. She meets Hannah's eyes for only a flickering second.

"It's cool," Hannah says.

There's a long, awkward pause, and then Clay reaches for the whiskey bottle again. "Well," he says, his voice embarrassingly hearty, "at least I know I was your best."

The next day, Monday, they sleep in late and don't trek down to the beach until noon. Wally and Clay convince Hannah to swim in the ocean with them, and even though Hannah feels irrationally sore at Clay, she agrees to go with them, mostly to avoid sitting awkwardly on the beach with Baker. They bob in the waves, scraping their toes against the mushy layer of sand that coats the bottom of the ocean, and Hannah's senses turn themselves over to everything saltwater: saltwater on her tongue, saltwater in her nose, saltwater stinging a half-healed blister on her ankle.

"I have to take a piss," Clay says, sweeping a hand through his wet, dark hair. "I'll be back."

He swims away from them, toward an open spot in the ocean, leaving Hannah and Wally to themselves. "Is he just gonna go in the water?" Hannah asks incredulously, straining her eyes against the sunlight.

"He's been doing it all week," Wally laughs. "Luke, too."

"Please tell me you haven't been doing that."

"I'm not saying anything either way."

"Ew."

"Everyone pees in the ocean, Han."

Something moves against Hannah's calf, startling her. She looks down to the water but can't see anything past the surface. Then Wally starts to laugh in that small, shy way he has.

"It was just me," he says. "Don't worry."

Hannah extends her arm outward, to the side, and sweeps water into Wally's face. He sputters and throws his arms up to shield himself, and Hannah starts to laugh.

"It was just me," she says. "Don't worry."

"Yeah, I see that," Wally says, his mouth curved into a smile, his eyes large and bright and vividly green in the absence of his glasses.

"Yo," Clay says, swimming back toward them. "Pretty sure I just unleashed about a liter of Jack Daniels into this ocean."

"You're disgusting," Hannah tells him.

"So Han," Clay continues, as if she hadn't said anything, "now that you know about Baker and me—"

Hannah's stomach knots in on itself.

"—What do you think I should do to get with her again?"

"What?"

"Come on, I like her. And I think she likes me. Or at least it seemed that way when she was making out with me." He waggles his eyebrows.

Hannah stares at him, unable to respond, feeling his words drop through her chest and sink all the way down to her stomach.

"So?" Clay prompts. "What do you think?"

"I don't—I don't know. She hasn't talked to me about it."

"Not even last night?"

"No."

"You should just talk to Baker directly," Wally says.

"And say what, Wall?" Clay says. "'Hey Bake, I think you're hot, wanna hook up again'?"

"Is that what this is?" Hannah says, her voice sharp with emotion. "You just want to hook up with her?"

Clay's entire countenance changes in an instant. His eyebrows draw together and his eyes narrow with scrutiny. He stares intently at Hannah, as if searching something out in her, and she remembers, with startling accuracy, the way she felt when they first became friends: that he possessed some secret truth she had never known, some kind of raw power that enabled him to understand people, to detect their insecurities, and ultimately to sway them to his side.

"No," Clay says finally, the intense look still present in his eyes. "Of course not. I think she's the prettiest girl I've ever seen—I've thought that for years—and I want to hook up with her again, yeah, but it's more than that. There's just something about her that makes me want to know her better. But I'm not sure how to do that. I'm not sure how to move beyond the physical stuff."

Neither Hannah nor Wally responds. Hannah feels a weird looseness inside of her, like her muscles have gone slack. Clay continues to look at her with his intense eyes, but there's a shade of uncertainty to them now, a tinge of pleading.

"I don't know," Hannah says after a moment.

Clay sighs in frustration and runs a hand through his hair. Hannah studies him—his tree-dark hair and eyes, his firm mouth, his strong jaw—and thinks inexplicably of the primordial Adam.

Clay shakes his head back and forth. "She's so hard to figure out. It feels like I've known her forever, but I still don't *get* her. I don't even know, like, the little shit about her. I mean, you know that stuff, Han. Like, her favorite book and color and everything. Don't you?"

Hannah looks away from him.

"Han?"

"Perks," she says.

"What?"

Her chest swells. "*The Perks of Being a Wallflower*," she says, unable to keep a sharpness from her voice. "She named her dog after it."

"Oh. Yeah. And what's her favorite color?"

Hannah looks at the sun until it blinds her. Then she looks back to Clay, but she can no longer see him through the imprint of the sun on her eyes.

"Yellow," she says.

"Yellow," he repeats. "Got it."

"I still think you should just talk to her," Wally says.

"Maybe," Clay says, his eyes focused on the water. "We'll see how it goes at Tyler's party tonight."

They eat a late dinner with the Landry's—Mrs. Landry cooks pork chops—and then shower in preparation for the party. "So you're telling me there's going to be no drinking there?" Dr. Landry says in an accusatory tone, staring Clay down when they're about to leave.

"Not that I've heard of," Clay says innocently. "If there is, we'll come home."

"Be back by one."

"One?"

"You want to make it 12:30?"

"No, sir."

"Stay together," Mrs. Landry says. "And *be good.*"

They walk through the cooling night air, down chalk-white sidewalks and past patches of grass so green they almost look fake. Clay and Baker take the lead, both of them dressed with social precision, Clay in a salmon-colored Polo shirt and Baker in her favorite navy sundress. Luke and Joanie walk behind them, swinging each other's hands loosely between them, Luke pointing out which beach houses he's going to buy when he's older, changing his mind on every new block. Hannah and Wally follow last, both of them quiet, an easy current of companionship between them.

"That one's just *lovely,*" Luke says, pointing to a flamingo-pink two-story. "I can buy that when I go through my gay phase."

"We should live here all the time," Joanie says, swinging Luke's hand with exaggerated silliness. "Let's just quit school and get jobs lifeguarding."

"We should all agree to come down here in the summers," Clay calls back to them. "You know, during college and when we're in our 20s and everything. We can all rent a house together."

"You and your fantasies," Joanie says. "It's like you think we're in a sorority or something."

"Six-Pack for life," Clay says, raising his left hand and right pointer finger in the air.

There are very few people at Tyler's house when they arrive. "What's *up*," Tyler says, drawing out the last syllable as he greets them at the door. "Y'all came on the earlier side of things."

"Didn't want to miss the fun," Clay says, clapping him on the shoulder. "Can you hook us up with some drinks? We couldn't sneak anything past my parents."

"No worries. Come on in and have whatever you want. This one's gonna be a rager."

Hannah catches Baker's eye as the six of them move to step over the threshold. *Rager*, Hannah mouths at her, lifting her eyebrows mockingly. Baker shakes her head and bites her lip, and Hannah can tell she's fighting a smile.

They follow Clay into the house, waving hi and calling hello to the classmates they pass as they walk by. Clay leads them to a high kitchen counter and they all circle around it, preparing to start their ritual.

Clay pours six shots of whiskey and raises his glass in a toast. "To an amazing spring break," he says, his deep voice resonating around their circle, "and to my amazing friends."

"To our beautiful sorority," Luke says, winking at Joanie.

"And our beautiful faces," Joanie says. "And just how beautiful we are in general."

"To Luke's future pink house," Wally says, saluting him with his shot glass.

"Amen," Luke says.

"Han?" Clay prompts, eyeing her from across the circle, and she can tell that he's feeling her out, that he's checking to see if the two of them are okay.

Hannah elevates her shot glass higher. "To our friends," she says, "just like Clay said."

"May we always stay friends," Baker says, "no matter what happens."

"Let's drink these already!" Joanie says, clanging her shot glass against the communal pile.

They throw their shots back and slam the glasses on the counter, each of them sticking their tongues out and gasping in reaction to the hard alcohol, and suddenly Tyler appears and hangs his arms over Clay and Luke.

"Well come on, y'all," he says. "Come join the rest of us heathens."

Half an hour later, the party has swelled to include another 40 or so St. Mary's kids, so that Hannah has a hard time moving from one side of the house to the other. The music blares so loudly that she has to yell to Joanie to make herself heard, and eventually Joanie throws her hands up and mouths *Can't hear* before she pulls Luke over to the middle of the room to dance.

Several of the other senior girls have drawn Baker into conversation, and Hannah watches them curiously, noting their excessive smiling, their arm grabbing, and the small sips they take from their Solo cups. Baker stands confidently before them, her hand on her hip and her hair hanging loose over her sundress.

"Some party," Wally says into Hannah's ear.

"What?"

He gestures toward the back patio and raises his eyebrows in a question—*Do you want to go outside?*—so she nods and follows his path through the packed house.

"Shit," Wally says when they step out onto the porch. "I couldn't even breathe."

"It's really fucking loud in there," Hannah says, covering her ears to stop the echoes of the music.

"I know. I'd much rather be back at the house right now."

"Why didn't you say so? Maybe everyone else would've wanted to stay, too."

"Nah. They love coming to these parties. And I don't mind them too much. I like the people watching."

"You love people watching," Hannah laughs.

"I do," Wally laughs, touching the frames of his glasses. "I like trying to understand people and how they see the world."

"Mr. Curiosity."

"I'm only curious about some things," Wally says, looking sideways at her.

Hannah breaks eye contact with him. She lets out a short laugh because she doesn't know what else to do.

"Hey, by the way," Wally says, "were you okay today? In the water?"

The question catches her off guard. "Oh. Yeah. I just—I don't know how I feel about Clay and—and Baker."

"He means well," Wally promises. "I know he talks callously sometimes, especially about girls, but I think he really likes her, Han. I think it's for real this time."

"He told you that?"

"Not exactly, but I can read Clay pretty well at this point."

"Oh."

"Are you worried?"

Wally looks so kind, and so sincerely concerned, that Hannah almost wants to run away. She looks away from him and leans against the balcony railing, touching her hands to the cold, smooth metal. "I just—" she says. She feels the words stirring within her, threatening to come up. "I—she's my best friend, you know? My *best* friend."

"Yeah," Wally says. "You care about her. You want her to be with the right guy."

Hannah says nothing. Her throat thickens with welled-up words.

"You want to stay out here for a bit?" Wally asks.

Hannah swallows. She breathes in the saltwater air. "Nah," she says, shaking her near-empty Solo cup. "I think I'll get another drink."

The party gets wilder as the hours go on. Tyler plays a quick succession of crowd-pleasing songs, and the party swells with peak noise when "Love Story" by Taylor Swift comes on. Everyone in the house, boys and girls alike, screams the lyrics with mad intensity, and suddenly all the girls are pointing dramatically at the boys when Taylor sings to her Romeo, and Luke's kneeling on the ground and serenading Joanie, and it sort of feels like everyone there has spent

144

their 16 or 17 or 18 years simply waiting to sing this song together at a beach house in Destin.

Hannah tries not to watch Baker and Clay dancing together on her right, but as the song goes on, they seem to grow larger in her peripheral vision. Their hands are matched together as they sing, and as Hannah turns to see them better, Clay twirls Baker in a circle and smiles his big cocky grin at her. She smiles radiantly back at him. Hannah's heart aches in her chest.

The song changes to a club song Hannah doesn't know, but the crowd around her shouts their approval and shifts easily into the beat. Hannah moves her body and gulps from her beer to have something to do. Wally smiles at her as he dances across from her, and she smiles back, fighting hard to stomp down her feelings.

But she can't ignore how Clay draws Baker in close to him and presses his forehead against hers. She can't ignore how their bodies move together and Clay's hand wraps around Baker's waist. She can't ignore how Baker seems to *want* it, how her hips move into his and her hand grips his upper arm.

"I need some air," Hannah says, though no one can hear her over the music anyway. She pushes her way through the packed room, and suddenly it's like she can't move fast enough, like her heart wants to push out of her throat before she makes it outside.

When she finally reaches the sanctuary of the balcony, her heart feels so high in her throat that she might choke. She takes long, deliberate breaths and orders herself to pay attention only to the here and now: what she can see, what she can feel, what she can smell and hear. She focuses hard on the smell of the saltwater air, on the distant moving of the ocean, but the pain rises out of her anyway.

Please. Please can you make it stop hurting it hurts so badly. I don't want it. It hurts and I don't want it. I'm trying to make it go away. Please, just make it go away, just make it go away.

But there's an ancient voice deep inside of her that knows it will never go away, no matter what she does or how hard she prays.

She would be content to stay out here all night, fighting this thing inside of her, gulping down sea air to try and clean out her insides, but some classmates interrupt her.

"Oh, sorry," Lisa says when she and Bryce stumble out onto the porch. Bryce pays hardly any attention; he's kissing at Lisa's neck. "What's up, Hannah," Lisa says drunkenly. "Do you mind if we hang out here?"

"No, that's totally fine," Hannah says shakily, tipping her cup toward them in a pathetic, long-distance cheers. "I was just cooling off."

She steps away from the balcony and walks past them, but right when she reaches the door, Lisa says, "Did you see your girl Baker making out with Clay on the dance floor? How cute are they! You have to tell her I said how cute they are."

"Yeah," Hannah says, fighting hard against the pain spreading over her heart. "I will."

She can't find her friends when she reenters the house. She circles the makeshift dance floor, searching for Baker's dark hair, for

146

Wally's glasses, for Joanie's neon headband and Luke's messy curls, even for Clay's cocky smile, but none of them are there.

She disappears up the steps to the second floor, slinking in the darkness like a thief, hoping no one notices her. Her body feels loose with alcohol but her heart feels tight with pain.

She finds them in a bedroom off the main landing. Wally, Joanie, Luke, and Clay sit with their backs against white furniture pieces. They beam up at her when she opens the door, and the relief she feels is so sudden that she almost yells at them.

"Where the hell have you been?" she says.

"Um, hello, I think it's pretty clear that we've been in here," Joanie giggles.

"Where's Baker?"

"She went looking for something...or someone...I don't remember," Clay says, tapping his head back against a dresser, a drunken grin plastered on his face. "But don't worry," he says, waggling his eyebrows, "she'll be back."

"Where were you?" Wally asks.

Hannah doesn't respond at first: she's too preoccupied with Clay's insinuation. After a pause, she sits down and mumbles, "Porch."

"Speaking poetry to the stars," Joanie sighs dramatically.

"Shut up."

"Oh, relax, Han," Clay says, nudging her. "Here, spend a minute with my friend Jack. He'll make you feel better."

She stares blankly at the handle of whiskey. "What, are you just drinking from the bottle?"

"Do you want a shot glass?" Joanie says. "You can have the one with the fat tourist's picture or the one Luke backwashed into."

"Thanks for saving me the good ones."

"Fat tourist it is," Joanie giggles, and passes her the glass.

They play a game where everyone has to say "—in Luke's pants" at the end of every sentence. They pass the whiskey around the circle and sip from it every few minutes, taking short pulls that burn their throats, the shot glasses discarded at their feet.

"Hannah, you're taking extra...in Luke's pants," Joanie says.

"Mind your own damn business...in Luke's pants."

"I will shank you."

"In Luke's pants?"

"Let's sing a song," says Wally, "...in Luke's pants."

"What do you want to sing in Luke's pants?" Joanie says.

"'Calling Baton Rouge.' In Luke's pants."

"Garrrrrth!" Joanie shouts.

"Let's sing Nicki Minaj," Luke says.

"You are so fucking gay," Clay laughs.

"Dude," says Luke. "'Super Bass.' *Super. Bass.*"

"Can't we plug in an iPod or something?" Joanie asks. "Where are the speakers? Hannah, where are the speakers?"

"What the hell are you talking about?"

"Our speakers! Where are they!"

"Oh my god, Joanie, they're at our house in Louisiana. They're not *here!*"

"Oh," Joanie says, looking lazily at the wall.

"I'll play something from my phone," Luke says.

148

He plays "Wagon Wheel," and they all tilt their heads back and sing along. Luke wraps his arms around Joanie and they sway back and forth, both of them singing loudly and obnoxiously; Clay and Wally strum invisible banjos, with Clay following Wally's example. They sing and laugh and laugh and sing, but Hannah can't bring herself to sing along, or even to smile.

"Let's play it again," Luke says when the song ends.

"Nah," says Clay, rising off the floor. "Let's go back downstairs. We're missing out on the party."

"Who needs that? We've got this whole handle of whiskey to ourselves."

"Come on, we came for the party, we can't just hide up here."

"Let's just head back, then."

"Dude, this is our one chance to really let loose this week. Come on. Let's all just go back downstairs."

"Calm down, Clay-Clay," Hannah says, knocking his calf with the whiskey bottle. "Your reputation won't expire just because you're up here."

"I hate when you call me that."

Hannah shrugs. "We all hate things sometimes."

"Baker's down there by herself," Clay says. "Don't you think we should go find her?"

Hannah sets down the whiskey bottle and narrows her eyes at him. There's a prolonged pause until Wally stands up and brushes his hands together. "Alright, let's all go down," he says. Luke makes a noise of protest from the floor, but Joanie kisses his cheek and says, with mock seriousness, "You can do it. I believe in you."

"Sweet," says Clay, nodding his head as they all stand up. He opens the door and leads them toward the stairs. "They've probably all been wondering where we went."

"Probably not," Hannah mutters under her breath, and Wally catches her eye and smiles.

Downstairs, the party has degenerated into messy, erratic chaos. The floor is littered with beer cans and red cups, and a group of underclassmen has hijacked the stereo. As Hannah and her friends descend the stairs, Clay and Wally get pulled into conversation with a group of raucously drunk guys, but Hannah notices Clay's eyes peering beyond them, searching for something. Hannah follows Joanie and Luke back into the heart of the room, where Tyler and some senior soccer players have taken to standing on top of the furniture and pumping their hands in the air. Everything in Hannah's vision is dim, like someone has covered the sides of her eyes and placed a film over her pupils.

"Let's jump on the furniture with them!" Joanie shouts into Hannah's ear. Hannah turns to give her an incredulous look, but Joanie only barks with laughter, grabs Luke's hand, and climbs on top of the kitchen table. As Hannah watches, Joanie sways back and forth with her blonde hair falling over her face, and Luke hops around in a circle next to her. The table thumps with their weight.

"Hey!" somebody shouts in Hannah's ear, and she turns to find Baker behind her.

"Hi!"

"Where've you been?!"

"Upstairs!"

Baker cups a hand around her ear to indicate that she can't hear, then takes Hannah's hand and tugs her out of the crowd and down the hallway. Hannah thinks they're going out to the porch, but Baker leads her through a side door into the garage. Hannah pulls the door closed behind them but hears it bounce off the lock.

"Leave it, it's fine," Baker says, walking further into the garage. "I just wanted some air."

"So you brought us to the garage instead of the porch?"

Baker smiles. Her eyelids look heavy; her eyes seem unfocused. She indicates the outdoor refrigerator and says, "I wanted a water, too."

"How'd you even know this was here?"

"I went looking for you. Where were you?"

"We were upstairs," Hannah says, stepping closer to the refrigerator. "I couldn't find you but I found everyone else in a bedroom up there. We were just drinking and hanging out."

"I thought you'd left me. I texted you like three times."

"I'd never do that," Hannah says, looking steadfastly at her. "You know that."

Baker opens the refrigerator and pulls out a water bottle. She uncaps it carefully and says, not looking at Hannah, "I'm sorry for not telling you about Clay."

There's a pause while neither one of them looks at each other. Hannah can hear the music booming inside, but from where they stand in the garage, she feels like she's hearing it from underwater.

"Why didn't you?" she asks.

Baker still doesn't look at her. Her eyes, unfocused and glazed over, cut an angular path to the cement floor. She inhales like she's about to speak, but then she closes her mouth.

"Bake?"

"I didn't know how I felt about it," Baker says.

"I made out with Wally again," Hannah offers, "and I didn't know how I felt about that, either."

Baker lifts her head. "You made out with Wally?"

"Yeah. Couple weeks ago."

"Oh."

"Yeah."

"That's great," Baker says listlessly. Then, as if asking the question causes her pain, she says, "How was it?"

Hannah gawps on the air. She takes in Baker's expression: the downward crinkle of her eyebrows, the jutting out of her bottom lip, and her eyes, bleary as they are, colored over with that perfect dark roast shade. There's something unnamable in her expression—some kind of bigger question that Hannah feels shimmering on the air.

"I liked kissing you better," Hannah whispers.

Baker breathes in quickly, almost like she might be hiccupping. Her eyes flit to Hannah's mouth, then back to Hannah's eyes.

Hannah leans forward and kisses her. Baker startles, but then she kisses back. The water bottle rests between their bodies, pressing coldness into Hannah's stomach.

They break the kiss to breathe, but Hannah doesn't dare pull away from her, not when either one of them might realize what they're doing. She kisses Baker again, and Baker kisses her, too, and the garage is quiet but for their wet kissing sounds and the throb of the music on the other side of the wall.

Baker moves her hand across Hannah's back, and Hannah mirrors her automatically, instinctively touching as much of her as she can. Baker kisses her with soft, rhythmic motions, her lips coming together and separating gracefully. And when Hannah opens her mouth wider and touches her tongue tentatively to Baker's, Baker responds with a hum and an equally eager tongue.

It's better than Hannah remembered, better than she imagined all those nights she lay awake in bed. It's hot and sweet and it *does* something to her; it awakens her body in a way kissing Wally never has. She feels it in her stomach, in her heart, and in that mysterious cavity at the base of her torso, propelling her to keep going, to kiss this girl until some unnamed need is filled.

Then, a noise. The slamming of a door.

They jolt apart and whip their eyes to the door, which is now fully closed. Hannah's stomach shrinks with dread.

"Someone saw us," Baker chokes out. In the dim light of the garage, her expression is wild with primal fear. She breathes erratically, her breath coming in short heaves, and her eyes are frenzied, like those of a trapped animal.

"It's okay," Hannah says, feeling equally panicked. She can hear the terror in her own voice and struggles to control it for Baker's sake. "I bet someone just bumped into the door on their way to the porch."

Baker doesn't seem to be listening. Her eyes dart all over the garage, but she doesn't look at Hannah. She places a hand on the refrigerator to steady herself, then falls against the wall of the garage, nearly hyperventilating.

"It's alright," Hannah says, pleading with her, or maybe just pleading with herself. The panic she feels is suffocating. "We'll just—we'll just go back into the party like everything's fine—"

"We need to go home," Baker rasps, her eyes still wild with fear.

"Okay," Hannah says, trying to breathe around her panic, "let's just go grab the others—come on—"

"No," Baker says, still refusing to look at Hannah. "We're not going anywhere together. We're not."

"Stop freaking out," Hannah says, hearing the flood of emotions in her own voice.

"You go inside. You go inside first, and I'll come in a few minutes—"

"I'm not leaving you here by yourself, you're too upset—"

"Just *go!*" Baker orders in a shrill whisper.

Hannah stumbles away from her, feeling like the whole night has been poisoned with fear. She sneaks back into the house and tries to catch her breath, but her heart hammers so fast that she thinks she might pass out from it.

She hurries out to the porch without thinking about it. It is, mercifully, devoid of people. She hangs her arms over the railing and gulps on the saltwater air, begging her head to clear and her heart rate to slow.

Please, she thinks, the words coming from deep inside of her. *Please, please, please help me.*

The walk home is fuzzy. Hannah is vaguely aware of Clay leading the pack and of Luke and Joanie walking behind her. She walks instep with Wally and says nothing, feeling lost in the labyrinth of her own mind.

The only thing she can focus her attention on is Baker, who walks next to Clay, her shoulders hunched and her sandals shuffling listlessly on the sidewalk.

"I'm going to bed, y'all," Clay says when they enter the house. In the dim light of the kitchen, he looks tired and worn. "Anybody need anything?"

"Nah, I'm going to bed, too," Luke mutters tiredly.

"Let me get everyone some water," Wally says.

"Everyone come take some aspirin," Joanie whispers, rifling through her purse.

Hannah stands uncertainly at the back of the group, hyperaware of Baker and the knotted tension that seems to be radiating off of her.

"Hey," Clay says, stepping over to Baker and speaking in a low voice. "You alright? Need anything?"

"I'm fine," Baker whispers. "Thanks, Clay."

"No problem," he smiles.

The boys head off to the basement and Joanie leads the way up the stairs, Hannah following behind her and Baker following several steps behind Hannah. Joanie steps into the bedroom on the first landing, waving silently behind her as she closes the door, and then Hannah leads the way to the bedroom on the top floor, her chest leaden with anxiety.

They don't speak as they get ready for bed. It feels clinical and depressing to Hannah, who can only remember nights of giddiness and muffled laughter and making cross-eyed faces at each other in the mirror. But now Baker won't look at her in the mirror or in person.

Hannah opens the windows while Baker brushes her teeth in the bathroom. The cool night air makes it easier for her to breathe. She leans her forehead against the window screen, trying to stay calm, trying to contextualize this night as just one disorienting event in what will otherwise be a long life of steadiness.

To her surprise, Baker speaks to her.

"I don't want the windows open."

Hannah turns around, entirely caught off guard. "What?"

Baker strides past the windows, staring determinedly away from her. "Not tonight. I can't handle it."

"What do the windows have to do with anything?"

"Just—shut them, please," Baker huffs. Her voice trembles with barely constrained anger.

Hannah stares at her, waiting for an explanation, but Baker climbs into the bed, rolls onto her side, and says nothing.

"Fine," Hannah says. She shuts the windows hard—for a half-second she startles, worrying that she might have woken the Landry's— but the room quickly dissolves into silence again.

Chapter Seven: The Only Two Humans on the Earth

Baker is gone from the bed when Hannah wakes the next day. Hannah finds her in the kitchen, eating a bowl of cereal and talking to Clay's mom.

"Good morning, Miss Hannah!" Clay's mom says, far too loudly and bubbly for Hannah's current state. She clutches a coffee mug and wears a floral-patterned robe. Baker sits next to her at the table, but she doesn't raise her eyes from her cereal.

"'Morning, Mrs. Landry," Hannah says.

"What would you like to eat?"

"I'm just going to get some Raisin Bran, thanks."

She pours the cereal into one of the delicate ceramic bowls, then fills a plastic cup with ice water. Clay's mom resumes her conversation with Baker, asking her about how she's going to choose a roommate for LSU. When Hannah sits at the table with them, Mrs. Landry glances away from Baker to give Hannah a welcome smile, but Baker keeps her eyes trained on Mrs. Landry.

Hannah tries hard to make eye contact with Baker, but Baker only looks between her cereal bowl and Mrs. Landry. A cell phone rings, and Mrs. Landry peels herself gracefully off her chair to answer it.

"Oh, hold on, girls, I've got to take this one, it's one of my bible study babes," she says. "Hello?" she answers. "Well, good morning to you, too!"

158

Hannah plays with the raisins in her bowl, burying them underneath the milk, until Mrs. Landry walks out onto the back porch and closes the door.

"Hey," Hannah says quietly, looking up at Baker. "You alright?"

Baker meets her eyes for a fraction of a second. "Fine. Are you?"

"Yeah." Hannah taps her spoon against her bowl.

They say nothing else to each other.

Baker doesn't speak directly to Hannah after their friends wake up and fill in the space around them. They all walk down to the beach again, and the sun beats hot on Hannah like it has every other day this week, but Baker doesn't catch her eye or smile at her, and every joke or remark Hannah says to the others seems to materialize from a scared, hollow place inside of her.

The boys spend a long time in the ocean. Hannah hangs out on the sand with Joanie and Baker, pretending to read while the two of them hit a volleyball back and forth. After a while, Joanie plops down onto her towel and puts her headphones into her ears, and Hannah and Baker are left in hot silence.

Baker kneels on her towel to apply sunscreen, and Hannah focuses so hard on the text of her book that the letters blur. She can see Baker out of her peripheral vision, squinting beneath her sunglasses as she lathers her shoulders and arms. Baker reaches behind her to rub in her back, and Hannah watches her struggle for a moment before she can no longer take it. She flops the book down onto her towel and sits up to help her.

"I'm fine," Baker says.

"Just let me get your back."

"I am getting it."

"Not very well. Just—here." Hannah rubs some lotion in-between Baker's shoulder blades, and Baker leans forward, her shoulders tense. Hannah pours more sunscreen onto Baker's back and lathers it down her spine, all the way down to her hips.

"Okay?" Hannah asks.

"Yep," Baker says, with an edge to her voice, and then she wrenches out of Hannah's grasp and walks purposefully down to the water, and Hannah is left kneeling on her towel.

There's pizza for dinner that night. Mrs. Landry apologizes to the group for not having the energy to cook something, and Dr. Landry waves off the apology and says, "This is fine, honey, we can eat pizza one night this week."

Hannah sits on the back porch after dinner and plays Apples to Apples with Wally, Luke, and Joanie. She tries not to think about how Baker is still sitting at the kitchen table with Clay and his parents.

"Clay's probably so uncomfortable," Joanie laughs. "You know he hates his mom getting too involved in anything."

"Yeah, but she wouldn't be Clay's mom if she didn't interview the prom date," Luke says. "Or girlfriend. Or whatever."

"I think she's been interviewing her here-and-there all week," says Joanie, choosing one of her cards and tossing it down to match the category. "Yesterday I heard her asking about Baker's brother and how he likes New Orleans and all that."

"Scopin' out the family," Luke says. "Mama Landry's got long-term plans."

"Could you imagine them married, though?" Joanie laughs. "Clay would be like, 'Honey, I'm home from coaching little league and junior football and all these other manly sports, is dinner on the table?' and Baker would be like, 'Hold on, Clay-Clay, I'm finishing up these city council papers and all of my other overachieving activities!' It'd be a nightmare."

Hannah's stomach clenches and the thing inside her chest hurts more than ever. *Please make it go away. Please just let me be normal. Please just let me find this funny, like they do.*

"Okay, really?" Wally says, holding up the selection of cards for the category he's judging. "'The dump,' 'Your grandma,' and 'Herpes'? For the *Delicious* card?"

"Guess we're all on the same wavelength here," says Luke.

"These are absolute shit."

"Oh, Walton, we always forget that you like to play this game *literally*," says Joanie.

"Aren't you the one who taught me that you're supposed to play to the judge? Alright, I'm gonna go with...'Your grandma.'"

"Yes!" says Luke. "That one was mine."

There's more drinking that night. Clay produces a bottle of Wild Turkey American Honey, which Hannah has never tried, and they all take turns swigging from it while they sit around the pool and talk. Wally makes everyone laugh by describing his series of Yu-Gi-Oh Halloween costumes from elementary school, and Joanie entertains the group with stories about growing up with Hannah.

"And we played doll house until we were, like, 12 and 13, didn't we, Han? We were way past the age where we should have been playing that. But we had a whole collection of families that lived together in this house, and we used to spend hours setting up the furniture and the decorations."

"And we had that butler," Hannah says. "That really ugly figurine that we took from some other play set, and you drew angry eyebrows on its face and we named it 'Hector.'"

"Yeah, and we used to laugh so hard because we would have the eight year-old daughter boss Hector around, but like only when the doll house parents weren't looking, so it became this whole subseries within our doll house universe."

"And we had the babies, too. The triplets."

"Oh, god. Okay, so Hannah's favorite character was this baby boy we named 'Oliver.' And he was definitely the cutest baby. And one day we just lost him. And Hannah spent two months looking for him, like absolutely upending the house on her search to find him. Like whenever she had a spare moment, she would go Oliver-hunting. And one time I caught her crying in the laundry room because she was so upset that she couldn't find him. And she was like, 'Joanie, now I understand what pain is.'"

Hannah laughs along with her friends, and without even meaning to, almost as a reflex, she looks at Baker, and she sees something deep and longing in Baker's face. Hannah catches it and holds onto it for a split second, but then Baker's eyes flicker away, almost in fear, and so Hannah looks away, too.

Wally tries to kiss Hannah a while after that. He intercepts her when she's returning from the bathroom and places his hands around her face before she fully realizes what's going on.

"Whoa," she says against his mouth. He kisses her again, then starts to run a hand through her hair.

"I've wanted to do this all week," he says. His stubble burns against her chin.

"Hold on. Wally, hold on."

He pulls away. His eyes are drunk; his lips are wet.

"Not tonight," Hannah says. "I just—I don't feel that great. Sorry."

"Okay." He nods his head a few times. "Okay. Can I—can I get you some medicine or something?"

"No, really, I'm okay."

"Okay," Wally says, his expression crestfallen. "Well...I'll meet you back out there, I guess."

And then he walks off toward the bathroom, and Hannah stands in the hallway that leads to the pool with her chin smarting and her chest aching.

On Wednesday, Hannah wakes before Baker. Her sleepy mind twitches with irritation, and she remembers, vaguely, that she dreamt of something sad.

Baker sleeps with her head turned toward the door. Hannah watches the rise and fall of her back. She thinks of Baker's lungs, working somewhere inside of her to keep her breathing—to keep her here with Hannah—and of her heart, pumping blood throughout her body and, most mysterious, keeping her deepest secrets nestled within her.

Hannah and Joanie leave the beach and walk back to the house around midday. They both have to pee and Joanie says she wants to make another sandwich, so they walk quietly up to the house, enjoying the break from the hot sand.

"What's going on with you and Baker?" Joanie asks while they mill about the kitchen.

"What do you mean?"

"Y'all are being weird. You're not, like, all obsessed with each other and laughing at each other's jokes like you usually do."

"We're fine," Hannah says. "I think she's just been in a bad mood. Stressed about college or something."

Joanie munches on her potato chips for a few seconds while she stares at Hannah long and hard. "Okay," she says finally, and then she grabs a water bottle and leads the way back to the beach.

On Thursday, their last full day in Destin, they stay on the beach until six at night, long after the sun's heat has thinned into cool air. The six of them lie on their backs on the sand, each of them facing the sky, the waves lulling them into that meditative state between life and sleep.

164

"I don't want to leave," Clay says, breaking the silence.

None of them respond, but Hannah knows they must all agree with him. She opens her eyes to the filter of her sunglasses and the rose-tinted sky. She wonders how the six of them must look to the clouds. Lined up across the sand, their half-naked bodies spread out in offering, their burnt skin and newly-formed freckles proof that they are not afraid of the sun, that they believe only in this day and their own immortality.

"I don't want to leave, either," Wally says.

"Me neither," Joanie says.

Hannah searches the clouds, the gulls, the sun. She wants to leave and she wants to stay. She wants to raise her hand to the heavens and command that everything stop, that time stills, that the rules and the laws retract their grip so nature can have her way. Hannah wants to sit up off her towel and look across her friends' lined-up bodies, frozen in time beneath the sky, and she wants to pull Baker out of their midst, out of time, and walk with her along the shoreline, following the infinite ocean, nothing moving on the whole green earth except for the two of them and the water and the sky.

And Hannah wants to ask her things. What does she think about in those last few seconds before she falls asleep at night? Does her mind swim in colors when she listens to music? How does she feel when she walks beneath the trees in the Garden District? When does she feel most afraid? Does she realize when she is acting brave? When she prays, does she mean it? Has she ever known God? Does she want to? When it's late at night, and the world feels uncontainable, and the air is warm on her skin, who does she think about?

"I want to stay here forever," Clay says.

Baker says nothing. Hannah says nothing.

Dr. and Mrs. Landry tell them to eat dinner on their own that night; they want to attend a Holy Thursday service at the local church and go out on their own afterwards. "Why don't you visit that salad bar restaurant?" Mrs. Landry says while she dabs aloe on Clay's sunburnt neck. "Eat something nice and healthy."

"Yeah, Mama, we probably will," Clay says.

After the Landry's leave, the six of them prepare a feast of macaroni and cheese, Hot Pockets, Ore Ida French fries, and Coca-Colas, and instead of sitting down at the table, they carry all the food out to the back porch and eat during the sunset.

"Talk about a Last Supper," Wally says between bites of French fries.

"This is my Hot Pocket," says Luke, holding it before Wally's face, "which will be given up for you."

They spend their last night swimming in the pool and the hot tub. The Landry's come home late and wave down at them from the balcony, and Hannah and her friends wave up at them and wish them a good night.

"I'm gonna miss this place," Wally says while Hannah sits with him in the hot tub.

Hannah looks down toward the pool, where Baker sits on Clay's shoulders and chicken fights Joanie and Luke. "Yeah," she says. "Yeah, me too."

Around midnight, feeling tired and wrinkly from staying in the pool for so long, they grab towels and tiptoe upstairs to the family room. Clay turns on a movie and they all lay around on the couches, clutching their towels around their wet bodies and trying to stay awake on their last night.

Wally dozes off halfway through the film, and when his head falls onto Hannah's bare shoulder, she let its stay there, thinking there's no point in fighting it.

When the movie ends, Clay rises sleepily from the couch and turns the television off. Joanie and Luke are asleep on the couch to Hannah's left; Wally is asleep on her shoulder; and Baker appears to be asleep on the couch to Hannah's right. Hannah closes her eyes before Clay turns around.

"I'm going to bed," he whispers. His footsteps move back toward the couch he and Baker were sharing. "You want to come?"

There's absolute silence for a moment—Hannah's heart dangles on the edge of something—but then Baker says, "Not tonight. Too tired."

Hannah opens her eyes a fraction of an inch and watches them. Clay stands over Baker, still cloaked in a pool towel. Baker sits motionless on the couch.

"Alright, fine," he says, and then he moves away from her and turns on a lamp.

Hannah keeps her eyes closed while Clay rouses Luke and Joanie, and then she feigns waking up when he draws close to her and Wally. They stretch and fix the cushions on the couch, and then everyone walks off toward their separate bedrooms, none of them speaking in their tired states.

Hannah has reached the first landing of the stairs before she realizes Baker hasn't left the couch. She's the only one who remains in the family room: the boys have already gone down to the lower level, and Joanie has already climbed the stairs ahead of Hannah.

"You coming?" Hannah whispers.

Baker tears her eyes away from whatever she was looking at and glances briefly up at Hannah—in the dim light of the lamp, her eyes look black and dead.

"In a minute," she says.

Hannah hesitates, wondering if she should go back down and talk to her, but Baker has already looked away.

Hannah lies awake for minutes and minutes, turning over the week's events, wondering if things will be better when they're back in Baton Rouge, desperately trying not to feel out the ache in her chest. She lies there for what seems like forever and still Baker does not come. One horrified part of Hannah thinks that maybe Baker changed her mind and went down to Clay's room. Another part of her starts to worry: she can't stop picturing that black, dead look in Baker's eyes.

She rises from bed and tiptoes downstairs. Baker is no longer in the family room, nor is she in the kitchen. Hannah walks out to the back porch, but Baker's not there, so she walks downstairs to the boys' room and pauses outside the door, listening. She opens the door as quietly as she can and hears the boys' even breathing. She looks around at their single beds, but Baker isn't in any of them. She breathes a sigh of relief. Then she walks outside to the pool, but Baker isn't there, either.

She's not sure why she does it, but she leaves the house and walks down toward the beach. A lone streetlamp lights her way as she walks, shivering slightly in her t-shirt and sleep shorts. She passes the outdoor shower at the edge of the beach, and then she takes off her sandals and walks onto the cool sand.

Baker's figure comes into view as Hannah walks farther toward the water. She can see her sitting on the sand, rigid and still, her outline illuminated by the bright white moon. Hannah's feet rub against the sand with that familiar slipper sound, and she doesn't try to take quieter steps, for she hopes that the sound of her feet will alert Baker to her presence.

Baker turns around when Hannah is still a few feet away. She lets out a defeated breath.

"Hey," Hannah says. "Can I sit?"

Baker says nothing. Hannah sits down next to her.

"What are you doing out here?" Hannah asks quietly.

Baker watches the ocean. She doesn't blink for almost a minute. Then she drops her head to look down at the sand.

Hannah eyes the bottle of Cabernet resting between Baker's knees. "Are you drinking?"

Baker sighs and finally opens her mouth. "You always were smart."

The sarcasm stings, but Hannah doesn't respond to it. She drops her head and studies the goosebumps on her legs. "Can I have some?" she asks.

Baker hands the bottle over but still doesn't look at her. Hannah swallows the warm, bitter wine, feeling it flood all the way down to her stomach.

"My dad always says," Hannah whispers, pausing to take another drink, "that when he drinks wine, he likes to imagine the hands of the person who picked the grapes that made it."

Baker sprinkles sand onto her calves. "That sounds like something your dad would say."

"Baker, I'm sorry," Hannah says with half a voice. She folds her hands around the wine bottle and breathes once, twice, three times, before she speaks again. "I shouldn't have done what I did—it's just—it's just that I felt so much, and I thought you felt it, too."

The waves stretch toward the sand, then pull back toward their indefinable center. They whisper their mesmerizing magic, saying *Yes, yes, Truth.*

"We can't have this conversation," Baker says.

"We have to have it. We can't keep doing this same thing and then not talking about it—"

"Hannah, I do not want to talk about this," Baker says, breathing in so fast that she might be choking.

"Do you think I do?!"

"Yes! I think that's exactly what you want! You always want to talk about things that shouldn't be talked about!"

"Because we NEED to! You can't just keep hiding from me, and hiding from whatever is going on between us, just because it might be messy and scary and require you to color outside the lines! I know you're scared, but guess what, I'm scared, too!"

"You're not scared!" Baker yells, wrenching herself off the sand and stalking away toward the ocean. "You're never scared!"

Hannah sits dumbfounded for a moment, but then she pushes up from the sand and follows Baker farther down the beach. "How do you know? How do you know I'm not scared?! Maybe I am scared! Maybe I'm terrified!"

Baker turns around, and there's dark fire blazing in her eyes. "Oh yeah?!" she shouts, her expression contorted with fear and madness Hannah has never seen before. "Tell me, Hannah, just how scared are you? Are you scared that someone saw us in the garage? Because you didn't seem very fazed by that. Are you scared that our friends are going to find out? Are you scared the boys are going to find out? How about our classmates? How about our entire school? How about our *parents*? And what about everything beyond that, Hannah? Tell me, how are you feeling about God at this point? Are you scared that He's going to reject you? Maybe that He already has? Are you scared that we're messing with something that goes all the way back to original creation? Are you scared that this is the one catch, the one thing that throws everything we've ever learned about God and religion into doubt? TELL ME, HANNAH," Baker screams, her voice breaking now, "HOW EXACTLY ARE YOU SCARED?!"

She whips around and pounds across the sand, farther down toward the water, and Hannah follows her without thinking about it, her heels aching as they hit the sand.

"I'm scared of all those things!" Hannah yells, kicking sand at Baker's legs. "Everything you just named—and God—and judgment—all of it!"

Baker spins around and kicks sand back at Hannah. "Just go away!" she cries. "Stop making this so hard!"

"No! I'm not leaving!" Hannah shouts, kicking more sand at Baker. "Not until you talk to me!"

Baker scoops up a handful of sand and throws it at Hannah's face. Hannah keels forward, the sand stinging her eyes and her cheeks. She spits sand from her mouth and hears it crunch in her teeth.

"I don't have to talk to you about everything," Baker says, her voice wet with tears.

Hannah wipes her face on her arm and spits into the sand again. Her blood rushes through her body and she snarls at Baker. "Did you seriously just throw sand in my face?"

Baker opens her mouth uncertainly, but then Hannah picks up a handful of sand and throws it back at her. Baker yells and falls to her knees, scratching madly at her face.

Hannah's furious now: she kicks at the sand over and over and over while Baker splutters and spits and crosses her arms over her face. Baker cowers until she falls prostrate with her head clutched between her hands, and then she begins to shake.

"Please," she cries. "Hannah, please."

Hannah freezes. Baker's breath comes in huge heaves as she cries with her face in the sand. "Please," she cries again, weaker this time. "Please, Hannah."

"Bake," Hannah says, dropping to her knees. "Bake, I'm sorry. I'm sorry."

"Please, Hannah—"

Hannah wraps her arms around her. Baker tries to throw Hannah off without shifting her position, making noises of pain and protest, but Hannah tightens her arms.

"Baker," Hannah says desperately, fighting to hold onto her, "I'm sorry. I'm sorry."

"Hannah," Baker cries. "Hannah, make it stop."

"Bake?"

"Make it stop," she repeats, no longer fighting but continuing to cry. "Make it stop."

Hannah places a hand on Baker's shoulder and pulls Baker back toward her, breaking her from the sand. She scoots around Baker until she's facing her, and then she touches her hands to Baker's face, wiping the sand away. Baker sobs helplessly, her eyes closed, tears streaming down her face. Hannah wipes the sand off of her forehead, out of her eyes, away from her mouth.

"Baker," Hannah says, her voice breaking.

Baker opens her eyes, and all the anger is gone from them. Now she only looks anguished and broken.

"Bake," Hannah whispers, "I'm sorry. I'm sorry." She places her hand on the side of Baker's face, and Baker leans into it. She pulls Baker into her arms, and Baker falls into her like a child, still crying and gasping. "It's okay," Hannah says. "It's okay."

"Hate—this."

Hannah cradles Baker's head under her chin. She kisses the crown of Baker's head over and over and over while she rocks her in her arms.

"It's okay," Hannah promises her. "It's okay. It's okay."

The waves break in the surf. Hannah knows that she and Baker are outside of time. She can tell by the whisper of the air and the pattern of the stars, by the swell of her heart and the immediacy of her pain. They are the only two humans on the earth tonight, she and Baker, and Hannah knows this. The sand is cool until their skin brings heat to its tiny grains. The heavens are unseen until they look upward, their eyes searching for luminaries in the great dome of the sky. The waves are still undiscovered, still naïve in their movements: they do not know anyone is watching them. *We're watching*, Hannah thinks.

"Do you really feel scared?" Baker asks, when they're calm.

"All the time." Hannah looks down at her. "But I still feel this—this pull towards you. Like I want to be around you every second. Like I can't be away."

Baker wipes at her eyes. In her barest voice, she says, "I don't want to feel this way."

"Me neither," Hannah says.

Baker turns toward her in the darkness. She wipes at her eyes again. "I want to be around you, too. All the time. I look at you and I just—I just—"

"I know," Hannah says, taking her hand. "Me too."

"But I'm scared, Han. I'm scared and I—I don't know if it's okay. I don't want to be wrong."

"I know," Hannah swallows.

Baker looks at her with desperate eyes, lit only by the brightness of the moon. "Do you think we're wrong?"

Hannah's heart hangs heavy in her chest. "No," she breathes, and in the silence that follows her admission, she cannot discern truth from lie.

Baker's eyes are sad but determined. She looks at Hannah, and now they are reading each other, reading each other's eyes, reading each other's selves, and Hannah's heart beats so strongly in her chest that she feels like it has only now been placed within her, an organ to confirm her humanity.

Baker's eyes are wet. "Hannah," she says, "Hannah—I want—"

Hannah nods and realizes her eyes are wet too. She sets a hand on the cold sand and pushes herself forward until her lips meet Baker's with the delicate touch of tree leaves. And there on the beach, with the sand, the sky, and the water as their witnesses, Baker kisses her back, and Hannah hopes desperately that the crashing of the waves is a celebration rather than a condemnation.

"Don't cry," Hannah whispers against Baker's mouth.

"Have to," Baker gasps.

They kiss each other beautifully but brokenly, each kiss imparting wishes and prayers and shame, their tears mixing on each other's mouths, and in a startling moment of clarity Hannah feels God there with her, pounding in her heart, flowing through her body and blood, but whether in jubilation or admonition, she doesn't know.

"Hold on," Baker whispers, drawing back and wiping her eyes. She turns her head from side to side, looking down the beach, then looking up at the sky, her eyes seeking something beyond Hannah. "Let's go back to the house."

"Right now?"

Baker's lip trembles. "I don't want to do this out here."

Hannah pauses. "Okay."

Their bedroom is a sanctuary, cradling them in its remote darkness, hiding them from the rest of the earth. It teems with the dark shapes of their clothes and towels, growing out of the carpet like familiar flora and fauna.

Hannah crosses to the windows to let some air into the room, but Baker's voice stops her.

"Don't," she says urgently. "Keep them closed." Her voice is shaking and pained. Hannah stills with her bare feet rubbing sand into the carpet.

They stare at each other's outlines, their eyes straining through the darkness.

"Hannah?"

"Yeah?" Hannah answers, her own voice shaking and pained now.

"It's just us, right?"

Hannah walks to her. She touches her cheek and finds her eyes. There is a desperate light hanging on her pupils. A flicker of passion, a flicker of shame.

"It's just us."

Baker nods, and Hannah can see in her half-lidded eyes that she's trying so hard to believe it. Tears bleed out of her eyes again, water and salt collecting on her face just as they did on Christ's face when he wept in the garden, just as they did on Eve's face when she wept beyond the garden.

Hannah presses close to her and kisses her tears. "Just us."

Baker raises an unsteady hand and grips the cotton of Hannah's shirt. "Will you—" she starts with a trembling breath. She shakes her head and grips Hannah's shirt tighter. "Will you—?"

Hannah kisses her gently, pressing against her lips with earliest innocence. Baker inhales like it might be the first time she's ever done so, her eyes closed and her hand still knotted in Hannah's shirt. They kiss again, more eagerly this time, until the kiss turns into a deeper hunger, each of them asking for their fill, both of them making offerings of lips and tongues and saliva.

Baker's hands wander over Hannah's hips and around to her back, and Hannah mirrors her actions, touching the stretchy fabric of Baker's bathing suit, then the soft nakedness of her skin. They kiss each other hard and touch each other with a frantic restlessness, and there is no sound in the room but the union of their wet lips and their panting. Baker kisses Hannah's jawline, her ear, her neck, her collarbone, and then walks her back toward the bed and eases her down onto her back, so that Hannah is sprawled out beneath the canopy of Baker's long, dark hair. Hannah surrenders with tentative willingness, opening herself bravely to the fate of these kisses, feeling her blood course through her body. She sits up and places her hands on Baker's hips to still her, and then she tugs her own shirt over her head. Baker draws back from Hannah and looks breathlessly over her body, and when Hannah meets Baker's eyes, she can still see that desperate light hanging in them, magnified in her enlarged pupils. Baker glides her hands down Hannah's stomach, seemingly in awe of the goosebumps that form at her touch, her face full of wonder, her eyes carrying that desperate light.

Then Baker takes off her bathing suit top, and Hannah can only breathe.

Baker hovers above Hannah, breathing hard, her face still wet with tears. Hannah's arms begin to shake, like branches of a tree in a rainstorm, and Baker's eyebrows crinkle in concern, but Hannah keeps eye contact with her and lies back down on the bed.

Baker kisses down Hannah's chest, down her stomach, across her bellybutton, at the bones of her hips. Hannah's body shakes more, and Baker looks at her with pained eyes, asking what to do, asking, wordlessly, whether they should keep going. Hannah looks back into Baker's dark eyes—darker and richer than the earth's oldest soil, but still with that desperate light hanging in them—and takes a deep breath. Then she nods.

Baker hesitates for a second, her wet lips parted in uncertainty, but then she nods, too. Hannah rolls down the waistband of her sleep shorts, and Baker watches Hannah's fingers move.

And then Baker's fingers are on Hannah's thighs, and then they're peeling Hannah's shorts down her legs, and then Baker looks at Hannah one more time, still blinking back tears, and Hannah holds her eyes and nods.

It's a feeling she never could have prepared for, having Baker inside of her like this. They breathe in at the same time, quick and sharp like they're hiccupping on air, and Baker looks at Hannah with such shy wonder that Hannah smiles, maybe out of nervousness or maybe out of shock, or maybe even out of joy, and then Baker's mouth upturns with the shadow of a smile, too, and Baker looks down at her hand like she can't believe it's connected to her body. Hannah closes her eyes, opens them to watch Baker, closes them when her feelings overtake her, opens them to watch Baker again.

 And then they're still, no sound in the room except for their ragged breathing. Hannah lies naked on the bed, one hand raised above her head, the other hand reaching for Baker's face so she can pull her down to kiss her. She can feel Baker's tears on her cheeks.

Baker moves her hand from between Hannah's legs to the plane of her stomach, and Hannah feels the wetness of Baker's fingers on her skin. They both stare at Baker's fingers, at the proof of their sin, at the seed of their salvation.

Hannah touches Baker's jaw to get her attention. Baker's eyes meet Hannah's again, and Hannah feels overwhelmed by the emotions she sees in them. She pulls Baker down and flips her onto her back, and Baker breathes as Hannah's fingers move to the buttons on her shorts.

And then Hannah has learned the oldest secret on earth, has connected herself to the long human story, has taken her place in the pattern of human unions. Baker's stomach rises and falls, her back arching off the sheets, and Hannah hovers over her on the bed, moving her fingers instinctively, touching something primitive and sacred deep inside the basin of Baker's body. Baker makes small sounds, woman's pleasure mixing with child's need, and then she starts to cry. "Please," she gasps, looking at Hannah, then looking away from her. "Please." Hannah moves one hand to Baker's forehead, brushes her hair away, combs a thumb across her eyebrow; she moves her other hand at the base of Baker's body, pulling prayers from deep within her, until, with one last petition, she comes.

There are fresh tears in Baker's eyes when she looks up at Hannah, both of them breathing rapidly in and out, trading air between their mouths. Hannah kisses her and rasps, "You okay?", and Baker doesn't answer except to pull Hannah toward her, and they lie with their bodies overlapping, skin on skin, beating heart on beating heart.

Baker sits up and hovers over Hannah again. She kisses her with an anguished tenderness, her tears bleeding onto Hannah's cheeks. She kisses her way down Hannah's neck and torso, her lips bringing fire to Hannah's skin. She kisses Hannah's naval, then her hipbones, and Hannah clenches on the bed sheets, waiting.

Then Baker kisses her way down Hannah's legs, her wet lips picking over the skin, until her mouth is at the inside of Hannah's thigh.

"Are you sure you want to—?" Hannah says desperately.

"Please?" Baker rasps, lifting her head to meet Hannah's eyes.

They hang silently on each other's questions. There is nothing in the room but darkness and themselves.

Then Hannah feels Baker's mouth on her, kissing her in this last, indisputable place.

She falls back on the sheets and listens to the new sound in the room—the sound of Baker tasting her—and for reasons she doesn't understand, her mind starts to meditate on words from the Mass, from the Last Supper—

This is my body....

She tangles a hand in Baker's hair and moves her fingers over the crown of Baker's head, asking wordlessly for more, turning her own head into her arm to stifle her gasps. Baker's mouth closes over her, tasting, eating, and Hannah finds herself praying, first in her mind and then aloud, her new voice begging and thanking, until she comes with the words *Oh my God* ringing around her.

Baker slides up Hannah's body afterwards, her breath fast and her lips wet. She wraps an arm around Hannah and kisses her on the mouth, and Hannah shares in the tasting of their covenant, of the fruit of their union. Baker kisses her again and buries her face into Hannah's neck, her tears still fresh on her face, and as Hannah strokes her hair, they fall asleep, naked in the darkness.

Chapter Eight: Broken

Hannah wakes to a knocking sound. "Girls," a voice calls through the door. "Are you awake?"

The first thing she realizes is that she is naked. The second thing she realizes is that Baker is naked too.

They stare at each other with terrified eyes.

"Girls," Mrs. Landry calls again, knocking louder this time. The doorknob rattles as she tries to turn it, and Hannah and Baker wrench the sheets over themselves. But the door stays closed, and Hannah remembers, through her adrenaline rush, that Baker had locked it the night before.

Get in the shower, Baker mouths as she scrambles off the bed. Her eyes are as frantic as a wild animal's. Hannah rushes into the bathroom and turns the shower on. Then she hovers near the bathroom door, listening to the sounds from the bedroom.

"Oh, good morning, Mrs. Landry," comes Baker's shaky voice. "Sorry, I just woke up."

"Are you two alright in here?"

"Yes, ma'am, we're fine, I think Hannah's in the shower."

"Did you mean to have the door locked, honey?"

"Oh—no, ma'am. I'm sorry. That was my fault. I heard weird noises last night and it kind of freaked me out, so I locked the door. Sorry."

There's a short pause before Mrs. Landry speaks again. "That's alright, honey. Are you two ready to start packing and cleaning? We have to be out by noon."

182

"Yes, ma'am. We'll clean up in here and then we'll come downstairs."

"Great. Let me get your sheets while I'm here. I need to start on the laundry."

"Oh—no! That's okay, we can get them."

"No, that's alright, I have to do everyone else's, too—"

"Please, no, my mom would be so embarrassed if she heard I didn't wash my own sheets. Really. I'll take care of them."

There's an awkward pause, and Hannah holds her breath at the door, the steady whistling of the shower the only thing she can hear.

"Well, alright," Mrs. Landry says hesitantly.

"Thanks," Baker says, her voice cheerful and overly polite. "We'll be right down!"

Then there's the sound of a door closing, followed by silence. Hannah opens the bathroom door a crack to see Baker standing limply by the bedroom door, her body slumped in humiliation, a long t-shirt covering her torso.

"Hey," Hannah calls softly. Baker doesn't turn around.

There's a bad energy in the room that makes Hannah's stomach clench. She stands still for a long second, her naked breasts pressing against the doorframe. Her heart beats fast in her chest.

She leaves the shower on and steps back into the bedroom, and still Baker does not turn around. Hannah walks up behind her and tucks in the tag on her sleep shirt. "You okay?"

Baker startles and turns to look at her, but she averts her eyes as soon as she realizes Hannah is still naked. She backs away toward the bed, her movements slow and graceless like she might be sick, and then she stands over the bed, gazing down at the sheets.

"Bake?"

Baker says nothing, just continues to look down at the bed. Hannah folds her arms over her breasts and crosses her legs together, suddenly very ashamed of her nakedness.

"You should get in the shower," Baker says tonelessly. She pauses. "Or at least put some clothes on."

Hannah feels a coldness spread up from her stomach and into her throat. Goosebumps rise on her skin. "Okay," she says, releasing the word into the room to see what happens. "But are you alright?"

Baker doesn't answer. Hannah takes a few steps toward her.

"Don't," Baker says, her body flinching.

"What's—?"

"Please just get in the shower."

Something in the room, some invisible line between them, has broken. Hannah can almost see it: a vine that had once connected them, had once wrapped them together, now lies, butchered, on the floor. She takes a step backward and feels her navel tugging on her broken half. It retracts into her, coils around her stomach, clogs her throat.

She retreats to the bathroom without another word. But after she locks the bathroom door behind her, she stands in front of the mirror and studies her naked body. She tries to remember every place Baker touched or kissed.

They clean their rooms, they clean the kitchen and the pool area, they load up their bags, and then it's time to leave. Hannah falls in line behind her friends to thank Dr. and Mrs. Landry, and she's not sure if it's her imagination, but Mrs. Landry seems to hug her with rigid arms.

They take a picture in front of the house—Hannah squeezes between Luke and Wally and smiles like she's the happiest 17-year-old girl on earth—and then separate between the two cars.

Hannah slides into Baker's passenger seat and listens to Luke and Joanie jabbering behind her. Baker scrolls through the music on her iPhone without asking Hannah to deejay like she normally does, and Hannah clutches her arms around her stomach, feeling hollow and sick. Then Baker starts the car and backs out of the driveway, away from the house, away from the upstairs bedroom, away from their barest selves.

They arrive back in Baton Rouge just before 4:30. Baker guides the car down familiar streets, past familiar banks and restaurants, and Hannah swells with a sudden hope that this anchoring, common place—this place their friendship is rooted in—will restore the two of them.

But Baker drops Hannah and Joanie off first, even though Luke's house would have been the more convenient one, and as Hannah grabs her bag out of the trunk and puts on a brave goodbye face, she realizes their shame has followed them all the way from Destin.

"Pizza for dinner tonight," her mom says while Hannah's gathering her dirty laundry into a pile. "Want any veggies on it?"

"Pepperoni," Hannah says listlessly.

"It's Good Friday. No meat."

Hannah hangs her head back. "The one time I want pepperoni."

"Why are you so moody?"

"I'm not moody."

"You walked in here with a dark cloud circling around your head. Did you not sleep this week?"

"I slept."

"Uh-huh." Her mom takes the laundry basket from her and cradles it under one arm. "Take a nap until the pizza gets here."

"I'm not tired."

"Then just lie down and relax. We're going to the Stations of the Cross after dinner and I want you at your best."

Hannah sighs and throws a rogue sock into the laundry basket. "Fine."

She fakes sick when her mom wakes her for pizza.

"I knew something was wrong with you," her mom says, feeling her forehead, "but you don't have a fever."

"It's a stomach bug or something," Hannah says, squinting into her pillow. "Or maybe cramps."

"Okay, well, just sleep, then. I'll wake you before we leave to see if you're feeling better."

She lies there in the dark until her mom comes back a while later.

"Still feel sick?"

"Yeah."

Her mom surveys her with critical eyes. "How about some ginger ale?"

"Yes, please."

Joanie brings it up to her a few minutes later. "You're such an ass," she says, setting the glass on Hannah's nightstand. "Faking sick to get out of Stations of the Cross."

"I'm not faking."

"Should we write out your will before I leave?"

"Shut up."

"I want those purple heart earrings from Express."

"Go away."

"Jeeze," Joanie says, backing out of the room. "I'm gonna pray for you to get a better sense of humor."

Hannah lies on her bed for hours and hours, faking sleep when her family comes home from church, faking sleep again when her mom checks her around 11 p.m., faking to herself that everything is okay.

She sneaks downstairs around one in the morning, no longer able to ignore the hunger in her stomach. She finds leftover pizza in the fridge and eats it cold while she slumps against the counter. In the darkness, her house looks strange to her, like a pattern of shapes she doesn't know.

She opens the backdoor as quietly as she can and tiptoes out into the yard. Her bare feet brush against the grass, her arms shiver in the cool night air. She tilts her head back until she's face to face with sky and stars. When her neck starts to hurt, she lies down on the ground, grass and dirt molding into her back, and folds her hands together over her stomach.

Is it okay?

The question bleeds forth from her and she imagines it rising into the sky, delivered on wind and air and atmospheric pressure until it reaches God.

Is it wrong? Were we wrong?

She lies there, bleeding into the sky, until the sky starts to bleed red with morning.

She doesn't hear from Baker at all on Saturday. Her texts go unanswered; her calls go to voicemail. She spends a lot of time lying in bed, pretending to read. But the words in her books mean nothing to her, and after awhile, she picks up her laptop and stares at Baker's Facebook page like she's praying to it.

"You are being such a lard," Joanie says when she steps into her room.

"I'm tired from the beach."

"Mom says to make sure you have a nice dress picked out for Mass tomorrow."

"Ugh."

Joanie shrugs her shoulders and eats the rest of the cookie in her hand. "Easter Sunday, champ."

Hannah sits through Easter Mass the next morning without actually absorbing anything that's going on. She follows along with the readings and the Gospel mostly out of habit, and the only thing that strikes her is a selection from the Gospel of John, which the lector reads in a solemn voice:

> On the first day of the week,
> Mary of Magdala came to the tomb early in the morning,
> while it was still dark,
> and saw the stone removed from the tomb.
> So she ran and went to Simon Peter
> and to the other disciple whom Jesus loved, and told them,
> "They have taken the Lord from the tomb,
> and we don't know where they put him."

And Hannah understands that even though today is supposed to be about the Resurrection—about hope, and rebirth, and renewed faith—the only thing that makes sense is Mary Magdalene's confusion and despair.

The lines for Communion are much longer than usual, swelled as they are with the people who come to Mass only on Christmas and Easter. Hannah watches as the faithful process to the front of the church to receive the Eucharist, all dressed in their Easter

Sunday best, some of the moms looking harried, some of the teenaged children looking annoyed. A familiar person comes into view in the long line on the right side of the church, and Hannah recognizes Nathan Hadley, dressed in a handsome Oxford shirt and with his kind eyes visible even from across the room. Mr. and Mrs. Hadley stand in line behind him, but Baker is not with them.

Hannah's stomach knots in on itself. An irrational part of her fears that Baker confessed everything to her family and they locked her in her room, too shamed by her transgressions to let her come to Easter Sunday Mass. Hannah's heart pounds hard when it's her family's turn to move along the pew and join the Communion line. She feels like the Hadley's eyes are on her, like the eyes of the whole congregation are on her, like they can all tell what she's done and what she's struggled with in her heart.

"Amen," she says when Father Simon raises the Eucharist in front of her. And then, for some reason, even though she was trained in how to passively receive the Communion bread years ago, she reaches up to snatch the Host. Father Simon raises the Host higher, almost as a knee-jerk reaction to her grabbing for it. His face shows his surprise, and Hannah's face flushes with embarrassment when she realizes her mistake. She lowers her eyes and cups her hands together, and Father Simon places the Eucharist on her left palm. She walks back to her pew with added shame, and it weighs her down through the end of Mass.

She doesn't sing the Recessional hymn. Neither does Joanie, who stands bored next to her while Father Simon, the deacon, and the

190

altar servers walk back up the center aisle with a magnificent Crucifix leading the way, balanced precariously in one of the altar server's hands.

Her parents file out of the pew after the song has officially ended—her mom doesn't condone leaving anytime before that—and she and Joanie shuffle behind them, smiling and nodding at the St. Mary's classmates they see.

She spots Nathan standing in a corner of the entrance hall, his hands in his pockets and his head down like he's trying not to be seen, and she steps around families with babies and old retired couples to go to him.

"Nate!"

His face lights up as soon as he sees her. "Hey, Han! Long time no see."

He pulls her into a hug and she holds on for a second too long.

"Everything okay?" he asks, his brown eyes, so much like his sister's, studying her carefully.

"Yeah, just haven't seen you in a while."

"I know, it's been way too long. How was Destin?"

She hesitates for a split-second. "Awesome. It was awesome."

"Good. I can't believe y'all are about to graduate."

"Yeah. Um. Where's Baker?"

"Sick, I guess." He shakes his head and puts his hands back in his pockets. "She hasn't really seemed like herself all weekend. It's weird—she usually loves Easter Mass, but my mom tried to wake her this morning and she just kept saying she thought she was going to throw up."

Hannah's stomach knots in on itself again. "Oh. Jeeze. I didn't realize."

"Yeah. I think she's just having anxiety about school. You know how worked up she gets about grades and everything."

"Yeah."

"Anyway, I'll tell her you said hi."

"Thanks."

"Sure. Bye, Han."

He turns to go find his parents, but she calls his name before she can think about it.

"Nate!"

"Yeah?"

She stares at him, tongue-tied, wishing she could tell him something that might help Baker, or wishing she could ask him how to help herself. He waits politely, his expression kind, but all she manages to say is, "It was great to see you."

He smiles. "You too. Enjoy these last few weeks of school. They'll be the best ones you'll have."

Saw Nate at church just now. He said you were sick. Can we please talk?

Baker never replies.

Hannah's mom spends all afternoon cooking the Easter ham. Hannah and Joanie's Aunt Ellie and Uncle Joel come over, towing their children, Colton and Sydney, behind them. "We brought the green beans," Aunt Ellie says, kissing Hannah and Joanie hello at the front door. "And the mutants," Uncle Joel huffs, nudging Colton and Sydney inside.

"Uncle Joel smells like beer already," Joanie says, scrunching up her nose in disgust. "He better not get drunk and start interrogating Luke again."

"Luke's coming?" Hannah asks.

"I already told you that, dum-dum. He didn't want to pick between his mom and his dad so Mom said he could come here for dinner."

"He's in for a treat," Hannah grumbles, eyeing Colton and Sydney as they run circles around the coffee table and shoot water guns at each other.

"Not in the house!" Uncle Joel yells from the kitchen.

"Oh, *now* you want to discipline them," Aunt Ellie says.

Joanie sighs and sets Aunt Ellie's gift of white wine on the decorative table near the front door. "I'd better get a tampon," she says. "You want one?"

"What?"

"To ward off Colton. You know he won't come near you with that stupid water gun if you dangle a tampon in front of his face."

"Are you serious?"

"Didn't you see me working that trick at Christmas? He tried to sneak-attack me, so I whipped a tampon out my purse and told him 'Up yours.' He ran away screaming."

"Oh my god, Joanie, you are insane," Hannah says, pushing past her to take the green beans to the kitchen.

"Take the stick out of your ass, Hannah," Joanie calls after her. "It's Easter Sunday."

Luke wears a button-down shirt and a handsome navy tie to dinner, prompting Hannah's mom and Aunt Ellie to gush over him. "Oh, Luke, you sweetheart!" Hannah's mom says, hugging him. "You didn't have to dress up!"

"It's a special occasion, Mrs. Eaden," Luke grins. "With a special family."

"*Stop*," Joanie beams, hitting him.

"Besides, how often do I get to wear a nice tie?"

"Every day at school," Hannah mutters.

"You are correct, Han," Luke says cheerily, "but how often do I get to wear this awesome *blue* tie?"

"You look great," Joanie says, her cheeks pink and her smile bright. "C'mere, come say hi to my dad. He's hiding in his office."

"Be right back," Luke smiles to Hannah's mom and Aunt Ellie.

"He is just the cutest thing," Aunt Ellie says after Joanie tugs Luke out of the kitchen. "With those curls and dimples....If I was 20 years younger, I'd pounce on him."

"You'd have to fight Joanie," Hannah's mom laughs. "She's crazy about him, hm, Han?"

"Yeah," Hannah says half-heartedly.

"Now what's up with your love life, Miss Hannah Banana?" Aunt Ellie asks. "How's the boy scene?"

"Oh, nothing to report," Hannah says, averting her eyes.

"What? A beautiful girl like you?"

"She never tells me anything about it," Hannah's mom says. She opens the oven and places a tray of rolls inside. "Like her dad that way."

"I tell you things," Hannah protests.

"You tell me things about your friends," her mom says, "but never about boys."

"Because there's nothing to say."

"That'll change in college," Aunt Ellie says. "Boys are so much more mature by that age. And college boys are *hot.*"

"How about Wally, though? Hm?" Hannah's mom prompts. "Does he still have a crush on you?"

"We're just friends, Mom, for the millionth time."

"You should see the way this kid looks at her," her mom tells Aunt Ellie. "He's absolutely crazy about her." She turns to Hannah and pushes her hair back behind her ears. "But Hannah's not interested, are you, Han?"

"Is he ugly?" Aunt Ellie asks.

"*No,*" Hannah says exasperatedly. "We are friends. That's it. We're in the same group of friends and it's great and that's all I need. Can't we just leave it at that?"

"Take it easy, Han, we're just curious!" Aunt Ellie says, patting her hand over Hannah's wrist. "Your mom and I are middle-aged and married and sometimes we like to hear about your fresh young love life!"

"I have a paper to do," Hannah says, pushing her stool back from the counter. "I'd better start on it before dinner."

"Make sure your sister and Luke aren't upstairs," Hannah's mom says. "Joanie knows the rules."

"Got it, Mom."

"And put a smile on your face. I made brownies for dessert."

"Okay," Hannah says, already halfway toward the stairs.

She hears Aunt Ellie talk about her just before she climbs the first step. "Just as touchy as she was when she was little," she says in a low voice.

"She's not touchy," Hannah's mom counters. "She's just feisty."

Hannah feels the trace of a smile on her face, but then Colton appears on the stairs and sprays her with a water gun.

"So, Luke," Uncle Joel says through a bite of ham when they're all seated at the table, and when Colton and Sydney have already been fed and instructed to play in the backyard, "what is it you'll be doing this summer? You working? You have a job? A real job?—not just 'working' as a camp counselor or something prissy like that?"

"Ease up, Joel," Aunt Ellie says, smacking his hand.

"He's fine," Uncle Joel says, gesturing at Luke with his fork. "He's not sweating through his shirt yet."

"Well, actually," Luke says confidently, "I won't have time to work this summer because I'll be training at a running camp."

"A running camp."

"Yes, sir. I got a track scholarship to Spring Hill, so I have to go to Alabama to start training with my coach."

"Huh," Uncle Joel says. "Well. That's nice. Congratulations."

"Thanks."

"And what about the rest of y'all's friends?" Aunt Ellie asks, tipping her wine glass towards Hannah, Joanie, and Luke. "Where are they going to school?"

"Our friend Wally's going to Georgia Tech," Luke says. "He's way smart—like great with math—and he got a partial scholarship there for doing so well on the SAT."

"Oooh," Aunt Ellie drawls, swiveling to look at Hannah. "*Wally.*" She winks.

Joanie starts to laugh. "Yeah," she says, smirking at Hannah. "*Wally.*"

Hannah rolls her eyes and stabs a piece of ham.

"And our friend Clay is going to LSU," Joanie says, "and so is our friend Baker—you remember her, right? Hannah's best friend?"

"The pretty girl?" Aunt Ellie asks. "The one with the cute little laugh?"

Hannah's stomach starts to ache.

"Yeah," Joanie says, "her. She got into LSU Honors so she's going there."

"So just the two are going to LSU?" Uncle Joel asks, sounding offended that the number isn't higher.

"Yeah, but they're probably happy about that," Joanie laughs, glancing sideways to Luke. "I don't think they'll mind it being just the two of them."

"What?" Hannah's mom asks, her eyes growing wide at this new piece of gossip. "Are they together now?"

"I don't know, kind of," Joanie says, shaking her head. "They're weird."

"Very weird," Luke agrees.

"I always thought they'd be cute together," Hannah's mom says.

"Is Clay going to play at LSU?" Hannah's dad asks, speaking for the first time since they sat down.

"He says he might try to walk on," Luke says. "But I don't think he's gotten his hopes up about it."

"Tell him to try," Uncle Joel says, pointing his finger at Luke. "No harm in trying. We need new talent. You tell him that."

"Joel, for heaven's sake," Aunt Ellie says. "Leave the poor kid alone. Anyway, I want to hear about Hannah's college plans."

"Oh," Hannah says. "I haven't decided yet."

"Don't they have deadlines for these things?" Uncle Joel says.

"She's got time," Hannah's mom says. "She has to choose between several schools that offered her admission. It's a good problem to have."

"She got into Emory," Hannah's dad says with a smile.

"I heard!" Aunt Ellie says. "That's beautiful news, Hannah. Beautiful. Are you leaning towards Emory?"

"I'm really not sure," Hannah says politely, feeling better now that the conversation has turned to something she can speak honestly and confidently about. "I got my acceptance letter just before we left for the beach, so I haven't had time to really sit down and think about it. And Atlanta's kind of far—"

"But isn't that where Georgia Tech is?" Aunt Ellie asks. "So you'll have your friend nearby?"

"Yeah, Han," Joanie smirks, "so you'll have your *friend* nearby?"

Aunt Ellie starts to laugh behind her hand. Joanie laughs, too, and Luke snorts into his napkin. Even Hannah's mom has to bite her lip to keep from laughing.

"Are we done?" Hannah says, her heart hammering. "Or did you want to keep being a stupid bitch, Joanie?"

Joanie's laughter dies in her throat. Her eyes narrow with anger. "Screw you, Hannah. Learn how to take a freaking joke."

"Stop being such a freaking gossip. Or do you just do that because you're insecure about how much of a baby you are compared to the rest of us?"

"Screw you!" Joanie says again, slamming her napkin onto the table. "God—you are such a—" she shakes her head with fury. "Come on, Luke," she says, pulling him up from the table, "let's go for a walk."

They stomp out of the dining room, Luke glancing uncomfortably back at the table. The front door slams and Hannah sits stock-still in her seat, unsure of what to do. After a long moment,

Hannah's mom starts to clean up the dishes, and Aunt Ellie gets up to help her. Uncle Joel shakes his head and takes another bite of ham.

Hannah's dad sighs at the other end of the table. When Hannah looks at him, begging him to say something, he takes his glasses off his face and stretches back in his chair, in a way that only fathers with teenaged daughters can do.

"You always had a way with words, Hannah," he says tiredly.

Hannah parks her car next to Baker's on Monday morning, just as she does every weekday morning, but today Baker isn't there waiting for her. Hannah looks over at Baker's car and imagines her sitting there in the driver's seat, tapping a pen against her student planner to make sure she's ahead of all her assignments, then smiling and stuffing the planner back into her booksack when she realizes Hannah has pulled in next to her.

Joanie gets out of the car without saying anything to Hannah. She slams the door behind her and Hannah watches, in the rearview mirror, as she walks over to Luke's car to take his hand.

Hannah sits through first period with her stomach in knots, hardly paying attention to Mr. Montgomery. During her unassigned period she sits in the senior lounge with Wally and tries to distract herself by working on her Theology paper. When she walks into the courtyard at lunchtime, with Wally peeling off to get food from the cafeteria, she finds that none of her other friends have gotten there yet, for the table they usually sit at is vacant. She sits down on the bench with a lead weight in her stomach, feeling nervous about the prospect of seeing Baker face to face for the first time since Friday.

"Yo," says Joanie, walking up to the table with Luke, Wally following behind them, "what's up with Clay and Baker ditching us?"

"What?" Hannah asks.

"Look," Joanie insists, pointing across the courtyard.

Hannah follows the direction of Joanie's outstretched arm and sees that Baker and Clay have gone to sit at a different table in the center of the courtyard. Some of their friends from the volleyball and football teams, and some of Baker's friends from student council, surround them. Hannah sits rigidly and watches them for a moment, hating how everyone at the table tunes their attention to the pretty pair of them, and how Clay smiles at Baker in-between every sentence he speaks.

"Is this some sort of like 'We're-dating-now-so-we're-going-to-branch-out-on-our-own' gesture?" Luke says.

"They're not dating," Hannah says before she can stop herself.

"Well, whatever they're doing, I have to admit that I feel pretty slighted," Luke says. "Shouldn't we at least have gotten some sort of friend group break-up memo about this?"

"Maybe they're subconsciously resentful toward us because they think we cock-blocked them in Destin," Joanie says.

Wally tilts his head, his eyes studying Baker and Clay across the courtyard. "What?" Hannah asks him. "What are you thinking?"

"It's just weird," Wally says after a moment. "It's not like them."

Hannah watches Baker bite into an apple slice, her mouth turning up in a smile as she talks to one of her friends from the volleyball team. Suddenly Hannah feels deeply lonely. Lonely and, in a sad but understanding way, betrayed.

When the bell rings to move to third block, Baker grabs onto Clay's booksack and follows him into the building. Hannah watches them from across the courtyard, her stomach emptier than when she sat down to lunch.

Hannah stares at her Calculus homework for a very long time that night.

We missed you at lunch today, she texts.

Baker doesn't reply.

Baker's car has moved four parking spaces down the next morning. Hannah's stomach drops when she sees it.

"What the hell?" Joanie says, momentarily distracted from applying her mascara. "What is going on?"

Hannah stares stupidly out the window. "I don't know," she says in a dead voice.

"Hannah. Seriously. What's going on?"

Hannah's torso aches like someone just rammed into her side.

"I don't know," she says.

Baker doesn't speak to Hannah during Ms. Carpenter's class. When the bell rings for lunch, Baker hurries out of the classroom before Hannah can catch up to her.

Baker and Clay sit at the other lunch table again. Hannah sits with her back facing them, determined to pay attention to Wally, Luke, and Joanie, and no one else. She pushes her feelings down in the same way that she pushes her plastic spoon into her pudding cup.

"I guess we're on Day Two of our trial separation?" Luke says, nodding his head toward Baker and Clay.

"Guess so," Joanie frowns. "I'm tempted to go confront them about it, those assholes."

"Don't," Hannah says.

"Why not? They're being so weird. Clay keeps doing this awkward guilty smile thing, like he knows he's being a piece of shit but doesn't want to acknowledge it, and Baker won't even look at me. I passed right by her on the way to lunch and she totally looked the other way. Like, on purpose. The fuck is that about?"

"She's been fine to me," Luke says between bites of his sandwich. "We worked on our Econ study guide together this morning. By which I mean, she worked on finding the answers while I worked on telling her some jokes."

"Do you think they walked in on us in the hot tub?" Joanie asks him under her breath. "Do you think that's why they're being weird?"

"Oh my god, stop," Hannah says, holding up her hand.

"I don't think this has anything to do with what y'all choose to do in hot tubs," Wally says seriously. "They're being weird for some other reason."

"You have to know, Hannah," Joanie says.

"What?"

"Come on. I know we're all close with each other, but you and Baker literally tell each other *everything*. I have a hard time believing you don't know what's going on."

"Joanie, I told you already, *I don't know.*"

Joanie takes on that challenging expression she used to get as a little kid, the one she'd wear when she and Hannah would sneak downstairs to watch the Disney Channel in the middle of the night. "You're lying," she says. "I can tell."

"I'm not lying," Hannah says heatedly.

"Hannah, your 'best friend' is sitting way over there, completely ignoring you, and completely ignoring us. So maybe it's time you let some other people in, huh? We're your best friends too, you know. Maybe it wouldn't kill you to share the truth with us—"

"That's not even—Jesus, Joanie—"

"Maybe we should all just take a breather—" Luke interjects.

"Just tell us, Hannah," Joanie huffs. "God, it's not like the rest of us are withholding information from each other—"

"Are you *kidding* me?" Hannah says dangerously, feeling her skin flush with fire. "Like you're some paragon of truth-telling? Fine, Joanie, then why don't you disclose all your secrets to the table? Maybe you could start with, oh, I don't know, how you're planning on dumping Luke right before he goes off to Alabama?"

Hannah wants to snatch the words back as soon as they leave her. A stunned silence spreads over the table, the kind that presses on and on until the point where nothing anyone could say would pull the conversation back from the edge.

Joanie sits frozen across from Hannah, her entire face aflame, her eyes wide in shock. Luke sits frozen next to her, his mouth half-open like he was just punched in the gut, no shadow of dimples on his face.

"I—" Hannah says.

Joanie's eyes cut loathingly into Hannah's. She breathes very fast, her face turning redder and redder, her expression murderous.

Luke pushes back from the lunch table. He swings his booksack onto his shoulders and moves to gather his snack wrappers, and Joanie grabs his wrist and pleads, "Luke—Luke, listen—"

He jerks his wrist out of her grip. "See y'all later," he huffs, not looking at any of them, and then he stalks away.

Joanie turns to Hannah with her face full of a horrible wrath Hannah has never seen before. "I hate you," she spits, scorching Hannah with her loathing eyes. She lunges aggressively for her sandwich and Diet Coke can, clenching her teeth against her anger and tears, and then heaves herself up from the table. "I—*hate*—you."

Then she turns and runs after Luke, and Hannah sits dumbly in her chair, unable to process the wave of sadness that comes over her.

She and Wally don't say anything for a long minute. Hannah is afraid to look at him, to face his disgusted reaction. They sit in heavy silence while Wally folds his napkin into tinier and tinier squares.

"I didn't mean to say that," Hannah says finally. She chances a glance at him and finds him staring hard at the napkin in his fingers, his face crinkled in thought.

He looks up at her, and the expression on his face is not judgmental. "I know," he says. "What are you gonna do?"

"Apologize to her when I can."

"Yeah," Wally agrees. "And to Luke."

"And to Luke."

Joanie doesn't speak to Hannah on their drive home from school. When they reach the stop sign at the corner of Kleinert and 22nd Street, Hannah takes a breath and reaches deep into her stomach for an apology. "I'm sorry," she mumbles.

Joanie's quiet for a long minute. Just before they turn onto Olive Street, she says, "I don't think you are."

Hannah glances sideways at her. Joanie stares straight ahead at the windshield, her jaw set and her eyes wet.

Please talk to me, Hannah texts that night.

At two in the morning, when Hannah is asleep, Baker responds.

I'm sorry Han. I can't.

On Wednesday, when Hannah and Joanie arrive at school, Baker's car once again sits four spots down. Hannah knew it would, but the sight still hurts her.

Joanie immediately pushes out of the car and sets off for the building. Hannah watches her go, feeling stupid and lonely. She sits forlornly in her car, half-heartedly applying her eyeliner, until she notices Wally's green Camry pull into its usual spot.

"'Morning," she says as they step out of their cars.

"Hey," he says as he fixes his tie. "How'd everything go with Joanie?"

"She won't talk to me."

Wally frowns. "She'll come around."

Just then, Luke's car drives by. He passes right by them and parks in a space much farther down the row, near the building entrance. Hannah and Wally watch as he ambles out of his car, his hair ruffled, his tie hanging loosely around his neck, and his shirt untucked.

"Manceau's gonna slam him with a ton of uniform infractions," Hannah says.

"I don't think he's worried about that right now," Wally says.

Hannah and Wally sit by themselves at lunch that day. Some of their classmates glance curiously at their table, wondering why Baker, Clay, Joanie, and Luke are no longer sitting with them. Michele watches them with a hungry look in her eyes, like she's desperate to know the gossip; as Hannah looks at her, Michele leans over to her friend Taylor and whispers behind her hand.

It goes on like that all week: Hannah and Joanie drive to school in silence; Hannah casts a longing look at Baker's car when they pull into the parking lot; Joanie dashes off into the building without speaking to Hannah; Luke pulls in just before the bell and hurries inside without looking at anyone; and Hannah and Wally continue to hang out by themselves, at lunch and in the parking lot, neither one of them mentioning how much they miss their friends.

"Wally," Hannah says on Friday afternoon, when she and Wally sit on the trunk of her car and wait for Joanie to come out to the parking lot so Hannah can go home, "you don't have to keep me company, you know. You should still hang out with the others. I feel bad."

"Don't worry about it," Wally says, lacing up his track shoes. "This thing'll fix itself. Friends have arguments, you know? It doesn't change anything."

"Wall...this whole thing is my fault. I really fucked up with Joanie and Luke. And—and with Baker and Clay. Joanie was right—I was lying before. Baker's avoiding me, and the rest of you, because of something that happened with us."

Wally squints at her in the spring sunlight. Hannah looks away from him and keeps talking.

"Baker and I—we had an issue. An issue that I don't know how to resolve."

"Yeah," Wally says. "I know that, actually."

"What?"

"I talked to Clay."

"You did? When?"

"Well, he came to talk to me. He felt pretty bad about not sitting with us at lunch."

"What'd he say?"

Wally rubs the back of his neck. "Baker went over to his house on Sunday night and told him she didn't want to be around you anymore."

Hannah's heart stops. "What?"

"Yeah."

"Did she tell him why?"

"No, she just said something had happened and she needed her space. Clay felt really torn up about it, but he said Baker was more upset than he'd ever seen her, so he thought he should support her for a few days, until this whole thing blows over."

"Until it 'blows over'? And what if it doesn't?"

"You really think it won't?"

"I—" The question nearly suffocates her. "I'm not sure."

"Well," Wally says slowly, setting his hands on his knees, "if it doesn't...then we'll adapt. All of us will."

"I just don't know if—Wally, I wish I could talk to you about what happened, but I don't know how...."

"You don't have to, Han," he says, nudging her with his shoulder. "Everything will be okay. And hey, it's not all bad. I think it's been good for Clay and Baker. Clay said they've started to talk more about their feelings for each other and everything. He's actually taking her out on a date this weekend—"

The words knock all the breath out of Hannah. "What?"

"Yeah, they're going out to dinner tomorrow night. He's actually way nervous about it, which is funny, you know, because we've never really seen him get nervous about anything before. But it's good for him." Wally hops down off the trunk and starts to stretch his calves. Hannah watches him as if he's not really there; she feels dazed and exhausted, and has the strongest urge to curl up in her bed and hide away from the world.

"I think they're both excited about it," Wally continues.

"Good," Hannah says, trying to infuse some heartiness into her voice.

"Hey," Wally says tenderly, stepping up to the trunk again. "It's gonna be okay. You'll work it out. That's what friends do."

"Yeah," Hannah rasps.

"I have to go—I'm gonna be late for practice."

"Yeah. Sure thing. Bye."

Wally starts to walk away, but then he glances at her and doubles back to the car. He wraps his arms around her in a sturdy, secure hold, and Hannah gives in to the embrace, drawing comfort from the warmth of his skin and the musky smell of his neck.

"It's gonna be okay," Wally says into her ear.

She hugs him hard and doesn't let herself think about anything else.

Hannah stays in bed until one in the afternoon on Saturday, her mind drifting in and out of sleep, her dreams splintered into fragments of memories. She wakes up to fogginess and slips back into darker fogginess. The memories ebb and flow, as real and powerful as the ocean.

Hey, come here, Baker says. *I want to show you this piece I've been learning.*

And Hannah watches, in the theater of her subconscious, as 14-year-old Baker, with braces and an overlarge sweater vest, plays the piano for her.

Tell me your favorite thing about nature, 16-year-old Hannah says.

Trees, Baker says. *Really old, beautiful trees.*

Hannah wakes again to the sound of the television playing downstairs. She hears her dad pacing around his first-floor study. That responsible voice inside of her berates her to get up and do her homework, do something productive, but she turns over on her stomach and slips back into the memories instead.

On Saturday night, she lies on her back on her bedroom floor and stares at the ceiling, at the glow-in-the-dark stars Baker helped her tape up there back in freshman year. She imagines everything Baker and Clay are doing right now.

The dress Baker wears. Is it the beige one with the brown belt? The lilac one with the lace sleeves?

Tell me if this looks good, Baker says as she stares at the mirror in the dressing room.

Of course it looks good, Hannah says. *Everything looks good on you.*

Does Clay wear a Polo shirt and khakis? Does he wear the cologne his mom gave him for Christmas? Does Baker like it?

You smell good, Baker says on the back porch at her house. *Are you wearing perfume?*

No, Hannah laughs.

I think it's just your shampoo, Baker says, shifting her head on Hannah's shoulder. *It smells like you.*

Hannah pictures them at a fancy restaurant, strolling in hand-in-hand, Baker in the dress and Clay in the khakis, pleasing the world with their complementarity. Clay must pull her chair out for her, and Baker must smile shyly and thank him.

Does she laugh at his jokes? Does he think about how pretty she is? Does he reach across the table for her hand? Does she let him take it? Do the older people sitting at the tables around them nudge each other and say *Look how cute?*

Hannah plays music through her iPod speakers. Eventually she starts to talk to God. Small phrases, monosyllabic words. *Why does this hurt. Can you hear me. Can you make this go away.* Her eyes fixate on a patch of green stars on the ceiling. *I love this pattern,* Baker says as she lies on Hannah's bed. *I wish I could sleep here all the time.*

You can, Hannah says.

Her back starts to hurt from the fibers in the carpet, but she doesn't move from her spot.

She folds her hands over her stomach and blinks at the ceiling and imagines what it would be like if she was the one out to dinner with Baker. She pictures Baker's smile and her dark chicory eyes and how she tucks her hair behind her ear. She sees her study the menu like it's a textbook chapter she's going to be quizzed on. She sees her order a sweet tea with two lemons, please, and she sees her fold her napkin over her lap.

What are you looking at? Baker asks.

Nothing, Hannah smiles.

She stands up and walks into her bathroom and stares at herself in the mirror. Her bloodshot eyes stare back at her. She turns around and lifts her shirt up, searching for the rug burn she knows will be there. Her upper back has scratchy pink marks all over it. She presses her fingers against her raw skin and watches the flesh shine white.

"So what do you want to do about prom pictures?" Wally asks her during Monday's unassigned period.

"What about them?"

"Do you still want to go to the picture party at Clay's house?"

"Oh. I didn't think about that."

"I think we should still go. I'd like to be with Clay and Baker. And I know Clay would want you to come."

"Is Luke still going?"

Wally frowns. "Luke's not going to prom."

"He's not?"

"No. Now that he and Joanie aren't going together, he doesn't want to go at all. Haven't you talked to him?"

Guilt sweeps over Hannah. She breaks eye contact from Wally, feeling embarrassed, and admits, "No, I haven't."

"Have you tried apologizing to Joanie again?"

"No," Hannah mumbles.

Wally sets down his pencil. "Really?"

"She won't talk to me."

Wally stares hard at her. Then he picks up his pencil and starts filling in his Calculus homework again. Hannah watches him, feeling both stubborn and shamed. "I don't know how to say sorry for what I did," she tells him. "I mean, I basically ruined their relationship. I broke Joanie's trust. I really hurt them both. How do you say sorry for that?"

"I can't tell you how to apologize, Han."

"But it's like the wrong is too big to be forgiven, you know?"

"No," Wally says, looking up from his textbook. "You just have to keep trying. You might have to work at it, especially when it comes to Joanie—I mean, you might have to sit down and *really* talk to her, you know, not like she's your little sister but like she's your friend. Like she's Baker."

"Joanie could never be Baker."

"See, there you go," Wally says, throwing his hand up to prove the point. "You're not trying, Han. You're not. They can forgive you if you try. Anyone can forgive you if you try. Christ, I'd probably even forgive my own father if he—" Wally stops abruptly, bites his lips into his mouth, takes a long breath. "Anyway, you need to keep trying."

He looks back down to his Calculus textbook. Hannah pulls at the pleats on her skirt while the silence fills up around them. Finally she says, "Thanks."

"No problem," Wally says, his voice much lighter now.

"Wally—I'm really lucky I have you. I'm really lucky you haven't left, too."

Wally raises his head again, his eyebrows knit together in seriousness, his jaw firm. "I'd never leave you," he says, and then, after checking her grateful expression, he goes back to his homework.

That afternoon, when Hannah and Joanie get home from school, Hannah follows Joanie into the kitchen. She leans against the counter and presses random applications on her phone while Joanie stands in front of the fridge, scanning her snack options.

"We could heat up that leftover meatloaf," Hannah offers.

Joanie ignores her.

"Joanie," Hannah says exasperatedly, "I'm sorry."

Still Joanie ignores her, moving the egg carton aside to see what's behind it. Hannah waits for about 15 seconds before she tries again.

"I know I was an asshole. I didn't mean to screw things up for you and Luke."

Finally Joanie turns around. Her eyes blaze with anger. "Are you kidding me?" she says bitterly. "You 'didn't mean to'? Is that a joke?"

"I wasn't thinking—"

"Luke hasn't spoken to me in six days," Joanie says. "Not a single word. He won't return my calls or my texts. He won't even look at me. And this is the guy who was my best friend. The only person in our group who ever made me feel like he absolutely wanted me to be there, even though I didn't always get that vibe from everyone else, and especially not from you, who always made me feel like I was stupid and a nuisance. But I tried so hard to be your friend anyway because I—" her voice starts to break—"I thought maybe if I was just a little bit funnier, or a little bit less annoying, then you'd let me in. And I trusted you because you're my sister. But I guess that was really fucking stupid of me, wasn't it? The only friend I truly had was Luke. He made me feel special and wanted and included, and now he can't even look at me. And you know whose fault that is, Hannah? It's yours."

She slams the refrigerator door shut and storms out of the kitchen. Hannah stands frozen in place. She hears Joanie pound up the stairs to her bedroom and slam the door. Then the house is absolutely silent but for the tick of the grandfather clock in the family room.

Hannah slides down the counter, her back bruising against the wood. She slides until she's sitting on the cold white tile of the kitchen floor, her elbows digging into her thighs and her sinuses pounding beneath her skin. And for the first time in months, she lets herself cry.

On Friday, the day before prom, Hannah trudges to her locker just before the first warning bell rings. She trades her French workbook for her Calculus binder and ignores the flurry of students around her, who are all buzzing with excitement and stored up energy as they talk about their plans for tomorrow night. Hannah hears words like "limo" and "pictures" and "afterparty," but she tries to block it all out.

But then, out of the corner of her eye, she catches a burst of bright color. She turns to her left and sees Baker and Clay, just a few yards down at Baker's locker, trading smiles as they look down at the bouquet of flowers in Baker's hands.

Roses. Clay has brought Baker a dozen roses. And they are a brilliant, cheerful, perfect yellow.

Chapter Nine: The Prom Queen

Wally looks handsome, in a classic all-American boy way, as he stands there in a tuxedo in Hannah's front hallway. Hannah watches him fidget with the corsage box in his hands while they wait for Hannah's mom to stop fussing over her dress and hair.

"Let's get some pictures here before we leave for the party," Hannah's mom says. "How about one with Wally giving Hannah the corsage?"

"Where's Joanie?" Hannah's dad asks. "Shouldn't she be in some of these?"

"Shhh," Hannah's mom says, swatting at his arm. "She's in her room. She wants to be left alone."

Hannah's mom snaps several photos on an outdated disposable Kodak while Hannah's dad stands quietly off to the side, a gentle smile playing on his face. Hannah smiles hard when Wally wraps his arm around her.

"You two look great together," Hannah's mom says, and when they all walk out to the cars to drive to Clay's house, she whispers, "He's the perfect boy for you, Han," right into Hannah's ear.

Hannah's sweating when she and Wally walk up the Landry's driveway. Her mom and dad walk behind them, hand in hand, two proud parents ready to see their daughter off to the dance. Wally leads them around to the backyard, from which they can already hear chatter and laughter, and Hannah's heart pounds hard when she sees the prom party and dozens of parents gathered on the back porch.

218

She spots Baker right away. She stands in the middle of the group, clutching Clay's arm, a big smile on her face as she talks to Mrs. Landry. She wears a long midnight blue halter dress that makes her shoulders look even more slender than they already are. She wears her hair in a fancy updo, thick strands of it weaving back past her ears like delicate rivulets. When she turns around to say something to Dr. Landry, the sun shines on the bare skin of her neck and her upper back, and Hannah is suddenly awash in the tactile memory of kissing her there.

When Wally pulls Hannah over to the porch, Baker meets her eyes for the quickest of seconds—almost like she did it by accident—but then tears her gaze away. Hannah's heart pounds faster. She greets several of the people around her, both classmates and parents, until Clay comes over to say hi.

"Hey," Clay says, sounding genuinely happy to see her. "I'm so pumped you came."

"I've missed you," Hannah says, hugging him hard.

He pulls away and gives her a very packed look, his eyes begging for her to understand. She smiles and holds onto his arm for a few seconds, and he smiles back. Several feet behind him, Baker looks pointedly away.

Hannah's parents say hi to the Landry's, Hannah's mom grabbing Mrs. Landry's arm as they laugh about something Hannah can't hear. Clay joins them to tell Hannah's parents hello, and Hannah's mom exclaims over how handsome he is while Hannah's dad shakes his hand. "And where's your pretty date?" Hannah's dad asks. "Yeah, where's Baker?" Hannah's mom says. Hannah's stomach turns over with anxiety, but Baker comes to greet them without missing a beat, hugging Hannah's mom as if nothing is wrong. Then Mr. and Mrs. Hadley join the group, Mrs. Hadley telling Hannah's mom all about their process for getting Baker ready. Hannah's mom pulls Hannah into the circle to say hi and talk about her own preparation process, and Hannah and Baker both act like everything's normal, though they avoid each other's eyes.

And then it's time for pictures. Hannah and Wally line up with the rest of their classmates—a whole line of them, handsome and beautiful 17- and 18-year-olds, stacked boy-girl-boy-girl all the way across the yard. Their proud parents stand across from them, holding up iPhones and fancy Canon cameras and, in Hannah's mom's case, disposable Kodak's, and the parents beg them all to smile, and to stand tall, and to remember this prom night forever. And in the midst of cameras clicking away, and of parents shouting out their ideas for clichéd photos, and of smelling Wally's cologne and brushing up against the itchy material of his tuxedo—in the midst of it all, Hannah feels the gravity of Baker's presence and aches to go stand next to her.

Clay's mom requests a picture of Clay, Baker, Wally, and Hannah after the large group photos have ended. Hannah feels Wally look over at her, but she doesn't look back, afraid she'll betray her discomfort. In her peripheral vision, she sees Baker shift and look away toward Clay's old swing set.

"Yeah, come on, you'll all treasure this one day when you're older," Hannah's mom says. "Go ahead, get together."

Then the four of them are posing together, and only Wally separates Hannah and Baker, so that each of them has an arm around

220

his back. For a brief second, when Wally leans forward in a laugh, Baker accidentally touches Hannah's wrist, and an electrifying charge surges through Hannah. But then Baker jerks her hand away as if she had been burned, and it becomes even more difficult for Hannah to smile for the camera.

And then it's time to go. Hannah hugs her mom and dad goodbye, and her mom whispers to be good and to have fun and to enjoy looking at Wally's handsome face all night. Hannah's dad shakes Wally's hand and instructs him to drive carefully.

"I will, Mr. Eaden," Wally says, sounding as serious as Hannah's ever heard him.

Hannah hugs the Landry's and Hadley's goodbye, and Mrs. Hadley holds her at arm's length and says, "Come by and see us soon, alright? Feels like it's been forever."

"I will," Hannah fake laughs.

On the drive to dinner, Wally says, "That wasn't as awkward as I thought it might be."

Hannah says nothing. She thinks about how that was the first time Baker's touched her since the beach.

The entryway to the ballroom at the Crowne Plaza is decorated with purple and yellow curtains. A hand painted sign—*Welcome to St. Mary's Prom 2012!*—hangs above the double doors. Hannah and Wally step into the ballroom, which has already filled up with juniors, seniors, and the counted-upon teachers who linger along the walls, including Ms. Carpenter, who sips from a Diet Coke can while she chats with Mrs. Shackleford. Purple and yellow balloons, packed together like organisms under a microscope, cling to the pillars on the wings of the room. A few people sit at scattered tables, but most of the student body has already taken to the center dance floor. Father Simon weaves his way through the slow-dancing couples, stopping here and there to request that each boy and girl leave room for the Holy Spirit.

"So what do you think?" Wally asks. "Want to dance?"

They join their classmates on the dance floor. People all around them say hi, the girls mouthing *So pretty!* or *Love your dress!* to Hannah, the guys reaching over to clasp Wally's hand in greeting. Wally loops his hands around Hannah's waist, and Hannah reaches up to lace her hands around his neck, and they start to dance.

She tries hard to lose herself in the soft rock song, to not picture Joanie sitting at home in her bedroom, or Luke watching TV at his mom or dad's house, or Baker and Clay taking their time at dinner before they arrive at the dance. She closes her eyes against Wally's chest and concentrates on shifting her body from side to side, following his lead.

It's about 15 minutes later that Hannah notices Baker and Clay on the dance floor. Baker faces away from Hannah, her back muscles visible as she strains to reach her arms around Clay's neck. Clay's talking to her, his whole face lit up with happiness, his boutonniere fastened a little lopsidedly on his tuxedo jacket. Hannah's heart starts to ache more acutely than it has all night as she watches them dance.

"So you know what my mom said to me before I left tonight?"

Wally asks.

"What?" Hannah says, glad for the distraction.

"She said, 'Hannah is much more beautiful than I was at 17, so you make sure you treat her well.'"

Hannah laughs. "Your mom's gorgeous."

"Try telling her that."

"I have. But that was nice of her to say."

Wally's mouth lifts in a gentle smile. "You are beautiful, though."

Hannah blushes, feeling touched that he would say that, but also sad that it doesn't matter.

Hannah and Wally dance on and off for an hour, lost in the middle of the crowd. Hannah watches Mackenzie dance with Jackson, Lisa dance with Bryce, Ellie Thomas dance with Michael Ramby. She even watches Michele dance with Cooper, though Michele scowls over his shoulder, her eyes on Clay and Baker.

Father Simon nods curtly at Hannah and Wally whenever he walks by. Ms. Carpenter smiles at them from her position on the edge of the dance floor. Clay catches their attention once or twice, but Baker never acknowledges them.

"Alright..." the deejay says, his voice hovering somewhere between manufactured enthusiasm and genuine boredom, "if I can have everyone gather 'round, it's now time for the Prom King and Queen announcement."

The sea of students turns toward the deejay platform, and several people break out into applause and whooping. "That's right," the deejay says, "...very exciting moment for everyone here."

Mr. Manceau waddles up to the deejay booth, rings of sweat darkening the underarms of his chartreuse button-down shirt. He hands a sealed envelope to the deejay and whispers something in his ear; the deejay nods his head a couple of times while the student body waits eagerly for the big reveal.

"Okay, here we go," the deejay says, his voice affecting more enthusiasm. "When I call out the Prom King and Queen's names, please step up here to the booth, where Mrs. Shackleford and Mr. Manceau will crown you. The official King and Queen dance will follow that. Y'all ready?"

The crowd responds with a heavy cheer and an ever-increasing amount of clapping. Hannah claps her hands limply together, feeling misgivings in her stomach.

"Your 2012 St. Mary's Prom King is..." the deejay says, inflecting his voice on the last few words, "...Mr. Clay Landry."

A huge cheer goes up around the ballroom. Hannah looks to her right and sees Clay, his smile too big for his face, standing momentarily frozen as he lets the moment soak in. The guys all around him, most of whom are other football players, clap him on the back and shove him forward toward the deejay booth.

"Nice job, man," the deejay says, seeming like he's just going through the motions. "How do you feel? Nervous?"

"Hell no," Clay calls as he walks to the booth, and a great roar of laughter and applause follows his assertion. Hannah hears more whooping from some of the football players.

"Are we allowed to say that at a Catholic prom?" the deejay

224

asks, glancing toward Mrs. Shackleford and Mr. Manceau and sounding truly amused for the first time all night. Mrs. Shackleford, standing with her arms folded, rolls her eyes but lifts her shoulders in a defeated gesture. Mr. Manceau frowns and tugs up the waistband of his pants.

"I didn't think so," the deejay continues, clearly trying to stir the pot now. "Maybe we should send this Prom King to Confession?"

"Get to the Prom Queen!" someone in the back yells out, and the surrounding students clap and echo his sentiment.

"Alright, alright. Just having some fun. Well, St. Mary's, your 2012 Prom Queen is..."

Hannah's stomach clenches.

"Miss Baker Hadley!"

A deafening roar goes up around the room. Wally cheers very loudly next to Hannah, pounding his hands together, and Hannah, standing there and feeling like she's watching this moment from above the dance floor, experiences a strange bittersweet feeling, like she wants to fall on the floor crying but run to Baker and hug her at the same time. Baker walks to the front of the crowd, her smile somehow both nervous and confident, mouthing thanks to the classmates who cheer her on. She walks to join Clay at the deejay booth, and Hannah's stomach surges upward to meet her heart with a feeling of love and pride.

But the feeling extinguishes as soon as Clay leans forward to hug Baker and the student body responds with even more amplified applause. Mrs. Shackleford and Mr. Manceau walk forward, shaking hands with both Baker and Clay, and then Mr. Manceau hands the crowns to Mrs. Shackleford, who places them carefully on top of Clay and Baker's heads.

"Let's hear it for your King and Queen!" the deejay shouts into his microphone, and the student body whoops and hollers and smacks their hands together, and someone on the far side of the room shouts "Get it, Landry!", and both Clay and Baker laugh, their whole faces shining like it's the happiest day of their life.

Then music starts to play, and the deejay signals to Clay that he should lead Baker to the dance floor. The students all around them part down the middle, and Clay steps forward with his hand clutching Baker's. He takes her right hand in his left and places his other hand around her waist; she wraps an arm around his neck and allows him to lead her in a slow dance. Hannah stands rooted to the spot, easily able to see them from her vantage point on the front ring of the crowd. She watches her classmates' reactions—how the girls look hungrily but fondly on the scene; how the guys nudge each other and mutter under their breath, probably joking about how they're glad it's not them who has to dance in front of everyone; how Michele Duquesne, standing on the far side of the crowd, clenches her jaw. Abby Frasier, one of Hannah's friends since freshman year, who stands just behind Hannah and watches the dance as if transfixed by magic, turns to Julia Grey and whispers, "Baker's so lucky. Can you imagine how amazing she must feel right now?"

Hannah wants so badly to leave, to run outside and gulp down fresh air. Her throat is tight with a choking sensation; her stomach aches so badly that she wants to throw up. But several girls are looking at her, gauging the reaction of the Prom Queen's best friend, even if they haven't seen Hannah and Baker interact much lately; so Hannah fixes her face into a happy expression, forcing herself to look absolutely delighted and proud, to look as if she cannot imagine anything better for her best friend, to take in the sight before her as if it's heartening her rather than killing her.

Finally the dance ends, and Baker pulls gently away from Clay. Clay runs a hand through his hair and grins down at her, his entire countenance suggesting that he's the luckiest guy on the earth.

"Okay, thank you to Clay and Baker," the deejay resumes. "I've got a few more songs for you, St. Mary's, and then it'll be time to wrap up this night. So enjoy these next few gems and dance with your date as long as you can."

He plays Eric Clapton's "Wonderful Tonight." Wally checks Hannah's expression, raising his eyebrows playfully to ask *Shall we?*, so Hannah wraps her arms around his neck again and allows him to sway her where they stand.

They're halfway through the song when she sees it. Baker and Clay, still dancing in the middle of the dance floor, are kissing. Baker's chin is tilted up to meet Clay's mouth, and Clay's hands are low on her back, and they're truly, freely, eagerly making out.

"Don't feel well," Hannah says, jerking away from Wally. She turns on the spot and hurries off the dance floor, toward the double doors that lead to the hotel lobby. She rushes down a hallway until she finds an exit, and almost as soon as she's out the door, she retches all over a patch of plants near the parking lot.

She falls against the building, her body weak and broken. She gasps for breath, begging it into her lungs, wanting so badly to clean these anguished feelings from her body. Cars rush past on the interstate across from the hotel, and Hannah wishes she was in one of them, heading somewhere far away.

Eventually, once she's able to catch her breath, she walks shakily to the sidewalk and sits down upon it, even though she knows her dress will snag on the concrete. She wraps her arms around her knees and demands that her mind think of something else, anything else, other than the images that keep floating to its surface: Baker grabbing Clay's arm at the picture party—Baker dancing with Clay in the middle of the dance floor—Baker kissing Clay, kissing him with those same lips that have kissed Hannah—

Please make it stop. Please take it away. Why can't you just take it away. What am I doing wrong. Why did you give me these feelings. Please help me. Please.

"Han? You okay?"

It's Wally, come to check on her. He lingers in the hotel doorway, his expression concerned but confused at the same time.

"Yeah," she says, steadying her breath, smiling as nonchalantly as she can. "Yeah, I'm fine. Just got overheated."

"You want me to sit with you for a little while?"

"You don't have to."

"I want to."

They sit next to each other on the sidewalk, Wally's shiny black shoes splayed out before him, Hannah's dress scratching on the concrete. They listen to the cars racing past in front of them.

"You sure you're alright?" Wally asks after a minute.

"I am. You want to go catch the last dance?"

He shakes his head. "Sitting out here is fine with me."

They follow a long line of cars to Clay's house for the afterparty, and Hannah, feeling relaxed from Wally's soothing company and from the ever-growing distance between them and the hotel ballroom, starts to feel marginally better. Dr. and Mrs. Landry greet the procession of teenagers at the front door. "Boys' things in the guest room, girls' things upstairs," Mrs. Landry recites, hugging Wally and Hannah and a few others, while Dr. Landry stands behind her with a glass of wine. "There's water and Coke in the coolers!"

The house feels as crowded as prom did, but everything is brighter and closer. Hannah weaves her way through the hallway, saying hi to some of her friends, Wally following behind her and echoing the hellos, occasionally placing a hand on the small of her back.

"Let's go outside," Wally says. "There are too many people in here."

The backyard is blissfully quiet—a welcome change from the loud music of prom and the booming bass in Clay's family room. Wally takes off his shoes and dress socks and rolls up his pants. "Come on," he says, extending a hand to Hannah, "let's take a ride on the swings."

She kicks off her high heels and hitches up her dress, then takes his extended hand. His palms are sweaty but warm, and she allows him to lead her across the dewy grass toward the swing set. He waits for her to sit down on the left swing; she tucks her dress under her and wraps her arms around the chains. He smiles and sits down upon the other swing, and then, wordlessly, they both kick off the dirt and start to swing up and down, surging higher and higher, lengthening their arcs each time, balanced by the two wooden triangular structures on either side of them.

"I'm trying to get in sync with you," Wally laughs, "but I can't."

"That's about the hardest thing in the world."

"Wait for it," Wally says, holding up his hand, daring her with his eyes. She watches as his body hiccups on the swing, so that he slows the arc of his swing to more closely match hers, and a few seconds later, after another hiccup, their swings move in sync so that they are perfectly paralleling each other, even down to the lift of their bare feet. And Hannah remembers, with a jolt, what she and Joanie and the neighborhood kids used to call this phenomenon when they were younger.

Look! We're married!

The memory startles her, so that her whole body falls out of rhythm and she loses her momentum. The synchrony between she and Wally breaks very suddenly. "Shit!" Wally yells, his voice brimming with laughter. "Catch up!"

She pumps her legs and arms hard, trying to recover from her mess up. She mimics Wally's hiccup maneuver, but she doesn't pull it off right: the gap between their swings grows more pronounced. "Han!" Wally calls, still laughing, and she yells, "I'm trying!", her voice pouring forth more desperately than she realized it would. She pumps her legs harder and harder and grows more and more frustrated, until Wally eventually does his hiccup maneuver again and restores their synchrony.

"Yo!" a voice shouts from the house. They whip their heads up to see a tall figure illuminated by the lights outside the door. It's Clay, his tuxedo gone and replaced by his normal clothes. "Stop flirting and get in here!" he shouts at them. "You're missing the party!"

"We're coming, you dick!" Wally yells back.

Clay swats his arm over the air as if to say *Yeah, yeah,* and then he turns back into the house and shuts the door behind him. Wally and Hannah slow their swinging until they reach a gradual stop, both of them kicking up dirt in the process. "I'm gonna ruin my pedicure," Hannah says, scrunching up her face, "but I don't really give a shit."

"I'm gonna hit Clay," Wally says, "but I don't give a shit, either."

Hannah can't fully see his face—not in the darkness, with only the lights on the back porch casting a dim blanket over the backyard—but she suspects his cheeks are red. "It's okay," Hannah says, affecting nonchalance. "You know Clay just likes to make people feel awkward."

"Should we head in?" Wally asks, extending his hand again.

They walk back over the damp grass. Wally doesn't let go of her hand. Just before they step onto the patio tile, he stops walking and pivots towards her.

He wants to kiss her. She knows it in an instant, even before she sees the look in his eyes.

Wally doesn't say anything; he just looks at her, his eyes making contact with hers before flitting down to stare at her mouth.

There is a hunger in his expression, and though Hannah has always caught glimpses of it, tonight she sees the full manifestation.

She stands unsteadily on the grass, unable to look away from his mouth, unable to make a decision. She wrestles with her instincts, remembering Baker and the beach, but also remembering Baker kissing Clay on the dance floor tonight.

Why should she fight this? Why fight it when Wally is standing in front of her, wanting to be with her? Wally, who is kind, and loving, and who believes in good things even though he doesn't always receive them? Wally, who sees her, who wants to understand her, who makes her feel like she might be better than she is?

"Hannah—" he says breathlessly, and when he says her name, she thinks, *Maybe this can be enough.*

So she arches her neck up to kiss him. His lips are warm and tinged with the minty flavor of the Altoids she saw him eating in the car. She kisses him hard, like she means to, and he kisses back hungrily, and though her gut has no reaction, and though she feels no burst of magic, she at least feels safe, and like she is standing, for the first time in months, on solid ground.

They kiss for several minutes, until the kiss turns heated and Wally pulls back from her. "Wow," he pants, his eyes wide behind his glasses. "Did I mention I'm glad you're my prom date?"

He stoops to pick up his socks and shoes. He picks up Hannah's heels, too. "Come on," he says, nudging her with his arm, "let's go in before Clay comes out and acts like an ass again."

It's past midnight now, and everyone at the party has changed out of their formal attire. Wally looks down at his tux, then over at Hannah in her dress, and says, "Guess we ought to follow suit?" He grins. "No pun intended."

Hannah smiles. "That was awful."

He shrugs, still grinning, and hands her her overnight bag. "I'll see you in a minute."

She takes the bag and winds her way through the forest of people in the house, her eyes on the staircase that leads upstairs to the second floor. She scoots around Ted and Kristen, who hug her as she goes by, and then, just before she reaches the stairs, she sees Baker.

Baker sits on the floor, her legs splayed out over the beige carpet, her hair taken down out of its elegant updo so that it now cascades down her back. Clay sits next to her, muttering something into her ear, his arm positioned behind her back. They sit in a larger circle of people, all of whom are paired off boy-girl, and Hannah notes the flask they seem to be passing around the group when they think no one is looking. At that moment, right when Hannah moves into their line of sight, Baker meets her eyes.

Her expression is hard to read. She doesn't move a single muscle in her face; she simply stares directly at Hannah, her eyes deep and loaded with a meaning Hannah can't understand. She seems almost hurt, and Hannah wonders for a lightning-quick second if Baker saw her kissing Wally in the yard.

But then Baker breaks eye contact and the moment is gone. Hannah keeps moving, walking toward the stairs, plastering a fake smile on her face when the other people in Baker's circle call hello to her. "Where you been?" they ask, some of them clearly tipsy already, and Hannah answers, "Outside," without pausing to explain. She waves at them all and promises to return, and then she makes herself climb the stairs to the second room. She carries the image of Baker's eyes the whole way.

Hannah spends most of the night huddled with Wally in a section of the family room, munching on Chex Mix and listening to David, one of their friends from their AP classes, tell stories. All around them, boys and girls flirt with each other, kiss each other, sneak outside or into bathrooms to hook up with each other, taking advantage of the fact that Clay's parents have surrendered to sleep.

Around two in the morning, with the party around them still in full swing, Wally asks Hannah if she wants to go for a walk.

"Right now?"

"Yeah," he says. "If you want to."

They walk the streets of Clay's neighborhood, accompanied by the whispers of water sprinklers and nighttime insects. Wally ambles along with his hands tucked into the pockets of his drawstring pajama pants, and Hannah holds her hands in her sweatshirt and reminds her heart that it should be here, with Wally, and not back at Clay's house.

"I like you," Wally says suddenly, after they've wandered down a couple of streets. "I've liked you for a really long time."

They reach the outskirts of the neighborhood, cross a quiet street, start a path toward the LSU lakes. Hannah wrestles with her instincts again, trying to think of an appropriate response to his admission.

"I guess I want to know," Wally says, kicking a pebble along as he walks, "do you like me back? Or am I just the friend you occasionally make out with?"

They reach the edge of the lake. She senses him looking at her, but in the darkness, it's hard to read his expression. They sit down on the earth and stare straight ahead at the lake—a dark mass reflecting the light of the moon. At this late hour, with only the two of them sitting calmly in front of the water, everything in the world feels predicated on hope, on possibility, and Hannah thinks, for the second time that night, *Maybe this can be enough.*

"I like you, too," Hannah says, and as soon as she speaks the words, she feels calmer, safer, like she's finally fitting into the world. For now, in the quiet peace of this night, she and Wally are the only two humans who exist, and it's easy to imagine that she could always feel this way. He's Boy, she's Girl, and maybe her teachers have been right all along, and maybe the churches have been right all along, and maybe Wally has been the divinely anointed one for her all along, ever since the beginning of time.

Wally kisses her there alongside the lake, and Hannah feels safe, and like she finally belongs.

They walk back to Clay's house with a looser quietness between them. Wally holds her hand and occasionally brushes his warm arm against hers, and Hannah's body and mind feel calmer, even relaxed.

When they walk back into the house, they find their classmates asleep on various parts of the floor. There is one lone light turned on near the staircase, and Wally leads Hannah toward it, both of them moving silently through the landmine of sleeping people.

"Looks like it's just guys down here now," Wally says. "Can I walk you upstairs?"

"No, I'll be okay," Hannah smiles.

He kisses her goodnight, and she tries to take that feeling of safety up the stairs with her.

She shines the light of her cell phone as she tiptoes up to the second floor. When she reaches the landing, she nearly bumps into a shadowy figure about to descend the stairs.

"Who's there?" the figure asks, and Hannah realizes, with a jolt, that it's Baker.

"It's me," Hannah answers. She raises her cell phone to shine its light on Baker. "What are you doing?"

Baker stands rigidly, as still and silent as a long-forgotten phantom. "Nothing," she says, her voice shaking. "Getting some water."

Hannah studies her in the weak light from her cell phone screen. She looks like she might have been crying. Her overlarge pajama shirt hangs loose and limp on her body. Just when Hannah's about to ask if she's okay, Baker opens her mouth and looks like she's on the verge of crying out, or begging for something, or spitting up something bad that she accidentally swallowed. For one heart-stopping moment, Hannah thinks Baker is going to let her in again.

But then Baker shuts her mouth as abruptly as she opened it and brushes past Hannah. She hurries down the stairs, her head bowed, and Hannah watches her forlornly, resigned to this new dynamic.

She finds the linen closet at the end of the upstairs hallway, just next to Ethan's old room. She grabs a dark cotton sheet and a thin flannel blanket, grateful to have something to warm her tonight.

She's walking past Clay's room when his door opens, startling her so that her heart lurches in her chest. "Whoa!" Clay shout-whispers, jerking back from the doorway. "Who is that?!"

"It's Hannah," she says, raising her cell phone to cast the dim light on herself. "I was just getting some blankets."

"God, you scared the shit out of me, Han."

Hannah doesn't apologize. She shines her cell phone light on him instead, noting his naked torso, which glistens with sweat, and his messy hair. He is wearing his boxers and nothing else.

"What are you doing?" Hannah asks.

"Nothing," he says hastily. "I was just brushing my teeth and everything."

"Oh."

A sick feeling spreads in Hannah's stomach—a kind of instinct that hints to something she doesn't want to know.

"Come on," Clay says. "Let's go to bed. I don't want to wake up my parents."

Hannah hesitates. That sick instinct fans out around her whole body, slipping up into the pipeline of her throat, making her think she might throw up.

"Your boxers are on inside-out," she whispers.

They stand in uncomfortable silence. "Oh," Clay says, fiddling with the waistband of his boxers. "Yeah. I pulled 'em on kind of quickly. Thanks."

He hurries away from her and sneaks down to the first floor. Hannah shuffles like a zombie to the second floor guest room, where she curls up in a ball on the floor, clutching her blanket around her.

Mrs. Landry cooks French toast for everyone the next morning, seeming to work with an infinite number of eggs and bread slices in order to feed all the hungry teenagers in her kitchen. Hannah feels like she's watching a modern interpretation of the Miracle of the Loaves and the Fish. Clay monitors the coffee pot, pouring mugs of dark roast for all of his many friends, his hair tousled and his eyes glazed with tiredness.

"He was up late," Wally says, following the direction of Hannah's gaze. "He didn't come to bed until after you and I got back."

"I know," Hannah says. "I bumped into him upstairs."

"Wonder what he was doing."

"I don't know," Hannah says. She picks apart the French toast on her plate and tries to focus on the here and now, especially the feeling of Wally holding her hand under the table. She squeezes Wally's fingers and commands herself to stop watching the hallway that leads to the stairs.

But it doesn't matter anyway: despite the scraping of silverware and the loud voices of the classmates around them, Baker never wanders into the kitchen.

Joanie comes into Hannah's bedroom when she gets home

238

that morning. She folds her arms over her chest and watches Hannah unpack her overnight bag and hang her dress on the door of her closet. "How was it?" Joanie says, her voice full of acid. "Did you have a *wonderful* time?"

"It was fine," Hannah says tiredly. "Not that exciting."

Joanie's voice quivers with anger when she responds. "Yeah, well, it was probably better than watching *Dateline* re-runs with Mom and Dad and trying to ignore all the pictures people were posting online. Oh, and trying to forget about the beautiful prom dress I had hanging in my closet—"

"I get it, Joanie, I'm sorry. I don't know what else to say other than that."

"—Not to mention Luke still hasn't talked to me at all, and yesterday was his parents' wedding anniversary, which is one of the main reasons he wanted to go to prom so badly. So he could forget about it."

Hannah's heart sinks. "I'm sorry."

"You're going to have to come up with something better than that," Joanie says, her face contorted with bitterness. She spins on her heel and storms away.

That week at school is a tough one. Baker continues to avoid Hannah; Clay speaks to her only sparingly; Joanie ignores Hannah altogether; and Luke, when Hannah tries to apologize to him, simply blinks at her a few times and then wanders away. Only Wally, with his concerned eyes and his warm hand wrapped around Hannah's, continues to talk to her.

It makes it harder and easier for her to make her college decision. She sits on the floor of her bedroom, barefoot and wet-haired from the shower, and fans her college decision letters in front of her. She eliminates three of them within minutes, and then she's left staring at her letter from Emory and her letter from LSU.

She reads through their admissions literature again. She browses their websites for hours, reading about libraries and campus life and student groups. She downloads course catalogs and lies on her stomach while she scrolls through class listings.

None of it matters. She knows, instinctively, which one she's going to choose anyway.

Her mom lifts her eyebrows in surprise when Hannah treads downstairs with the college letters in her hand. "Did you decide?" she asks, setting her reading glasses over her nightgown. Hannah's dad, sitting in his beaten up old armchair, lifts his eyes from his book.

"Yeah," Hannah breathes.

Her mom's mouth lifts as she prepares to smile. "What's it going to be, honey?"

Hannah bites her lip. "What do you think I chose?"

Her parents study her for a moment. Her mom tilts her head with her mouth upturned in a thoughtful smile. Her dad sits very still, his gray eyes unblinking as he reads her with his engineer's mind.

"Emory," her dad says.

Hannah smiles. "Yeah."

They stand up to hug her, and she holds her Emory letter tight to her chest as they wrap their arms around her.

"So have you heard the news about your *best* friend?" Joanie says after school on Wednesday. She struts up to the car, her hands tucked under her booksack straps, and waits for Hannah and Wally to break off their conversation.

Hannah squints in the sunlight, shocked that Joanie is willingly speaking to her. "What news?"

"The news about Clay and Baker and their little four a.m. *tryst.*"

Hannah's stomach turns over. "What?"

"Joanie—" Wally says warningly.

"Yep," Joanie says cockily, flinging her bag onto the pavement. "They done the deed, condoms and all. Kind of clichéd in my opinion, having sex on prom night, but whatever gets them off, I guess."

"What are you talking about?" Hannah says desperately.

"Emily Zydeig just told me. Apparently Clay had to ask Walker for some condoms. Clay was trying to keep it quiet because Baker didn't want anyone to know, but it sounds like everybody's hearing about it anyway."

Hannah looks desperately at Wally. He doesn't meet her eyes. "Did you know about this?" she asks him.

Wally's jaw clenches. Hannah can't look away from him, not until he refutes what Joanie said, not until he gives her a sign that this whole conversation is an elaborate joke.

He doesn't look at her, though.

"Oh god, Hannah," Joanie says disdainfully. "Stop being so goddamn dramatic. It's just sex. Lots of people are doing it. Except you, apparently."

"Stop talking, Joanie," Wally says harshly.

Joanie falters under Wally's glare. Hannah feels dizzy in the silence, her stomach quaking with that sick feeling. "How did you know?" Hannah asks finally.

Wally meets her eyes. "Clay talked to me about it. He asked me to keep it in confidence."

"So you kept it from me, too?"

"It wasn't mine to tell." Wally looks pointedly at Joanie. "It wasn't anyone's to tell."

The three of them wither in the silence. The sun beats down on the crown of Hannah's head, burning through her hair. She's not sure what to do, where to look, so she stares at the black asphalt of the parking lot, her thoughts and emotions rocking around her body like a ship tossed about in a storm.

"That's pretty crazy," Hannah says at last. She swallows and forces herself to smile at Wally. "I feel pretty dumb, not knowing about it—"

Wally opens his mouth uncertainly.

"I've gotta go," Hannah says, backing away toward the car, aware of a spreading hollowness inside of her. "Big paper due tomorrow. Come on, Joanie."

"Han—" Wally says.

"See you tomorrow," she says, her voice catching in her throat. She shuts herself in the car, waits for Joanie to do the same, and then drives away from the St. Mary's parking lot.

Joanie narrows her eyes at Hannah on the drive home. "What's wrong with you?" she asks, her voice coming out aggressively, and yet tinged with a small trace of doubt.

"Nothing," Hannah says, punching the radio dial.

She drops her booksack on her bedroom floor. She locks the door. She leans her head into the wall.

Clay and Baker and their little four a.m. tryst.

She mouths the words to life again. She mouths them a second time. She mouths them over and over and over until the badness inside of her finally leaks out.

She cries against her bedroom wall. She cries out in broken breaths. They are half-formed cries, not fully imbued with the magnitude of the suffering she feels. They are all air—broken, disrupted air—and no voice. But she cannot lend her voice to her suffering. Joanie might hear.

She touches her palms to the wallpaper. She brushes her cheek against the filmy surface. Her tears bleed into the paper. Her tears. These offerings from her body. She can smell them and taste them.

Chapter Ten: Shards of Glass

If Hannah thought she knew what pain was before, she was wrong. Every part of her—her body, her heart, her soul—aches with suffering. She has the sensation of being crushed in on all sides, compressed until she can hardly breathe, until she wants to do nothing more than run away as far as she can go.

She wonders about this suffering. Was it designed by God, a lesson to turn her away from her sin? Is it absolute proof that she can never be with Baker, and she should just stop trying?

Wally wants to understand. She can tell by the way he looks at her with those open, concerned eyes. They talk at her locker and he silently implores her to tell him what's going on, but she can't.

Ms. Carpenter wants to understand, too. Hannah knows by the way Ms. Carpenter watches her pack up her things at the end of class. "Everything good with you, Hannah?" she asks, her angular eyebrows drawn together in concern, but Hannah just half-smiles and insists that she's fine, she's fine.

Late at night, after her parents and Joanie have already gone to sleep, she drives to City Park and sits in her car beneath the canopy of trees. She looks up at these trees and marvels at their existence, at how they just *are* what they were created to be, how they tower proudly on their wooden trunks, how they sway in the breeze and move their leaves like piano keys, and she prays that she can be like them, that she can innately grasp her existence and live it out without questioning.

Am I wrong? she asks. *Just tell me if I am.*

She never receives an answer.

It feels like her sadness will stay with her forever. The future, a vague notion that at one time felt very exciting to her because it contained only possibilities, now seems like a prison sentence, a condemnation. For now that she understands the yearnings of her heart, what is she supposed to do?

Lose-lose situation.

Marry Wally. Marry a boy. Have the beautiful wedding in early autumn, when the air is warm and football season is in full swing. Have sex and make babies. Give them a mother and a father, that they may have casserole on the table and baseball in the yard. Go to the office holiday parties, hold onto Wally's arm, wear a black cocktail dress and the necklace he bought her for Christmas. Grow old together. Watch him lose his hair only to grow a paunch on his waistline. Babysit the grandkids on the weekends.

All the while, ignore the hole, the falsehood, in her heart. Discipline herself not to look over at her bridesmaids—at Baker— when she stands on the altar. Never allow herself to pretend that it's Baker's arms wrapped around her in bed at night.

Or fuck it all and fight to be with her. Take her to the movies and buy her her favorite candy when she goes to the restroom before the show. Find a house with her in a safe part of town and fill it with animals and books. Stay in on Friday nights and fall asleep on the couch watching Netflix with their bodies lined up next to each other under the blanket. Learn each other's secrets. Love each other's faults. Promise her the world.

But give up the traditional church wedding. Give up the possibility of children who are a perfect half of each of them. Find a different church, or sit in the very back pew where fewer people will see the electricity between them when they hold hands during the "Our Father," or forgo church all together. Resign themselves to the lifelong burden of explaining their relationship to every new person they meet.

How can her feelings be right? How can they, when no matter what she chooses, she will never be whole? Somewhere, somehow, something must have gone wrong when she was born. Something got switched in the wiring. Something in her brain, or in her body, or in her blood. Everything she's learned about union with another person, about her body's purpose—none of that can transfer to a girl, to Baker.

Disordered. She is disordered.

She stops texting Baker. Stops trying to talk to her in English class. Stops trying to catch her eye at lunch. Surrenders herself to this new reality in which she and Baker have no relationship at all, and in which the only person who will talk to her is Wally.

But it doesn't stop her heart from longing. It doesn't stop her from thinking about Baker with every song she hears and every beautiful sky she sees. It doesn't stop her from dreaming about hugging Baker, holding her close, promising her that everything is okay.

She knows they are trapped. She wonders if Baker is trying to show her the way—show her the way they are supposed to live and the way they are supposed to love. Sometimes she is absolutely convinced that Baker is right: that it's better for them to forget their sin, and to focus instead on their relationships with Clay and Wally. But other times she wonders if Baker has it wrong—if the world has it wrong.

She tries to ask God, but she can't seem to find God anywhere.

She doesn't know what's right or wrong anymore; all she knows is this vast hollowness inside of herself—this place where God used to be, where the church used to be, where her parents used to be, where she used to be. Now there's a heaviness inside her esophagus; a lodged stone that refuses to move, that she would like to vomit up if she could, that she could coax out with tears if only she was free enough to cry.

She goes to Mass on Sunday and Father Simon speaks about Truth, about how many people in the world don't want to hear the Truth. "Our Church, the bride of Christ, is persecuted every day," he says, and Hannah thinks on that and cannot understand how it is true.

She goes to Ms. Carpenter.

"What's up, Hannah?" Ms. Carpenter says, glancing up from her computer when Hannah hovers in her doorway after school.

"Can I talk to you?"

Ms. Carpenter trains her eyes on her, searching her. "Of course," she says. "Come on in."

Hannah shuts the door against the sounds from the hallway: people talking, lockers slamming, clothing and booksacks rustling as students leave the building.

"What's going on?" Ms. Carpenter asks. "Everything okay?"

Hannah stops in front of her desk. She taps her knuckles on the wood. "No."

"No?"

"No."

Ms. Carpenter nods. "You want to sit down and tell me about it?"

Hannah accepts the chair Ms. Carpenter pulls over for her. She folds her hands together on her skirt and bounces her right leg off the floor. Ms. Carpenter sits silently at her desk, waiting.

"I feel...alone," Hannah says. "I feel lost."

Ms. Carpenter blinks, but her expression betrays no judgment.

"There's something going on with me," Hannah continues, "that doesn't fit with my conception of who I am. Or what I want my life to be. It doesn't...it doesn't fit the paradigm of what other people want my life to be."

"Okay," Ms. Carpenter nods.

"I just..." She inhales; she twists her tongue around the words. "I don't know how to say it."

Ms. Carpenter waits.

"I...it's like...it's like my deepest nature isn't what it's supposed to be. It's different from what everyone says God wants it to be."

"And what's that?"

"I...remember my comment about Father Simon? I think maybe I said that out of anger...out of anger because...because I...."

Ms. Carpenter swallows. "Hannah," she says, her voice weaker than it normally is. "There is nothing you could be that God wouldn't love. Your deepest nature—whatever it is—is who you are, and God loves you for it. You are good. And no matter what people might say, you need to believe that."

"Yeah," Hannah breathes, tears springing into her eyes. "It's just—"

There's a knock on the door, and Hannah whips her head up. Joanie's face peers through the rectangular window, her expression annoyed.

Ms. Carpenter's angular eyebrows pull tight together. She clears her throat and walks to open the door.

"Hi, Joanie."

"Hi. Sorry to bother you. I was just looking for Hannah."

Ms. Carpenter looks back to Hannah. Her eyes are pained. Hannah stands up and swings her booksack over her shoulder.

"Thanks, Ms. C," Hannah says, not looking at her. "I'll get that revised essay to you tomorrow."

"Sure thing, Hannah," Ms. Carpenter says, her voice gentle. "Stop by anytime if you need to talk through it again."

"Why do you look so depressed?" Joanie asks as they walk to the car.

"I'm just tired."

"What were you talking to Ms. Carpenter about?"

"Are you speaking to me again?" Hannah snaps.

Joanie shuts up, but on the drive home, Hannah feels her watching her.

"First day of May," Wally says at lunch on Tuesday. "It's officially graduation month."

"God, I can't even process that," Hannah says.

"That means finals and AP exams start next week."

"Well, fuck me."

Wally stifles his smile. "Want to meet me after practice today and we can study?"

"Sure."

"Great. I need your help on some AP Gov stuff."

"Cool."

Then they run out of things to say. Hannah doesn't mind: she lets herself be absorbed by the lunchtime chatter, her mind drifting back to Ms. Carpenter's words yesterday. But she's distracted when Father Simon walks into the senior courtyard with a proud smile on his face: she recognizes it as the one he wears when he thinks he's going to win students over.

He takes a red sharpie and writes something on the outdoor poster that Baker and Michele hung to track the rankings for the Diocesan Cup. The seniors in the courtyard slip into silence, waiting to see what he wrote. After a minute, he steps back from the poster, caps the sharpie, and smiles his proud close-lipped smile again.

"Our service hours log just pushed us a mile ahead of Mount Sinai," he says.

The courtyard breaks into applause. Michele looks smug where she sits with her friends. Clay wraps his arm around Baker, and Hannah knows he's thinking of the service projects she organized in the fall.

Wally doesn't clap much.

"Not excited about the Cup?" Hannah asks him.

"It's like you said months ago," he says. "The whole thing is kind of weird."

Hannah shrugs. "Whatever gets people excited."

Wally frowns. He rustles his hand around a bag of Cheetos, lost in thought.

"Hey," he says after a moment, "I've been meaning to ask you...have you talked to Baker at all?"

"You know I haven't. Why?"

Wally hesitates. "Clay's really worried about her."

"What? Why?"

"We went for a run yesterday and he was telling me that she hasn't really been eating."

Hannah's chest constricts. "She's not eating?"

"No, no, I mean, she is, I think she's just not eating as much as she used to, you know? She told Clay she hasn't really had an appetite."

Hannah shifts on the bench to get a good look at Baker. She sits in the middle of her crowded, lively table, smiling and talking to the people all around her. But there's something different about her, and Hannah can see it now that she's truly looking for the first time in days. Baker is skinnier. Paler. Her smile less bright.

"She's probably missing you, Han," Wally says.

Hannah says nothing.

As they shift into May, the days grow longer and the earth

grows greener. Hannah hears the birds when she wakes and the crickets when she falls to sleep. The whole world holds a feeling of balance, like a tightrope walker poised on a wire, waiting for something, restless in the heat.

The ache in Hannah's heart starts to scar over, so that it no longer feels fresh, but more like a routine part of her. She sits on the back porch at night and wonders how long she will carry it within her. She breathes slowly, asking air into her lungs, and feels the air shape around the outline of the ache, as if too frightened to go near it.

On the first Saturday of May, Hannah rearranges the jewelry on her sink while Joanie gets ready to go out to a party. "Turn off that stupid emo music," Joanie says when she comes into the bathroom to grab her makeup bag. "You're making me depressed."

Hannah hangs out with her parents after Joanie leaves. She helps her mom cook baked ziti while her dad plays Fleetwood Mac songs through his laptop speakers, and then she and her parents fall into the big couch in the family room and watch *One Flew Over the Cuckoo's Nest* on AMC.

Joanie calls her sometime after midnight, an hour after their parents have gone up to bed. Hannah ignores it. Joanie calls again.

"What?" Hannah answers. "I don't want to pick you up, Joanie, I thought you were staying the night there."

"You need to come over here," Joanie says urgently.

"What?"

"It's Baker. She's really sick."

"What happened?"

"She drank too much. She won't let me help her. Please just come over."

"I'll be right there," Hannah breathes, rushing to grab her keys. "Just stay with her. I'll be right there."

She speeds out of the Garden District, across South Acadian, down into Liz Freeman's neighborhood. She squints through the darkness and sees Liz's house on the corner, a whole gaggle of cars parked outside of it. She parks on a median and sprints up to the house with one of her shoes halfway off.

She can't find Joanie anywhere on the first floor of the house. Several of her confused classmates call out to her, drunkenly teasing her about her messy hair and her panicked face. "Where's the fire, Hannah?" someone laughs, but Hannah pushes past him and rushes up the stairs.

With a swell of relief, she finds Joanie in one of the upstairs bedrooms, crouched against a door.

"Where is she?" Hannah asks, her heart racing with fear and adrenaline. "What's going on?"

"She's in here," Joanie says, spreading her fingers over the bathroom door. "She won't let me in."

Hannah tries the door handle. It's locked. She drops to her knees in front of the door. "Baker?" she calls. "Bake? Can you hear me?"

She listens through the wood of the door, but Baker doesn't respond. Hannah taps on the door, calls Baker's name again, and then hears a retching sound coming from the bathroom.

"How much did she have to drink?" she asks Joanie.

"I don't know, I wasn't with her for most of the night, but Liz said she was drinking straight vodka for the last hour."

"And no one stopped her?"

"I don't think they realized."

"Where the hell is Clay?"

Joanie shakes her head. "I don't know. I found her slumped over the kitchen sink and tried to take her into the downstairs bathroom, but she wanted to come up here. I don't think she wanted anyone to see her."

Hannah lays her head on the carpet and peers through the crack beneath the door. She can see Baker's bare legs and feet spread over the tile floor. "Baker?" she calls again. "Baker, it's me, it's Hannah. Can you let me in, please?"

"I tried to use a bobby pin," Joanie says, her eyes wide and frightened, "but I couldn't get it to work."

"Let me see it. Where's your phone? Look up how to unlock doors with bobby pins."

Joanie finds a helpful article and reads it aloud while Hannah works the bobby pin in the keyhole.

"Come on," Hannah pleads with the bobby bin, "come on."

Finally, something clicks, and Hannah rotates the doorknob until the door pushes open and she falls forward onto her hands.

Baker is slumped against the bathtub with her feet extended toward the toilet. Hannah crawls toward her, calling her name, Joanie right behind her.

"Baker? You okay?" Hannah asks when she reaches her. Baker rolls her head on the edge of the bathtub, moaning and clutching her stomach. She has vomit on the corner of her mouth and in her hair. "Bake," Hannah says, wrapping her arms around her, "are you alright? What happened?"

Baker nestles her head into Hannah's shirt and starts to cry.

"Joanie," Hannah says, looking up at her sister's anxious face, "can you wet some toilet paper?"

They wipe Baker's mouth and her hair. Hannah pulls her into her lap and rubs her back, whispering calming things to her and promising that it's going to be all right.

"She needs to throw up more," Joanie says.

"Baker," Hannah says softly, tucking her hair back, "we need you to vomit more, okay? Okay? We'll help you."

Baker scrunches up her face and cries. "Can't," she whispers. "Hurts."

"I know," Hannah coos, pulling Baker's hair back into a ponytail, "but it's going to make you feel better, okay? I promise. Come on, we'll help you."

"Come on, Baker," Joanie says kindly, "you can do it."

Baker turns her head away from them; two more tears streak down her face. "Come on, B," Hannah says, "let's sit up."

She and Joanie guide Baker to the toilet. They stand on either side of her, poised like bodyguards, Joanie gripping Baker's arm and Hannah rubbing Baker's back.

"Doing great," Hannah coaches her. "Now try to make yourself vomit, okay?"

"Just stick a couple of fingers down your throat," Joanie adds, miming the action.

Baker bends forward and heaves. Joanie looks away with her face screwed up in distaste, and Hannah stares at a hand towel near the sink and focuses on drawing circular patterns over Baker's shirt.

They stay that way for several minutes, the sound of Baker's retching echoing around the bathroom, the vibrations from the music downstairs pulsing through their blood. Then Baker stills.

"Feel better?" Hannah asks.

"Yeah," Baker rasps. Hannah hears the pump of the toilet flushing.

"Careful," Hannah guides. "Sit down slowly. We'll get you some water, okay?"

She sits down and pulls Baker into her arms again. Joanie squats next to them, her eyes still crinkled with worry. "Do you think you got it all out?" Joanie asks.

Baker nods against Hannah's chest. Hannah strokes through her hair and smoothes a thumb over the light sheen on her forehead.

"Can you get me a wet washcloth, Joanie? Or a wet piece of toilet paper?"

Joanie finds a washcloth under the sink, wets it, wrings it out. Hannah presses the blue cloth against Baker's forehead, then her cheeks, then her collarbone. "How you feeling, B? Any better?"

"Yeah," Baker breathes, sounding more like herself even though she keeps her eyes closed. She tucks her head further into Hannah's shirt. "Thank you."

"We'll just sit here for a little while, alright?"

The three of them rest in silence for a few minutes, Joanie sitting with her back against the wall, Hannah sitting with her back against the bathtub and Baker tucked into her side. She can feel Baker breathing against her body, and she pulls her fingers through Baker's hair in the same rhythm.

"It's a good thing I called you," Joanie says.

Hannah looks up. Joanie is wearing an unusual expression: she seems calmer and older somehow.

"Yeah," Hannah agrees, shifting her eyes to the tile floor. "I'm glad you did."

"I'm gonna get her a glass of water. I'll be back in a minute."

"Thanks."

Then Joanie is gone, and Hannah is left with Baker in her arms.

"What the hell happened?" Clay yells, bursting into the bathroom. Joanie trails behind him with her mouth open in protest and a glass of water in her hand. Luke follows last, his usually bright face falling into worry.

"She got sick," Hannah says, sitting forward. "Keep your voice down."

"Why didn't anyone come get me?"

"What?"

"Baker, are you okay?" he says, falling to his knees in front of her. He runs his hands up and down her arms. "What happened, baby?"

Baby. The word echoes loudly in Hannah's head, then drops

into her stomach and pierces her sharply.

"Don't move her, Clay," Joanie snaps, stepping forward. "Here, Hannah, give her some water."

"I'm going to get my keys," Luke says from the doorway. "Bring her out to the car in a minute."

"Thanks, man," Clay says. He inches closer to Baker and brushes his knuckles down her face. "You alright, Bake? What were you drinking?"

"She can't talk, Clay," Joanie says impatiently. "She just vomited up a whole swimming pool of alcohol. Give her some space."

"Here," Clay says, reaching for the water glass from Hannah, "I'll do it. You and Joanie go help Luke with the car."

"What?" Hannah says, nothing making sense in her head, her impulse to hold Baker strengthening by the second.

"I'll take care of her. I can carry her down the stairs."

"I don't think we should move her yet," Hannah says.

"Hannah, she's my *girlfriend*, okay, I can handle this. C'mere, Bake."

Hannah watches numbly as he transfers Baker's body weight to himself and holds the glass of water to her lips to drink. "Open up, baby," he says, his deep voice stripped down to a gentler sound.

Hannah stands slowly and backs into the sink, words swimming around her head, worry still clutching at her stomach, and beyond it all, that ache, that terrible ache, suffocating her heart.

"Hannah," Joanie says softly.

Hannah doesn't look at her.

"Up we go," Clay says, lifting Baker in his arms. "Han, can

you get that water glass?"

She does as he asks and follows him out of the bathroom, out of the bedroom, out of the house. Luke's car idles in the driveway, waiting for them.

"Are y'all coming?" Clay asks, turning around briefly.

Hannah can't find her voice.

"We're good," Joanie answers him. "Text us once you get her home, okay?"

"I will," Clay promises, and then he climbs into Luke's car with Baker resting in his lap. Hannah and Joanie stand still and watch them drive away.

"I can drive home, if you want," Joanie says tentatively.

"Yeah."

"Han? You should put that water glass down."

"What?"

"That water glass. In your hand. Maybe you should go put it on the porch."

"Yeah."

She walks it numbly to the front porch, but then, just as she's about to set it down, a deep pain overtakes her, a pain so sudden and blinding that she channels it without thinking—she throws the glass at the brick wall of the house—she hears it smash into a million fragments, fragments as numerous as the hairs on her head, as the sands on the seashore—she hears Joanie gasp behind her but she doesn't care—the pain is debilitating and she wants to vomit, she wants to vomit, she wants to vomit, but she can't.

"Hannah," Joanie says, approaching her cautiously. There are tears in her eyes.

Hannah opens her mouth to speak, but only dry sobs come out. She shakes her head back and forth, back and forth, trying to erase everything.

"Hannah, please," Joanie says, grabbing her wrist. "Let's go home."

Chapter Eleven: Possibility

Hannah stays in bed for a long time on Sunday morning. She blinks at the sunlight streaming through the crack in her crimson curtains, but all she sees is Baker on the bathroom floor, vomit on her mouth and in her hair.

Hannah, she's my girlfriend, okay, I can handle this.

"Hannah?" Joanie calls through the door. "Can I come in?"

Hannah hides her face in her covers, but Joanie enters the room anyway. Hannah hears her set something on the dresser. Then she feels Joanie's weight settle onto the bed, right over Hannah's feet.

"You should probably get up," Joanie says. "It's past noon."

"So what."

"So you're being a total lard-ass."

Hannah doesn't respond. A heavy silence falls over them, a silence that Hannah can feel wrapped all around her.

"Han?" Joanie says, her voice fragile. Hannah can imagine her face, sad and anxious like it was the time Hannah fell off her bike and sprained her wrist when she was in first grade and Joanie was in kindergarten. "Is there anything I can do to make you feel better?"

Hannah breathes into her pillow. Unexpected tears spring into her throat. "No," she says.

Joanie shifts her weight on the bed, and Hannah feels a lighter pressure on her foot, the pressure of Joanie's hand.

"Han?" Joanie's voice is so, so fragile. "Is there something you want to talk about?"

Hannah breathes. "Where are Mom and Dad?"

"They're at Home Depot."

"Oh."

"Hannah? What's going on with you?"

Hannah sits up and wipes at her eyes. Her heart sprints away in her chest, like it knows what's coming before she does.

"I—" she says.

"Yeah?"

"I—I don't know how to explain this."

"Okay...well, does it have something to do with Baker and Clay?"

Hannah swallows. "Yeah."

Joanie studies her for a moment, and Hannah keeps her head down, bracing for the question that might come. "Okay," Joanie says, and her voice sounds nervous all of a sudden. Hannah looks at her. There is something fearful and expectant in her eyes. "What is it?" she asks.

The question hangs between them for a second. Hannah searches Joanie's expression, looking for signs that Joanie already knows what she needs to say. Joanie stares back with her jaw set.

Hannah's face sears with heat. Her whole body revs up for danger, her primal instincts kicking into gear like those of a trapped animal. She can hear her heart pounding in her head.

"I have—feelings," Hannah says carefully, her voice shaking. "Feelings for—for—"

"For Clay?" Joanie suggests, her eyes too hopeful.

They look at each other for a long second. Hannah considers capitulating to the lie Joanie has handed her. Joanie looks scared, yet defiant.

"No," Hannah says finally, the word wrestling its way out of her throat. She takes a breath. "Not for Clay. For Baker."

Joanie stares hard at Hannah. She blinks once, twice. The entire moment feels surreal, like they're playacting the way they used to as children.

"Okay," Joanie says finally.

"Okay?"

"Yeah," Joanie nods. "That makes sense. I mean, I always wondered if maybe—" She nods her head again. "Okay. I'm glad you told me."

"You're not—it's not weird?"

"Why would it be weird?" Joanie says, and the question is so affectedly defiant—grounded in heartiness, like Joanie expected to be asked this question and rehearsed this inauthentic answer to preempt any real analysis—that Hannah starts to cry. She opens her mouth and tries to respond, but her response turns into a sob, a sob as quick and surprising as a hiccup, and now Hannah is sobbing into her pillow, sobbing so loudly and physically that her body starts to feel like it isn't even hers, like it's functioning independently, casting out demons at the command of the Christ.

Then she feels Joanie's weight on her body, feels Joanie hugging her through the duvet cover, hears Joanie whispering to her that it's okay, it's okay, it's okay. She cries and shakes and thinks of Baker, drowning in toxic shame, fighting to exorcise it from inside of her, wondering to what depth it goes.

She cries for long minutes while Joanie holds her through the covers. "It's okay," Joanie says, her voice raspy, her weight still on Hannah's body. "It's okay."

When Hannah's last cry pours out, she breathes hard into the pillowcase, inhaling its laundry detergent scent, drawing comfort from the familiarity of it.

Then it's quiet, and Hannah listens to the hum of the air conditioning running through the house.

"Sit up," Joanie says. "I brought you some Sprite."

She feeds the glass into Hannah's hand, and Hannah gulps down the soda, imagining it flooding over her empty body and fizzing away all the bad things.

"Why didn't you tell me?" Joanie asks. Her eyes are large and pained and bluer than usual.

"How could I have?" Hannah says.

"Hannah, I'm your sister. You can tell me these things. You can tell me how you feel."

"I didn't know how."

Joanie picks at a snag on the comforter. "Um," she says. She raises her eyes carefully to Hannah's. "Do you like other girls, too? Or is it just Baker?"

Hannah drops her eyes to the floral pattern on her comforter. The question hangs between her sister and herself, delicate and important like the long threads they used to swing their stuffed animals on when they were younger.

"I think," Hannah says evenly, tasting the words, "that I like girls in general. I think I always have."

"How long have you known?"

"I don't know—I mean, it's like, how long have you known your own name?"

"Yeah." Joanie pauses. "Do you think Baker feels the same way?"

Hannah glances around her bedroom—at the clothes on the floor, at the hairbrush on the dresser. Her eyes settle on a picture of Baker and herself from last summer. They're sitting on the back porch at Wally's house—Hannah on Baker's lap, Baker's arms clasped around Hannah's waist—while Joanie and Luke photobomb the picture from behind. Baker's mouth is open mid-laugh, her eyes dark and happy, a piece of gum visible on her back teeth. They had all been drinking Bud Lights and eating Doritos on the porch that night, while Wally's mom was away with his two younger brothers, and it had started to rain, one of those light, humid rains that made the backyard feel like a sauna, and they had all stood up to go into the house until Baker had said, in a voice full of wonder, "Wait—why don't we just stay out here and experience it?" So they had stayed sitting on the porch, yelling at each other about how they were all dumbasses, watching the rain drip down their wrists, feeling it slide down their noses, until they were all wearing the rainwater like another layer of clothing.

That was one of the stupidest things I've ever done, Hannah had laughed later.

Don't knock it, Clay had said.

She's not, Baker had said, her eyes lighting on Hannah. *That's just Hannah-speak for loving something.*

"What are you thinking, Han?" Joanie asks.

"Just remembering something."

"About Baker?"

"Yeah."

"What happened at the beach?"

"What?"

"The beach," Joanie says. "Everything was all fine and great while we were there, but then it went to shit when we came back. What happened?"

"I don't know, we just...."

"Did you tell her how you feel?" Joanie guesses. "Did you, like, confess to her?"

"In a way," Hannah says dazedly.

"What did she say? Did she feel the same way?"

Hannah hesitates. "It's hard to explain. I think—that even if she did, she wouldn't allow herself to let anything come of it."

"What do you mean?"

"Like, she has these ideas, you know, of how she's supposed to be. Of what it means to be the good girl."

Joanie sighs. "I cannot figure her out."

Hannah says nothing.

"Han?"

"Yeah?"

"What about Wally?"

Hannah's heart drops. "I love him, too," she says, her voice sad and wistful, "but it's not the same."

Joanie swallows. "I worry that he really loves you."

"I do, too."

"Han—I'm sorry that I didn't talk to you for so long. Especially when you were going through this."

"Don't be sorry. I deserved it."

"I didn't understand."

"I didn't know how to explain."

They lapse into silence, until Hannah starts to blow bubbles in her Sprite glass.

Hannah stares at her phone screen for a long time that afternoon, until her fingers can no longer stay still.

How are you feeling?

Baker doesn't reply.

School is better and worse on Monday. Better because Joanie is talking to Hannah again, worse because Baker is not.

"She could at least, like, acknowledge that you took care of her on Saturday night," Joanie says at lunch. "A simple 'Hey Han, thanks for wiping all that vom off my face' would suffice."

Hannah, Joanie, and Wally gaze in the direction of Baker's lunch table. Baker sits in her usual place—right in the middle of the table—and Clay sits next to her, occasionally reaching out an arm to squeeze her protectively around the middle, his leather letterman's jacket creasing every time he does so. Baker looks thin and sallow; her hair looks unkempt and her eyes seem smaller on her face.

"Exactly how sick was she?" Wally asks.

Hannah shakes her head and looks to Joanie.

"*Sick*," Joanie answers. "Like, totally incapacitated. She was heaving her freaking guts out."

Wally looks sideways at Hannah. "And she let you take care of her?"

"I think she was too out of it to argue."

"That's not true," Joanie says. "It's more like, she was so out of it that she acted like her true self instead of this weird person she's been lately."

"I don't get her," Wally says. "I mean, I've never understood her the way you do, Han, but now I understand her even less."

"You and I are in agreement on that, Walton," Joanie says.

"Did Clay tell you anything more about what happened on Saturday?" Hannah asks.

"Nothing that you haven't told me," Wally says.

"She looks so skinny," Joanie says. "And like she needs a really long nap."

Hannah watches Baker again, and the ache in her heart bleeds anew.

Hannah charges her way through her final exams, feeling grateful for the distraction of intense studying. She and Wally continue to meet at Garden District Coffee to trade notes and make outlines together, and now Joanie comes, too, and buys them all sugar cookies when they need a break. "You look like you're just drawing lines of gibberish," Joanie says as she watches them work through a calculus problem. "Why the hell would you take AP Calc anyway?"

"Because now I won't have to take Calculus in college," Hannah answers distractedly. "I can just take all the English and humanities classes I want."

"Yeah, and I can nerd out with even crazier math classes," Wally says.

"That's why we love you, Wall," Joanie says. "But don't expect me to root for the Yellow Jackets."

"I would never lay that ridiculous expectation on you, J. But I might expect you to come visit."

"Are you kidding? Fucking duh. I'll be there anyway to see Han. We can all hang out together."

"Yeah," Wally agrees, nudging Hannah's leg under the table. "It'll be awesome."

On Tuesday, after her Theology final, Hannah spots Luke standing alone at his locker. "Hey," she says, approaching him tentatively. "How'd you do?"

Luke turns around in a daze, like he wasn't prepared for her to speak to him. "Hey," he says after a moment. "I did okay. How about you? Did you blow it out of the water?"

"I think I did alright."

"I forgot a lot of that stuff about Vatican II."

"Yeah, there's a lot to remember."

"So then I just played dumb and wrote down that Vatican II was the sequel to a really bad sci-fi movie."

Hannah grins for the first time in a long while. "Did you really?"

"No," he laughs, and she sees that old familiar hitch in his smile, and for a second she forgets that anything ever came between herself and her friends.

But then Luke's grin shrinks into an expression of sadness, like he has just remembered himself. "Anyway, I better go," he says, swinging his booksack over his shoulder. "See you later, Han."

He walks away before she can think of anything else to say to him.

"I didn't think the end of high school would be like this," she tells Joanie when they're washing dishes on Tuesday night.

"Like what?"

"Like—so messed up. So fragmented. I mean, just a few weeks ago we were all getting drunk together and talking about our future trips to Destin. And now our group's totally split up. I always imagined the end of high school would be bittersweet, not just bitter."

Joanie is silent as she towel dries a saucepan. "Yeah," she says finally.

"I'm sorry," Hannah says hurriedly. "I didn't—sorry."

"It's okay."

"I talked to him today."

"You did?"

"At the lockers."

"How was he?"

Hannah tells her about the joke Luke made, and Joanie takes on a soft, yearning expression. "I miss him so much," she says.

"I'm really sorry."

"It's okay. When it all comes down to it, it's my fault."

"Do you still want to be with him?"

Joanie doesn't hesitate to answer. "Every second of every day," she says, and Hannah knows exactly what she means.

Hannah and Wally sit for the national AP Calculus exam on Wednesday morning. It's a grueling exam—long and full of complicated problem sets—and by the end of it, Hannah's wrist aches from writing, and the eraser on her mechanical pencil has been beaten down to a nub. "I am so done with math," she tells Wally afterwards, when they're walking back to their classes. "Like, don't even show me another number for the rest of my life."

Wally holds up three fingers. "What number is this?"

"Stop," she laughs, hitting him in the ribs, and he recoils and pretends like she hurt him. And then, right there in the hallway, with the rest of the student body still in their regular classes, Wally kisses her.

"Oh," Hannah says in surprise.

"We haven't done this in way too long," Wally says against her mouth.

"Maybe here isn't the best place."

They hear a catcall, and both of them whip around to see a handful of their AP Calculus classmates crossing down a perpendicular hallway. "Get it, Sumner!" David calls, and Wally turns red and raises his middle finger.

"One," Hannah says.

"What?"

She laughs. In the middle of this hallway, where her classmates just spotted her kissing Wally, she feels wholly normal and beautifully conventional. "One," she repeats, her voice giddy now. "You just held up one finger."

Wally's face breaks into a huge smile. He kisses her again, and Hannah lets him, and she feels so, so safe.

When she gets home from school that day, Hannah pours herself a bowl of Apple Jacks and eats the green and orange cereal bits one by one, striving to keep an even ratio between the two colors. She studies a page from her AP Literature notebook ("Notes on 'The Friar's Tale'") and focuses her eyes away from the sketch of a bald, dumpy little friar, drawn in blue ink pen, that Baker had scribbled on her paper in the middle of class that day (*Where's my hair?* the friar's speech bubble reads).

"Han," Joanie says, coming into the kitchen and clutching her cell phone in front of her body, "have you seen the news today?"

"No," Hannah says, only half-listening.

"The president came out in favor of same-sex marriage."

"What?"

"I just saw it on my news feed. I read the transcript. Look—"

Hannah reads the transcript of the president's words with her heart beating fast in her throat. Joanie hovers over her shoulder and reads down the screen with her.

"Wow," Hannah says when she's through.

"This is great," Joanie says earnestly. "Hannah, this is really, really good. He's the first president in history to support same-sex marriage—"

Hannah slams her notebook. "Yeah," she says, standing up at the counter, her mind racing and her heart still hammering. She carries her cereal bowl to the sink, turns the faucet on, waits for the water to turn from cold to hot.

"Aren't you excited?" Joanie asks.

"Can we not talk about this right now?"

"What's wrong? Don't you want to get married one day?"

"Who says I can't, Joanie? Just because I'm—I mean, just because I told you about all this confusing stuff with Baker, doesn't mean I'm—like, I might not even be—"

"What?"

"You know 'what.'"

"I'm not gonna say it for you."

Hannah jams her cereal bowl into the dishwasher. "Maybe I still want to marry a guy, okay? Maybe I don't have to be this way."

"What are you talking about?"

"Wally's been really great to me. He's a good person and he understands me. And we're both going to be in Atlanta for the next four years. Don't you think that's significant? Don't you think maybe it's a sign?"

Joanie scrunches up her face in distaste. "A sign about what?"

"That maybe that's the right path for me! I mean, just because I feel a certain way, doesn't mean I have to indulge it—doesn't mean I have to go down that life path—"

"Are you saying you like Wally now? Like, *really* like him?"

"You ask that like it can be a straight answer."

"It *is* a straight answer."

"I could grow to like him! I really feel like I could. I love him in a way. I really do. He's smart and sweet and totally devoted to his family—"

"Does he make you happy?"

"What?"

"Does he make you happy?"

Hannah hangs on the question. "Of course he does," she says.

Joanie narrows her eyes at her. She picks up her cell phone again and moves her thumb over the screen.

"Does he make you happier than this person?" she asks, thrusting her phone at Hannah.

Hannah stares at the picture on the screen. She and Baker stand in front of Baker's birthday cake, their arms around each other's shoulders, Baker's other arm looped around Hannah's stomach. The picture captures them mid-laugh, with Hannah gesturing down at the King Cake, her mouth open in sheer joy, and Baker looking at Hannah, her eyes lit up and her smile conveying absolute happiness.

"Well?" Joanie prompts.

"What do you want me to say? This—" she jabs at the picture with her index finger—"is not a possibility."

"It could be."

"In what world, Joanie?"

"In this world! Things are starting to change!"

"That's bullshit and you know it."

Joanie flings her cell phone onto the counter. She steps nearer to Hannah, her eyes blazing and her arms folded. "You need to talk to her."

"I can't."

"Yes, you can."

"I can't!" Hannah shouts, her arms extended in front of her in madness. "Joanie, do you not get it? Everything is different between us! We're not the same people we used to be! I don't know what we are to each other anymore. I don't even know if it's *okay* for us to be what we are—"

"Stop it!" Joanie yells, pushing Hannah back against the sink. "Stop! Stop saying that!"

"It's true!"

"It's not true!"

"THEN LOOK ME IN THE EYE," Hannah roars, "AND TELL ME, WITH ABSOLUTE CERTAINTY, THAT HOW I FEEL ISN'T WRONG, THAT IT'S NOT BAD, THAT IT'S NOT DISGUSTING AND PERVERTED AND FUCKED UP—"

"IT'S NOT!" Joanie screams, shoving Hannah hard.

Hannah falls back against the sink; at once, she feels a bruise bloom on the skin of her back. Joanie glares at her, her eyes still blazing, and Hannah breathes heavily and blinks against the warm tears forming in her eyes.

"I don't believe you," Hannah says.

Joanie screws up her face and flares her nostrils. Her chest rises and falls rapidly, the St. Mary's logo on her Oxford shirt moving up and down with the motion. When she speaks, her voice quivers.

"Start believing."

Hannah hears the quick intake of her own breath. She swats at the tears in her eyes and leans forward off the sink, her back aching with the new bruise from Joanie's push. "I need some ice," Hannah says, trying hard to steady her voice.

Joanie gathers some ice cubes into a Ziploc bag and wraps a dishcloth around it. Hannah hitches up her shirt and presses the cold compress to her skin. Joanie turns away as Hannah continues to swat at her tears and sniff against her sinuses.

"You should probably just let it all out," Joanie says in a deliberately cavalier voice. She opens the refrigerator but stands listlessly in front of it.

"I don't need to let anything out."

"Don't make me push you again," Joanie says, still staring into the refrigerator. "I'll hurt you worse than Baker did."

Hannah starts to cry in full. She tucks her face into the collar of her uniform shirt and heaves great, expansive sobs into the fabric. Her sinuses clog, her throat aches, her eyes floods with tears.

Joanie shuts the refrigerator door and sits down at the counter. She rests her chin on her hand and looks away toward the family room.

Hannah tries to stop crying, but she can't stem this release. She cries for a long three minutes while Joanie waits at the counter.

When Hannah's sobs slow, and when she's able to take gulping breaths down into her stomach, Joanie stands up and walks back over to her. "Here," she says, proffering a tissue box. "You have disgusting snot all over your face."

Hannah laughs, short and hiccup-like, into her tissue. She laughs in that sweet way of finding the shore after the storm, of tethering herself to something she knows.

"Feel better?" Joanie asks.

"Yeah," Hannah breathes.

"Hannah...you need to talk to her. You're both hurting. But I worry that she's not as strong as you."

"Don't say that."

"It's true," Joanie says, her face falling. "I'm worried that she's going to hurt herself even more. If she's not eating, and she's destructively drinking, and she's not talking to her best friend—"

Hannah turns away to throw her tissues into the trashcan. "Joanie, I can't make sense of how I feel about this. It feels like the whole world has rolled over in the air and I can't tell which way is up. So how am I supposed to talk to her when I haven't even figured out what I believe? I don't know the truth anymore. I don't know what's right and what's wrong."

"Jesus, Han," Joanie says. "Nobody knows that."

Late that night, Hannah lies on her stomach on her unmade bed and watches the news clip of the president five times in a row. His words flow through her headphones and into her ears, and her heart pounds fast, and she holds her hands together in front of the screen, her palms turned upward as if yearning to receive the Eucharist.

Maybe... she thinks, but she pulls herself back when she's right at the edge of that possibility. It's still too unfathomable. Or perhaps it's just too miraculous to think about.

But the possibility stays with her as she finally tucks in to sleep, and she wonders who the president was thinking about when he spoke those words. Was he imagining a scared teenaged girl in Louisiana? Was he imagining her?

Chapter Twelve: Good Friday

On Thursday, a few minutes after the end of Hannah's AP Literature exam, the bell signals for late-morning assembly. Hannah files into the gym amongst hordes of people and spots Wally sitting with David and Jackson a dozen rows up in the bleachers. He hails her, and she climbs the bleachers to meet him.

"Last school Mass," Wally says.

"Can't say I'm bummed about it," Hannah says.

Father Simon closes his eyes as he walks in during the procession. The music group sings one of their favorite contemporary Christian songs, but none of the people in the bleachers with Hannah sing along. Wally stands with his hands in his pockets, his eyes glazed over as he stares out over the sea of classmates below them.

Hannah listens to the readings with mild interest, but mostly she counts the number of juniors across the gym who have their eyes closed. She picks out Joanie sitting on the end of a row with her head in her hand.

Then the music group sings the "Alleluia," and Father Simon walks to the portable wooden lectern to proclaim the Gospel reading. Hannah choruses "Amen" with the rest of the living bodies in the gym, and then Father Simon tucks the liturgical book away and places his hands firmly on the edges of the lectern.

"Good morning," he says in his robust voice.

"Good morning," the hundreds of people around the gym respond.

"I had originally written a homily intended for our Senior

Class friends, since this is their last all-school Mass at St. Mary's—" Father Simon looks over toward the senior class and smiles—"but I felt I could not ignore an issue that has come to the forefront of our national conversation lately, and which begs us to meet it with compassionate—but firm—truth. And then I realized, Seniors, that this was the perfect thing to talk about in my homily today, as it exemplifies the hard questions you will be met with as you leave St. Mary's and enter into the real world as faithful, educated, Catholic adults. This is the first of many times that you will be tested in your faith, and in your understanding of morality, as you attempt to balance God's eternal truth with the reality of the world we live in.

"Yesterday," Father Simon says, "the president made a statement that challenges our beliefs about what's right and what's wrong, and about the kind of culture we want to promote in this country."

Hannah's heart starts drilling so fast that she can hardly breathe. Her palms and underarms sweat. Searing heat flares up beneath the skin of her face. Across the gym, Joanie sits straight-backed on the bleachers.

"Yesterday, our president said that he supports 'same-sex marriage.'" Father Simon pauses with his fingers still pulled over the air in a quote-making gesture. He pulls his plump lips into his mouth and stares down at the surface of the lectern.

"Students, I know you know, from your theology classes and from your interactions with our faith community, that marriage—Holy Matrimony—is an ordained act between a man and a woman. The sacrament of Holy Matrimony is one of the most precious gifts our

God has given us—as old as Adam and Eve, yet constantly renewed and reflected by Christ's love for His bride, the Church. It is a sacrament that we celebrate, that we honor, and that we want to protect. The sexual union that takes place within marriage leads to increased love between partners and, with God's blessing, to life.

"Now. Forgive me for repeating that which you already know. But I offer you this reminder if only to contrast this truth with the statement our president made yesterday. Same-sex marriage cannot exist because it is an oxymoron in and of itself, and because it undermines the very sanctity of Holy Matrimony.

"But there is an even more insidious side to political statements like this one, and it is precisely this snakelike temptation that I want you to watch for as you move beyond St. Mary's. In this case, the president's insidious suggestion was meant to trick us into thinking that Christ has nothing bigger in store for our homosexual brothers and sisters than a false, culturally-approved but eternally-unsound imitation of a marriage—that they might as well give up on their principles, give up on their conviction of right versus wrong, and settle for a sham—settle for something less-than.

"It is a lie," Father Simon roars, clasping his hands together and pointing them beseechingly at the student body, "that Christ wants his homosexual children to settle for this kind of life. It is a lie that He cannot renew them, cannot fulfill them, cannot call them to a life in the Church. We all have our Crosses to carry, we must all suffer with our Lord, but to reject the promise of our salvation is to live half a life. To live brokenly. To live in sin, separated from our loving God.

"God wants more than that for His children. He wants all of

you to walk with Him in faith, and to reject shameful imitations of His love, and to lead all of your brothers and sisters into a family of faith so we can worship our Creator and Savior. He wants the absolute fullness of life for you, and sometimes that means rejecting the empty promises that society—"

There is a commotion on the other side of the gym. Hannah whips her head up, her face still searing with heat, to see Ms. Carpenter thundering down the first four rows of the bleachers, her heels pounding, her heavy brown hair flying behind her, her angry expression visible even from Hannah's vantage point. Father Simon looks up politely, expectantly, as if Ms. Carpenter might interrupt him to say that someone has gotten sick or fainted, but she thunders straight past the row of curious juniors on the ground floor and huffs toward the exit doors. Just before she disappears around the corner of the bleachers, she sweeps her hand across a card table and knocks a stack of Mass programs off the top. They *swish* to the gymnasium floor with that uncomfortable landing sound that Hannah associates with someone dropping a book in a library. Then Ms. Carpenter shoves her hands against the exit bar of the gym doors—there's the loud echo of flesh hitting metal—and is gone from the gym.

Father Simon sputters and flushes red at the lectern. He settles his eyes on something over in the sophomore section, and following his line of sight, Hannah sees Mrs. Shackleford pursing her lips and folding her hands over her dress. The student body starts to murmur and gossip; everywhere around Hannah, people shift in their seats and whisper behind their hands and drop curse words under their breath. Wally side-eyes Hannah and says, "The hell was that about?"

Father Simon calls for everyone's attention and wraps up his homily with short, jarring sentences. The music group plays a song during the Preparation of the Gifts and a dull normalcy settles over the gym again. Father Simon plods through the Consecration as if nothing has gone amiss, but his face stays a bright red color and his hands shake when he raises the Host above the altar.

Hannah stands to join the Communion line with her hands clasped in front of her and her heartbeat still faster than normal. She receives the Body of Christ from Father Simon without looking into his eyes.

When she has settled back onto the bleachers, Wally wraps his hand around hers. His warm skin meets her clammy palms and she twitches in her seat. Wally smiles, mistaking her twitch for embarrassment. "I don't mind," he whispers.

Below them, on the floor of the gymnasium, Baker stands behind Clay in the Communion line. Her Oxford shirt fits loosely on her back—looser than it ever did before. She takes Communion and pivots to climb the bleachers back to her seat, her eyes trained on the steps in front of her. As she climbs higher, coming closer to Hannah's row, Hannah gets her first good look at her since Saturday night. Her skin looks ashen; her eyes loom much larger in her gaunt face; her hair looks thinner. She passes by Hannah's row on slender, unsteady legs, and Hannah's heart wants to climb the rest of the bleachers with her.

She's not sure what prompts her to do it. Maybe it's Joanie's warning echoing in her head. Maybe it's the image of Baker climbing the bleachers after Communion. Maybe it's the instinct in her stomach.

She drives to Baker's house at ten o'clock that night.

I'm outside your house, she texts. *Come out and talk to me or I'm going to pound on your front door and tell your mom everything.*

The curtains in Baker's window move aside, and Hannah can see her, her skinny outline lit from behind.

Hannah's standing on the driveway when Baker slips out the garage door.

"What is wrong with you?" Baker whisper-shouts, her eyes bulging, her hair hanging in lank strands around her face.

"I need to talk to you."

"So you threaten to tell my mom everything?"

"You know I wouldn't do that. But I had to talk to you."

"I don't have time for this," Baker says, looking away from her. "My AP Bio exam is tomorrow."

"You need to talk to someone," Hannah says, her voice pleading. "You're making yourself sick."

"I'm fine."

"You're not fine. I've known you for four years and you've never looked the way you look right now. Please, Bake. You could talk to Ms. Carpenter. You saw how she reacted at Mass today. You know she can't believe all that stuff Father Simon was saying."

Baker says nothing. The garage lights stream down onto her gaunt face, making her dark eyes look bigger than ever.

"I know you have to be thinking about it," Hannah says. "I've been thinking about it, too. Whether he's right."

"Of course he's right," Baker rasps, her eyes glistening.

"What if he's not?"

Baker shakes her head. "Don't," she says, swallowing visibly in the white light. "Don't. It's not a possibility. None of this is a possibility—"

"We can make it a possibility—"

"Don't," Baker says, stepping back from her, her eyes large and wet. She shakes her head and swallows hard. "We can't, Hannah. We can't."

"What about the beach?" Hannah says desperately. "What about everything that happened?"

"I meant it," Baker cries, rubbing her hands feverishly up and down her arms. "I meant every word I said to you. It's killing me not to talk to you. You have to believe me that it is. But Hannah, there's no alternative. You heard Father Simon today. You heard what he said about people like us. And everyone believes that, Hannah. Even if they say they don't, deep down they really do. We don't have a choice. I mean, if we tried to—God, my parents would never look at me again—"

"Talk to Ms. Carpenter," Hannah begs. "Please. You know she's always told us the truth."

"I have to go."

"Baker, please—" Hannah calls.

But Baker hurries back into the garage and disappears into her house without another word.

Hannah drives to City Park. Though she would normally sit in her car, tonight she roams onto the golf course and lies on her back beneath the sky. She raises her hand into the humid air and imagines that she can stir it with her fingers, like a child discovering paint for the first time.

"I'm here to talk to you," she tells the sky.

The leaves on the oak trees tickle with the breeze. The earth buzzes with insects and secrets, and Hannah listens carefully, wanting to know what they say.

"Tell me what to do," she says. "Tell me what's right. I can't sort the bullshit from the truth."

The stars sit still in the overwhelming sky. Hannah narrows her eyes, trying to determine the colors she sees, but she can't distinguish blue from black. The mass of the sky is impenetrable.

Father Simon's words wrap themselves about her heart. She thinks about Christ. How she'd like to lay everything down at his feet. "Here you go," she'd say, dropping everything down like a pile of wood. "You gave me this, and I have no idea what to do with it."

Then she'd take out a key, a big, clunky, golden key, and she'd reach to unlock her heart with it. Her heart would open up and all kinds of wondrous things would come spilling out—maybe rushing forth like a powerful waterfall, or maybe fluttering out like a gentle butterfly. "Here it is," she'd tell him. "Everything that's in my heart, for you and me to see."

She'd ask him to stand in her kitchen when Baker came over to hang out. She'd have him witness Baker's laughter, her smile, her kind heart, her vulnerability. Baker wouldn't see him, but he would see everything: the goodness of her heart and the light in her eyes.

And afterwards, Hannah would ask him, "How could I not love her?"

She'd ask him about the other people. The ones like her, the ones unlike her. "There are so many people who make me hate myself," she'd say. "Who make me feel ashamed. They claim to know what you want. They say I'm turning away from you if I fall in love with a girl. Is it true?"

He'd glide along, the giant of mankind who calmed the waves with his hand, the heart of humanity who loved the lepers and the prostitutes, the silent spirit of Christmas Future, the gentle silver doe, the quiet lamb.

"Please," she'd beg him. "Please tell me."

Maybe he still wouldn't give her an answer, and she'd tell him this was all bullshit. Surely he should know *why* he made her the way she is. Surely he should know *why* her heart beats the way it does. If he knows every hair on her head, why can he not recognize the truth of her heart?

"Please," Hannah cries, sitting up on her knees and sobbing to the sky. She chokes, shudders, blinks away the tears. "Please, either help me or take this away from me. I don't want this anymore."

But her stormy heart does not settle. Her muscles do not relax. She looks at the stars and wonders why God made them so good, so brilliant, but made her so wrong and broken. Her eyes spill over with tears and her throat burns. She pounds her fists into the earth, into the grass and the soil, and emits an animal-like cry from the depths of her body.

"Please," she sobs, digging her hands into the soil. *"Please."*

She wakes Friday morning with a pit in her stomach. She walks to the window and lifts it open, and the humid air collects on her skin. The fragile light of early morning stretches across the sky and the birds sing to each other about its promise. Hannah leaves the window open, though her parents would chide her about letting the air conditioning out, and walks to the bathroom to wash her face.

She enjoys an easy morning with no exams, and the lack of stress allows her to forget about her venture to Baker's house and the park the night before. During second block, in Ms. Carpenter's class, they talk about how the AP Literature exam went for them, but no one dares to hint at Ms. Carpenter's behavior during Mass the previous day. Hannah relaxes and talks easily with her classmates, for once not distracted by Baker's presence, as Baker is sitting for her AP Biology exam in the gym.

Mr. Manceau interrupts with a knock on the door halfway through the class period. Ms. Carpenter steps into the hall and closes the door behind her, and Hannah's classmates trade knowing looks with each other.

Mr. Manceau shuffles into the room a minute later. He leans against the whiteboard and folds his arms over his protruding stomach. "Ms. Carpenter has to go take care of something," he says, breathing heavily beneath his black mustache. "I'll be here with you until the end of the period. So get on back to work now."

"What does Ms. Carpenter have to take care of?"

"Don't you be worrying about that, Collins," Mr. Manceau says. His beady eyes gleam with satisfaction. "Just get on back to work.

288

Well? Why aren't y'all pullin' out your workbooks?"

"We don't have any work to do," Collins says. "We had our exam yesterday."

Mr. Manceau huffs and swivels his eyes to the ceiling, as if begging for patience. "Why am I not surprised," he mutters under his breath. Hannah and her classmates wait on bated breath for him to continue, but he merely claps his hands together and says, "Well, in that case, each one of y'all needs to write me an essay about the things you've learned in this class this year."

"Are you serious?"

"*Yes*, Davies, I'm serious. And watch your mouth."

"How long does it have to be?"

"Are you kidding me right now? Have you not made it to the 12th grade? It needs to be as long as it needs to be."

Hannah and her classmates roll their eyes and begrudgingly pull out loose-leaf paper and pens. Hannah makes eye contact with a few of the people around her—Emily, Christina, Josh—as if to check with them: *Are we really doing this?*

"Are you going to read these?" Christina asks.

Mr. Manceau widens his eyes to signal that she has asked a good question. "I don't know if I will..." he says slowly, "but there are people who might be interested in reading them, I would think."

Hannah glares at him from her desk. Mr. Manceau pays no attention: he starts examining his nails, then chewing on them with short, aggressive bites.

Hannah takes pen to paper and writes a title across the top of the page: *A Condensed Summary of the Material* I Have Learned* *from the Best Teacher in This School.* She then drops her pen to the bottom of the page and writes, below the margin, **Note that I am limiting this summary to academic material. I could never capture everything Ms. Carpenter has taught me about everything else.*

Mr. Manceau stretches his neck against the whiteboard while the classroom of students writes in silence. Hannah's hand races across her paper, writing *Hurston's dialect technique in* Their Eyes Were Watching God and *the influence of colonization on "ethnic" literature* and *the importance of questioning the narrator.*

Ms. Carpenter never returns.

The senior courtyard buzzes with talk when Hannah goes to lunch. Joanie intercepts her before she can sit down, pulling her into a spare corner away from the tables.

"Han—" Joanie says. Her expression is frantic; her eyes dart all over the courtyard, checking to make sure no one can overhear them.

"What's wrong?"

"Do you—have you heard what people are saying?"

"No?"

Joanie pulls her lips into her mouth and turns her head to check behind them. In a hushed voice, she asks, "Did you know Ms. Carpenter is in the front office?"

"Yeah, Manceau came to our class and pulled her out—Joanie, what's wrong? Is she getting fired?"

"Hannah—"

"What? What is it?"

"Did you send her that e-mail?"

290

"What e-mail?"

"Someone sent Ms. Carpenter an e-mail. And she replied to it."

"So?"

Joanie swallows. "The e-mail was about—it was about all that stuff Father Simon ranted about yesterday—the person who wrote it said she was confused about her feelings for her friend—"

All the breath goes out of Hannah. Her limbs start to tingle. "How do you know this?"

"Everyone's talking about it—Michele overheard the front office staff whispering about it during her work study—she got a copy of the e-mail and she's showing it to people—"

"Jesus Christ."

"Hannah," Joanie says tentatively, "you really didn't—?"

"No," Hannah says, her head reeling. "No. I really didn't."

Joanie's face looks momentarily relieved, but then her eyebrows crinkle and she voices the fear Hannah has tried to push down for the last minute.

"Han, do you think Baker might have—?"

"Hey," Wally calls, striding toward them with his lunch tray. "What's up? Y'all coming to sit?"

Hannah and Joanie freeze. Wally hovers five feet away, his eyebrows lifting as he takes in their expressions.

"We're coming," Hannah says. "Sorry. We were just talking about something our mom asked us to do."

They follow him to their usual lunch table. Hannah sits down next to him and Joanie sits across from them, trying to catch Hannah's eye. Hannah unpacks her lunch bag and picks the bread off her sandwich, chewing it in small bites that make her feel like she might throw up. Wally stirs the red beans on his lunch tray and says, "So during Econ today—"

Hannah doesn't listen: Michele has just strutted into the courtyard, her face alight with a power Hannah has never seen on it before, her friends trailing her with satisfied smirks on their faces. Whole tables of students look around to her, and all at once people start calling out to her.

"What's going on?"

"Is it true?"

"Do you have it with you?"

The ruckus is enough to distract Wally from his story and to quell the other conversations taking place at all the different lunch tables. A hushed silence falls over the courtyard: no one talks, no one eats, no one shifts a lunch tray or crinkles a bag. Michele struts to a table in the middle of the courtyard—the table where Baker and Clay sit—and leans down to whisper to someone. Hannah's stomach chills; she waits in absolute stillness, unable to breathe or blink.

Wally leans over. "What's going—?"

His words are cut off by a yell from the middle table.

"—AND GET THE HELL AWAY!"

Hannah cranes her neck to get a better look, but she need not move at all: Clay is half-rising from his seat, his face blotchy red and his eyes narrowed in fury, his shoulders tight with tension.

"Calm down, Clay," Michele says, her voice carrying around the courtyard. "I'm just saying—"

"Well shut up and move on," Clay spits. He turns away from her and gazes out over the sea of onlookers. "Go back to your tacos," he says. "She's just talking out of her ass, like usual."

"Why don't you let Baker speak for herself?" Michele retorts, her voice dangerous.

The whole courtyard balances on a pin.

"Great, Clay, you've gone and alerted our whole class," Michele says, crossing her arms. "I was trying to be discrete. This is a sensitive issue. Although...it's probably fair that everyone should know who's responsible for getting Ms. Carpenter in trouble. Right, Baker?"

Hannah's stomach turns over.

"She has nothing to do with it," Clay says. He speaks in a deliberately low voice now, but his voice carries around the silent courtyard anyway.

"Then why do you look so scared, Baker?" Michele says. "If you had nothing to do with the e-mail, then why did I see you crying in Ms. Carpenter's room before school this morning?"

Hannah shifts down the bench, straining her eyes. Then she sees her: Baker sits as still as a statue, her face flushed red, her eyes stretched with fear.

"Kind of makes sense, doesn't it?" Michele continues, shrugging a shoulder. "I mean, the writer mentioned that she had been trying to cover up her feelings by dating a guy. She said she worried about hurting her tight-knit group of friends. Yes, Clay, *the Six-Pack*. She said she was drunk and had started drinking a lot more lately. And we all know that has to be you, Baker, right? I mean, you had that embarrassing episode at Liz's party last weekend—"

"Shut your mouth!" Clay yells, jumping up from his bench.

"Can't you see I'm trying to help? If she's the one who wrote the e-mail, then she obviously needs our support as she tries to figure out these difficult feelings. We're her friends. We're all a family. You're the one who always says that, Clay, right? Maybe if we had known about this sooner, then she wouldn't have had to send that e-mail that got Ms. Carpenter in trouble...."

Hannah scans the faces of everyone in the courtyard. Nearly all of them wear the same expression: a mixture between shock and confusion.

"So?" Michele says, speaking down to Baker. "Was it you, or what?"

Baker opens her mouth, but no sound comes out.

"I'm not trying to accuse you," Michele says. "I just think whoever got Carpenter in trouble owes us all an apology. Don't you think that's fair, Baker?"

"I didn't write it," Baker says, her voice weaker than Hannah's ever heard it.

"I don't understand why you're acting so funny, then," Michele says, peering down at her. She hangs her head, like the whole encounter is causing her pain, and sighs. "It was you, Baker. Right?"

There is a long, pressured silence, and Hannah's heart hammers inside her chest.

"You're supposed to be our *president*, remember?" Michele sneers. "You're not supposed to go getting our favorite teacher fired. Or, you know, decide to be a *lesbian*."

Baker breathes very fast; even though she sits yards away, Hannah can see her shaking.

"Well, since you're not saying anything," Michele says, "I guess we can take that as a yes."

Hannah stands up without thinking and knows what she's about to do before she actually processes it.

"It wasn't her," Hannah says. Her voice spreads out around the courtyard, and she hears it echo in her head, almost like it isn't hers. Every face in the vicinity turns to look at her.

"What are you doing?!" Joanie whispers. "Sit down!"

"She didn't write it," Hannah says, making eye contact with as many people as she can, but hardly seeing them at all. "I wrote it."

"Stop trying to cover for her, Hannah," Michele says.

"I'm not. She was trying to cover for me."

"That doesn't make any sense, Hannah, just sit down—"

"I sent the e-mail last night," Hannah says, her mind working furiously to keep up with her words. "I was drunk—and panicking—I had been feeling that way for a really long time—" her voice starts to break—"and Ms. Carpenter has always been my favorite teacher, and I saw how she acted at Mass yesterday..." She shakes her head with genuine tears in her eyes. "I sent her the e-mail without thinking about it."

"Then why did I see Baker crying to Ms. Carpenter this morning?" Michele says angrily.

Hannah swallows down the tears in her throat. "I called Baker in the middle of the night and told her everything. She said she would try to help. She told me everything would be okay. She promised she'd talk to Ms. Carpenter for me and explain everything so that I wouldn't get in trouble. I was worried that I—I might jeopardize my acceptance to Emory. I begged her to go talk to Ms. Carpenter first thing this morning."

"Oh, this is a bunch of crap," Michele says, but Hannah looks around at her peers' faces and knows that they believe her—that they are desperate to believe her.

"Baker has nothing to do with this," Hannah says, her voice shaking, her eyes still wet with tears.

"That doesn't even make sense," Michele says. "You two haven't even talked in, like, weeks. We've all noticed it."

"She was trying to distance herself from me," Hannah says, lowering her eyes to the table. "I told her how I've been feeling about—about girls—and—" she swallows—"she wasn't sure we should be friends anymore. She didn't want to compromise her beliefs."

Clay's voice is the first one to break the courtyard's silence. "Is that true, Bake?"

Every face turns away from Hannah and back to Baker. Baker meets Hannah's eyes, her expression still terrified. For an infinite moment they read each other, and Hannah nods her head forward a fraction of an inch.

"Yes," Baker says.

Hannah breathes.

"So, what, you were gonna take the fall for Hannah?" Clay asks incredulously.

Baker doesn't answer. In the distance, somewhere far, far away, Hannah hears the bell ring. The sound of it seems to startle everyone back into the reality of the school day. In an uncomfortable silence, people all around the courtyard pick up their trash and step away from their tables. Then the silence gives way to a buzzing whispering, and Hannah watches in a daze, feeling like she's in a movie, as classmates walk past her, some of them staring, some of them ignoring her, others outright glaring at her.

But the only person Hannah watches is Baker. She rises unsteadily from her table and seems unaware that Clay is speaking into her ear. She meets Hannah's eyes one more time, and Hannah feels the weight of the world between them. Then Baker walks loosely and clumsily toward the B-Hall doors, her head down and her hair hanging over her eyes.

And then everyone is gone. Everyone except for Joanie and Wally.

Hannah slumps down into her seat. Everything around her seems dim, surreal. Joanie gawps at her. Wally sits with his back rigid and his hands clenched.

"Wally—" Hannah says.

"Don't talk to me."

"Wally, wait—"

But he jerks himself away from the table and yanks his booksack over his shoulder. He throws his bag of trash at the trashcan; it hits off the side and falls to the ground, but he doesn't stop to pick it up.

Joanie gathers up the contents of her lunch, sealing her sandwich bag with trembling thumbs. She reaches for her water bottle but knocks it over onto the table. Hannah watches the water spread over the wood while Joanie picks up the bottle with shaking hands.

"I had to," Hannah says.

"Bullshit," Joanie says. She stands up and tucks her blouse into her skirt over and over and over, until the fabric is stretched taut across her stomach. "Do you realize Mom and Dad are gonna find out now? Is that how you wanted this to go?"

Joanie's hands continue to shake as she raises her water bottle to her mouth and takes a clumsy gulp from it. Hannah still sits at the table, her arms and legs numb, her mind foggy.

"Stupidest thing you've ever done in your life," Joanie says.

Her classmates stare at her all through third block. The only person who doesn't look at her is Wally, who sits with his jaw clenched and his head bent over the desk. Hannah's mind replays the scene in the courtyard again and again while Mr. Creary prattles on about the format of their Government exam.

And then the overhead intercom beeps.

"Mr. Creary?"

"Mm?"

"Please send Hannah Eaden to the office."

She tries hard to ignore the stares of her two-dozen classmates, but she can feel their eyes on her as she crosses the classroom. She closes Mr. Creary's door and stands in the hallway with a feeling of panic in her stomach. Her vision dims. When she starts to walk, she can feel air beating against her sweaty palms. She stops off into the bathroom and throws up.

The front office secretaries seem to be waiting for her. "Hello, Hannah," one of them says, her smile forced. "Mrs. Shackleford would like to see you. You can go on back to her office."

Hannah opens Mrs. Shackleford's door to find a half-dozen people inside. Mrs. Shackleford sits at her desk, her expression grim; Mr. Manceau and Father Simon stand together at one window, Mr. Manceau's arms crossed over his stomach and Father Simon's hands clasped behind his back; Ms. Carpenter stands at the opposite window, her angular eyebrows drawn together; and Hannah's parents hover just inside the door, their skin pale and their eyes nervous.

"Hi, honey," her mom says. She looks like it's costing her everything she has to look at Hannah. Hannah's dad stands silently at her side, mechanically rubbing at his elbow.

"Hello, Hannah," Mrs. Shackleford says. "Have a seat, please."

Hannah sits in the designated chair in front of Mrs. Shackleford's desk, with the adults circled around her. She feels like the center pawn in a child's game of Duck-Duck-Goose.

"Hannah, do you know why we called you in?" Mrs. Shackleford asks.

"Is this about the e-mail?" Hannah says, trying to sound braver than she feels.

Mrs. Shackleford nods a few times. "Yes, it is. Hannah, we've had several students tell us that you've taken ownership of that e-mail. That you told some friends that you're the one who wrote it."

"I told the whole senior courtyard," Hannah says. In her peripheral vision, she can see her mom flinch.

"Hannah..." Mrs. Shackleford brings her hands together and stares hard at her. "Do you understand the implications of telling people you wrote this e-mail?"

Hannah casts her eyes to the objects on Mrs. Shackleford's desk: the name placard, the dove-shaped paperweight, the photographs of her husband and children. She feels acutely aware of everyone watching her. "Yes, ma'am. Everyone will think that I'm—um." She clears her throat. Out of the corner of her eye, she sees Ms. Carpenter tuck her head down.

"It's a bit more complicated than that, Hannah," Mrs. Shackleford says.

"How?"

"So you did write the e-mail?" Mr. Manceau cuts in.

"Bob—" Mrs. Shackleford says.

"I think you should let her answer the question, Mrs. Shackleford," Father Simon says. "She hasn't confirmed yet."

"Can you confirm that you wrote this e-mail?" Mr. Manceau says, thrusting a piece of paper into Hannah's hand. Hannah smoothes out the paper and reads the topmost line, but then her parents step up behind her and peer over her shoulder.

"Don't," Hannah says.

"We've already read it," her mom says.

"What?"

Her mom swallows. "Mr. Manceau already showed us."

Hannah glares at Mr. Manceau. He raises his eyebrows, and his challenge is clear: *What are you gonna do about it?*

"Please just give me a minute," Hannah asks her parents.

Her mom nods in a resigned way. Her dad continues to rub his elbow. Hannah, with the force of a hammer on her heart, reads:

DATE May 11, 2012
TIME 1:03 AM
FROM intheoven94@gmail.com
TO kcarpenter@smmcatholic.org

Ms. Carpenter, please, I need your help. You're the only person I know who can hlep me. I'm so scared right now. I have feelings for another girl, feelings I'm not supposed to have. We did things together that you're not supposed to do, things I only should have done with a boy. i'm so shocked at myself that I feel like it didn't even happen, like it's not real. Sometimes when I think about it I'm just disgusted with myself and I feel so dirty, I feel so wrong and like god hates me. But the scariest part is I was so happy when we were togehter. It felt so amazing, it felt like everything I always wanted to have with someone. But I know that can't be true, I know that can't be what god wants for me. But then why did he make me like this? Why did he put this inside of me? Why did he make me feel like I'm always happiest when I'm with her?? I don't understand because I didn't ask for this and I've tried really hard to make it go away. Every time I get these feelings I feel like there's a monster inside of me, an evil monster that's trying to take me away from god and lead me to sin. I wish I could be better. Everyone esle expects me to be better. I'm dating a boy right now to try and make everything better but it's not working, it's nto working, and now I'm ruining my group of best friends too. Everything is getting out of control, I can't stop crying all the time, and now I'm drinking a lot too and I don't know hwy. I'm sorry to bother you with this but it's late and I've been drinking and I'm crying and I'm just so scared.

Hannah blinks back the tears in her eyes and raises her head to face the room again. Mr. Manceau leans forward off the window, his fat face hungry for an answer; Father Simon wears that too-kind expression Hannah has seen him wear during Confession; Mrs. Shackleford stares hard at Hannah over the knuckles of her folded hands; Ms. Carpenter still leans against the window and says nothing.

"Ms. Carpenter?" Hannah says.

"Yes, Hannah?"

"Where's your response?"

"Do you really need to read it?" Mr. Manceau says, holding up another piece of paper. "Don't you have it starred in your inbox?"

"Bob—" Mrs. Shackleford says.

"Did you write it or not?" Mr. Manceau demands.

Hannah grips the seat of her chair. She commands herself not to look back at her parents. Instead, she looks defiantly at Mr. Manceau and Father Simon. "Yes," she says. "I wrote it."

Her mom makes an involuntary sound behind her. Mrs. Shackleford drops her head onto her folded hands. Mr. Manceau smirks and glances to Father Simon, who taps his fingers to his mouth and says, "Well, I think that settles it."

"What?" Hannah asks.

Mrs. Shackleford leans back in her chair and moves her glasses up to the crown of her head. She rubs her eyes and takes a deep breath. "The thing is, Hannah," she says, her voice weary, "until now, we had no way of proving that this e-mail was written by one of our students. It could have been written by any random person with Internet access. If that had been the case, then Ms. Carpenter's response to the e-mail would have been...less of an issue. But because you're a St. Mary's student, and because Ms. Carpenter, your teacher, replied to your e-mail with advice that—" she stops, clears her throat, glares at the two men by the window—"advice that some in this diocese would deem *inconsistent* with the views of our Church and school..." She trails off and gestures at the air.

"What?" Hannah asks again. She shifts in her chair to look at Ms. Carpenter, who smiles sadly at her.

"It means they can fire me, Hannah," Ms. Carpenter says.

Hannah's stomach drops. "What? But—I don't understand—"

"It's okay, Hannah," Father Simon says kindly.

"No, it's not! Ms. Carpenter didn't do anything wrong!"

"Ms. Carpenter gave you guidance that is absolutely contradictory to the practice of our faith," Father Simon says patiently. "You trusted her, Hannah, and she failed you."

"She didn't fail me! And why are you talking about her like she's not in the room?"

Father Simon looks over to Mrs. Shackleford. "This is exactly what I was talking about, Brenda. She inspires this sort of misplaced passion in her students."

"Excuse me," a new voice says. Hannah's dad steps forward and the faces in the room turn toward him. "Did you know you were writing to Hannah?" he asks Ms. Carpenter. He looks to Mr. Manceau and Father Simon. "If we follow the logic you're using, then Ms. Carpenter can't be fired if she didn't realize she was writing to a student."

"Actually, Tom," Father Simon says, "just based on the fact that she was using her St. Mary's e-mail address, she can absolutely be fired."

"Thank you, Mr. Eaden," Ms. Carpenter says, still wearing her sad smile. "I did actually know I was communicating with a St. Mary's student. That's why I had to respond."

Mr. Manceau shakes his head. Father Simon moves his mouth around as if experiencing lockjaw.

"Mr. Manceau," Hannah's mom says, "I'd like to see Ms. Carpenter's response to Hannah."

"I'd rather we not go into that," Father Simon interjects. "Suffice it to say, Anne, that the e-mail encouraged Hannah to give in to her feelings of same-sex attraction—"

"With all due respect, Father Simon, I'd like to see for myself what Ms. Carpenter wrote to my daughter."

Mr. Manceau hands Hannah's mom the other piece of paper. Hannah's mom reads the e-mail slowly, her face expressionless, and then hands the paper to Hannah's dad. He reads it fast, his eyes jumping down the page and a muscle jumping in his jaw.

"Thank you," Hannah's dad says when he's finished. Hannah looks at him, then at her mother, and waits for them to meet her eyes. They both stare at the carpet instead.

"Tom, Anne, please let me be clear," Father Simon says. "Not a single one of us in this room thinks there is anything wrong with Hannah. Every person has her own burdens—every disciple of Christ has her own Cross to carry—and same-sex attraction is a particularly difficult one. But I don't want Hannah to settle for thinking that she has to resign herself to living this way. Same-sex attraction is something she can move past and heal from."

"You make it sound like Hannah has a disease," Hannah's mom says.

"Of course not," Father Simon says patiently. "Though don't forget that Christ tended to those with the meanest forms of disease. But, no, I would never suggest that Hannah has a disease. Same-sex attraction is not a disease, but rather a disorder. Counter to the natural law, counter to God's plan for humanity—"

"A disorder?" Hannah's mom says. "Father, with all due respect, Hannah doesn't have a *disorder.*"

"Then how would you classify it, Anne? SSA is a deviation from the natural law. It is particularly sinister because many people—especially in our current culture—would have us believe that it's normal, that it's hereditary, that it can't be helped and so we might as well give in to it, but the reality is that it *can* be helped and that people who experience SSA have a special place in the Church, either through the vocation of prayerful single life or, in some cases, Holy Matrimony with another person of the opposite sex. Hannah *will* be able to move past this. Through prayer, through choosing chastity, through faith in our generous God—"

"That's not true," Hannah says. She grips the seat of her chair until her knuckles hurt. When she speaks again, her voice is low and raspy. "I tried to believe all that stuff. I tried to trust that God could help me move past it. He couldn't. He didn't."

"Hannah," Father Simon says gently, stepping forward to place a hand on her shoulder. "He can. He will. And in the meantime, we're going to make sure you don't have to listen to the sort of outrageous heresy that you read in that e-mail—"

"Enough, Simon," Mrs. Shackleford says, holding up her hand. "I'd like to speak to Hannah and Ms. Carpenter alone."

"I don't think that's a good idea, Brenda—"

"I don't give a lick what you think right now," Mrs. Shackleford says in a loud, harsh voice, her eyes narrowed dangerously at Father Simon. "Personally, Simon, I don't consider it a good idea to hack into our teachers' e-mail accounts. And yet here we are, and so we will proceed accordingly. But first, as St. Mary's *principal*, I am going to have a word with Hannah and Ms. Carpenter *alone*."

"We're staying, too," Hannah's mom says, her voice quivering.

"Of course, Anne."

Father Simon and Mr. Manceau stand silent and motionless. Father Simon swallows hard with his jaw still clenched. Mr. Manceau's giant stomach moves up and down with his heavy breathing. Finally, after a long few seconds, both men turn and walk rigidly out of the office, closing the thick wooden door behind them.

"Well," Mrs. Shackleford says, leaning her head against her hands, "here we find ourselves in uncharted territory."

"I'm sorry," Hannah says.

"Don't be sorry, Hannah. This situation has been made into something much bigger than it should be because of politics and ignorance. It's not your fault."

"Ms. Carpenter," Hannah says timidly, "I'm so sorry. I didn't realize what would happen."

"There's nothing to be sorry for," Ms. Carpenter says, stepping up to the desk and resting her hand on the corner of it. "Mrs. Shackleford's right, Hannah—this is about things outside of your control. What happens to me isn't important. I'll be just fine. But you, Hannah—are you sure *you* want to claim responsibility for this burden?"

Her eyes bore into Hannah's, and Hannah cannot look away even if she wants to: she feels like Ms. Carpenter is seeing into her soul. For a fleeting second, she wants to tell the truth, wants to shrug off this burden and be taken into her mother's arms. But then she remembers Baker's face, terrified beyond help as she sat in the courtyard.

"Yes," Hannah answers. "Yes, I want to claim responsibility."

Ms. Carpenter looks at her for another long moment, and then her eyes go soft.

"Hannah—Anne—Tom—" Mrs. Shackleford says. "I don't know exactly what's going to happen here. I'm going to fight hard to keep Ms. Carpenter at St. Mary's, but that decision might be beyond the scope of my control. Either way, Hannah is going to take some heat from her classmates. This community will not be happy about losing a beloved teacher."

"Yes, ma'am," Hannah says.

"Hannah—you're going to hear conflicting opinions about the content of your e-mail. Some of them will not be kind. They may even be judgmental—"

"Yes, ma'am, I know—"

"But I want you to know that I support you. Understand?"

Hannah finds it hard to answer around the heaviness in her chest. "Yes, ma'am, I understand."

"You can go home with your parents now. I'll have Mrs. Stewart check you out of fourth block. If you need me for anything—" Mrs. Shackleford turns her eyes now to Hannah's parents—"don't hesitate to call."

"Thank you," Hannah's mom says. Hannah's dad clears his throat and nods.

Hannah stands to leave, but Ms. Carpenter rests a hand on her arm. "Hannah," she says, "I want you to know I'm proud of you. Keep going, okay? Don't lose faith."

There is a great surge of emotion in Hannah's throat. She takes a slow breath to speak around it, but she starts to cry anyway. "Thanks, Ms. Carpenter."

Then she turns and walks to the door. Her parents flank her on either side, their posture slumped and their eyes focused straight ahead. Hannah takes one last look as she steps out of the room: Mrs. Shackleford sits at her desk, her shoulders hunched and her hand raised to her forehead; Ms. Carpenter stands next to her, her eyes trained on Hannah, and she is smiling and smiling and smiling.

Chapter Thirteen: The Arms of Hanging Men

"You can meet us at home," her mom says once Hannah has retrieved her booksack. "We'll get Joanie later."

"You don't have to go back to work?" Hannah asks.

"No, Hannah," her dad says sadly. "Not today."

Hannah's hands shake on the steering wheel. She winds her way through the Garden District, over the black asphalt damp with rainwater and under the tall, lush trees that stretch above the streets, their branches twisted out to the side like the arms of hanging men. Her wrists ache from having gripped the chair in Mrs. Shackleford's office for so long. The collar of her uniform shirt rubs against her neck, choking her.

Her parents' cars sit in the carport. Hannah parks on the empty street and looks into the front windows of her house. She can imagine her parents inside, her father's head in his hands as he bends over the kitchen table, her mother scrubbing at dirty dishes while furious tears run over the faded freckles on her cheeks.

Hannah's throat burns with thick, hot emotion. She drops her hands from the steering wheel, but they still shake in her lap. She looks through the windshield at the tall oak trees that guard her neighborhood street, and she wants nothing more than to climb to the top of them and hide beneath their leaves.

She finds her parents standing on opposite sides of the kitchen, both of them silent as she walks into the room. Her dad leans against the stove and wipes his palms with a dishtowel. Her mom stands at the kitchen window, glancing out over the back porch.

Hannah drops her booksack on the floor and waits.

A long minute passes. Hannah's dad drops the dishtowel over the stove plates, then picks it back up again and wipes at his left palm, then his right, back and forth, back and forth. Hannah's mom stands as still as a deer, so that Hannah wonders if she even noticed her come into the house.

But then her mom speaks.

"You should have talked to us."

"I didn't know how."

"But you knew how to drunkenly e-mail your teacher about it?"

"I wasn't thinking," Hannah says, her voice shaking. "I didn't know what to do. I didn't know if you and Dad would be angry with me—"

"Well it looks like you managed to avoid that, huh?"

"Mama, I'm sorry—"

"Now we're finding out at the same time as the entire school and church community," her mom says in a thick voice. She turns around and crosses her arms over her chest. Her lip trembles. "No time to process—no time to figure out how to defend you—"

"You don't have to defend me! I'm fine!"

"Don't be so naïve, Hannah! If you think people aren't going to talk about this—if you think people aren't going to treat you differently—"

"Let them! I don't care! I don't give a shit what anyone thinks of me!"

"WELL WE DO!" her mom yells, slamming her hand down on the counter. "We do! You're our daughter—you're our daughter and we love you—we've loved you since the day we found out we were going to have you—and we don't want you treated unfairly! We don't want you discriminated against and shamed and hated! We don't ever want to see you treated the way you were treated in that office today!"

Her mom starts to cry, her eyes swinging up at an angle as she tries to block the tears in frustration, and Hannah cries, too, her sinuses swelling and her tears falling onto her collared shirt.

Her dad clears his throat. His voice scratches when he speaks. "Joanie texted me. I'm going to pick her up." He rubs at his chin as he leaves the room. A moment later, he returns. He clears his throat again. "Forgot my keys."

Hannah slumps down onto one of the counter stools. She and her mom wipe their eyes and do not look at each other.

"I'm making you some soup," her mom says. "What do you want?"

"I'm not hungry."

"Tomato or chicken noodle?"

"I don't want anything."

Her mom fills a midsized pot with water and places it on the stovetop. She steps into the pantry and grabs a can of soup.

"I don't want it," Hannah repeats.

Her mom sniffles and winds her hand around the can opener. "You need to eat something."

Hannah relents. Her mom stands at the stovetop and stirs a

spoon around the pot, occasionally tapping metal against metal. She sets crackers in front of Hannah without looking at her.

"Here you go," she says a few minutes later, placing a white ceramic bowl in front of Hannah. Hannah swirls the tomato soup around the bowl, watching the thick orange-red liquid curve along her spoon.

"Mama? You haven't said anything about the actual content of the e-mail."

Her mom makes fleeting eye contact with her. "Let's not talk about it right now. Just eat and put everything out of your mind."

"But—how do you feel about it? Is it okay?"

Her mom carries the soup pot to the sink and flushes water over it. She scrubs hard at it with a soap sponge, her arm working fast as if she's trying to shove the pot down the garbage disposal.

"Mom?"

"Give me some time, Hannah."

Hannah's tears drop into the tomato soup. She bites her lip to stop herself from crying again, but her whole body shakes and her breaths come out sharp and edgy, as if someone has taken a knife to her voice.

"Oh, Hannah..." her mom says, turning around.

Her mom gathers her against her body and holds her. Hannah sobs into her mother's satin shirt but keeps her hands balled at her sides, afraid to give herself over completely.

"Honey," her mom coos. "It's okay. I love you. Dad and I love you. Nothing could ever change that."

Hannah cries until she hears the back door turn. Then she

darts out of her seat, leaving her soup bowl and her mom in the kitchen.

She stays in her room on Saturday. She spends hours clicking around the Emory website, researching classes, memorizing the calendar, reading up on campus traditions. She hears her family walking around downstairs, hears them talking in the kitchen, hears the jarring music of TV commercials. She waits for her mom or dad to come check on her. They send Joanie instead.

"Will you get me some hash browns from Zeeland?" Hannah asks her. "I'm craving them."

"Go get them yourself, lazy."

Hannah turns back to her computer. "Never mind."

"Ugh, fine, I'll go with you."

"That's okay."

"No, seriously, let's go. I'll drive."

"No, I'm good."

"You could use some fresh air. Come on."

"Joanie. I don't want to go."

"You just said you were craving the hash browns."

"I—never mind."

"What?" Joanie shuts Hannah's laptop screen. "Let's go."

"I don't *want* to go."

"Stop being such a brat."

"I don't want to go, okay?!"

Joanie pulls away from her. "Jeeze. I was just trying to be nice."

Hannah pulls her lips into her mouth. "I don't want to walk into Zeeland and see one of our classmates. Or one of their parents. Okay?"

Joanie drops her head and taps her fingers against her thigh. "Sorry," she says quietly.

"It's fine."

"You want to watch a movie or something?"

"No, I'm okay. I'm just gonna take a nap."

Joanie leaves, and Hannah falls into a restless sleep. When she wakes, she finds a Styrofoam box on her nightstand. She opens it. It's full of Zeeland Street hash browns.

Her parents call her downstairs for dinner around seven o'clock. Joanie looks up when Hannah walks into the kitchen. Her eyes ask a question. Hannah smiles in answer.

The four of them sit subdued around the table, each of them paying too much attention to their chicken. Joanie makes a valiant effort to stir the conversation, asking about everything from their dad's friends at Albemarle to their mom's recent tennis match. Neither one of their parents says much in response.

"Okay, this is just awkward," Joanie says, dropping her fork. "Can we please address the rainbow-colored elephant in the room? So Hannah might not have a fairytale plantation wedding. So what?"

"Don't start, Joanie," their mom says.

"I think it's brave what Hannah did."

Their mom pauses with her fork in midair. "In what way?"

Hannah shoots Joanie a warning look. Joanie drops her eyes

and says, clumsily, "In—telling the truth about how she feels."

Their parents push pieces of chicken around their plates. Hannah drinks from her water glass for something to do, but the cold water makes the pit in her stomach feel even more hollowed.

Hannah wakes up late on Sunday morning and startles when she realizes her family is supposed to leave for Mass in three minutes.

"Don't bother," Joanie says when Hannah rushes into the bathroom and reaches for the toothpaste. "They already left."

"What? They never let us miss church."

Joanie shrugs. "I heard the backdoor slam, and then I looked out the window and saw them driving away."

Hannah's heart sinks. "They don't want me there with them."

"Don't be dumb. Of course they do. They probably just—they probably don't want you to feel uncomfortable, you know?"

The worst part of Sunday is when Aunt Ellie calls after lunch. Hannah stands outside the locked door of the study, listening to her mom whisper into the phone, listening to the breaths of silence that pour forth from her mom's mouth.

"No," her mom says after a few minutes, "never made it there. Couldn't bring ourselves to face all those stares. We went to lunch on the other side of town instead."

Hannah crawls back into her bed and stays there for the rest of the day.

Her stomach knots in on itself when she wakes on Monday morning. Joanie makes her toast, which Hannah takes only one bite of before she feels sick, and then they get into the car, neither one of them speaking. By the time they arrive at St. Mary's, Hannah's underarms are soaked through with sweat.

There aren't many people in the parking lot when they pull in. Hannah looks automatically at Baker's car, parked far down the lot next to Clay's truck.

"Ready?" Joanie asks, her face pale.

"No," Hannah breathes. "But let's go."

Several people cast her looks when she steps out of the car. She averts her eyes and follows Joanie's path to the A-Hall doors. Just as they're about to walk inside, a voice from behind them calls, "Hey, H'Eaden, wanna go out with me tonight?"

She falters in her steps, but Joanie clutches her arm and keeps her facing forward. "Go fuck yourself, Guthrie!" Joanie yells, her voice loud in Hannah's ear.

"It's fine," Hannah says.

"He's always been a jackass. Whatever. Come on."

They walk into the building, and whereas Joanie would normally turn left for the junior hallway, today she turns right for the senior hallway.

"You don't have to lead me the whole way," Hannah tells her.

"I was just going to stop by Mrs. Paulk's room to ask her something about our study guide."

"Joanie. I'll be okay. I don't need an escort. Seriously."

Joanie eyes the hall behind her and sighs. "Alright. I'm sure everything will be fine."

"It will be. Thanks."

The walk to her locker is full of stares and hushed gossip. A few people smile nicely at her, but most of her classmates openly gawk. She clears her throat just to reassure herself that she is still there.

She spots Wally at the end of the hallway, his booksack propped against his side as he switches out his books. She yearns to go to him, to find reassurance in his steady expression, but she stops at her own locker instead.

Ms. Carpenter isn't at school. Hannah's heart drops as soon as she sees the substitute teacher standing in Ms. Carpenter's doorway.

By late Monday morning, the news that Ms. Carpenter has been fired has spread around the entire school. "The diocese called for her immediate dismissal," Michele says pointedly as Hannah walks past her during class change. "I heard Ms. Gramley telling Mr. Jasper. The teachers are just as pissed about it as we are."

"Carpenter was the only cool teacher at this school," Jonah says. "This is so fucked up."

All eyes are on Hannah when she walks into the lunch courtyard that day. She walks to her usual table, her blood pounding in her ears, and opens her lunch bag as if everything is normal, as if she's not absolutely alone in this hell. She scans the courtyard for Wally and spots him at Luke's table, the sun reflecting off his glasses.

He does not so much as look at her. She checks Clay and Baker's table: Baker sits on the opposite bench today, so that her back is to Hannah. Hannah stabs a fork into her salad and swallows against the burning lump in her throat.

Joanie joins her a minute later, brushing her hair back from her red face. "We just had the dumbest assignment in Pre-Calc," she says. "I almost got into an argument with Ms. Hersch about it. Just because she got dumped doesn't mean she can force us to recap everything we learned last semester."

"You don't have to talk to me like everything's normal," Hannah says. "Let's just acknowledge it."

Joanie's face falls. "How's it been?"

"Shitty. Really shitty." Her voice breaks on the last syllable.

"Four more days. That's it. Just four more days."

Hannah looks up and makes eye contact with a table of guys who are clearly talking about her. As she watches, Bradford leans into the center of the table and says something that makes all the guys roar with laughter.

"How was school?" her mom asks when she gets home from work that evening. She asks the question offhandedly, but Hannah notices the anxious look in her eyes.

"Fine," Hannah says. "Nothing different."

"No one said anything about it?"

"Nope."

"Well that's good," her mom says. Her hands fumble over the grocery bags on the counter. "Will you help me put these away?"

On Tuesday morning, when Hannah opens her locker, a crumpled note falls out.

Nice going lesbeaux.

She tries to intercept Wally in the parking lot after school, but he marches straight past her to his car. She follows him and knocks on his window, but he does not turn to look at her. He blares his music and reverses out of his parking spot with fast, jerky movements.

"Maybe you shouldn't have fucked with his heart," someone says, and when she whips around, she comes face to face with Luke.

"I never meant to."

Luke stuffs his hands into his pockets and squints at her. Up close, he looks haggard and more jaded than he ever did before. "Look, Hannah," he says, "I'm sorry that you've been going through all this stuff. I really am. I wish we'd been able to help you. But just because you were confused or going through a hard time or whatever, doesn't mean you had the right to string him along. You hurt him. You hurt him just like my parents hurt each other and Joanie hurt me."

"Joanie loves you," Hannah says thickly. "You know she loves you."

Luke swallows. "This isn't about that. Just leave him alone. I hope you figure things out and I hope you feel better, but leave him alone."

He shuffles away, his hands still in his pockets, his shoes scuffing against the asphalt.

Clay's end-of-year party is scheduled for the Friday night of graduation weekend. The seniors gossip about it all week, trading ideas for how to lie to their parents, bragging about how wasted they plan to get, whispering to their friends about which person they want one last chance to hook up with.

"Hannah," Joanie asks her timidly one night, "are you considering going to Clay's party at all?"

Hannah looks at her like she's gone insane. "Are you joking?"

Joanie lowers her eyes. "I want to hang out with Luke one last time. See if he'll talk to me." She pauses. "But I don't have the guts to go alone."

Hannah sets her makeup remover on the bathroom sink. She stares hard at the faucet for a long moment.

"I'm sorry, Joanie," she says. "I can't."

Joanie nods her head, her expression sad but understanding.

Michele Duquesne wanders up to Hannah after graduation practice on Friday morning. "Crazy that I'm invited to the party and you're not," she says.

"Leave me alone," Hannah says.

"I'm not actually trying to be mean," Michele says, and by looking at her, Hannah can tell that she's speaking the truth. "I wanted to tell you that it's not personal, what happened with the e-mail. I was trying to get at Baker, not at you."

"I don't care who you were trying to get at," Hannah says. "What you did was disgusting."

"I'm trying to be nice to you."

"I don't need you to be nice to me. You're a jealous snake."

Michele's eyes thin to slits. "Remember who ultimately betrayed you, Hannah. It wasn't me. It was her. It was your friends. They saw something they didn't like and they left you."

"That's not true."

"Isn't it, though?"

"You're a piece of shit," Hannah says. "You're a hateful, bitter piece of shit, and whatever I have left to hope for, it's not your friendship."

She storms out of the gymnasium while Michele glowers behind her. She makes her way down empty hallways, listening to the classrooms full of freshmen, sophomores, and juniors, pausing outside Ms. Carpenter's room to see if her energy still lingers around its doorway.

She wanders down the senior hallway and counts her friends' lockers as she passes. 142—Luke's. 151—her own. 159—Baker's. 174—Clay's. 203—Wally's.

She stops at the end of the hallway and peers through the empty space between the two rows of burgundy lockers. She can see the echoes of herself and her friends in front of each section of the lockers, their Oxford shirts sticking out of their skirts or khakis, their shoes scuffing against the tiled floor, their laughs reverberating off these sacred walls.

I don't want to hate this place.

Joanie approaches her again that evening. "I'm gonna go to Clay's party," she says.

"Are you sure?"

"Luke leaves for Alabama on Monday. And I probably won't get a chance to talk to him at graduation." She pauses. "This might be my last chance to talk to him."

Hannah nods. "Good luck. I hope it works out."

"Han—will you please go with me?"

"No."

Joanie rubs her left elbow. She stares hard at the grandfather clock in the family room. "Hannah..." she says, her voice small, "I need you to go with me. Please. We only have to go for ten minutes. I just have to tell him that I love him."

Hannah sighs. "I can't, Joanie."

"No one has to know you're there. Even if they do, it's not like they'll say anything. Please, Hannah. I mean, isn't there a part of you that wants to go anyway?"

"No," Hannah lies.

Joanie rubs her elbow harder. "Alright," she says, her voice only half-there. "I'll just try to go see him tomorrow instead."

Hannah sighs into the pages of her book. She presses her hands to her eyes. "Fine," she mutters, her heart pumping faster. "Fine. I'll go with you."

Joanie's eyes shine with gratitude when Hannah gets off the couch. They drive to Clay's house in silence.

Chapter Fourteen: The Fall

There's music blaring from a set of speakers mounted on the outdoor bar. Two long card tables have been set up at the top of the lawn, covered with plastic red cups and beer cans, and dozens of Hannah's classmates crowd around them, watching as the players shoot bone-white ping pong balls back and forth into each other's cups. Beyond them, swarms of people cover the backyard, all of them dressed alike in Polo button-downs and khaki shorts, in sundresses and pearl earrings, their sandaled feet planted on the summer green grass and their hands cupping Natty Light cans.

Clay has lit the torches along the perimeter of the backyard, just like he did on Mardi Gras. The torches blaze with primitive fire, adding a ritualistic feel to this final high school party. The old swing set sits motionless at the back of the yard, the worn away wooden beams and rusted metal chains speaking eerily to Hannah, as if from some haunted place she knew a long time ago, though she sat upon the swings just last month with Wally.

The rest of the property is shrouded in darkness, but Hannah can sense the silent majesty of the age-old trees reaching into the sky in the woods below the backyard. The trees peer out over the party like uninvited guests, their status made clear by the rickety old fence that runs along the edge of the backyard, protecting these backyard partiers from falling down the hill into the trees' thick dark mass.

"Clay's looking at us," Joanie says, and Hannah turns to see Clay eyeing them from across the yard, his expression unreadable.

"Maybe he wants us to leave."

Clay takes a long sip from his beer can, his gaze still on Hannah. Then he shifts his body away and responds to one of the players at the beer pong table, who shoves the ball into Clay's palm and claps him on the arm. Clay grins and moves closer to the table, raising his arms in the air and shouting something that makes everyone around him laugh.

"Guess he doesn't care," Joanie says.

"I want to leave," Hannah says nervously.

"Just help me find Luke first, okay?"

They walk silently around the perimeter of the party, leaving several feet between themselves and everyone else. Joanie carries a cup of vodka-lemonade but Hannah walks empty-handed, her arms crossed over her chest, her eyes darting all over the backyard. A few of her classmates make eye contact with her, some of them smiling politely or nodding uncomfortably, but most people ignore her.

At last they find Luke. He stands in a small circle of guys in the back right corner of the yard, his curls catching the light off the torches. As Hannah and Joanie approach him, Hannah recognizes Wally standing across from him.

"Shit," she whispers. "I'd better hang back. Go ahead. Do your thing."

Joanie clears her throat and hands Hannah her drink. She straightens her back and walks confidently up to Luke, her hair now carrying the torches' light too. The circle of guys stops talking as she approaches, and Luke turns just a fraction of an inch to face her. Wally's eyes land on the two of them—his eyes look thoughtful— before flitting over to meet Hannah's. Hannah pulls her lips together

324

and nods her head very slowly, keeping her eyes on him. He gives a quick jerk of the head in response, then looks down to his beer.

Joanie has spoken to Luke for less than thirty seconds when the music abruptly cuts off and there's a commotion at the front of the yard. Clay has jumped up onto the short brick wall that encloses the outdoor bar, and even from her spot at the very back of the yard, Hannah can see him, his tall, muscular form towering over his party guests, his smile huge and easy.

"Thank you for coming!" he shouts, and the partygoers all around the yard holler and cheer and raise their beer cans and plastic cups into the night. Luke, Joanie, Wally, and the rest of their circle stand in silence, waiting to see what Clay wants to say.

"It's just after midnight," Clay continues, his deep voice spilling out over the yard, "which means we've officially finished our last ever day as high school students—yeah, yeah, I know!—but anyway, I'm drunk and I just wanted to say that St. Mary's Class of 2012 is the best damn class that school has ever had, and I'm really glad I was a part of it with all of y'all!"

A deafening cheer goes up through the yard. People yell and whistle and shout Clay's name, and in the back right corner of the yard, Hannah claps tepidly along with Luke, Joanie, and Wally.

"Before I turn the music back on and get totally wasted," Clay says, "I just need to thank my girlfriend for helping to set this whole thing up. Where are you, Bake?"

A collective cheer goes up at the sound of Baker's name. Clay surveys the yard, his tree-dark hair falling onto his sweaty forehead, until he spots her, for he grins and extends his hand chivalrously into the crowd. Hannah squints through the mass of people in front of her, but she can't see Baker's face.

"Baker, you are the *best*," Clay says, slurring the last word. "And we all know what a hard time you've had lately with some of this nasty bullshit that's been going on, but we all love you!"

An even bigger cheer goes up around the yard, a cheer that lasts for a full minute, with whistles and whooping and drunken shouts of "Yeahhhhhh!" Hannah's stomach goes cold. She has a hard time swallowing. She feels Joanie's eyes on her, and when she turns, almost against her will, to make eye contact, she finds that not only is Joanie watching her, but Luke and Wally are, too.

He's an asshole, Joanie mouths.

Hannah bites her teeth together. She feels a growing desperation inside of her, like her heart is drowning and doesn't know where to reach.

"Everyone give Baker a drink tonight!" Clay shouts from the front of the party.

"I'm gonna go," Hannah mouths to Joanie, and then she drops Joanie's vodka drink on the grass and turns to walk along the perimeter of the yard.

"Hannah, wait!" Joanie says sharply, and Hannah hears racing footsteps behind her and feels Joanie's grip on her arm. "Let me go with you, okay?"

They've walked five paces when they hear another commotion. "Wait, wait, what?" Clay shouts from his post on the brick wall. "What are you saying?"

Someone at the front of the crowd is talking, but the distance and the crowd muffle their words. Hannah and Joanie stop walking, and Hannah experiences an inexplicable feeling of dread.

"Are you fucking kidding me?" Clay says, his voice hoarse, his face fallen.

"What's going on?" someone shouts.

Hannah stands still as Clay looks out over the yard, his face white underneath the lights from the deck. He drops his drink as his arms fall to his sides. "We lost the Diocesan Cup."

"What?"

"What?"

"No!"

The backyard is suddenly riotous, with people yelling all at once, their cacophonous voices scraping against the night heat. "Hold on!" Clay says, throwing his arms down as if trying to slam a car trunk.

"What happened?" someone shouts.

Clay looks down to the same spot in the crowd, and a suffocating silence blankets the night. Hannah strains her ears to hear the words of the person talking.

"We can't hear back here!" one of the guys standing near Luke says.

Clay raises his head again. There's a murderous look on his face.

"Kasey just got a text from her friend whose mom works at the diocese office," he says, his voice cutting over the backyard. "They're rescinding the Cup. They're awarding it to Mount Sinai instead."

"What?"

"They can't do that!"

"Why?!"

Clay's jaw clenches. He stands completely still, his shoulders tight and his fists balled at his sides. Under the glare of the deck lights, his eyes flicker out to the very back of the yard, searching for something. Hannah's chest surges with fear.

"You know why," he says, his voice deadly.

There is one packed second of silence, and Hannah has the sensation of tumbling over a ledge, her heart in her throat and her body out of her control.

Then, noise. Roaring, angry noise.

"We need to go," Joanie says, her eyes frantic. She pushes Hannah forward, causing them both to trip in their haste to get out of the backyard.

The next thing Hannah knows, Wally is at her side, helping her up, his glasses reflecting fire. "It's okay," he says, his voice as steady as always. "They're not gonna do anything."

"I need to get out of here," Hannah pants.

"We'll come with you," someone else says, and Hannah looks behind her to see Luke at Joanie's side.

"Hey, what's going on back there?" Clay's angry drunken voice shouts, and in her peripheral vision, Hannah sees dark figures turn their heads toward her.

"Come on," she says, leading the way forward along the torch-lit perimeter.

"Yeah, that's right, leave!" Clay shouts. "We don't need your bullshit anymore!"

328

"Shut up!" Wally yells, his voice grating on Hannah's ears.

"Get the fuck out of here!" Clay shouts back, and then the sea of people between them starts to shout, too, their voices yelling indecipherable things, and Joanie starts to shout back at them, screaming herself hoarse, catapulting profanities into the air.

And then Wally starts yelling at Clay.

"You're a spineless asshole!" Wally roars. "You're a self-obsessed prick who never gave a shit about his friends!"

"You fucking—!"

Then Clay's moving off the wall, jumping down into the crowd, storming through the mass of people until he's within feet of Hannah and the others. "What's your problem, huh?" he says, shoving Wally in the chest.

"Back off, man!" Wally shouts, pushing him back. "You crossed the line!"

"Are you *kidding* me?!" Clay snarls, his nostrils flaring and his face burning red. "Open your eyes, man! *She* crossed the line! She crossed all of us and she used you and now she's making you and our whole school look like fucking idiots!"

Wally lunges, his sprinter's legs propelling him forward, and throws a solid punch at Clay's jaw. Clay stumbles backwards into the crowd of people, his face registering shock and pain. He lets out a primal roar before launching himself at Wally and throwing his own punch.

Then they're both throwing punches, and Hannah ducks down to the ground with them, begging Wally to stop, begging Clay to stop, and one of their hands goes awry and smacks her in the face, and she stands up, dazed, her left cheek smarting, the shouts of people all around her. More people jump into the brawl—Luke barrels in and tries to pull Clay and Wally apart, and then Jackson drops down to the ground and hits Wally, and then Luke hits Jackson until Bradford hits Luke—

"Way to go, H'Eaden," says a venomous voice, and Hannah turns to see Michele and her friends glaring at her. "I guess it's not enough to get Carpenter fired and cost us the Cup, right, I mean now you've gotta pit the whole school against each other—"

"I had nothing to do with this," Hannah says, tears springing into her eyes.

"Bullcrap you didn't," Michele says, stepping nearer to her. "Everything was *normal* until you started in with your crap—"

But then Hannah doesn't hear what Michele has to say anymore, because Baker appears in the circle of onlookers, her eyes terrified as she looks down at Clay, Wally, Luke, and the other boys on the ground. Hannah's heart jumps into her throat, and as she stares across the circle at Baker, Baker looks up and meets her eyes, and there's something in them that Hannah recognizes: there's something in them that tells Hannah nothing is finished—

"Hey!" Michele shouts, pushing Hannah backward. "Give it up! Stop lusting after her!"

"Don't push me!"

"If anyone deserves to be hurt tonight, it's you!"

Below them, the fight finally breaks up, with multiple guys holding Wally, Clay, and Luke apart from each other. Hannah looks at the blood smeared across their mouths and down their shirts, at

330

Wally's broken glasses hanging off his face, at Joanie's horrified expression as she rushes to tend to Luke, but before Hannah can go to help them, something smacks against her right cheek with the force of a wooden plank—

"How's that feel?" Michele says, retracting her hand.

Hannah's whole face is stinging now, her throat full of tears. Across the circle, Baker looks at her with anguished eyes, her mouth open on a silent cry, but she does not move.

Michele takes a cup from one of her friends and Hannah knows what's going to happen before it does. She tries to turn away, but the beer hits her full on in the face, seeping into her eyes and mouth before she can process what happened.

"HEY!" Joanie shouts, lunging at them from where she was tending to Luke. "Get away from her!"

"Back off, Baby Eaden!" Michele yells.

Joanie launches herself at Michele, slapping her and pushing her with all the force she has, until Hannah jumps forward and pulls her off, begging "Joanie, Joanie, stop, please stop—"

One of Michele's friends jabs Joanie hard in the stomach. Joanie stumbles backwards into Hannah, toppling them both over with sudden force.

"HEY!" Luke roars. He jerks himself free from Cooper's stronghold and starts to run at Michele, but Miles and Walker grab him.

"I'm giving you three seconds to run, H'Eaden," Michele says, her low voice slithering across the silent onlookers. "And then we're kicking you out of this party."

Hannah blinks up at her, wondering how serious she could be. The crowd all around them stands still and silent, their faces contorted with hatred. Wally and Luke writhe against their strongholds, Wally panting and sputtering. Joanie starts to rise off the ground, her hand clamped on her stomach, but Hannah pushes her down with a firm hand.

And then she looks to Baker, who stands stock-still, her eyes full of tears and her mouth still open on a silent cry.

"Get out of here!" Michele screams, and then she and her friends lunge forward, and Hannah moves without thinking, jumping up from the dark grass and running back along the same path she'd earlier walked, making a wide circle around the lawn, blood rushing in her head. She runs until she's at the far edge of the yard, just before the rickety fence and the steep downward slope to the woods, and as these boundaries come into view she switches her path to sprint back around the opposite side of the yard, away from the angry mass of people.

But some of Michele's friends run towards her from the opposite side of the yard, and she halts, terror gripping her, wondering which way to go. She starts to cut a path down the middle of the yard, but her pursuers weave their way toward the middle so that she can't run that way, and she has no choice but to stop and back away from them toward the edge of the yard. She backs up until she's only a couple of feet from the rickety fence, equidistant from two of the blazing torches.

"Funny predicament you find yourself in," Michele pants as she draws near. "It's like, which way should you run? Two choices, right? Two directions to go? And you picked the wrong one."

"You need to calm down," Hannah says, feeling seriously scared for the first time, for it's clear to her, as they stumble and laugh unrestrainedly, how drunk these people are.

"I think *you* need to shut up."

"No, Michele, really, there's steep woods behind us—Clay's mom is always warning us about them—"

"There's also a fence behind you, you imbecile," Michele sneers. She steps forward and pushes Hannah again, laughing delightedly in her face. The heel of Hannah's foot brushes against the fence, and the blood rushes to her head so fast she feels dizzy with it. Behind Michele, the crowd of people grows larger, and Hannah sees Clay, now free from his hold and calm again, walking nearer to the scene.

"I bet you wouldn't have done all that crap if you knew this would happen, huh?" Michele taunts. "Bet you wish you could get us that Diocesan Cup back, huh?"

"I didn't mean for any of this to happen," Hannah cries.

"But it *did*. You couldn't keep your mouth shut—couldn't sit quietly on your little problem—and now you've screwed us all over. So screw—you—" Michele says, shoving Hannah again.

"Stop!" someone cries. "Stop!"

Hannah's breath catches in her chest.

Baker walks out of the crowd, her dark eyes reflecting the torches' light. She looks fragile and small—smaller than Hannah's ever seen her.

"You're standing at the weakest part of the fence," Baker says, her voice shaking.

"Relax, Baker," Michele says, sounding exasperated. "We're not gonna do anything."

"You'd better not," Baker says, stepping closer and closer to Hannah.

"Stop giving orders," Michele says, her voice quivering with anger. "You're not the president here, you got it?"

"This isn't about that," Baker says.

"You already saved your lesbo pal once, remember? Your good deed is done, blah blah blah, you can go be Saint Baker somewhere else."

"Stay away from her," Baker says, her voice still shaking but loud enough to be heard by the crowd of people. "I mean it. Walk away."

"So, what," Michele says, turning to face her. "You ignore H'Eaden for weeks, and now you want to save her?"

"She's my best friend."

"Some best friend you've been. You try to negotiate for her, but when it doesn't work out, you walk away, right?"

"*Leave*," Baker says through gritted teeth.

"Fine," Michele growls. "But before I do, let's be honest for a second, Baker: Why do you *care* what happens to her?"

Baker flushes red in the firelight. Her eyes narrow. Her chest heaves. She opens her mouth to speak, but her words catch, and she clenches her jaw, seeming to struggle with something.

"Wow," Michele says, "so much love for your *best friend.*"

Baker swallows hard. She turns to Hannah, and her expression is tortured. Their eyes lock.

"I wrote it," Baker says, her eyes on Hannah.

"What?" Michele says.

"The e-mail," Baker says, her eyes watering. "I wrote it. I sent it. It wasn't Hannah. It was me."

"No," Clay says from his spot in the crowd.

"I'm sorry," Baker rasps, her voice barely audible, but she's not apologizing to the crowd: she is apologizing to Hannah. Her eyes fill with tears, and the soul shining forth from those eyes is so beaten and bare, so afflicted and terrified, but still so very much the girl Hannah loves. Baker reaches over with trembling fingers and, for the first time in an eternity, she touches Hannah. She trails her fingers lightly over Hannah's smarting cheek, her expression still tortured, before she drops her arm to take Hannah's hand.

"Oh my God, is this a freaking joke?" Michele shrieks.

Everything happens very slowly. Hannah looks up to see Michele running at her, her ugly face blazing with rage, and in the same instant, in her peripheral vision, she sees Baker throw herself behind her with the same speed and skill she had on the volleyball court—

And the next thing Hannah feels is a barreling into her chest, a blow that knocks all the breath out of her, and yet in the same instant she feels her body knock into something behind her, something solid and strong, something that feels like a human body—

And then Hannah is on the ground, and there are splinters of wood falling onto her limbs. She looks up, dizzy, to see a break in the fence. The crowd of people starts to scream into the night, their panicked voices mixing on the heat. Hannah rolls onto her side and crawls toward the broken fence, her breath coming in short gasps. She peers out over the edge of the yard with her very soul caught in her throat.

"Where is she?" someone's panicked voice shouts, and then Clay is kneeling next to the broken fence with Hannah, his hands clawing on the edge of the yard like frightened crabs in the sand.

Hannah crawls headfirst down the slope of the yard, the weight of her body leaning forward on her elbows, her knees scraping against the earth beneath her, her hands combing over plants and stones and dirt, her heart screaming in her throat. She crawls farther and farther down, the force of gravity pulling her torso before her legs, and then she hears Clay's voice behind her again, hears it erupt from his throat in a mangled cry, and she knows he's crawling down the slope, too, and that Wally and Luke and Joanie must be as well—that they're all crawling down this slope, poised to fall, desperate to stay upright if only to find their friend—

Something catches Hannah's attention, and a few yards to her right, she sees the trunk of a mammoth tree with a dark shape twitching in front of it.

"HERE!" she shouts, her voice desperate and wet.

She can still hear people yelling, and now she hears police sirens blaring distantly in the night, but all she cares about is the girl in front of her, the girl whose body has been pinned against this massive tree—this tree that broke her fall—

"Baker," Hannah whispers, reaching her at last. "Can you hear me?"

"Han," Baker whispers.

"Are you okay?"

Baker takes a breath, and her whole body seems to rattle with it.

"HELP!" Hannah screams up toward the yard. "HELP! Call an ambulance!"

"Han," Baker says.

"I'm here. I'm here. You're going to be okay. You're fine. You're fine."

"I'm sorry."

"Don't be sorry. There's nothing to worry about." Hannah wipes furiously at her eyes, the tears wetting her hands. She bends forward and kisses Baker's forehead. "Everything's okay, Bake. Everything's okay. Just hang in there. Stay with me, okay? Stay with me."

Then Clay appears, his strong body crumpled in fear. "Baker," he cries, reaching out an arm to her, "Baker—I'm sorry— Baker—"

Hannah's not sure what makes her do it, but she reaches toward him and clasps his hand. He jerks his head toward her, his tears glistening in the darkness, and Hannah doesn't look away.

And they stay like that, holding hands, each of them holding one of Baker's hands, until the paramedics reach them.

Chapter Fifteen: The Tree

The EMT workers tell them to stay back as they wheel Baker's stretcher out to the ambulance. But Hannah follows them anyway, and so does Clay, and so do Joanie and Wally and Luke. They file past the policemen, who speak into their radios with weary expressions on their faces, and past dozens of St. Mary's kids, all of whom call out to them in confusion in-between their breathalyzer tests. The police car sirens light up the street, casting everyone's faces in blue, and the nosy neighbors in the cul-de-sac stand on their front porches and watch the scene, clad in bathrobes and frayed LSU shirts.

One of the EMTs, a middle-aged guy with a ponytail, turns back toward the group of them. "You can't ride with us," he says. "You have to stay with the police until your parents pick you up."

"No!" Hannah says. "No, I have to go with you!"

"Not our rules," the ponytailed guy says.

"But I haven't even been drinking! I was just trying to help her! Please! You have to let me go with you—she's my best friend!"

The EMT gives her a hard look. Behind him, his coworker loads Baker's stretcher into the ambulance.

"I'd better not see you get in," he says, "or my neck's on the line."

"No, sir," Hannah says hastily. "Thank you."

Joanie approaches her as soon as the EMT worker walks away. "We'll meet you there as soon as we can," she says, her face blotchy and tear-streaked. "I already called Mom and Dad."

"Bring the boys," Hannah says, glancing beyond Joanie to where Wally, Clay, and Luke stand uncertainly on the sidewalk. Clay meets Hannah's eyes and heaves a great breath, his expression broken.

Baker has passed out by the time Hannah takes her place next to her. The EMTs have secured an oxygen mask over her mouth. In the yellow lights of the ambulance interior, Hannah can see her clearly for the first time since her fall. Her face is covered in cuts and abrasions and there are thorns of blood all along her hairline. Her neck, shoulders, arms, legs—anywhere there is skin, Hannah can see streaks of red mixed with dirt.

"Hey," Hannah whispers, taking her hand.

The ponytailed EMT slams the ambulance doors shut and a moment later the vehicle lurches with movement, reminding Hannah that her heart still works. The siren on the roof wails its desperate song, and Hannah's mind takes up the familiar refrain of *Please, please, please* while the ambulance speeds them toward salvation.

The hospital waiting room is so devoid of sound that Hannah feels like she might be underwater. The only other person in the vicinity is a middle-aged nurse posted at the front desk with her eyes closed and her hand around a coffee mug.

Hannah's heart drills so fast that she might pass out from it. She sits erectly in the waiting room chair, perched to react to news at any moment, while Baker's name circles around her head over and over and over.

She stands up and paces the lobby for a few minutes. The front desk nurse opens one bleary eye to watch her. "It's gonna be okay, sweetheart," she says.

"I don't know if it will be," Hannah says. When she hears how her voice sounds, she stops walking and stares at the nurse. "That's not what I usually sound like," she says stupidly.

The nurse's cheeks move with a tired laugh. "I don't think anyone sounds the same when they're waiting in here. Is that girl your friend?"

The tears prick at her eyes. "Yes, ma'am," she answers, her throat aching.

She paces all around the waiting room, her mind hopscotching through hundreds of images, her muscles trying to jump out of her skin. Her lungs tighten every time she breathes. When she looks down at her arms, she can almost see the blood rushing through her veins, sweeping through everything like a great flood.

She startles when the automatic doors open and Mrs. Shackleford hurries into the room, dressed in loose jeans and an over-large sweater, her eyes glassy and her face wan.

"Are you alright?" Mrs. Shackleford asks, hurrying over to her. "Hannah, you're bleeding!"

Hannah opens her mouth to answer, but the lobby doors open again and Mrs. Hadley comes running in. "Ginny!" Mrs. Shackleford calls, but Mrs. Hadley only raises a hand in response and rushes toward the nurse's desk. "My daughter is here," she says, her voice panicky, her eyes wet, her fingers shaking as they grip the top of the desk. "Baker Hadley. Please tell me where she is."

"Let me go speak to the doctor, ma'am," the nurse says.

"I'm coming with you."

"Ma'am, I'm afraid you'll have to—"

But Mrs. Hadley rushes past her and through the doors to the emergency rooms. The nurse heaves an irritated sigh and follows her at a much slower pace. Mr. Hadley runs into the lobby a moment later, car keys shaking in his hands, his dark hair windswept and his temples glistening with sweat. "Where?" he says abruptly, looking toward Mrs. Shackleford, and Mrs. Shackleford simply points toward the ward Mrs. Hadley just rushed into, and Mr. Hadley goes running through the same doors.

Then Hannah's parents and Joanie arrive, and Hannah's mom pulls her into a hug and holds her tight. "You smell like beer," she says, her tone more a worried question than an accusation, and Hannah can't help the way her voice breaks when she whispers, without even planning to, that someone threw one on her. Her mom's eyes are broken when she pulls away, and Hannah doesn't want to see that, doesn't want to remember the shame she felt when it happened, so she turns away and hugs her dad instead. Her mom says nothing else, just accepts the chair that Mrs. Shackleford pulls over for her and sits down with her hand resting over Hannah's arm.

Luke and Mr. Broussard are next, and Wally and Ms. Sumner after that. Mrs. Shackleford gasps at Luke's and Wally's bruised faces, at Wally's broken glasses, at the blood on their button-down shirts. "I can't understand how this happened," Mrs. Shackleford says, her normally strong persona withering away before them, and Mr. Broussard and Ms. Sumner and Hannah's parents swallow and shake their heads, at a loss for what to say.

And then Father Simon sweeps through the waiting room doors, his bald head shining with sweat. He touches their shoulders paternally and asks to know what happened. No one answers him. Finally, Mrs. Shackleford rubs the bridge of her nose and starts to recount everything the police told her over the phone. Father Simon's eyes widen in shock, and he looks at them and mutters their names— "*Luke*"—"*Joanie*"—"*Wally*"—"*Hannah*"—like he doesn't want to believe they could have fallen so far.

"And I thought we'd already hit the heart of our struggle," he says, knocking his folded hands against his forehead. His face is grave when he raises it to address them. "This is not the life I want for you."

"But I don't understand how this whole thing started," Ms. Sumner says desperately. "What were you all fighting about?"

Hannah's heart pounds so fast that she can't breathe. She keeps her head bowed, waiting for someone to explain, waiting for it all to come back to her. But no one speaks. The silence between them all is heavier than Hannah has ever known. Until—

"One of our students has been struggling with same-sex attraction," Father Simon says, and Hannah's stomach splits open. She feels her mom's hand tighten on her arm and Joanie's posture stiffen next to her.

"And I'm assuming, from everything I've heard just now, that there was a clash over this issue," Father Simon continues, his voice despondent, "and our student body resorted to violence rather than compassion."

"But what about Baker?" Ms. Sumner says. "What does she have to do with this?" Her voice drops all of a sudden, and she looks back to Father Simon. "Was she the student? The one that—?"

"No," Hannah says firmly. She raises her eyes to meet Wally's mom's. "I am, Ms. Sumner."

"Oh—Hannah—"

"And there's nothing wrong with that," Hannah's mom says loudly. "And as far as I'm concerned, Mrs. Shackleford, all of the kids who were bullying Hannah should be expelled!"

"We're going to take care of it, I promise you, Anne," Mrs. Shackleford says. "But first I want to make sure everyone is okay. Especially Baker."

"We've seen a lot of brokenness over the last month," Father Simon says. "Our whole community needs to work through it together." He pauses. "I think the sacrament of Reconciliation would be a good place to start. Would any of you like to come to Confession now, while we're waiting?"

No one answers him.

"Hannah?" he prompts. "Maybe we could start with you?"

"No," Hannah says.

Father Simon licks his lips. "Hannah..." he says patiently. "This brokenness is going to continue until you make your peace with—"

"I'm not going to Confession!" Hannah screams at him. "I'm not going anywhere! I'm staying right here until Baker walks out of those doors!"

"You are blinded," Father Simon says. "You are blinded by sin and stubbornness and your resentment of our faith—"

"I'm not blinded!" Hannah screams. "I'm seeing clearly for the first time in my life!"

"Then you are lost!" Father Simon roars, his whole face turning purple, his neck straining against his clerical collar. "You are lost and you need the saving power of—!"

"Stand down!" a new voice says.

Hannah's heart reels when she realizes her father is speaking. He jumps up from his seat and positions himself in front of Hannah, blocking Father Simon from her sight.

"I beg your pardon?" Father Simon sputters.

"Stand down, man!" Hannah's dad repeats, his voice shaking. He breathes hard—his back moves up and down—and when he speaks again, his voice is more controlled. "I respect your vocation," he says, "but I will not let you speak to my child like this—"

"I am a father of the church—"

"And I'm Hannah's father, and I'm telling you to walk away. Walk away before you hurt these kids any more than you already have."

There is a long beat of silence, followed by the sound of Father Simon sucking air over his teeth.

"Fine," he says.

Hannah pulls away from her father to watch him leave. He looks back at their group when he reaches the doors, and there is a vein throbbing in his red temple. "I'll be praying for you all," he says, swallowing hard. Then the automatic doors open, and he has gone out into the night.

"Dad—" Hannah says. "You didn't have to—"

"No, Hannah, I did," her dad says, breathing heavily, his voice shaking. "Hate like that—when it's disguised as love, or righteousness or pity—I'm not going to subject you to hate like that. I'm not going to let that happen, honey."

Hannah hugs him hard. She presses her face into his sweatshirt and breathes in the scent. It smells of his aftershave and the cedar in his office and her mother's laundry detergent and the candles Joanie likes to burn all over their house. She loses herself in the smell of his sweatshirt and thinks about nothing else.

It's a little over an hour later when Clay walks into the waiting room, flanked by his parents on each side. His eyes are still bleary with alcohol and tears, and his nose and left eye have swollen from fighting.

Dr. Landry pulls out a chair for his wife and then commands Clay to sit in another one. "Not a word," Dr. Landry says to Clay, his voice deadly. "Sit there silently and do not move."

Hannah and her friends turn their faces away as new tears fill Clay's eyes. The adults—Mr. Broussard, Ms. Sumner, Mrs. Shackleford, the Landry's, and Hannah and Joanie's parents—start to talk about the party damage, with Dr. Landry sharing all the details from his conversation with the police department. "Drove all the way up from New Orleans just to be told that it's the biggest party they've had to break up in a decade. And now this one—" he jerks his thumb at Clay—"may not even be eligible to walk on at LSU. We're lucky they haven't revoked his acceptance yet." Dr. Landry squeezes his hands together over his knees, and Clay hangs his head next to him.

Mrs. Landry stares straight ahead, her eyes glassy. When she speaks, it sounds as if she's coming out of a trance.

"We never should have bought that house," she says, her voice lifeless. "We never should have risked that hill."

Dr. Landry says nothing; none of the other adults speak either.

Hannah stands up where she sits between her parents. She turns to Joanie, then to Wally, then to Luke, and at last to Clay. "Come with me," she says.

"Where are we going?" Joanie says.

"For a walk." She turns to the parents. "We won't go far. I just thought you all might want some privacy."

Joanie, Wally, and Luke stand up to follow her. Dr. Landry nods at Clay, who lumbers gracelessly off his chair, still hanging his head.

Hannah leads them down a new corridor—away from the double doors that lead to the emergency ward—and into the deep silence of the hospital. "Where are we going?" Joanie asks again, but Hannah shushes her and scans one of the hospital maps.

They reach their destination a few minutes later. Hannah pulls the door open and leads the way inside, saying nothing. The others follow behind her without question.

She chooses a row of chairs in the back. She files in first and kneels with her hands folded on the chair in front of her. Joanie follows after her, then Wally, then Luke, then Clay.

They kneel in silence. Clay and Wally hang forward over the chairs in front of them, their heads bowed. Luke kneels with erect shoulders, his face screwed up like he's trying hard to understand something. Joanie, kneeling next to Hannah, closes her eyes and moves her mouth around silent words.

Hannah stares at the skin of her folded hands until the sight starts to blur through her tears.

Please help her. Please take care of her. Please take care of us all.

Clay stands up at the end of the row. Hannah opens her mouth to protest, to tell him to sit back down with them and pray, but the words die in her throat when she sees what he is doing. He has walked to the front of the room to light a candle. It flickers with a tiny, yellow flame, drawing their eyes to its light.

Clay sits back down and takes Luke's hand. Luke takes Wally's hand, and Wally takes Joanie's hand. And Hannah, upon seeing what they're doing, reaches for Joanie's hand before Joanie can reach for hers.

In the anxious silence of a hospital chapel, with one small candle to light the darkness, five teenagers hold hands and pray.

They wander back to the waiting room a while later. The silent, sleepy adults look up when they reach their circle of chairs. "Anything?" Hannah asks, but her mom shakes her head no.

Hannah and her friends slump down into the vacant chairs, and their group of 12 sits in a circle, as if joined at table, waiting for news.

Hannah's heart stops when Mrs. Hadley walks back into the waiting room. They all look round at her. Mrs. Hadley wipes a shaky hand across her eyes and breathes out.

"She's going to be okay."

It's the most forceful feeling of relief Hannah's ever experienced. Her heart stops pounding immediately and her whole body seems to cool over as it comes down from its adrenaline rush. She drops her face into her hands and the only thing she can think is *Thank you. Thank you.*

"She just regained consciousness," Mrs. Hadley says, her voice worn. "She has a broken rib and some bad bruising. They had to stitch up some cuts on her hairline. But the doctor said it could have been a lot worse. She's alright, thank God."

Hannah loves the collective sigh that runs around their circle of chairs, loves the way Clay leans back against the wall and laughs in relief, loves the way Mrs. Shackleford closes her eyes and smiles into her fingertips.

"Jack's sitting with her now," Mrs. Hadley continues. "She needs rest. They're not going to release her until late tomorrow, at the earliest. You all don't have to stay."

"We'll bring you dinner tomorrow night," Hannah's mom says.

"I'll bring it Sunday night," Ms. Sumner says.

"Thank you," Mrs. Hadley says. Then she pulls her lips together and blinks very fast at the floor, as if steeling herself for something.

"Hannah," she says.

Hannah looks up, her heart beating fast again.

"She's asking for you," Mrs. Hadley says. She swallows; her lips press into a tight line. "Will you come see her?"

The rest of the circle looks at Hannah. Hannah looks past them all, her eyes on Mrs. Hadley. She stands and follows her through the double doors.

"Hannah..." Mrs. Hadley says when they're on the other side of the doors.

Hannah waits.

"I don't know everything that happened tonight," Mrs. Hadley says. "I don't know what's been going on with you and Baker." She swallows and closes her eyes for an extended second. Her chin quivers as she breathes in through her nose. "But I have an inkling."

Hannah feels the blood rush to her face.

"This is difficult for me," Mrs. Hadley says. "This isn't what I—" She cuts herself off, swallowing hard again. She twists her hands together, her beautiful diamond ring catching the light. "I love my daughter, Hannah. Above everything else, I love her."

Hannah nods her head fast. "Yes, ma'am," she says, her voice small. "I know you do."

Mrs. Hadley takes a Kleenex from her purse and dabs at her eyes. She bats her eyelashes toward the ceiling, trying to ward off tears.

"Be patient with me, Hannah," she says, her voice thick. "Help Baker be patient with me, too."

"Yes, ma'am," Hannah says, her heart rising. "I will."

Mrs. Hadley closes her eyes and nods to herself. When she opens her eyes, she gives a short, quick laugh, almost in embarrassment. "I'm a silly woman," she says, shaking her head.

"No you're not."

"I am, honey, but that's okay." She fixes a smile on her face. "Let's go see Baker now, hm?"

It's funny how Hannah can't think of anything to say to her. Funny, because all she's done for the last few weeks is think of everything she wants to say, everything she wants to confess and profess. Now she stands in this hospital room and blinks at Baker through her tears, but the swelling of her heart seems to have taken the words away.

"We'll give you some privacy," Mrs. Hadley says, her tone outlined by a softness Hannah hasn't heard before. She pats Mr. Hadley's arm and the two of them step out of the room.

Hannah stares at Baker, wondering how to start. Baker looks back at her, her eyes dark and familiar.

"How bad is it?" Baker asks, her voice raspy. "Do I still look like a prom queen?"

Hannah laughs through her tears. She can feel her heart in her throat. "Not too bad."

Baker's bottom lip, split open and shining red, lifts in a smile. "Liar."

"You look like you're hurting."

"I am," Baker says. "But not from the fall."

"You shouldn't have done that."

"I should have done it ages ago."

They look at each other, and the eye contact is so powerful that Hannah might collapse from it. She steps closer, waiting for Baker to look away at any second, but Baker never does. Hannah steps closer until she's right there at her side, close enough to touch her.

Baker swallows hard. She keeps looking at Hannah, but tears start to pool in her eyes. Hannah watches her try to blink them away.

"Han—" she says, her chest rattling.

"Don't cry, Bake. Please don't cry."

"I'm not. I'm just, I'm just, breathing," she heaves.

Hannah touches her cheek. "Don't cry."

Baker turns her head so that Hannah touches more of her cheek. She closes her eyes and Hannah watches her struggle to keep her sobs down. Tears slide out beneath her eyelids and down onto Hannah's hand.

"Baker," Hannah says, her voice catching on the name.

"I'm so sorry," Baker says.

"Shh, it's okay. It's okay."

"I'm so sorry," Baker heaves, opening her eyes again to look at Hannah. Her tears spill out freely. "So sorry, Han, so sorry. I was so wrong—I was so awful to you—to *you*—"

"You were scared—I know you were scared—"

"It doesn't matter," Baker says in a rush, her voice reaching a high pitch.

"Baker," Hannah pleads, insistent tears spilling down her own cheeks, "Baker, please, don't cry. Please don't. You're going to hurt yourself more. You broke your rib. Please."

Baker gasps and heaves, and Hannah tries in vain to steady her shaking shoulders. She leans her head down close to Baker's, so that she doesn't know whose tears are making her hair wet.

"I hurt you," Baker cries. "I hurt the one person I love more than anyone else in the world."

The swelling in Hannah's throat threatens to explode. Her sinuses prickle; her body rushes with uncontrollable feeling.

"I hurt you, Han. I hurt you," Baker says, her body convulsing.

The sobs burst out of Hannah's throat. "Yeah," she cries, choking on the word, hating that she needs to release it. "Yeah, you did. You hurt me. You really hurt me."

Baker's face contorts with anguish. Her chin trembles; her mouth gasps around shuddering breaths. Her eyes bleed with agony. "I'm so—" she heaves. "I'm so—"

"But Baker," Hannah says, touching a hand to her tears, "you also saved me."

Baker's face screws up again. She heaves with more sobs, placing a hand over her ribs.

"You saved me, too," she cries.

It takes long minutes for Baker's sobs to subside. Hannah holds her the whole time, crying along with her.

And then everything is calm. Their sobs soften into normal breaths. Hannah tries to inhale through the blockage in her nose and hears Baker doing the same thing.

"You alright?" Hannah asks.

"Yeah," Baker breathes, her voice wet and nasally.

"Let me get some tissues."

She brings a trash bin, too, and the two of them sit on the bed, Baker under the blankets and Hannah next to her feet, both of them blowing their noses and wiping their eyes, until, after each of them has gone through five tissues, they both start to laugh.

"*Now* you don't look like a prom queen," Hannah says.

Baker smiles like Hannah is the greatest person in the world.

"What do we do now?" Hannah asks.

Baker casts her red, puffy eyes to the hospital blanket. Her left eyebrow creases downward, and Hannah knows she is thinking.

"We need some time," she says.

"Time?"

Baker picks at a snag on the blanket. Her eyebrow is still creased in thought. "There's a lot I need to think about. A lot I need to figure out about myself."

Hannah's heart sinks. "I thought—I thought everything that happened—"

Baker pulls Hannah's fingers into her hand. "I'm not trying to run away again," she says, her eyes unblinking. "I'm not trying to hide.

I'm trying to make sure that—that I'm ready. Completely ready. That I'm not scared anymore. If I'm going to be with you, I want to do it right."

Hannah looks down to their intertwined fingers. She thinks of her shame, of her anger, of her broken friendships.

"I probably need that time, too," she says.

They rest in silence for a while, just looking at each other. And then Hannah knows it's time for her to go.

She kisses Baker's forehead with a lingering, tender kiss. Baker closes her eyes and her face assumes an expression of peace.

"Don't take too long," Hannah says.

Baker kisses the back of Hannah's hand. "I won't," she promises.

Hannah's parents send Joanie to bed when they walk into their silent, unlit house. "We need to speak to Hannah alone," Hannah's mom says.

Joanie trudges up the stairs without a word.

"Hannah," her mom says, gathering her into her arms, "Hannah, my sweet girl—"

Hannah's tears come in full again. They rush up from her insides with unexpected force, flooding out from her eyes and her mouth before she can stop them. Her dad wraps his arms around her, too, and she closes her eyes and nestles further into her parents' embrace.

"We're sorry," her mom whispers.

"We are," her dad says.

"I'm sorry," Hannah says. "I'm sorry for putting you through this—I'm sorry for not telling you—I'm sorry for being the way I am—"

"Don't you say that," her mom says, jerking back from her and shaking her shoulders.

"Don't you ever say that," her dad says, tears spilling forth from his eyes.

Her mom looks at her straight on, and her expression is resolute. "God knew exactly what He was doing when He created you, Hannah."

Hannah sobs into her mom's shoulder, and her dad presses his arms around her again, and as she draws in great, gulping breaths, she wishes desperately that she held the same conviction.

She can't fall asleep. She turns back and forth beneath her sheets, her mind buzzing with agitation, until she finally climbs out of bed with a yearning to be somewhere else. She dresses in the early morning darkness, tugging an old St. Mary's pullover over her head.

And just as the sun's coming up, while the whole world around her is still sleeping through the earliest hours of the morning, she drives to the St. Mary's chapel. The air is already heavy with heat. The birds are already singing.

She finds a single unlocked door at the back of the chapel. The air inside is stuffy the way it always is in churches: it smells of incense and old ladies' perfume and long-forgotten books.

She walks behind the half-dozen pews, trailing her hand along the smooth wooden surface where the faithful rest their backs. The chapel is dark, but the early morning sun brings a faint glow to the stained glass windows that decorate the walls.

She chooses a pew near the back. She kneels on the floor the same way she did in the hospital chapel. Words and ideas and questions wrestle with each other in the deepest recesses of her mind.

And then she whispers a word without meaning to.

"Gay."

She opens her eyes in surprise. She tastes the echo of the word on her tongue, raises her head to the statues of Mary and Joseph to see if they heard. They stare back at her serenely.

"Gay," she says again, louder this time.

The life-size statue of Mary Magdalene, the one that stands in the corner of the chapel, shimmers with morning sunlight.

"Gay," Hannah says, her voice at its normal volume now. "Gay."

The chapel stays silent. The statues do not reprimand her. She raises her eyes to the Crucifix that hangs above the altar and stares beseechingly at it.

"Gay," she says, her voice swelling in her throat. "Gay! I'm gay!"

The Jesus on the Crucifix stays motionless. His face stays anguished.

"Did you hear me?!" Hannah says, shouting now. "I'm gay! I'm gay!"

A door shuts behind her, and Hannah spins around in her pew, terrified.

Ms. Carpenter stands frozen just inside the chapel door, her eyebrows pulled high in surprise. She drops her hand from the door and the hint of a smile shows on her face. "Hi, Hannah," she says.

Hannah grips the top of her pew, her muscles rigid with astonishment. "Hi," she says. "What are you doing here?"

"I'm here to pray. There's usually no one else here this early." She steps into the heart of the chapel and scrutinizes Hannah. "Are you okay?"

"Yeah," Hannah says, nodding her head fast.

Ms. Carpenter smiles in a way that means she doesn't believe her. She genuflects on the stone floor and slides into the pew behind Hannah. Hannah sits breathlessly, still stunned at the sight of her teacher.

"Everyone missed you after you left," Hannah says, the words tumbling out of her mouth.

Ms. Carpenter smiles sadly. "I missed all of you, too. It was really hard to leave."

"I'm sorry I lost you your job."

"You didn't lose me my job."

"But if...if it hadn't been for that e-mail, they wouldn't have been able to fire you."

"They would have found a way sooner or later. I knew as soon as I read the e-mail that something like this would probably happen, but what was there to do? There is no way in the world I could not have responded to that e-mail. Or that I could not have done something during Father Simon's homily that day."

"But you loved it here."

"I did," Ms. Carpenter says, nodding. She clears her throat. "But I'll love it somewhere else, too. And this isn't about me. This is about something much bigger. You know what I mean?"

"Yeah."

"How are things with you, Hannah?"

Hannah shifts her eyes away. She prepares to tell Ms. Carpenter that things are fine, that she's getting along okay, but a different answer comes out instead.

"Things have been pretty bad," she says. The words taste honest, but she's surprised to find there's nothing frightening about them.

Ms. Carpenter stares intently at her. "So I heard. Mrs. Shackleford called me."

"She called you?"

"Late last night, when she was on her way to the hospital."

"Why didn't you come?"

"You were in good hands, and I didn't want to make the situation any worse. I figured I'd come here instead."

"Did you come to pray for us?"

"I'm always praying for you all." She pauses. "Hannah. Are you okay?"

Hannah's throat starts to swell, but she takes a long breath and invites the calm of the chapel to wash over her. Ms. Carpenter waits patiently, and when Hannah turns in the pew to face her, she finds a compassionate expression on her teacher's face.

"Can I tell you the story?" Hannah asks.

"Of course," Ms. Carpenter says, more breath than voice.

Hannah tells the story haphazardly, parenthesizing her feelings and speaking quickly through the parts where Michele hit her and threw the beer. The whole while, she feels her emotions building in her chest, staying with her until she reaches the part where Baker joined her at the edge of the yard. Then her words start to feel insufficient and she wishes there was a way she could color the feelings inside of her, outlining them so they're easier to see, highlighting details like Baker's scared eyes and the texture of the dirt under her hands while she crawled down to her.

Ms. Carpenter's expression does not change the whole time. She sits absolutely still, her eyebrows turned down and her hands folded in her lap. When Hannah finishes talking, Ms. Carpenter bows her head and closes her eyes for a long moment.

"Ms. Carpenter?"

Ms. Carpenter's shoulders rise with a breath. Behind her, the sunlight grows stronger in the windows. "The unnecessary pain of this whole thing," she says finally. "It kills me."

Hannah waits for her to elaborate. She doesn't.

"I've been wondering," Hannah says, "if the pain—if the pain *is* necessary."

Ms. Carpenter blinks as if coming out of a daydream. "Hm?"

"I just—I just keep coming back to this same question—I just keep worrying—What if I *am* wrong? What if there *is* something wrong with me? I mean, look at everything that's happened. Look at what happened to you. Look at—look at what happened to Baker."

"Pain isn't always a reflection of what's right or wrong, Hannah."

360

"But if things were different, if I was *straight,* then there wouldn't be any of this pain. You'd be okay, Baker would be okay, I would be okay. Ms. Carpenter, I just feel—I feel so lost. I can't tell what's right or wrong anymore. I can't figure out the truth. I wish so badly that I could find Jesus, or God, or whatever—I just wish I could find him in the park or something, and sit down with him on the grass and *ask* him what I'm supposed to do. Or why any of this happened. I wish I could look into his face and say, 'Why do I have these feelings in my heart? Are they bad? Why does everyone say they're bad? And if they are bad, why did you make me like this?'"

Ms. Carpenter swallows. She clears her throat. "And what do you think he would say?"

"I don't *know,*" Hannah says. She can feel the telltale signs that she is about to cry. "Everything Father Simon said at Mass—everything people say about Adam and Eve and what God intended for our relationships—how do I know what to believe?"

She takes a rattling breath, but it's not enough to stop her from crying. Ms. Carpenter brings her a box of tissues from the back of the chapel, and Hannah dabs at her eyes and nose until she gets her breathing under control. "I'm sorry," she says awkwardly.

"Don't be," Ms. Carpenter says, taking the box back from her, sniffling and using a tissue herself. "Someone needs to use these old tissues."

Hannah laughs gratefully.

"Hannah," Ms. Carpenter says, peering curiously at her, "why did you take the blame for that e-mail?"

Hannah crumples a tissue between her fingers. "Because I wrote it."

"We both know that's not true."

A beat of silence passes, and Hannah looks away.

"I was trying to—to protect—"

"Protect Baker?"

"I—well—"

"It's okay," Ms. Carpenter says kindly. "I know she wrote it. She came and talked to me about it, as I'm sure you no doubt heard from Michele."

"What did you say to her?"

Ms. Carpenter's face lifts with a small smile. "That's between us. I'm sure Baker will tell you when she's ready. But you wanted to protect her? Why?"

"Because—well, because I didn't want her to get hurt. Because I could tell how scared she was."

"And you weren't scared?"

"No, I was, but I wasn't really thinking about it. All I could think about was her."

"Why?"

"Because," Hannah says, her heart pounding with the answer, "I love her."

Sunlight illuminates the smile on Ms. Carpenter's face. "It's amazing," she says, folding her tissue over in her palm, "the things we'll do when we love another person."

Hannah swallows. "But I still don't know whether that love is good or bad."

Ms. Carpenter turns her head and squints at the altar. Her sharp, dark eyebrows draw together the way they do when she's unearthing the heart of a novel. "You mentioned Adam and Eve," she says, her eyes narrowing further and further. "Which is pretty perfect for this conversation, since they represent both love and sin."

Hannah follows Ms. Carpenter's line of sight toward the altar, but she finds she can't look steadily at it. "And how do I—how do I know which one I'm playing into?"

"Oh, I think we're always playing into both," Ms. Carpenter says easily. "That's what makes us human, right? Now look—I'm not a Creationist, Hannah. I don't believe the story of Genesis is supposed to be taken literally at all. I think humanity, at the moment—I think we're trapping ourselves in the story of Adam and Eve. That we're getting too caught up in the specifics and forgetting the larger meaning of the story."

"What's the larger meaning?"

"Well, you tell me. What do you think?"

"I don't know. I think about that story in my head and—all I see is a man and a woman and no way to reconcile who I am with who they were."

Ms. Carpenter crumples her face in sadness. "You know what I think?"

"What?"

"I think the most essential thing is that God didn't want Adam to be alone. God wanted Adam to be able to love someone. To have a relationship that reflected God's own love. And so he made Eve so that Adam could love her. So that Adam could be fully human. And when he made Eve, he gave her the miraculous capacity to love Adam back. Do you ever think about how crazy that is?—Our miraculous capacity to love? We don't know why, we don't know how, but our hearts and souls are drawn to others. We weren't made to be alone. We were made to love. And when we love, we automatically know God without even trying to, because God *is* love. If we love as he made us to love—if we love with our hearts instead of our criteria— then we simply *are* love."

Hannah exhales. "So—you're saying it's okay for me to love Baker?"

"That has to be your call. I can't sit here and pretend to know the mysteries of your heart. That's between you and God. If you love her, and if you know God's love by loving her, then it's up to you to decide whether that love is worth seeking."

"Okay."

"But Hannah," Ms. Carpenter says tentatively, "I can tell you that I believe—that the human heart's mysterious ability to love others is never wrong. Your heart will never ask your permission to love. It's going to love whomever it was made to love, and the best thing you can do is follow it."

"It's just—it's scary when other people don't understand that."

"Yeah," Ms. Carpenter says, nodding with sad eyes.

"I've tried to pretend like I don't care," Hannah says. "Like I'm not afraid to break the rules. But deep down...I'm really scared."

"You've been very brave so far."

"No," Hannah says.

"You have. Not just with other people, but with yourself. It takes overwhelming amounts of bravery to call yourself out on who you are."

"It wasn't bravery so much as an inevitability."

"There's nothing inevitable about it, Hannah. Some people go entire lifetimes without facing the truth about who they really are."

"But I'm still working through it," Hannah says. "I think Baker is, too. I think we're both so ashamed of our feelings." She swallows. "It's hard to love someone when loving them makes you feel ashamed of yourself."

Ms. Carpenter dips her head. Hannah releases a shaky breath and twists up the corners of her tissue. When she looks up, Ms. Carpenter is peering at the altar again.

"What are you thinking about?" Hannah asks.

Ms. Carpenter meets her eyes. "Shame," she says.

Hannah nods. "It sucks."

"Do you remember everything from the story of the Fall?" Ms. Carpenter asks. "Not just the part about picking the fruit from the tree, or about Adam and Eve sharing the fruit. Do you remember what happened afterwards?"

"God was angry with them."

"No, before that. Right after their eyes were opened."

Their eyes were opened, and they saw that they were naked...

"They covered themselves up," Hannah says.

"Exactly," Ms. Carpenter says. "They were ashamed. It's the second part of the sin."

"Their shame? But—they should have felt ashamed. They

disobeyed God."

"Sure, but think about it in a bigger context. What does it mean about humanity?"

Hannah turns her hands in her lap, staring hard at the prints of her fingers. "That we shame ourselves? That we hide from God?"

"Right. Sometimes I think God reacted the way he did because he was so, so anguished that Adam and Eve hated something about themselves. They didn't realize how beautiful they were in the Garden. They didn't realize how perfect they were in their love. When their eyes were opened—when they saw that they were naked— they felt as if they had to cover themselves. They thought what God had made was shameful and embarrassing and wrong. Can you imagine how that made God feel? How his heart must have ached to see them denying their beauty, their humanity, in front of him like that? It's the most heartrending part of the story."

"I'm like them," Hannah tells her. "I'm hiding from God because I'm ashamed of how he made me. I hate him for the way he made me."

"Hannah," Ms. Carpenter says softly. "I think we all hide from God sometimes. We all have things we're ashamed of. The essential thing is that you work through it."

"How am I supposed to do that?"

Ms. Carpenter turns her head from side to side, her eyes glazed over in thought. "You refuse to be imprisoned by that shame. You realize that you are good—you are good because God made you— and you claim that goodness."

Hannah shifts her body so that she faces the altar just the

tiniest bit. The rectangular table is draped in white cloth, with sunlight streaming across its surface. Hannah lets her eyes linger on it until her vision glazes over, and now the white altar looks like a girl's hospital bed, or like a man's tomb.

"Hannah..." Ms. Carpenter says softly. "You know what I love about the story of the Fall?"

"What?"

"I love how beautifully it matches up with the story of Christ. It makes a perfect palindrome. It's what makes the Bible such a magnificent work of literature."

Hannah keeps her eyes on the altar as she listens.

"In the end," Ms. Carpenter says, "Adam and Eve's shame can't imprison us. It doesn't matter that they took the fruit from that tree and clothed themselves in garments of shame, sparking that long story of human suffering and filling the Bible with broken words—because after everything that happened, Christ, the new Word, sacrificed himself on that same tree. And after he died for us—after he showed us his love—he came back to life and shrugged off those garments of shame and death. The story of Genesis cannot trap us anymore. The tree of sin becomes the tree of salvation, those garments of shame become the garments of the Resurrection, and the garden that Eve was banished from becomes the garden Mary Magdalene walks through when she goes to Christ's tomb on the Third Day. *That's* the garden you go looking for, Hannah—the one that leads to the risen Christ, who saves us with his radical, unconditional love. The same love you have for Baker—the love that prompted you to carry the cross of her shame. The same love she has for you—the love that prompted her to sacrifice herself to that fall and that tree. Love ultimately wins, Hannah. Love ultimately saves."

Hannah is stunned. The air in the chapel is suddenly alight with magic. "Wow," she breathes, her eyes filling with tears as she looks at the altar.

"Hannah," Ms. Carpenter says.

"Yes?"

"You have to forgive yourself. You have to work past that harmful, murderous shame and start to love yourself. Love yourself the way God loves you. The way Baker loves you."

"I will," Hannah says.

She and Ms. Carpenter both turn to face the altar now, and the sunlight coats everything in the chapel—the altar, the Crucifix, Hannah's own body—in a beautiful, hopeful gold.

Chapter Sixteen: The Third Day

Hours later, Hannah wakes to a hot, sunny afternoon. Joanie drives her to Zeeland Street for hash browns, and then they drive to Baker's house to take Charlie out so the Hadley's don't have to leave the hospital.

Charlie bounds up to Hannah and licks her face with unrestrained joy. She laughs against his fur and coos into his ear. "She'll be home soon," Hannah promises him, kissing his face. "She'll be home and she'll be so excited to see you."

Hannah's mom helps her try on her graduation gown that afternoon. "It looks like a circus tent," Joanie says, regarding the garment with distaste. "Like a cheap, red circus tent."

"You'll have to wear one next year," Hannah says, "and it'll look even uglier on you."

Joanie smirks before reaching for her phone. "Hold on," she says, spinning away from them, "it's Luke."

She takes the call with pink cheeks and bright eyes. "Yeah," she says into the phone, as breathless as she was when Luke first asked her out two years ago. "Yeah, I'd love to."

Hannah eats dinner with her parents by herself that night, after Joanie leaves to go out with Luke. Her mom cooks her favorite dinner—jambalaya—and surprises her with brownies for dessert. They talk about Emory and what Hannah's major might be and when she wants to start shopping for her new dorm room.

"Hannah," her mom says tentatively when they've all finished eating, "this whole thing—you and girls—it's going to be very new for your dad and me. We won't always know what we're supposed to do or say."

"I know," Hannah says, meeting her mom's eyes.

"But we want you to know," her mom continues, twisting her hands together, "that we're both praying for you to find love. With whomever that may be."

Hannah's dad takes her mom's hand. He smiles at her in his quiet way, and a lump builds in Hannah's throat.

"Thank you," she says, looking hard at them both.

"We love you," her dad says.

"I love you, too," she says, and it's never been truer.

On Sunday morning, Hannah walks into St. Mary's for the last time. The senior hallway bursts with colorful red gowns as everyone lines up for graduation. Hannah slips through the crowd, not talking to anyone, but not ducking her head, either. She takes her place in line directly behind the spot where Michele would have stood.

Her classmates look curiously at her, but she looks past them for the only people in this line whom she truly cares about. She recognizes Luke's messy curls toward the front of the line; when she turns to search behind her, she finds Clay's tall form and Wally's glasses. They both stand subdued, neither one of them talking, Clay in the middle of the line and Wally toward the back. Hannah makes eye contact with each of them. Clay nods. Wally raises his palm to say hello.

She doesn't see Baker in the line. She didn't expect to.

The graduation march starts to play from the gym and the seniors in line shift with excitement. Then they're walking forward, each of them processing toward the end of their high school story, and then the gym doors open and Hannah opens her right hand onto the air at her side, wishing Baker was there next to her.

Long after graduation has ended—long after the cameras have stopped clicking, after Joanie has stopped mocking her red gown, after her St. Mary's diploma has been flattened underneath a stack of books—Hannah stands naked in front of her bathroom mirror and looks at herself—really looks at herself—for the first time in months.

Her ash blonde hair, with the split ends tickling halfway down her back. She'll have to get a haircut before Emory. Her blue-gray eyes, always narrowed in thought, curtained by brittle eyelashes. Her small, thin lips on a mouth that eats and drinks and speaks and prays. There is so much more for her to taste in this life.

The skin on her body. Skin that has withheld and has given, skin that has absorbed alcohol thrown in violence and tears wept in redemption. Cold skin. Hot skin. Clothed skin. Naked skin.

And this neck—this neck that has leaned forward so she could pray over a chair, that has tilted back so she could see the heavens, that has turned to the side so she could hide from her demons, that has propelled her forward so she could kiss a girl.

The legs that have carried her when she wanted to separate, that have parted when she wanted to unite. The arms that have shaken when she gripped her chair with terror, that have quivered when she touched another with courage. And her hands—the hands that have white-knuckled on railings when she needed to breathe, that have folded together in chapels when she needed to pray, that have entered another when she needed to live. When she needed to love.

She sees herself, and she does not look away.

Early Monday morning, after she drops Joanie off for her last week of school, Hannah drives to Luke's mom's house. Luke sits on the front porch steps, waiting for her, a glass of water in his hand.

"Hey," he says when she walks up to sit next to him. "Have you eaten breakfast yet?"

He brings out a crate of oranges and places it on the step below their feet. They dig their thumbnails into the oranges and peel off the skin with lazy, early-morning movements, the undersides of their nails turning a yellow-orange color.

"What time do you leave?" Hannah asks.

"Probably around 10. Wally's coming at 9:30 to help me load up the car."

"And Clay?"

Luke frowns as he drops a peel on the porch. "Haven't heard from him."

The air smells like citrus. At this early hour, when it's not yet eight o'clock, the heat is gentle and balmy.

"I owe you so many apologies," Hannah says.

"I owe you some, too," Luke says.

"My sister loves you. Really loves you."

Luke smiles. Smiles in a way he rarely does—not like the world is bursting with hilarity, but rather like the world has given him something he never thought he deserved.

"I love her, too," he says.

They eat their oranges in silence, sitting side by side on the porch, until Luke turns to Hannah and says, "I wish I had been there for you."

"I wish I had told you what was going on," Hannah says. "I think I knew, deep down, that you would understand. That you would be able to talk to me in a way Wally and Clay couldn't. But I was afraid."

Luke nods. He picks up another orange and tosses it up and down in his palm. Then a slow grin spreads across his face.

"Well," he says, looking her in the eye, that old familiar hitch in his smile, "*Orange* you glad you told me now?"

She talks to Clay next. She walks up to his front door on Tuesday afternoon, her heart beating anxiously as it remembers this place.

"He's grounded," Mrs. Landry says when she answers the door. Her voice has lost its normal warmth. "Pete and I are only letting him out to do community service."

"I have some things I want to apologize for," Hannah says, begging Mrs. Landry with her eyes.

Mrs. Landry scrutinizes her with an uncomfortable expression on her face, and Hannah realizes that Mrs. Landry must now see her as someone foreign, someone unfathomable, someone unknown. But

Hannah stands upright, feeling her breath in her lungs and her pulse in her chest.

"He's out back," Mrs. Landry says finally. "You can talk to him for a few minutes."

"Thank you," Hannah says, and then she turns away from the door and walks around the side of the house instead.

She finds Clay at the back of the yard, one knee in the dirt, his quarterback's hands hammering nails into the wooden fence.

"Need some help?" Hannah calls.

Clay startles. "Oh," he says, his tone uncertain. "No, I'm alright."

"Can we talk?"

Clay looks at her for an extended second. Then he drops his hammer into the dirt and walks over to her.

They sit on the swings and scrape their heels against the ground. Clay bounces a tennis ball up and down off the dirt, his tree-dark hair reflecting sunlight.

"I'm not sure how to start," Hannah mutters.

Clay clutches the tennis ball in his hand. "Yeah."

"And it's weird," Hannah continues, "because I've always known how to talk to you. I've always felt like I could tell you anything."

Clay's eyebrows draw together. He bounces the tennis ball into the dirt.

"I saw y'all kissing," he says.

"What?"

"At the beach. At Tyler's party. I went looking for Baker. I opened the garage door, and I saw y'all kissing."

"That was you?"

"It freaked me out," Clay says, his eyebrows still drawn close together. "Not because I thought it was bad, or wrong, or any of that shit, but because it made sense. It made so much sense. And I didn't want it to. I didn't want her to be with you. And I didn't want to hate you."

A long beat of silence. Hannah winds her arms around her swing. She digs her sandals into the dirt and waits.

"I was an ass," Clay says finally. "Wally was right. I was so blinded by wanting to be with her, and wanting everyone to love the two of us, and trying so hard not to resent you...that I messed everything up. I ruined us. I ruined our friends."

"No," Hannah says. "It's not your fault. All this stuff that happened—it's too big to be anyone's fault. Maybe there's no fault at all. Maybe it's just stuff that had to happen."

"No. I shouldn't have abandoned you. I shouldn't have said all those ugly things I said and I shouldn't have started that fight." He pauses. "I shouldn't have waited to see what Michele would do."

"There's a lot of things I shouldn't have done, either," Hannah says.

"You know the worst part? I knew she didn't want to be with me. I knew it deep down. She never seemed to want to talk to me on the phone. One time she started crying when I was driving us home from the movies—she said she was just stressed about college stuff, but I knew that wasn't it. Even when we—even when we, you know, had sex, she was really distant afterwards. She wouldn't let me hold her or anything, and then we both just kinda lay there for a few minutes until she started to cry."

Hannah's chest aches. Clay raises his head to look at her.

"And the way she looked whenever someone said your name," he says. "I knew, somehow, that she wanted to be with you. That she had always wanted to be with you."

Hannah's throat thickens. She swallows and shakes the hair out of her eyes.

"She," Clay says, stopping himself when his voice shakes. He clears his throat and stares down at the tennis ball in his palm. "She was telling the truth about the e-mail. When she said she wrote it. Right?"

He's looking hard at Hannah, begging her for the truth. Hannah pulls her lips into her mouth and stares back at him, unsure of what to say.

But Clay nods, and then he passes the tennis ball into Hannah's hand. "You're brave, Han," he says, looking meekly at her. "You're braver and stronger than I've ever been."

"No," Hannah says, turning the tennis ball over in her hand.

"I really missed you when all of this was going down. Even though I didn't want to, I did. I really missed our whole group. Even now, after all the shit that's happened, all I want is for all of us to hang out again."

Hannah tosses the tennis ball to him. "I want that, too."

"You gonna talk to Wally?"

"I'm going to try."

"He'll listen," Clay says, tossing the ball back her way.

"Are you going to talk to him?"

Clay hangs his head. "I need to," he says. "I need to talk to him and Luke and Joanie."

They fall back into silence, each of them bouncing the tennis ball a few times before tossing it back to the other, until Clay stands and tells her that he needs to finish repairing the fence.

"Can we hang out when you're no longer grounded?" Hannah asks.

Clay ducks his head into the sun. "Yeah," he says, with the trace of a smile on his face. "I'd love that."

He hugs her for a long minute before she turns to leave. "I hope you figure everything out," he says, talking quietly into her hair. "You're one of my best friends, and even after everything, so is she, and I'd be a pretty awful guy if I didn't want my friends to be happy."

And then it's time to talk to Wally. She drives to his house on Thursday morning, knowing that his mom will be at work and his brothers will still have one more day of school, and parks in the driveway next to his old Camry. She knocks on the garage door and listens to the steady sound of his feet moving toward her.

He opens the door and blinks quickly at her, like he's not sure whether or not she's there. He wears the same flannel pajama pants he wore at the beach, but his glasses are missing from his face.

"Can we talk?" she says.

He studies her for a moment. "Yeah, of course," he says, pulling the door aside to let her in.

She sits down at the kitchen counter, and he stands across from her, his back jutting up against the sink. "Do you want some water?" he asks, his arms folded across his ribs.

She shakes her head no. "I just want to talk to you," she says.

It's hard at first. She doesn't know how to articulate so many of her feelings, doesn't know how to convince him that she thought she was living out truth. "I wasn't trying to hurt you," she says, her eyes lowered to the counter. "I thought I was doing what I was supposed to. I thought if I tried hard to be with you, then the romantic feelings would follow."

They never discuss the e-mail, but when they talk about Clay's party and Baker's fall through the fence, Wally lifts his eyes to look at her, and she knows he understands.

"I really did love you, Hannah," he says, his voice honest and bare. "I thought you were the most amazing girl in the world. I still do." He pauses and shifts sideways, then turns the sink faucet on and off, on and off, his fingers brushing through the water. Hannah waits.

"But you know," he says, his expression changing to the one she has seen him wear when he learns something new in class, "one of the reasons I find you so amazing is that you've always seemed to know who you are. So if you're now learning more about who that is, then how can I be anything but happy for you?"

Hannah exhales. Wally shuts the faucet off and turns back around to face her.

"Can we still be friends?" Hannah asks. "Because I don't think—" she struggles against the break in her voice—"I don't think I could ever give up our friendship."

"I could never give up our friendship, either," he says, "but I need some time."

"Time?" Hannah repeats.

"Time to get over everything," he explains.

"I'm sorry."

"It's okay," he says, his voice steady. "I just—need to step back and get some clarity. Get my head on straight."

"Okay."

"We'll be friends again, Han. I promise."

She looks at him and sees the young, earnest boy she met on the first day of P.E. class, the boy who recognized her from Geography and asked her if she wanted to be stretch partners.

"I'm holding you to that," Hannah says.

Wally smiles. "You got it."

She picks up Joanie from her last final exam that day. The temperature climbs to the high 80s, so they drive to the snowball stand near Country Corner and order two mango-flavored cups and sit at one of the outdoor benches while the sun warms their hair. Joanie fills Hannah in on Luke's experience at running camp so far, telling her all about his new friends at Spring Hill and his plans to visit home in two weeks.

"That's awesome," Hannah says, "but let's talk about you. You're a rising senior now. You feeling okay about it?"

Joanie falters, her face showing her surprise, but then she leans her elbow on the table and adopts a deliberately casual expression, as if it doesn't mean the world to her that Hannah has asked the question. "Yeah, I'm okay," she says, swirling her spoon around her cup. "It's just one year."

"Joanie."

"Yeah."

"I'm your sister. You can tell me these things."

Joanie looks at her the same way she did when they were little and Hannah caught her in a fib. "Fine," she says. "I'm scared as hell. I know I have other friends, I know there are some pretty cool people in my class, but I can't imagine not having Luke there, or going to volleyball practice without Baker, or eating lunch without any of y'all." She pauses and scratches casually at her elbow. "Or driving to school without you."

"You're going to be fine," Hannah promises.

They don't look at each other as they talk through it—they scrape at their snowballs instead—but afterwards, on the drive home, Hannah feels like they are 11 and 10 years old again, riding their bikes home after buying candy at the gas station.

"Han," Joanie says, "what are you gonna do now?"

"What do you mean?"

"Baker. What are you gonna do?"

The sun streams through the leaves of the live oaks as Hannah steers the car onto Olive Street. "I'm going to wait," she says. "I'm going to wait until she's ready."

"What if she's never ready?"

Hannah guides the car onto their driveway. She thinks about how she has waited for Baker all week, how she's thought about Baker's broken rib and the cuts on her hairline and the bruises on her skin. How she's kept her phone in her hand like a talisman. How she's looked out the window with the sound of every car that's driven by.

"I'll just keep waiting," she says.

May melts into June. Hannah doesn't see Wally, nor does she see Clay. She and Joanie sit on the back porch in the mid-morning heat and eat Apple Jacks and toast, and Hannah swells with hope that today might be the day she sees Baker again.

She goes to Mass with her parents. Some people look at her differently than they used to, but Hannah remembers Ms. Carpenter's words and looks up at the Crucifix without shame. When it comes time for her to receive the Eucharist, she stands confidently in front of Father Simon. He holds the Host in front of her for a lingering second, his clerical collar tight on his red neck.

She reaches up and takes the Host out of his hand. It melts onto her tongue as she walks back to her pew.

It rains every day during the first week of June. The wet heat of the morning transforms into the warm showers of the afternoon, and by early evening, it rains so hard that the streets flood. Hannah presses her fingers to the dining room window, watching the Dupuis' trash can fall over from the wind and rain.

She steps outside on Friday afternoon, her tennis shoes laced tightly on her feet, just as the first rumbles of thunder reverberate on the air. The earth is muggy and still as she jogs down the street, her body moving under the protection of the strong, sturdy trees.

Just as she turns onto Drehr, a light rain starts to fall, sprinkling her face and melting into the sidewalk. She keeps running, her wrists damp with sweat and water, the streets damp and smelling of rain and steam.

By the time she reaches Kleinert, the rain has strengthened into a regular shower, but she keeps running anyway. The rain feels good on her skin and she feels good in her skin.

She's soaking wet by the time she reaches St. Mary's. Something builds in her heart as she runs past the familiar blond brick buildings. She looks at the statue of Jesus, visible from the street, and smiles as she runs by.

On the second Sunday of June, late in the evening, when Hannah is washing the dinner dishes, there's a knock on the back door.

"I'll get it," Joanie says, abandoning the cloth she was using to wipe the table.

Hannah turns the faucet off, her heart dangling high above her.

"Oh," Joanie says, pulling the door open. "Hannah—"

Hannah walks into view of the door, and there she is, standing outside Hannah's house, her hands tucked into the back pockets of her shorts.

"Hi," Baker says.

"Hi," Hannah breathes.

Baker's eyes are nervous, but she steadies them on Hannah's face. She pulls her lips into her mouth. She shifts her weight from one foot to the other.

"Want to go for a walk?" she asks.

"Yeah," Hannah says, her heart swelling. "Joanie, can you—?"

"I'll finish the dishes," Joanie says, a smile playing on her face. "You two go walk."

The earth is buzzing when Hannah steps outside. She smells the perfume of flowers all around her, hears the trilling of insects deep in her ears. The sky is painted with the colors of dusk. She stands in front of Baker and just looks at her, and Baker lets her.

"You're here," Hannah says.

"I am," Baker says.

Hannah nods. They stand across from each other, their arms hanging at their sides, and keep looking at each other.

"Will you walk with me?" Baker asks.

They turn right onto Olive Street and pad along beneath the cover of the trees. The sunset filters through the leaves, creating latticework patches of golden light on the asphalt road. Hannah breathes in the summer air and tries to absorb the life all around her.

"How've you been?" Baker asks.

Hannah thinks about it. "I've been good," she says, and she's happy to realize she means it. "I feel—like I'm me."

Baker's eyes shine with a smile. "Good."

Hannah kicks a pebble down the street ahead of them. It skips across the pavement, the only sound in the world.

"You haven't been here," Hannah says. "Where did you go?"

Baker bites her lip. "New Orleans," she says. "I went down to stay with Nate as soon as my mom would let me."

"How was it?"

Baker nods to herself, trying to articulate her answer. "It was what I needed."

They cross over Drehr and continue down Olive, Hannah's sandals scraping against the asphalt, Baker's sandals making no sound with her light steps.

"Hannah..." Baker says.

"Yeah?"

"When I was there—when I was in New Orleans—I figured out a lot of things. I didn't want to just leave town without telling you, especially after everything that happened, but I felt like I had to. Like I had to escape, you know? Like I had to take myself out of here so I could step back and try to understand everything. Not just the stuff with you and me, but, like, how I feel even beyond you. About girls, and boys, and religion, and my family...and it was really hard to do. It was really hard to figure out the truth."

"Yeah," Hannah says. "I know what you mean."

"I talked to my brother. I told him the whole story."

"You did? What'd he say?"

"That it was important for me to figure out what it all meant, and that I couldn't listen to anyone but myself. And he hugged me a lot."

Hannah smiles. "I love Nate."

"He loves you, too." Baker takes a sharp breath. "I went to Confession, too."

"You did?"

She nods. "I asked for forgiveness for everything I did to you."

"What did the priest say?"

"He said a lot of things. Some of them made me feel better and some of them made me feel worse. But Han, when I was there, what I realized was—I realized I was afraid of the truth. I was scared. I felt, like—I felt like I was trapped by these feelings I didn't want to have, and I didn't want to deal with what it meant, and what people would say, and how I would negotiate with my faith...and I resented you for finding your way into my heart like you did. I was scared of you. Being around you, it was like—you were everything I wasn't supposed to want. You're—no one told me about you. When I was growing up, it was always, 'One day, when you meet a nice boy,' or, 'When you have a husband....' No one ever told me that it might be different. That it would be okay to be different. So I just—I had this deep sense of shame about myself. About the way that I felt."

"I had that, too," Hannah says. "I talked to Ms. Carpenter about it."

"I talked to my brother."

"Did it help?"

"Yeah. But mostly—I think mostly it was just talking to myself. Really forcing myself to confront the truth, you know? And praying. A lot of praying. Because—ultimately I realized something."

"What?"

"I realized...that I had to deal with it. All of it. The fear, and the guilt, and the shame...because otherwise there was no way to be with you. And I realized that's what I really want, when it comes down to it. I want to be with you. I've wanted to be with you for a while. I wish I'd realized it sooner. I wish someone had told me that it might be you. I wish someone had said, 'One day, your heart will feel a lot bigger than it was before, and that's when you know.' Because—that's how it is with you, Han. You make me feel, like—God, I don't even know. Like being with you makes me a thousand times better than I am. Like my eyes are clearer when I look at things. And when I'm not with you, it's like—like my heart can't breathe.

"I'm sorry for everything I did," she says, her eyes shining with tears. "For playing games, for hiding from you, for—for Clay—"

Hannah ducks her head.

Baker wipes at her eyes. "I know," she says, tears spilling down her face. "I'm sorry. Hannah, I'm so sorry. For that, and for the e-mail, for everything I did to you. I was scared and ashamed. I was a coward." She pauses and looks at Hannah, her eyes pleading. "But Han...I'm tired of being scared. I'm tired of being ashamed. And I'm tired of not being with you. I still might get scared sometimes, and I still might feel a little ashamed, but I want to work through it because—because all I want is to be with you. I know you might not want that anymore after everything that's happened, but I just had to tell you this because—because I love you."

Hannah stops walking. Baker stops, too. And, finally, they face each other.

"Hannah," Baker says, searching her with those deep brown eyes.

She speaks her name again, in the way that only she can do, and it rings in Hannah's head over and over. "Hannah," she says, her voice arching. "I love you. I've loved you for a while. I fought against it before, but I get it now. I get it." She shakes her head, breathing shallowly. "I love you so much."

And Hannah knows it's true, because she sees the proof in Baker's eyes: they are vulnerable, and full of wonder, and begging Hannah to love her in return. And something happens in Hannah's heart: something spreads throughout it, warm and unstoppable and steady like the sun.

She steps forward and takes Baker's hand.

"I love you, too."

Baker breathes. "Really?"

"Yeah," Hannah says, her voice wet.

Baker's mouth upturns in a smile. She pushes more tears away from her eyes. "This is—" she says. "I mean, it's like—"

"I know," Hannah laughs.

"I need to ask you something, though."

"Sure. What is it?"

Baker opens her mouth but holds the question in; she ducks her head, her hair falling over her face, and when she raises her head back up, her tears are falling fast again. She struggles for another few seconds, blinking fast through her tears. She clears her eyes and looks at Hannah. "Do you forgive me?" she asks. "For everything I did?"

Hannah inhales. "Yes," she says.

Baker's whole body seems to sigh in release. Hannah pulls Baker against her, wrapping her arms around her as tightly as she can, nudging Baker's head down onto her shoulder. She can feel Baker breathing hard against her, her tears bleeding through Hannah's tank top and into her skin; she cradles Baker's head with one hand, feeling her soft, warm hair under her palm, and secures her body with her other, spreading her fingers over the back of her shirt so that she can feel her spine and her deep, shuddering breaths.

"It's okay," Hannah promises her, kissing the side of her head. "It's okay."

Hannah holds her until her cries die away. Baker sniffles against her, swallows, breathes out. She wraps both her arms around Hannah's body, too, so that they're both holding onto each other, right there on the sidewalk on Cherokee Street.

"You okay?" Hannah whispers.

"Yeah," Baker says. She takes a few deep breaths.

Hannah draws back from her so she can see her face. Her eyes are red and her eyelashes are wet, and she wipes at her mouth and her nose, embarrassed.

"You're beautiful," Hannah tells her.

Baker blushes and shakes her head, then holds her fingers up to her eyes, trying to collect the remaining tears from her lashes. "Let's keep walking," she says.

"Where do you want to go?" Hannah asks.

"Home," Baker says. "Let's just go home."

That feeling comes back into Hannah's chest, that growing, drumming feeling that warms her, and she begins to laugh, a wonderful, relieved laugh that shimmers around her in the heat. She laughs again, and it comes out mixed with a joyful cry, so that a couple of tears wind down her face and she has to wipe them away.

Baker looks over at her, and a smile breaks out on her face—a smile that's all mouth and eyes and soul.

There are so many more things Hannah wants to talk about with her, and she knows Baker wants to talk about them, too, but for tonight they simply fall onto the big couch in the family room and watch an old movie with Joanie. Joanie doesn't say anything to them, just smiles knowingly when they sit down next to her.

Baker's right side brushes up against Hannah's left, and for the first time in months Hannah feels whole.

She walks Baker out to her car when the movie ends. Baker leans against the driver-side door, her complexion flushed beneath the light from the street lamps.

"Thanks for...tonight," Baker says, her voice nervous.

"Thank you," Hannah says.

"You're the bravest person I've ever known."

"So are you."

"No," Baker says, ducking her head. "But I'm going to try to be right now when I ask you for something."

"What?"

Baker fidgets with her car keys. "Um. Can I—can I kiss you?"

And it's too perfect, and Baker is too pretty standing there against the car, and Hannah's heart is too, too full. "Are you sure?" Hannah asks, trying to fight down her silly grin. "Out here?"

Baker smiles one of the happiest smiles Hannah has ever seen. "Out here, Hannah-bear."

Hannah steps closer to her, places a hand on her hip where her halter meets her shorts, leans into her. Baker inhales quickly, like she's surprised, and her eyelids close over her eyes.

And then, with a simple touch of her lips, Baker kisses Hannah beneath the lights of a street lamp and the leaves of an oak tree.

Chapter Seventeen: In the Garden

It's heavy, the August heat. Hannah's mom calls it "oppressive" when she comes home from work in the evenings, her forehead glistening with a light sheen of sweat. Joanie calls it "the Luzianna plague" when she and Hannah drive around in the early afternoons, their underarms sweating as they run back-to-school errands. But to Hannah, the heat feels like a blanket. Warm and secure. And lucky for her, Baker agrees.

"Can you pass me that cake pan?" Baker says, her dark chicory eyes drifting down the counter, past Hannah's hand.

They stand in Hannah's kitchen with the screen door open to the earth outside. They hear the mysteries of late summer taking place beyond the porch: the insistent nighttime crickets, the engines and wheels of the cars that drive past at this late hour. Hannah's parents are in bed, content with their air conditioning and their summer quilt. They don't know that Hannah and Baker have propped the porch door open.

"Do you think your dorm will have a kitchen?" Hannah asks.

Baker's arm, beating the brownie batter around the mixing bowl, stills for a pocket of a moment. "I hope so," she says.

"Well hey," Hannah says, trying to keep the moment light, "even if it doesn't, we'll just leave campus and come home for a night."

Baker smiles, her eyes still on the brownie batter. "Is it bad if I don't want to come home for a night? I want to have the whole weekend to ourselves when you visit. And I want to be able to, you know—" her face turns pink—"actually sleep in the same bed."

Hannah pokes at her hip. "Are you having dirty thoughts?"

"No!" Baker laughs, kicking at Hannah with her arms still poised over the mixing bowl.

"I think you are."

"I'm going to fling this batter at you."

"No you're not," Hannah says, hugging her from behind. She squeezes Baker's middle and drops her head onto her shoulder. "But anyway, I'll be back for lots of visits. I figure we can come home for at least *one* night."

Baker releases the mixer, letting it fall back against the glass of the mixing bowl. She spins in Hannah's arms so they're facing each other.

"You got it," she says, and she kisses Hannah.

It's hard, that second week of August. It's bittersweet. Hannah's stomach is anxious when she wakes in the morning. She thinks of how far she and Baker have come, and she wishes they could go on forever, growing and learning together, without the impending separation that college will bring.

She stands in the middle of her childhood bedroom, with sticky old stuffed animals lumped together in the corner, with pictures of her friends adorning the walls, with Baker's sweatshirt strewn over the bed, with piles of clothes that she has already set aside for Emory.

And all she can see, as she stands in the middle of this room, is Baker asking her to dance.

"What are we doing?" Hannah laughs, her heart rate accelerating as Baker steps away from Hannah's music speakers.

"Dancing," Baker says, pulling Hannah into her. "Like we should have done at prom."

The song is soft, rhythmic, mesmerizing. Baker sways Hannah from side to side, her head resting against Hannah's, their hair mixing together, brown into blonde. Hannah turns her head into Baker's neck, and Baker's left hand holds Hannah steady at the base of her back while her right hand grips Hannah's shoulder like she never plans to let her go, and the music drifts over them, a song that exists only for them.

"You looked so beautiful at prom," Baker says.

Hannah wraps her arm tighter around Baker's waist. "So did you."

Baker kisses the side of Hannah's face, right where her skin meets her hairline. "I didn't feel like I did," she says. "But I do now."

Every time Hannah gets into her car, she sees Baker in the passenger seat next to her, wearing her brother's faded old LSU baseball cap, laughing around the straw of her Sonic milkshake.

"Let's go out to dinner," Hannah says, reaching across the console to trace a finger over Baker's palm.

"Dinner?"

"Yeah, like on a date. We can dress all fancy, and I'll pick you up with a bouquet of roses or something, and I'll take you to dinner." She pauses. "If you don't like it, we don't have to do it again."

Baker's eyes tick over to hers. "How could I not like that?"

So they go on a date. Hannah wears her prettiest dress and her favorite perfume. Baker steps out of her garage with her navy sundress on, her hair pulled half up, the bobby pins glinting in the evening sunlight.

"I don't know why you brought that," Hannah says, eyeing Baker's clutch as they drive down Perkins. "You know I'm gonna pay."

Baker raises her eyebrows. "Not if I fight you for it."

They go to Parrain's. The hostess seats them on the porch outside, and it's crowded and busy in a good way. They order sweet tea and boudin balls, and Baker asks, "So—since this is an official date, does that mean we have to talk about different things than when we were just best friends?"

"No," Hannah laughs, "I'm just gonna make fun of the way you fidget with your napkin, like I always do."

"Don't," Baker laughs, her smile shy. "I'm fidgeting because I'm nervous."

"Why are you nervous?"

"Because this is the first date I've been on where I actually *like* the person," Baker says, and Hannah blushes all over.

They drive to City Park afterwards and sit in Hannah's car, and Hannah thinks of all the times she came here late at night and wished for something better for them. "Did you know," Hannah says, surprising herself, "that being around you is my favorite thing in the world?"

Baker answers by kissing her. It's sudden, but soft. They let the kiss linger, and Baker raises a hand to Hannah's neck, and they kiss again.

"Holy shit," Hannah says afterwards. "I don't know how I *ever* thought kissing anybody else was good."

Baker smiles, her eyes lit with magic, and says, "Yeah? I'm that good?"

"Stop," Hannah laughs, tugging on her wrists. "Don't act like you don't like it too."

Baker kisses her again and says, "No, you're right," in a breathless voice.

They hold hands and listen to the radio while they drive back to Baker's house. Hannah pulls into the driveway and turns the car off, and they turn to look at each other.

"Did you want this?" Baker asks, holding up her empty to-go cup of sweet tea, her voice silly. "Maybe as a souvenir of our first date?"

"Nah, wasn't that memorable," Hannah says.

Baker lunges across the console to tickle Hannah's side. Hannah squirms away from her, her laughter high-pitched and joyful.

"That was hurtful, Hannah," Baker says. "You shouldn't say things like that to your girlfriend."

Hannah heats all over when she hears the word. She stills with her back against the window, her hands still held up to ward off Baker's tickling. "Girlfriend?" she asks. "Really?"

Baker's eyes become hesitant, but then she says, in her brave voice, "Yeah—isn't that what we are now?"

Hannah feels brand new. "Yes," she says. "Yes, we absolutely are."

Baker leans across the console and kisses her. "I'll see you in the morning, right?"

"Right."

"Night, Han."

Hannah guides her in for one more kiss. They hold their lips together and Hannah breathes in Baker's scent, and then Baker squeezes her hand and climbs out of the car.

When Hannah lies in bed at night, all she knows is the feeling of Baker waking her up on the 22nd of July, her hands warm on Hannah's shoulders, her mouth dropping kisses to Hannah's face like pennies into a fountain. "Wake up, Birthday Girl," Baker says, her voice in that halfway place between whispering and speaking.

Hannah smiles without planning to, the way she used to smile as a kid when her mom would wake her on Christmas morning.

Baker takes her to Zeeland Street for breakfast, and they sit in their favorite booth, and Baker pulls one leg up on the bench like she always does. They feast on eggs and bacon and grits and hash browns, and Hannah looks across the table at Baker, sitting there in her tank top and shorts with her hair pulled back from her face, and she cannot remember ever being happier.

They eat spice cake with Hannah's family that night. Joanie cuts the slices for everyone, her voice proud as she brags about how this is the best cake she's ever made. Hannah's mom and dad sit at the far side of the table, both of them wearing content smiles, Hannah's dad laying his hand on the table for her mom to take.

"Can't believe we have an 18-year-old," Hannah's mom says.

"That makes y'all pretty old, doesn't it?" Joanie says.

"Feels like you were just born, Hannah," her mom continues.

"It was one of the two best days of my life," her dad says, smiling at Hannah and Joanie.

Baker sits next to her on the back porch steps later that night. "Can I give you your birthday present?" she says, her voice breathless.

They walk in silence up the stairs to Hannah's bedroom, their hands clasped between them, a growing excitement, a restless energy, palpable on the air between their bodies. Baker guides Hannah to sit on the bed and closes the door behind them, her chest heaving with breaths. Then she crosses to the far side of the room and opens the windows.

The room swells with humidity and the scent of flowers and the song of crickets. Baker comes back to the bed and places her palm over Hannah's heart—Hannah can feel it drumming within her—and eases her down onto her back.

"I couldn't figure out what to get you," Baker says, pushing Hannah's hair back from her face. "What do you get for the person who gave you everything?"

Hannah's arms begin to shake, but this time she is not afraid.

"And I realized," Baker says, taking a breath, "that there's one thing I haven't truly given you yet, and that's me. My self. My whole self. Without the fear or the shame. Just with love, and abandon." Her voice shakes, but her eyes are clear. "Is that okay?"

Her words sling through the room with the force of David's stone, defiant and brave. Hannah searches her eyes and finds a new light in them. Not the desperate one, full of shame, but the light of love, the light that rolls aside the stone, that pierces the tomb to find the miracle of salvation.

"That's all I've ever wanted," Hannah says.

Baker kisses her with tenderness. Hannah feels the weight of Baker's body on her torso, pressing against her ribs and stomach, warming her. They kiss, and then they move their hands over each other's clothes, and then they are naked on the bed, their bodies cupped together and open to the outside world.

And Hannah finds herself praying again, and she feels God coursing through her body and blood, but this time she knows it's with jubilation.

"You're crying," Baker says.

Hannah raises a hand to her own cheek. She touches the tears and laughs in disbelief. "Yeah," she says, her voice wet, "but I think it's in a good way."

Baker's smile starts small, just her lips parted in wonder, but then it grows until it lights up her whole face.

"I love you," she says.

"I love you," Hannah says.

And they show each other.

And then it's the second Friday of August, and Baker has to start freshman orientation on Monday. Hannah sits on Baker's bed while Baker darts distractedly around her bedroom, categorizing her belongings into piles of toiletries and clothes and school supplies and cleaning products.

"I pity your roommate," Hannah says. "You're gonna color coordinate her closet while she's out of the room, and then she's gonna come back and not know how to find her own clothes."

"I pity *your* roommate," Baker says while she fits her shampoo into a shower caddy. "You're going to scare her off with all your bad puns. She'll be terrified to have a conversation with you."

Hannah narrows her eyes. Baker looks up from where she's seated on the floor, and she shakes her head and says, "Oh, no. Don't even."

"What?"

"I know what you're doing. You're trying to make a pun about something. I can tell by your expression."

"I am not," Hannah laughs.

"You so are."

"Fine."

The corners of Baker's mouth lift. "Did you come up with anything?"

"No," Hannah admits. She pauses. "I've had a hard time concentrating lately."

Baker's smile falters. She drops her hand from the shower caddy. "We're gonna be fine, Han," she says. "We're going to miss each other, but we'll be fine."

"I know," Hannah says. "I'm just not looking forward to the missing each other part."

"Me neither."

Hannah chews the inside of her lip. "I'm going to miss our friends, too. I already do."

Baker holds her eyes. They stare at each other through the space of Baker's bedroom, surrounded by proof that their lives are changing again.

"Me too," Baker says.

They spend all of Saturday together. They eat breakfast and lunch together and share snacks in-between. They take Charlie to the dog park. They watch the first *Harry Potter* movie on Hannah's couch, lying under the same blanket with Hannah's back against Baker's stomach. They drive Baker's car to the St. Mary's parking lot and gaze through the windshield at the familiar blond brick buildings, the buildings that always felt like home, while they hold hands across the console. They eat dinner with Hannah's parents, talking excitedly about college while they pass the green beans around the table, both of them masking the nostalgia they already feel for their old life.

And after dinner, while Hannah washes the dishes and Baker dries them with an old dishtowel, Baker's cell phone chimes in her pocket. Hannah pays no attention while Baker reads the text message.

"Hey," Baker says, stepping up behind Hannah and kissing the underside of her ear. "Let's take a break now, okay? There's something I want to show you."

"What?"

"C'mere," Baker says, tugging on her hand.

"What are we doing?"

Baker smiles. "We're going to play outside."

They leave the kitchen and walk out the back door. They step beyond the carport and into the muggy evening air, and there, standing in the road, Hannah sees them.

Luke, Joanie, Wally, and Clay, their figures larger than life on the sunset backdrop. They grin at her as she approaches. Each one of them stands in front of a bicycle, and Wally and Clay each have a hand on two additional bicycles balanced at their sides.

"What—?" Hannah says, breathless.

"Don't look so surprised, dummy," Joanie says.

"It's the last night we can all be together," Clay says.

"Together?" Hannah says. "You mean...we're all okay?"

"Of course we're okay," Clay says, looking sideways to Wally, Joanie, and Luke. He clasps hands with Wally and looks back to Hannah. "Six-Pack for life."

Hannah steps toward them. Wally meets her eyes. His smile is gentle and steady.

"What do you say, Han?" he asks.

Hannah feels her smile all over her body, from the roots of her hair down to the bones of her feet.

"We thought an evening bike ride would be really clichéd and disgustingly romantic," Luke says.

"Which is how we knew you'd like it," Joanie says.

"Come on," Clay says, tilting the bicycle at his side. "I've got ice-cold Coke and a bag of chips in my booksack. We'll make a picnic out of it."

Hannah turns to Baker. "Did you plan all this?"

Baker pulls her eyes away from the group to look at Hannah.

"Maybe."

They hold each other's eyes for a second, and then Hannah swings her smile from Baker to the others. "I'm down," she says.

Wally holds his extra bike out for her. She steps forward to take it, thanking him with disbelieving eyes. He pulls his lips up in a smile.

Clay balances the other bike as Baker steps forward to take it. She kicks her sandals up onto the pedals and looks sideways to Hannah.

"Ready?" she asks.

"Ready," Hannah says.

They bike away from the yard, first Clay, then Wally, then Baker, then Hannah, then Joanie and Luke laughing in the back. They bike down Olive Street and into the core of the Garden District, and Hannah watches Clay's booksack flapping with the wind, watches the evening sunlight glint off Wally's glasses when he turns his head to the side, hears Joanie and Luke's shouts of laughter behind her, feels Baker's presence at her side. Clay raises his hands in the air—his left hand with all five fingers spread apart, his right hand with just one finger pointing in the air—and they all copy him, whooping and yelling before hastily grabbing onto their bikes again. They ride over pebbles and patches of dusk-colored sunlight, underneath the spread arms of the live oaks and the promise of their green leaves, past houses full of people and rules and prayers and magic. Hannah looks at Baker, and Baker extends her hand outward into the space between them, holding it palm-up for Hannah to take, right there in the heart of the garden.

Acknowledgements

My deepest thanks to:

JJ and Ruth, for reading early drafts and cheering me on when I so desperately needed it; and to all the Brittana writers, for leading me back to the joy of writing.

Srice, for all the long talks and the wise advice you gave me about the end of this story, and for believing in me from the beginning.

Melissa (Sis), for your thorough and dedicated reading, and for being with me through the lighter and darker moments.

Elise, for providing critical and insightful feedback on rough drafts, for your unfailing encouragement, and for being one of life's little oases.

My Louisiana family, for the adventures and the joie de vivre, and for making me fall in love with such a uniquely beautiful place.

Faf and Nik, for assuring me early on that everything would be okay, and for anchoring me through stormier times.

Hamy, for your patient heart and your steady friendship--you have seeped into so much of this story.

Mom-mom & Pop-pop and Grandmom & Grandpop, for championing me in my education and my dreams of writing.

Maria, for your gentle criticism on early drafts (you were right, of course), for putting up with me through this whole thing, and for refusing to be ashamed. I love you.

Deb, for all your feedback, your support, your enthusiasm, and your patience, and for tackling all those formatting issues. You are irreplaceable.

Eric, for sharing your artistic talents and your generous heart. You are one of a kind in the best way.

Freida, for being my confidante through this whole process, for taking my whiny phone calls, for kicking my ass when I needed it, and for being the one "who heard this one first." If this book is any good, it's because of you. #yourejoanie

Mom and Dad, for everything you have given me and for being the truest example of love I know. I would be lost without your guidance, support, and unmatched senses of humor. This work of love is for you.

About the Author

Kelly Quindlen began writing *Her Name in the Sky* while teaching middle school in Louisiana. She is the co-creator of the original web series "The Family Business" (www.tfbwebseries.com). She lives in Atlanta.

Follow Kelly on Twitter: https://twitter.com/kellyquindlen
Follow Kelly on Tumblr: kellyquindlen.tumblr.com

Credits

Cover art and design by Eric Ehrnschwender.

Visit esehrnschwender.blogspot.com for prints and original artwork.